# ZONES OF SILENCE

"The highest quality spi-fi. No one, including le Carré, conveys the secret game of moles and sleepers better than Garner, while preserving the strong human identity of his characters."  *City Limits*

"John le Carré is not the only one writing espionage novels that do all the work of the novel proper and carry with them an extra edge"  *Times*

"William Garner is one of our most satisfying spy writers"  *Mail on Sunday*

"A very superior brand of cloak and dagger ... sharp, worldly with a sense of backroom man-oeuvering. And cryptic, very.  *The Literary Review*

Books by
**WILLIAM GARNER**

Overkill
The Deep Deep Freeze
The Us or Them War
The Puppet-Masters
The Andra Fiasco
Ditto, Brother Rat!
A Big Enough Wreath
The Möbius Trip

*The Morpurgo Trilogy*
Think Big, Think Dirty*
Rats' Alley*
Zones of Silence*


*Available in Methuen Paperbacks

William Garner

# ZONES
# OF SILENCE

A Methuen Paperback

A Methuen Paperback

ZONES OF SILENCE

**British Library Cataloguing in Publication Data**

Garner, William, *1920–*
Zones of silence.
I. Title
823'.914[F]         PR6057.A675

ISBN 0–413–41220–2

First published in Great Britain 1986
by William Heinemann Ltd
This edition published 1987
by Methuen London Ltd
11 New Fetter Lane, London EC4P 4EE
Copyright © William Garner 1986
Printed and bound in Great Britain
by Cox & Wyman Ltd, Reading

My wife and WordStar,
without whom and which

We have all lost very much,
Don't fool yourself; me and you also.
We were born open to the world.
Now we keep the doors closed
to him and her and them . . .

Eva Strittmatter
*Ich schwing mich auf die Schauckel*


A subject thought: because he had a verb
With several objects that he ruled a sentence . . .
*Subject*, the dictionary warned, means 'Someone ruled by
Person or thing'. Was he not *having's* slave?

Stephen Spender,
*Subect, Object, Sentence*

# THE
# OUTER
# ZONE

# ONE

The year was still sharp-edged night and morning, the room barely warm. The Engineer was a careful man, fine-tuning the thermostat a dozen times a day with painstaking frugality. But then, the Viennese have learned to be careful with everything, especially time. History has taught them that the next minute is as much as can be relied on. The trick is to mock everything, miss nothing.

The Frau Engineer had missed very little. The day before, she had noticed, Herr Aske had not done his usual weekly shopping at Meinl's and the Alserbach market. And – she stressed the point to the police and later to the men from Department One – Herr Aske, normally the tidiest of young men, she had to say that about him, had left his bed unmade, his wash-basin dirty, his pyjamas on the floor.

Not, said the plump little Engineer, bobbing his glossy pink pate, washing his soft pink paws obsessively, with endless seated half-bows to Authority, that you would have known anything was wrong, seeing Herr Aske depart.

"Herr Doctor Aske, really," the Frau Engineer interrupted. "It was on some of the letters he got from London. But he wouldn't have it at all. Wouldn't be called Herr Doctor, not for anything." Her quick sideways glances invited everyone to draw their own, very Viennese conclusions: a man with a title he refused to use!

"Yes, but he was a foreigner." The Engineer was confused and irritated by the frequent interruptions. "And a Jew as well. Not," he hastened to add, "that that makes any difference." Authority had treated the Engineer with due respect, even calling him Herr Professor, which, strictly speaking, he was not. But after all, they

3

were gentlefolk, retired professionals with a decent *pension*, not the sort of people who ran a common rooming house.

"Same old trip?" he had asked on that particular morning.

"Same old trip, Herr Stiegelbauer." Then the little smile. Herr Aske always had the little smile.

"Though he didn't like to look you in the eye." The Frau Engineer had interrupted a great deal. "Not directly in the eye, not if he could avoid it."

The Engineer took a deep breath to restrain his irritation. "Back on Friday?" he had asked.

"Back on Friday, Engineer Stiegelbauer." Again the smile, although when the Engineer had come to think about it, Herr Aske might have been, well, just a little bit edgy, something on his mind perhaps.

"Well then, have a good trip." The Engineer had quite liked Herr Aske because he allowed himself to be patronised. Some Jews, especially since the war, could be very objectionable. It had been the Engineer's theory, not to be conveyed to Authority, that a Herr Doctor who wouldn't allow himself to be called Herr Doctor probably had something to hide, quite apart from the fact that he was a Jew. It had given Stefan Stiegelbauer, Dip. Ing., Präs. Prof., a pleasant feeling of superiority, even of power. And now events had proved him right, hadn't they?

Anyway, as he was saying, Herr Aske, carrying nothing but his usual soft-topped case, not new, not old, had gone, a last little nod and smile. "Thank you, Herr Engineer. *Wiedersehen. Wiedersehen*, Frau Stiegelbauer."

"Only" – the Engineer laboured the joke in his anxiety to be agreeable to Authority – "see him again on Friday we did not."

After that, Frau Dohnal, Frau Prassl, Fräulein Minge and the Austrian State Railways inspector had all plotted his passage without, naturally, ever coming close to plotting his thoughts.

At the junction of Währingerstrasse and Spitalgasse there was a cab on the rank. According to Frau Dohnal, watching him from the corner fruit shop, he had signalled to it, waited for the lights to change, crossed under the high red prow of a halted streetcar. After buying a paper at the newsstand, he had crossed Spitalgasse for his usual apples. Then Frau Dohnal saw him get into the taxi.

A woman driver, but no, she couldn't really describe her or the cab.

Frau Hanna Prassl. Sergeant Stenkowitz, who traced and

found her, definitely fancied prematurely widowed Frau Hanna. Taxi primped and tasselled like a cosy corner of her own little apartment in Favoriten. The Blessed Virgin in a silver frame dangling from her rear view mirror. Bright yellow hair, dyed, of course, framing a still pretty face. Yes, definitely fancied her.

She remembered the man all right, first customer of the morning. Dark, medium height, fortyish, shy smile, nice-looking in a sad, shut-in sort of way, know what I mean? Soft-topped case, newspaper, bag of fruit that he put in a zipper compartment of the case, nothing else. German? Oh, perfect, absolutely.

She had taken him to the Franz Josef Station. No, not chat, not really. He didn't want it, something on his mind, you got to recognise that sort of thing in her job. What did she mean, sad? Oh, hard to say, really. But permanent, if you could put it that way. A smile for everyone, but only a front.

Anyway, she'd put him down at the side entrance and he'd tipped above the odds, although sort of – you know? – absent-mindedly, thoughts somewhere else and – you'll laugh at this – the somewhere else wasn't a place he was looking forward to.

"Momenterl, bitte," she had said, thinking he would want change, but he'd just waved it away and gone up the steps as if he'd rather have been coming down them instead, know what I mean?

The sergeant saw Frau Hanna more times than were strictly necessary, but never made it with her. When he finally put his proposition outright, she listened, smiling, said, mockingly, "Nein, danke, Exzellenz," and walked out of his paper-ridden, smoke-smelling cubbyhole, still smiling.

The sergeant had made no such proposition to Fräulein Trudi, skinny, hair like rusty steel wool, thin red hands with straggly fingers that somehow didn't fit. She remembered the man, yes. Been there quite often, yes, definitely! Same time, always just before nine, pretty well always the same table, jo, sure of it. Always a double mokka, case right at his side like someone might pinch it. Might, too, all them Böhmen, East Germans and such on their way back home where there wasn't nothing to buy, so they said.

Anyway, this time, yes, definitely! Comes in a bit before nine, plenty of time if he's catching the Berliner. Sits there sort of in a daydream, little smile on his face, sad though, letting his coffee go cold. Then, last minute, looks at his watch, sort of jumps, chucks money on the table, grabs his case and runs, train due out in minutes. Over there quick to check the money, she was, but it was okay.

He caught the train. Kriminalpolizei Sergeant Stenkowitz had confirmed that too. Reserved seat, duplicate documentation, a return from Prague booked for the following Friday. Oberinspektor Lubimov remembered Aske, breathless, boarding at the last moment, remembered directing him to his seat as well as inspecting his ticket later.

After that? The Herr Oberinspektor shrugged. Czechoslovakia, yes? The Böhmen *Grenzpolizei*, the soldiers, the Zoll . . . Whoever knew, after that?

And there, from the point of view of the police, the luck ran out. Five fellow passengers in a crowded compartment, Vienna playing a soccer cup tie with Prague. Two other reserved seats, both one-way trips, one to Lauchhammer, one to East Berlin. The rest? Unreserved. Untraceable.

Had Aske actually crossed the border? The inspector grew testy. Worked for Austrian State Railways, didn't he? Checked them as far as Gmünd, didn't he? Want to know what happened after Gmünd, better ask the Böhmen, hadn't they?

There was little point in making enquiries of the Czechoslovakian authorities, whose uniformed minions swarmed over the train in khaki waves between Gmünd and Vesilí nad Lůznicí. The Austrians were not fools. It was pretty clear what had been going on. Protocol obliged them to make formal enquiries just the same.

But if a Czech functionary at the highest level declared, with a finality that froze the fingertips of those who read the communication, that a passenger known to be on the train as far as Gmünd had not been on the train when it reached Veselí, the only thing left was to say thank you.

The news – or the lack of it – moved slowly through *höh* – them up there – spinning off flurries of paperwork, producing a series of cool little meetings between officials, very correct, in the Austrian Ministries for the Interior and Foreign Affairs, and other officials, diffident but urbane, from the British embassy in Reisnerstrasse.

The meetings were invariably short. The only worthwhile questions were those which could be neither asked nor answered. The State Treaty of 1955 pledged Austria to permanent neutrality. Being neutral, as the Swiss learned long ago, is to a large extent the art of dodging questions.

6

That Vienna, a perpetually revolving door between East and West, has long been the spy capital of the world is universally recognised. So long as those with a claim to be *Ausserordentlicher und Bevollmächtiger Botschafter*, as diplomats in that city of titles may call themselves, refrained from behaving boorishly, there was seldom need to talk about it.

At the British embassy, two second secretaries and the assistant to the cultural attaché were quite casually replaced: doesn't do to let chaps in the Dip feel settled for too long.

Almost at once the routine disapproval of Austrian authority switched to the *Ausserordentlicher und etcetera Botschafter* at the United States embassy, clear across the Innere Stadt, as the civilising mission of the CIA in Central America became everyone's cause of the year. The matter of Simon Aske was transferred to the back burner. In due course, assiduously neglected, the back burner went out.

\*   \*   \*

Late one evening, a man alighted from the Vindobona express at the Franz Josef Station. He had had a compartment to himself all the way from Prague. He carried one small, soft-topped case. A light, dank breeze blew from the Danube. The sky was a starless darkness daubed with the yellow melancholy of sodium street lights and little excitements of neon.

After the rush hour Vienna is a city in which traffic all but vanishes, just occasional small bursts of cars, bunched by the traffic lights. They race along the wide, empty streets, their tyres zipping shrilly over the stone setts of the central strips down which the streetcars run.

The newly arrived traveller wasted no time looking for a cab. Crossing Julius Tandler Platz, he headed confidently down Porzellangasse. Pedestrians were even scarcer than cars, although the weinstuben produced a warm hum of conversation and the occasional laugh or alcoholic shout.

Each time he passed through the dead wash of illumination from a shop window, his face showed pale and blank. As he walked, not fast, not slow, he hummed. No recognisable tune or rhythm, simply a sound to set against silence.

In Währingerstrasse, at the hotdog stand outside the Chemical Institute, he bought lebwurst in brötchen, which he ate mechanically. He watched the streetcars whine towards the Schottentor, stared at the distant, floodlit spires of the Votivkirche. His face had the vacuity of a baroque angel.

Finishing his snack, he went on past the General Hospital with its constellated lights. Past the Spitalgasse junction, the shutters down on the little fruit shop, past the medical bookshop, past the revolving orange ball of the savings bank. West at Zimmermann, north at Schumann, finally arriving at the high, arched entrance with its massive oak doors and column of bell pushes.

Letting himself in through the wicket door, he stepped into the long, tiled hall, gloomy and cavernous under its high ceiling. The notice board displaying city ordinances was a tatty collage, nothing new. He mounted the stairway to the shiny oak door on the fourth floor, used his other key. Silence inside; a small lobby with a table, the telephone, the directories and commercial guides. Silence from the private quarters.

Treading softly, the traveller went towards the guest rooms. In the same instant, the Engineer, always inquisitive, appeared in the archway, stumpy, pigeon-toed in his worn red slippers, woollen cardigan fastened over his pot-belly with the top button and the bottom buttonhole unpartnered. His pate glistened in the shaded light.

"Herr Aske!" He stood there like a man experiencing a small, unexpected stroke.

Her Britannic Majesty's ambassador to Austria, first early night in weeks, was livid when the news came through via the criminal police, Department One and the embassy duty officer. He had as little time for Six's bogeys as for that bloody awful monstrosity of a building they infested in Lambeth.

# TWO

Pierre Weber stuck his head in. "Hi! The Yanks are in town. How's my girl? Street door opened when I pushed."

"Pierre!" Sylvie Morpurgo, washing developing equipment, a preliminary to getting her new darkroom into working order, reached for a towel. "Workmen! Gone to the pub for lunch. They think just because I'm here . . ."

"You are. I'm glad." Far from looking glad, he seemed more melancholy than ever, his thin face with its foxy hair and quizzical mouth, one side up, the other drooped, giving him the look of a poet of quiet despair.

"Go through. This isn't where I entertain. Who told you we'd moved? I don't remember sending Langley a card."

"The Cousins know everything. That's the party line, anyway."

In the living room she waved him to a seat. "Johnny's not here."

"I came to see you. Incidentally, this trip's secret."

"You're in London in secret?"

"In your home in secret."

Sylvie, who could make castoffs and a kerchief look like a new fashion trend, pushed a fallen strand of honey-coloured hair away from one eye. "You people! I think I could manage to live without you."

"You don't mean that. How's the boy?"

"You came to talk about Johnny?"

"I came to see *you*, damn it. How" – he indicated his surroundings – "does he reconcile fashionable Chelsea with his puritan conscience?"

9

"He's working on it. And finding it hard."

"I'll bet." He looking at her with open pleasure, Mrs John Morpurgo, who, as Sylvie Markham, would be on anybody's list of top photographers. She improved, he thought, all the time.

He produced his pothook smile. "Must be tough at that. You rich and famous, him a professional nobody, just like me."

"Security's just that, isn't it? Full of professional nobodies. If you want to be famous, do something else, and that goes for the pair of you."

"I guess it goes for being rich, too." Sylvie, not Morpurgo, was the moneyed one, even though what she had she had worked for. John Morpurgo, humble background, had been recruited into MI5 from the trade union movement as a token represent-ative of the moderate left and the common man.

Twenty years had taken him to the top of K section, culmin-ating in the brilliant stroke that rounded up the Sattin spy ring. Next thing you knew, clobbered by his political enemies as a potential security risk.

A triple charge: leftish politics, being too clever if not outright tricky, and a seducer of his betters' wives. Even Sylvie had left him for a while.

Well, it had all worked out in the end, thanks to a great girl like Sylvie. And to Lawrence Epworth. "Sorry," he said. "Just thinking."

"Carry on," she said. "There isn't a lot of it about." Laid back and very collected, that was Sylvie. He wouldn't put it past her to read his thoughts.

"Anyway," he said, "how are things these days? For you and the boy?"

"No thanks to you, but things are okay."

"Me? Why me? What did I do?"

"The collective you. The species. Does Johnny know you're here? Meaning in the country, not my house."

"Lawrence Epworth knows. How's the boy – "

This time she was swift. "The boy will soon be fifty."

He gave her a look of anguished apology. "How's he making out south of the Thames?"

"With the king over the water?" She smiled at his puzzlement. "So the Cousins don't know everything after all. That's how their supporters referred to the Stuart kings after they were kicked off the throne in the seventeenth century. Loyalists like Steve used to call them the Pretenders. I gather he calls Epworth both."

"Hey, success must be honing Steve's wits."

Everyone in the business knew that Sir Stephen Archer, once Morpurgo's second-in-command and now head of Five, was not exactly a friend. His wife, since divorced, had been the nominal cause of Johnny's downfall.

Lawrence Epworth, operational head of the Secret Intelligence Service, had picked up the bits, including the discredited John Morpurgo. His was the only name above Johnny's on the list of men Steve Archer could do without.

"Johnny's making out," Sylvie said. "Let's leave it at that."

"Still don't care for friend Lawrence?"

"I like his wife. I like Amaryllis a lot."

"There is nothing," Weber said tactfully, "like the love of a good woman," and looked so wistful that Sylvie warmed to him.

No use asking Pierre Weber about his wife. Rumour had it that she was dead after giving Weber a hard time. Rumour had it that the son took after his mother.

Weber returned his attention to his surroundings. The move from an unfashionable area of Kensington had been Sylvie's idea. Most of the money had been Sylvie's, too. The way Weber had heard it, Morpurgo had fought hard to stay in the old house. It was he who had bought it, way back, raising a mortgage on a then meagre salary.

His other reason for fighting had been even more typically Morpurgo. More than two decades on in the security business, first MI5, now SIS and lucky to make it, the wrong side of Holland Park – Shepherd's Bush *bis*, as Epworth had called it – had sustained an illusion. A house in fashionable Chelsea would not.

"It's the idea, right?" He knew there was no need to explain.

She smiled. "All these years as an Establishment watchdog, and he still sees himself as a typical member of the proletariat. Sweet, really."

The furnishing was pretty well the way it had been in the old house, little obviously new. Sylvie had been typically thoughtful about that. The most striking feature, as always, was her own pictures, few in number, but all, in their way, works of art.

"Love that one." He nodded. "The old woman on the donkey."

Somewhere that was not England, a harsh and arid land. An old woman astride a donkey piled high with fodder, both of them in silhouette, the donkey caught in the act of snatching a mouthful of hay.

11

The drama lay behind them. An ancient tree stretched out gnarled and tortured arms, its bole hiding the setting sun. Light flared all about it as if, from the heart of darkness, a universe were in the explosive moment of birth. Sylvie, lord knew how, had captured the scene as the tree had captured the sun; patience and poverty, transience and awesome eternity.

An old woman on a donkey! It was as if you were to take a picture of Jesus entering into Jerusalem and call it "Young man on a donkey." And me, Weber thought, not even a practising atheist.

"Spain." Sylvie said it casually, and then, equally casually, "Why are you really here?"

"Warren Claas's last day as head of London station, what else? Someone has to be around to count the spoons."

"We dined him a couple of nights ago." Warren Claas was another of them about whom Sylvie had ambivalent views.

"So you know your people are throwing a shindig for Warren tonight?"

"Johnny's people, not mine."

"Sorry to hear about John's mother," Weber said diplomatically. "I guess he took it hard."

Next door, in the converted garage, the workmen had returned. Almost at once, an electric drill produced sound effects of torture.

Sylvie kicked off her shoes, tucked up her feet in the big, plump chair. "It hit him hard. Still does. What else might hit him hard, Pierre?"

He sidestepped. "Too bad. I know he thought a lot of her."

"She lay for hours, until a neighbour found her; died two days later, pneumonia. You can imagine the field day his conscience has been having."

"So you're sticking around a while, right? Can't leave the poor guy all by himself, nothing to do but brood. A house he didn't want. His ma. His fate. His future."

Sylvie Markham, who was a genuine lady, smiled sweetly. "You fink bastard! Just where did you hear I might be going?"

"Sylvie, I swear – !"

"Stop dodging questions."

"I just said. He needs you here. Do you still want him out?"

She laughed with a kind of dismay. "You know too much."

"Oh, look!" He was genuinely hurt. "You're not the girl I think you are if you haven't thought, often, that things would be a

12

whole heap better with the guy in a normal, decent job."

He gave a wry little shake of the head. "Sometimes have the same idea, but who'd have me?"

"Yes, I'd like him out of the Service." She spoke quickly, get it out of the way. "I had the idea, once we were over that stupid business of Helga Archer, he could come in with me as my manager. But then . . ."

"Don't tell me. The right to live his life his own way?"

"Right." She said it ruefully.

"He's a lucky guy."

"Maybe I'm a lucky woman."

The drilling started up again next door. When it paused, Weber said, "I like him, will you believe that?"

"Johnny? Yes, I'll believe that."

"They have a hit list, the anti-Epworth club."

"Meaning Steve Archer and his friends."

"Spell that with a capital F. Johnny and brother Epworth share the same enemies, Sylvie. And for the same reasons."

"If Lawrence Epworth's left of centre, it's news to me."

"Nobody knows what he is, except that he's not one of them. Doesn't play by their rules. The same goes for Johnny. Makes people like Archer and his pals goddam uncomfortable."

"Oh, I know I'm not the only one who'd like Johnny out."

"You'd like him to quit. Archer and his pals wouldn't give him the option. Or Epworth either."

"He nearly resigned. I stopped him. Now it's too late."

"They wouldn't let him resign, honey. Back home you can quit and write a book. Over here, the rules are tougher. I guess you could blame us for that."

"Langley? Or Washington?"

"Both. Your people are so scared about losing the special relationship – hey, listen, use that expression back home and people think you're talking about a couple of gays – they're so scared Uncle Sam will show them the door they'll do damn near anything to curry favour."

"Getting rid of Epworth and Johnny is currying favour?"

"Getting rid of people you can't be sure are really your kind of people, the kind of people the top brass over here tend to call Them, meaning not Us . . ."

"You sound just like Johnny."

"Next thing you know, you'll be trusting me. Did I tell you my story about this guy at Langley who was being given the standard

13

polygraph test?"

"Lie detectors."

"They're supposed to detect the truth, too. Like Diogenes looking for an honest man. Anyway, the operator gets everything set up, then he asks what they call calibration questions, straight stuff, okay? So he starts by asking the guy his name, age, where he lives, then he says, 'Did you ever think you were Napoleon?' 'I am Napoleon,' the guy says, and the polygraph says he's not lying. The operator readjusts everything, then says, 'That was a lie, right?' 'Sure,' the guy says. 'That was a hell of a lie,' and the polygraph shows he's lying."

They both laughed a little before Sylvie said, "Johnny's going to have to take a polygraph test?"

"Not Johnny. Them. Meaning Us, with the capital U."

"Steve Archer!"

"His people. Sacrificed on the altar of the special relationship."

"Meaning Washington insisted."

"Didn't have to. Your people stay awake nights, second-guessing Washington before Washington asks."

Sylvie stirred at last. "I've had enough riddles. If it's all to do with Five, what's it matter to Johnny?"

"Steve's out for blood. Secret Intelligence is just about the only arm of British security that still keeps us Yanks out. No kowtowing, no joint vetting, no polygraphs."

"Steve's looking for a way to keep his end up in Whitehall and he thinks he might be able to get at Epworth through Johnny?"

"Close enough. When it comes to national security, I never forget how few steps it is from the street to the dock for you British."

"It's still a free country."

"You're free to think so. Getting to be so it's subversive to say so."

"Steve hasn't forgiven Johnny for Helga, but I don't think he's vengeful."

"Maybe, but people like Steve feel the way some folk feel back home: a lefty's one step short of a commie, and commie's another word for traitor."

"Johnny's no more a communist than you are."

Weber nodded vigorously. "I know that. It's all beside the point." He made a tentative gesture. "I could have told you less. I'd rather not tell you more."

She wondered if Weber's wife had ever shared her own present feeling, always disturbing, sometimes worse, of being inextricably entangled in matters it was an offence to know anything at all about.

"Damn them!" she said. "Damn all of you! That's why I nearly left him. Not just Helga. The bloody job."

"You didn't leave him. And you'll pry him loose, sooner or later."

"I wish I could think so. I've got to go on my travels again soon, a quickie to Vienna, then New York, not so quick. I wanted him to take a few days off, come with me to Vienna, but oh no, always loyal, even when he doesn't really believe what he's being loyal to. Would you like a drink or something?"

"He wouldn't go with you to Vienna?"

"So it's Vienna that brought you round to pry. Quite a relief to find you don't know everything. No, he's not. Disappointed?"

He stroked the arm of his chair, admiring the room. "Used a light touch here, didn't you? Just this one big change, the house. He'll adjust. You make more changes, little by little, until, one day . . . Oh yes, you'll pry him loose."

He pointed to the baby grand. "Time to play piano, be his own man." He gave her a quick grin, complicit. "No. Not entirely his own man. More than a little yours, but he won't know that. You're too smart." He stood up. "No drink, thanks, honey. Things to do."

"Stay to lunch." Suddenly she wanted to know much more.

"Next time. Thanks all the same."

"You know you won't see him tonight? Top brass only."

"I won't see him, period. Off to Europe, no rest for the wicked."

"No," she said. "That's why I want him out. Do I tell him you called?"

"You will anyway."

She smiled. "Just wanted to know what you'd say."

He stood smiling back, a slightly-built man with a smile as cryptic as a shorthand symbol and brown eyes that, if they were doggy, were the eyes of a much-thrashed hound.

"He won't come just because you whistle, Sylvie. He'll come when he's ready for home. But you know that." He left her thinking that it was a doggy thing to say.

# THREE

Century House, an exemplary specimen of Property Developer's Primitive, is in Lambeth. Lambeth is a London borough twinned by an aggressively left-wing council with the Moscow district of Moskvoretsky. One of the few things with which Lambeth is well-endowed is poverty, but inexplicably it has no queues against the day when the Soviet Union opens its borders to the yearning masses of the West.

A select few, commuters all, of those who work in Century House know Moskvoretsky well enough, but ageing aesthetes among its six hundred or so government employees tend to yearn more for the days when Her Majesty's Secret Service operated principally from an antique labyrinth of offices in Queen Anne's Gate.

True, it was easy to lose oneself in a warren of ill-lit, drearily painted and virtually identical corridors. True, the prospect from a cliffy myriad of grimy windows was of another myriad of grimy windows across Petty France. But the offices of the top people had an antique dignity, and one was at least on the right side of the river, old boy. St James's Park was one's pleasant front garden, the Army and Navy Stores, not yet vulgarised, still a decent place for a gentleman to make his purchases, and one could actually stroll to most of the places that matter.

All gone now, together with a past in which SIS not only lived with an illusion of globally omniscient power, but persuaded others to share it. The present twenty-storey eyesore in the clogged heart of Lambeth has achieved a symbolism its architects never intended.

Lawrence Epworth, most outwardly ethereal of latter-day

aesthetes, preferred any street in Lambeth to the gruesome cheerfulness of the Century House cafeteria. Fortunately, he and his companions were only passing through. The farewell wining and dining of Warren Claas was over.

Sir Edward Inch, the new SIS knight, and the heads of the six operational departments had gathered at White's in St James's the previous evening. There, Sir Edward, short on experience, had proved long on platitudes and notably unfunny stories. There, Hugo Pendleton of the Foreign and Commonwealth Office, privately referred to by Epworth as the – mmmm – androgynous android, had made a speech, laced with obscure classicisms, that had left Warren Claas all but speechless.

John Morpurgo had not been invited. Yet now, by Claas's express wish, he was accompanying him on what Claas insisted was no more than a last nostalgic tour of Century House. In Morpurgo's opinion, anyone who could extract nostalgia from Century House was a closet coprophiliac.

Epworth was wearing his Gioconda smile. Tall, stooped, hollow-chested, with a barely visible down of hair above a high, pallid forehead, he might have been the donor of an unwise amount of blood, and Claas, a crew-cut, freckle-faced country boy even in middle age, the bouncing beneficiary.

Claas had lingered everywhere. He even lingered in the cafeteria, as if the blue polyvinyl floor, the orange polycarbonate chairs and polyester curtains gave him the emotional charge of the Sistine Chapel. What's his game? wondered Morpurgo.

"If you persist in loitering," Epworth said, "we shall oblige you to stay to lunch. Then you'll look back nostalgically on White's."

"White's?" Claas showed his teeth, the better to lie through them. "Why, last night was just terrific. All that history, that atmosphere, the heady smell of power or whatever it is your old English clubs smell of."

He aimed a jab at Epworth's slender bicep. "See, I don't have to snow you guys now. C'mon, let's take a last look at the flower of cities all."

He punched again, this time at Morpurgo. " 'Earth hath not anything to show more fair', right? Nobody wrote a poem about Langley yet, not fit to print."

Morpurgo, tallish, darkish, nothing very special though given to moods, had known Claas for quite some time. They had had their battles: seven years of veiled mistrust and a running banter of insults in disguise. Anyone would think, he told himself, that

17

he's finally decided to like me.

A bit late now, and yet, in this surreal world into which they all stepped when they left wives, kids, firesides to go to what, still more surrealistically, they called work, it was a cause for suspicion. Such, Morpurgo thought, as they emerged on the roof, was the nature of the game, such the nature of those who played it.

Leaning dangerously forward over the drop, Claas reverted to the rebarbative image so carefully cultivated during his time in London.

"We bought London Bridge and the old *Queen Elizabeth* from you. That heap of mock-Gothic junk over there in Westminster sure would pull them in in Disneyland."

Epworth smiled his protosmile. "Perhaps we could arrange a swap, the Houses of Parliament for your presidential elections. British children still enjoy – mmmm – a travelling circus."

Morpurgo, watching the clowning, no less subtle on Claas's side for all the rodomontade, knew when to keep his mouth shut. Lawrence Epworth ran the SIS roadshow, and Claas knew it. Claas would get nothing unless Epworth chose to give, but it was Morpurgo's opinion that Claas was giving it a try.

"Okay," Claas said, "so I'm shooting my mouth off. But this is my swan song. Tomorrow you'll be dealing with Di Pasolino. The king is dead, long live the king, right?" Epworth's tiny smile turned the Mona Lisa into a giggler.

"I mean" – Claas the unsuspected actor, farewell performance – "seven years sitting on my butt over there in Grosvenor Square, watching, listening, learning the ropes." The hazy sunlight, mellow as honey, softened the guileful candour of his gaze. "I mean," he said, "I was willing to learn from you boys.

"These guys, I would think, were cloak-and-daggering when America belonged to the Indians. 'Listen,' I would say to Ella, days when Ella and me were talking, 'listen, these babies not only have more history than we have kooks in California, they know what to do with it.' "

All these years, Morpurgo thought, and he had had this man tagged and filed in the wrong box. Now, at the moment of his departure, the truth shone through. Steely-bright, sapient, shrewd as a moneylender.

"Sure, you had your bad spells," Claas was saying. "Your moles and spies and cover-ups. You had your Director-Generals who might have been Moscow Centre agents, and your Moscow

18

Centre agents who damn near got to be Director-Generals."

He switched his attention to Morpurgo, an odd blend of speculation and wintry warmth. "Looks like whatever they did, though, they ended up knights. I told Ella I figured that was the trick of it all."

He waited for someone to be offended. All about them the city hummed polyphonically. A tug twinkled downstream on the morning tide. Epworth, listening with the rapt attention of a music lover, which he was, at a recital, which in a way it also was, said, "Ah," and giggled, a sound that could raise eyebrows at first encounter but was somehow never mocked.

"My Lord," Claas said, "Your Grace, My Right Honourable Friend. The Queen in Parliament, the country, right or wrong. Only for country read party in power. Boy, that is one hell of a con trick."

He hoisted himself on to the parapet, put his hands in his pockets. One quick shove, Morpurgo thought, and Britain avenged.

"Playing your tune, John my friend, right?" Claas was openly mocking him. "Back there in Langley they make cracks about Warren Claas being too long among the British. So long, they say, he's maybe been turned around."

Morpurgo, middle-aged man of a kind of world, blushed inwardly. Claas was signalling his awareness of seven years of anti-Claasness. Was he signalling something more?

"Well," Claas said, "maybe they're right at that. Maybe I went even farther than my good friend John Morpurgo, who took an oath to defend and protect what he doesn't entirely believe in. And maybe that's because I figured out the trick."

He grinned, a stocky man with a bas-relief face whose cold button-eyes, anywhere west of the Allegheny Mountains, might have been more interested in checking grain futures or the price of hog on the trotter.

"Maybe," he said, "because I realised that what I was looking at was no tinpot charade. Maybe I realised I was wrong in thinking that tradition was something the British invented as an excuse for dressing up in screwy clothes. Maybe I realised that knighthoods, all that kind of stuff, come cheaper than pork barrel projects and political favours, which is the way we do things back home."

He shifted his queasy perch on the parapet without removing his hands from his pockets. "In the US we have the Freedom of

19

Information Act, nothing refused without good reason. Over here, you stand it on its head, for no good reason. Over there, a Senate committee can haul up the Director, CIA, for a grilling in front of the TV cameras and the press. Over here, Her Majesty's Secret Intelligence Service doesn't even exist."

He chuckled. "Okay, you can challenge the government in the courts. But first you have to know what questions to ask, and second, if the government doesn't like the questions, it pleads the safety of the realm, no safety, no law.

" 'Just one little minute here,' you say. 'You claim something's above the law on grounds of national security, you're going to have to prove it.' 'Sorry, fellers,' says your government, 'you just have to take our word for it. Can't give you the facts. That would imperil national security.' "

He shook his head in mock awe. "No wonder Lewis Carroll was British! Joseph Heller, eat your heart out!"

Morpurgo mostly agreed with what Claas had said, but since Epworth stayed silent, he made a joke. "Whose side are you on, Warren?"

The joke rebounded. "Whose side are *you* on, John my friend? Maybe one of these days you'll have to decide." Claas pretended to inspect his hand-lasted English shoes. "I just spent seven years watching a bunch of magicians at work. I figure you for the sorcerer's apprentice."

Morpurgo felt himself begin to flush, but Claas slid down to link arms with him.

"Only kidding." He looked at the panorama. "Tell me one last time where everything is. Back there in Langley, they're going to have me down as an expert on everything British."

Morpurgo pointed at Westminster. "Well, starting from the left . . ."

"Which you usually do," Claas said, and squeezed his arm.

". . . Government, Civil Service, Law, Press, Church and Big Business." Two, he thought, could play Claas's little game.

"A panorama," Epworth said, "of – mmmm – power."

Smiling broadly, Claas pretended to revert to type, a Kansas City boy, third-generation American, with ancestors in the wrong Germany.

"A panorama of power? Well, gee whizz, how about that? And here's me thinking it was maybe just – you know? – kind of like a stage set. Kind of a Hollywood thing, all the actors gone someplace else."

20

He turned suddenly to Epworth. "Ever been to Vienna, Lawrence? It was there, too, once upon a time. I mean power. Now all that's left is the fancy goddam buildings."

Epworth's china-blue eyes filmed like the early autumn sky. "Mmmm. I can't claim to know it well."

Claas looked at Morpurgo. "How about Sylvie? This be her first trip?" They had finally arrived, Morpurgo guessed, at Claas's destination.

A moment later he was roaring with laughter. "Why don't I mind my own business, right? Old Warren, having his last fling before pulling out."

He flung up an arm to look at the gold and platinum Omega on his thick, dark-thatched wrist. "Hey, Lawrence my old buddy, I almost forgot. You're on vacation. You come all the way up from the sticks to indulge a sentimental prairie boy and he doesn't have the grace to know when to quit yacking."

"Our time," Epworth murmured, "is yours. Incidentally" – Morpurgo pricked up his ears – "when were you last in Vienna?"

"Me?" Claas stepped through the steel door on to the bare concrete steps. "I never was. Just heard a lot about the place. From other people." He started down.

\*     \*     \*

When they had seen Claas off, Epworth said, "Walk with me to the car." Morpurgo was determined not to ask what was so important about Vienna.

Orson had brought up Epworth's old Volvo estate from the underground carpark. It stood in the little bay normally fenced off by no-parking cones.

"You didn't tell me Sylvie was going to Vienna." Epworth tossed a grubby, beaten-up panda into the back seat by its one remaining ear.

"She doesn't work for SIS."

"It came up when you and she took Claas out to dinner?"

"Never mentioned. Anyway, it's her business." First one to give something away's a sissy, Morpurgo told himself.

"Interesting." Epworth had absently pushed in the cigar lighter. It popped out with a smell of burning dust. "*Do* you know Vienna?"

"I went there once. When I was still with Five."

"Oh yes. Irish National Liberation Army on a shopping spree. High velocity rifles, wasn't it?" It was something he had not learned from Morpurgo.

"Come to lunch tomorrow." Epworth released the handbrake. "Bring Sylvie. Amaryllis would like it."

"I think Sylvie may be busy."

Epworth ignored the small rebuff. "He's wrong, you know. There's a bit of power left. It's all a question of who wields it."

"In Vienna?"

"Oh, there too, I dare say." The car pulled away, scattering and squashing plastic cones. Orson, emerging from the lobby to set them up again, tried to catch Morpurgo's eye with an unspoken comment. Morpurgo, playing the Epworth game, looked the other way.

# FOUR

Sid was about fifty-five, which gave him authority by unspoken
consent. The others, all in their twenties, fast-talking, flippant,
were aware of working for an attractive woman. Damian, not
knowing that Sylvie was within earshot, had referred to her as 'a
tasty slice of boiler'. Sid kept that kind of thing well under
control.

There was another thing about him from which Sylvie drew
secret joy. As well as opening the door to visitors when he was
around, he answered telephone calls and brought any mail that
arrived. Letters were almost always addressed to Sylvie Markham, usually prefixed by Ms.

Beginning by calling her Mrs Morpurgo, Sid had soon fallen
prey to doubt. He had never, like the young ones, called her
missus or, to his undisguised outrage – it stopped immediately –
love. He solved his private problem by changing to calling her
lady. From Sid it was a product of infinite grace.

Each evening, after supervising the others while they cleared
and tidied, he came to seek Sylvie out.

"Scuse me, lady, got a minute, have you?"

"Of course, Sid." She had tried calling him Mr Timpson. He
had steered her, politely but firmly, on to Sid. Even Johnny's
remark about the serf syndrome had been half-hearted. Sid's
dignity was adamantine.

"Another two days and the lads'll be out, lady. Just like to be
straight in my mind about while you're away." Sid was the
painter and decorator, his work the far from perfunctory seal of
approval on plumbing, electrical work and joinery.

"Darkroom's finished," he said, "barring a bit of plastering.

23

Electricity board's coming in to approve connecting up the wiring tomorrow. Damian" – he sucked a tooth, not really approving of cheaply witty, disco-crazy Damian with his dyed hair and earrings – "reckons he'll have them cupboards ready for painting Thursday. Made him change them hinges, though. Cheap and nasty, they were."

He felt for the tin from which he rolled cigarettes. "Working evenings, that's nothing to me, it's doing a good job. But" – his hands were conjuring a spindly cigarette into existence – "it's Mr Morpurgo, see? On account of disturbing."

"Yes," she said. "I do see."

"If you could, I dunno, sort of persuade him to stay out a couple of nights, I'd be out of this room come Tuesday." He stuck his cigarette in his mouth. It would remain unlit until he left, no use trying to persuade him. Wandering to the baby grand, he touched its gleam with careful, craftsman's fingers, silently approving.

Hearing Johnny play for the first time, he had made a polite enquiry. "Mozart? Is that what it is? Reckon they knew something in them days." She was going to miss Sid.

Wiry, nervy, sunken cheeks, with dark eyes that could glow when fanned by thoughts he mostly kept to himself, he said, "Plays this thing a treat. Shame to have me taking his mind off it."

She laughed. "I'll see what I can do, Sid."

He nodded, satisfied. "Out there in the street now, Mr Morpurgo is."

Unconscious of being watched, Johnny was on the opposite pavement, studying his own home. She knew what he was thinking.

"Get my things then," Sid said. "Bloke's entitled to a bit of peace when he's finished work." She wondered what he would say if he knew what kind of work it was.

\*        \*        \*

When Morpurgo came downstairs the drinks were ready, Schubert rippling from the hi-fi speakers. Mozart, Schubert, Bach transcriptions, he played them all superbly, he would say, on the hi-fi.

She patted the sofa. "Sit here. Now, tell me you're getting used to it. Tell me you actually, secretly, like it."

He slipped an arm about her. "I quite like it, your new house."

24

"Home. Our new home."

"Home, then. Yes, I quite like it. It's . . . handier. More in the middle of things." He drank some Scotch.

She squeezed hard, making his breath whoosh. "You bloody well like it. Only to say so out loud makes you feel – "

He grinned. "A class traitor."

"Class traitor!" She thrust him away. "Tell Sid that. He'd say, 'What class is that, then?' Openly admiring your own house isn't a crime."

"Where I come from, standing in the street staring at a house like this would have the nearest copper pulling you in on sus."

"Where you came from! All those years ago! If you'd called yourself working class in front of your mother, she'd have murdered you."

"*She* was working class, that's the point, even if she was determined to haul us up by the bootstraps, make us respectable."

"Well she did, didn't she? If she'd lived to come here, she'd have adjusted quicker than you: look what my Johnny's done."

"Her Johnny did nothing, except neglect her. And marry a girl who turned out to be clever."

"Who does that make cleverest? Anyway, nothing clever about pressing a button. Relax and enjoy, that's what I say. Go on. Smile."

He made the effort. "It's the image. All these years, man and boy, first Five, then Six, as the token prole. The posh end of the King's Road is going to wreck my image. By the way, has Warren Claas been in touch since we took him out?"

His by-the-ways, when they concerned work, were seldom casual.

"Yes," she said. "He wanted a final romp in bed before he left. I said it would upset the workmen."

"Maybe you and Warren had a date in Vienna."

She had been on the point of telling him about Pierre Weber. Now, suspicious, she decided to wait.

Perhaps sensing something, he changed the subject. "Before I forget, the Epworths have invited us to lunch tomorrow. Their place, he's still on leave."

"Funny. I called Amaryllis only yesterday. She didn't say anything." She was less and less inclined, at least for the time being, to mention Pierre's visit.

"A casual sort of thing," he said. "Anyway, it should be

25

pleasant. You're the one who always enjoys the country life."

"I'll give Rylla a call. Stella's coming here for a snack and a quick run through the schedule. Can't cancel it, worse luck."

Stella was Sylvie's agent. She had an agent, an accountant, a part-time secretary, not to mention a separate bank account that would make his own look like her petty cash book. It was an old sore, but from time to time it still itched.

It led him to another subject, dormant but not yet extinct. "You've been at home a couple of weeks and I've hardly seen you. Now you're off again. Before we know it we shall be waving as we pass in the street."

"So come with me to Vienna." Looking back, she was to decide that she had said it less in defiance of Weber's cryptic probing than to see what he would say.

"You know I'd like to." He was certain that Epworth had invited them both to lunch so that when the subject of Sylvie's trip came up – and he would have made sure that it did – he could make the casual suggestion that they should go together.

Sylvie was tempted into a sudden thrust. "Has anything happened to make you change your mind?"

"Damn it, Sylvie!" He allowed himself to sound injured. "It just struck me it might be rather pleasant after all." If he were mistaken about Epworth's intentions, he could always say that he had been refused leave.

Sylvie experienced a pang of conscience. Moving house had enabled her to give up the premises off Baker Street. From now on she would be working from home. As Pierre Weber had guessed, the other and more difficult part of the plan was to get him to quit without feeling that she had forced him. It made the idea of having him with her on a working trip doubly attractive.

Vienna was just a couple of meetings to discuss the possibility of a commission. There would be plenty of free time. If he enjoyed the experience, he might develop a taste for it.

There was something else. She was a little unhappy about leaving him alone in a house he had not yet adjusted to. Men could be such babies about things like that. And he was still oppressed by the circumstances of his mother's death.

Coincidentally, he said, "It might do me good to get away a bit. I keep thinking, if we hadn't been held up so much over moving, she'd have been in. Then it wouldn't have happened."

That did it, Sylvie thought. The old girl, gutsy, proud, wilful, had also been incurably prejudiced against almost everything:

the young, the blacks, the way we live now. Having her living with them would have been an on-and-off kind of purgatory, but after a lifelong love-hate relationship, Johnny had been freed to wallow in unjustified guilt.

"All right," she said, Weber and his mysteries forgotten, "I'm sorry I can't come tomorrow, but don't ask him about Vienna, bloody well tell him you're coming with me. I shall be off all over the place after that."

"Remind me. Might come in handy as ammunition."

"Well, New York's not fixed yet, but it could come up any time. Otherwise, the Royal Shakespeare and ICI. Quite a plateful."

"Plus Vienna."

"Yes, no, maybe. You did some history. What do you think? It seems to me that huge, illustrated books on the Holy Roman Empire might just as well be sold with a set of legs and a socket in each corner."

"I thought they raked through the archives for that kind of illustration."

"They do and they will, all except mine."

"People." People and places were Sylvie's speciality.

"People. Flattering, I suppose, but somehow I don't see them getting permission for me to go poking a camera around in Hungary, Czechoslovakia, those places. That's one of the things I have to talk about."

"And the RSC, that's Stratford and London?"

"The RSC's a year's work, off and on. Whatever they do, wherever they go. Not just productions, a full year's photographic record, everything. Rehearsals, workshops, management, press and publicity, front-of-the-house staff, audiences, restaurants and bars, even loo attendants if they've got any. A free hand." She pointed a mock camera at him and clicked her tongue. "Terrific! Best theatre company in the world, and I get my name linked with theirs in a permanent record. Exhibition next year, then a book. Super chance, super compliment."

"For them, too," he said, and meant it. "If the RSC deserves Sylvie Markham, Sylvie Markham deserves the RSC." But his heart sank at the prospect. "All that plus ICI and the Holy Roman Empire? I'll be lucky if I ever see you again."

So why don't you get out of your lousy business and come in with me? she wanted to say, but instead she said, "ICI's different, just twelve shots, prestige stuff, fit it in over a period of months."

27

"Just twelve shots in the end, but you'll take hundreds, I know you."

"Take a bit of organising, that's one of the reasons Stella's coming tomorrow, but I'll be around, don't you fret."

She was working on him now, he knew that. Back often enough to assure him he wasn't being neglected, away often enough to let him persuade himself that he was.

There was a way out; partnership. If they went to Vienna together, it would probably come up on the agenda. And yet . . . and yet . . .

Although she hated it, the limelight was beginning to follow Sylvie everywhere. Full partner, maybe. But Stella, when she zoomed in and out in the course of her agenting, tended to call him Mr Markham and make things worse by the effusiveness of her apologies before she did it again.

If he quit, it would be Mr Sylvie Markham who booked her flights and carried her baggage. The alternative; a minor figure among the dedicatedly anonymous, operating in a world of professional silence. Would working for Sylvie, he wondered, be better than being Lawrence Epworth's poodle?

# FIVE

Born and bred in London, Morpurgo saw the countryside as little more than a vaguely agreeable way of preventing towns from running into each other. The fact that the Epworths' house had been standing in its Surrey woodlands for four centuries impressed him without giving him any wish to own it. Through the kitchen window, open on to an explosion of hibiscus, hydrangeas and late-flowering buddleia, Amaryllis waved a floury hand.

"Bother about Sylvie. I was looking forward to a natter. Bung the car in the shade, then come round and rub noses before you kiss hands with His Grace." She had once achieved the effect of gross blasphemy by telling Morpurgo that Lawrence Epworth, lord of the high, the middle and the low, was the only son of 'a piffling colonial bishop'.

It was almost all he knew about the man. Epworth on his private life was like Count Moltke, silent in seven languages.

Pinkly pretty and pushing a well-distributed one hundred and forty pounds, Amaryllis was making bread, her floral print dress reminding him of one of her herbaceous borders. She presented a slightly floury cheek to be kissed, simultaneously hitching up a stray strap.

"I know," she said. "Bust is springing out all over. Lucky Sylvie, no calorie crises. Here, sloosh your hands under the tap and thump this stuff about a bit while I dash to the loo. Jolly difficult bashing the hundred per cent stoneground with your legs crossed. How's Sylvie? How's the house? Remember to tell me later." On her way out she punted aside a grubby rag doll with one of her bare, surprisingly small feet.

"There, that's better." She came to look at the dough. "Given it a good socking, have you? Super! Don't think you and his lordship are going to plot and plan until the little woman announces luncheon is served. Nought on the double damask before I've downed one or two swifties, and I never drink alone. Leastways, that's my story.

"Incidentally, a word 'twixt thee and me. Are you supposed to be going to Vienna to please Sylvie?" She poked the dough with an experimental finger. "Ah, jolly good, make a baker out of you yet."

She pretended to misread his surprise. "Like a baby's bum, good bread dough. Prod it and it should pop back. Don't suppose you've kneaded many babies. Oh lordy, sorry!" She knew he and Sylvie couldn't have kids.

"Anyway," she said, "what's the party line? Wouldn't want to let any kitties out of the bag."

So he was going to Vienna. "The story will be that I thought it would please Sylvie," he said.

"Good-oh! Now I shan't blab. Come on then, doesn't do to keep old cleverclogs waiting once he knows you're around."

The hall, with its chintzy window seats and late summer flowers, had its usual smell of lavender. Opening a door she shouted, "Hoy, Moriarty, one o'clock on the dot if you don't want to find me sloshed."

The room, low-ceilinged like the rest of the house, had its own run of massive, adze-hewn beams. Its three mullioned windows commanded terraces, lawns spattered with the small change of summer's end and, in the middle distance, the ragged wall of woodland. It was a room of books, heterogeneous furnishings, organised muddle; shabbiness made distinguished by the loving care with which everything had passed through time's fingers.

Epworth was seated at an old desk, doing something delicate. His sparse gossamer hair, backlit, gave him a halo. "Sorry about Sylvie. Another time, perhaps. We call this the – mmmm – music room."

Looking at the ranged instruments, Morpurgo was impressed. "Good lord, I'd no idea you had so many."

"Early woodwinds come in all shapes and sizes."

Morpurgo picked up a thing bent into the shape of a pothook. "Shawm? Or crumhorn? I never remember."

"The shawm is straight. The crumhorn is – mmmm – horn-shaped. That one is the granddaddy of the consort, basso grande."

Epworth was a founder member of an early music group calling itself the Cornysh Consort after some obscure composer of the fifteenth – or was it sixteenth? – century. Highly proficient, it specialised in music of the late Middle Ages and early Renaissance. Epworth played shawm, crumhorn and, as he put it, doubled on the bombard. He also sang male soprano.

Morpurgo turned the crumhorn curiously. "Is this thing real? I mean original, an antique?"

Epworth came to relieve him of it. "Munich, around 1520. My only other original is sixteenth-century Italian, Ferrara. The rest are modern, Körber in Berlin, Moeck in Celle, and a chap who lives in Essex. Shouldn't be out of their cases really, but I'm re-reeding."

"You're what?"

Epworth removed a mouthpiece. "See? Double reed, they all are. Well, you don't buy them at the nearest supermarket."

"What do you do? Grow 'em yourself?"

Sarcasm was wasted on Epworth. He giggled. "All but, in my case."

There was no easy way through Epworth's mental maze. "All right, how do you reed?"

Epworth took him back to the desk. There was a wooden board to work on, a small pair of pliers, an old-fashioned cutthroat razor, blade ground lethally slim. There was also a fragment of something, presumably reed. Epworth handed it delicately to Morpurgo. It was, in fact, two pieces of reed, bound with fine wire. "Double. When you blow, the air makes the reeds vibrate. You scrape and adjust to make them behave the way you want. Doubles are dodgy things."

He fitted the reed in the mouthpiece, the mouthpiece on the crumhorn, sucked several times, blew, producing a deep-throated snarl.

"Sounds terminal." Morpurgo, a Mozart and Schubert lover, found early music interesting rather than mellifluous.

Epworth ran up and down a scale before rasping out something approaching a melody. "Praetorius. Michael, not Hieronymous. A snatch, of course, a mere snatch." On early music, as on unblended sherries, he could talk like a Thurber archetype, yet his recondite interests were no more mocked than was his giggle. He removed the reed. "Never leave them in

31

longer than necessary," he said as if Morpurgo were contemplating such a thing. "Sometimes leads to a broken reed. Of course" – he produced a bottle and a glass – "the vital part is selection. Handpicked, that's the only sure way." Epworth preached condensed sermons on the iniquity of drinking anything but sherry before good wine. There would be wine for lunch, yet that was a bottle of vodka.

"Arles," Epworth continued. "You know the Camargue? *Arundo donax*, otherwise known as sative. Other people, other preferences. I find sative effective." He took a small feather, worked it between the blades of the double reed, wiggled it delicately. "Still, all tricky, and doubles can be particularly tiresome."

For the first time Morpurgo began to listen seriously. Doubles and broken reeds. Epworth could effortlessly sustain conversations on two levels of meaning.

"Stolnichaya." He poured out a generous measure of vodka. "The best. Only the *nomenklatura* can buy it in the Soviet workers' paradise." He dropped the reed in the vodka, stirring it carefully.

"Five years for curing. Distilled water for softening. Vodka for sterilising." He fished out the reed and laid it on a sheet of blotting paper. "Of course, vodka wouldn't be everyone's choice. Remind me, what do you know about Fish?"

It was a question of phonetics. If someone, out of the blue, said "*Arundo donax*," it could take a while to identify the language. It was the same with "Fish", while "double", in Morpurgo's line of country, had its own special problems.

In the aftermath of the breaking of the Sattin spy ring, others beside Morpurgo had fallen from grace. They had included a Foreign Secretary ill-advised by SIS's then Director-General and, like Belial tumbling after Lucifer, the Director-General himself. Into the vacuum had moved Lawrence Epworth. His ruthlessly brilliant opportunism the more effective for being as unexpected as assault and battery from a village curate, he had elbowed out the heir apparent, one Humphrey Fish.

"What do I know about Fish?" No doubt about it, half of this discourse on the art of reed-making could be put down to Epworth's Byzantine sense of humour. "Not much. Head of Sovbloc intelligence when I was still with Five. Early retirement following your rise to power. Dead soon after that."

"Is that all?"

"Gassed himself to death in his garage. Nicely hushed up, of course."

"Any more?"

"Double garage. Posh Georgian house in Esher."

"Mmmm – mock Georgian. Almost everything is mock in Esher. Do you recall the first time you met Fish?"

"How could I forget? It was my first meeting with you."

"Reactions?"

It was like prodding a barely healed wound. In the midst of the Sattin turmoil, encountering Epworth for the first time at a meeting between Five and Six, Morpurgo had made the mistake of dismissing him as of minor importance. Epworth had later saved Morpurgo from the suspicion of being a Security Director-ate mole, but only at the expense of having Sylvie find out about Helga.

Humphrey Fish, very public school and Esher, had made a far greater impression; a high-speed palsy of suppressed impatience and nervous energy.

"Jumpy. Very jumpy, but nobody's fool." Morpurgo frowned. "What's so special about the first impression? He was still there for a while after I came to Century House." When I was going cheap, said his memory, and you bought me.

"Poor Humphrey," Epworth said unpityingly. "Not the smallest skill in music, but an unwise urge to play solo."

According to Sylvie, Epworth could have denied the Lord three times before cockcrow and left everyone unsure whether it was some kind of joke.

"The exhaust pipe of a car, even a BMW, is an instrument of limited capacity," he said. "But then, his penultimate perform-ance was hardly more successful."

"Was he running something special before he . . . retired?"

"A little show of his own, around the time of your – mmmm – modified success with the Sattin ring. A PE exercise."

PE – private enterprise – was the abbreviation SIS used for operations run single-handed on the grounds that wider know-ledge might put them at risk. Rare things, the only justification was an exceptionally high-quality product.

"You'll remember," Epworth said, "why we all met on that occasion?"

Did he not! He and Steve Archer had just swept Sattin and his dupes into the bag. SIS, for once, had not disdained the rival establishment's success. The reason soon emerged. Recently, in East Germany, they had lost an agent of their own.

"I remember," Morpurgo said. "Nominally, you were

interested in what we might squeeze out of Sattin. Actually, you didn't give a damn. What you really wanted was to swap him for your own bloke."

"Not I. Fish."

"Look." In imagination, Morpurgo was back with Five, SIS the aloof rival. "We had a spy. Your lot wanted him. Anyway" – he discovered he could still be bitter about it – "it made no difference in the end, did it? Sattin died. Too bad for you. Too bad for me as well. They kicked me out."

"Not for that," Epworth said dispassionately. "And it made a difference to Fish. He's dead too."

Morpurgo glimpsed light. "The bloke the Hauptverwaltung had picked up in the DDR was part of Fish's PE operation?"

"He *was* Fish's PE operation. Operation Highflyer."

Think, Morpurgo commanded himself. This is why you're going to Vienna.

"That's why Fish was so agitated at that meeting. Couldn't wait to get his agent back. But Sattin died, so the swap fell through. Is that why he resigned?"

"No," Epworth said, "it's not why he resigned. It may be why he killed himself."

Outside, the surrounding woods were motionless in the airless noon; dark, crenellated walls. Amaryllis, still barefoot, padded across the lawn to collect a tricycle and started back. In imagination, Morpurgo was smelling the lethal fumes of car exhaust.

"Are the Sovs still holding Fish's field man?"

"We don't know. The cryptonym was Gossip. Real name. . . ?" Epworth shrugged, put the cap back on the Stolichnaya.

"Was Gossip a broken reed? Or a double?"

"Gossip was a first-class source. Fish wouldn't have got away with acting directly as Gossip's case officer if the product hadn't been – mmmm – of the first water."

"What's the link with Vienna?"

Epworth underwent one of his subtle metamorphoses. It reminded Morpurgo of the sensuous stretch and bend of a cat that, waking, prepares to take a predatory interest in life.

"Fish ran a courier between himself and Gossip. Simon Benjamin Aske, British citizen, professional expatriate, normal place of residence, Vienna. An – mmmm – *Einzelgänger*."

"A loner." Morpurgo spoke fair German, the only language he had to set against Sylvie's effortless, almost osmotic ability in the Latin tongues.

"And a linguist. Czech as well as German."

"What was his cover?"

"Some long-term research project for a man at the University of London who's a recognised authority on abstruse aspects of the Habsburg dynasty."

"Vienna as a base, but travelling. Where?"

"Prague, principally. Anyway, there we had Master Aske, funded by this man Masius – who was partly funded by us, incidentally – living modestly in Vienna, spending a good deal of his time in specialist libraries and, of course, making little trips."

"And Masius is kosher."

"A naturalised Slovak, distinguished in his field, and an SIS crypto since way back."

Most Sovbloc refugees sang their hate from the rooftops. SIS cryptos kept the lowest of profiles, publicly interested in nothing but family and career, privately providing the kind of service Masius had given to Fish.

"I gather Operation Highflyer was blue chip."

"You might never have uncovered Sattin and the Stringers if we hadn't given you absolute proof of that leakage of information from Underwater Weapons."

"That was Highflyer?"

"That was Highflyer. And Highflyer, to all intents and purposes, was Gossip. The product quality was so high that we were – mmmm – obliged to multi-attribute."

"Gossip got it to Prague, Aske brought it to London each time he came to see Masius, that it?"

"Aske never came to London. Fish always dealt with him direct."

"Sovbloc security obviously knew all about Aske if he was making regular trips through the Curtain. He must have been good to stay clean."

"So it would seem." Epworth's face had assumed the polished blandness of soapstone.

Aware from noises off that Epworth's youngest and her nanny had just returned from parts unknown, Morpurgo said, "I suppose Aske has some kind of academic background?"

"Aske was vouched for by Fish. Masius had no complaints."

"Someone must have known Aske's qualifications. They're on record, presumably."

"Presumably." Epworth put his hands behind his domed

35

head. "Is that really all you know about Fish?"

Morpurgo was experiencing a growing bewilderment. "Fish didn't give much away," he said. "He radiated suspicion the way your kids radiate trust."

"My children," Epworth said, "may seem to you to radiate trust."

What he felt for Epworth, Morpurgo decided, was a kind of Platonic hate. "The inquest gave nothing away, either," he said. "There was an internal enquiry, obviously."

"We had to make sure brother Humphrey hadn't been talking to Moscow during those trips to Vienna."

"Had he?"

"We decided not, so far" – Epworth pulled a small face – "as one can ever be sure of such things. That apart, there was evidence of stress. Depression. Wife trouble."

Stress, depression, wife trouble: the intelligence service equivalent of long service awards. "What did his wife say?" Morpurgo asked.

"She was somewhat uncooperative."

"Surprise, surprise! Wouldn't you say he had plenty of cause for stress and depression? I mean, quite apart from losing his agent?"

"I suppose so. There was his – mmmm – unfortunate fall from grace." Epworth the palace revolutionary had been the principal cause of Fish's fall from grace. "And of course, he didn't awfully care for the reorganisation. Didn't like losing the Sovbloc desk." Epworth himself had done the reorganising and taken the Sovbloc desk.

"What was his wife trouble?"

"Have you ever had to question a woman whose husband has left her abruptly and – mmmm – somewhat inconsiderately? I told you, uncooperative."

"Any other women?"

"We turned nothing up."

"Family?"

"One daughter, married, in Australia. It seems, from the daughter, that Humphrey was quite the little sadist. Dominate, humiliate, this hurts me more than it hurts you. He was considerably older."

"Did she love him, Mrs Fish?"

"She stayed married to him. She was the one who discovered him, all rosy-pink, the carbon monoxide. Alma Fish" – Epworth

36

simulated regret – "is not a great fan of the Service."

"So it all comes back to this chap Aske. How much did he know?"

"Ah," Epworth said. "Aske. Poor Humphrey. I suppose that must have been the – mmmm – *coup de grâce*. Didn't I say? Aske went missing in Prague, just about the time you joined us from Security Directorate."

"You bloody well know you didn't say. Are you telling me he was picked up by the" – he racked his brains – "the SB?"

"The Služba Bezpečnosti" – it was quite possible, Morpurgo thought, depressed, that Epworth, who spoke fluent German, also spoke Czech – "might have picked up Aske in Prague. He might" – it was all back to speculation, then? – "have languished in the Čtyrka until Cousin Ivan came to – mmmm – collect. Humphrey went to Vienna again, stayed some days. It was after his return that he shut himself up in his garage."

Come on, Morpurgo urged himself. This isn't SIS hocus-pocus. This is good down-to-earth Five stuff: who? what? where? why? when?

"Humphrey was desperate about Gossip," Epworth was saying. "Still hoping for some kind of swap. The Aske thing finally knocked the stuffing out of him. The more so since we could discover nothing at all about Aske."

"No talk of a trade there?"

"Nothing to trade with."

"So Fish lost everything. Seniority, the Sovbloc desk, a successful operation and two good blokes."

"I'd have done something about him anyway." Epworth was unmoved. "Too pally with your old friend Steve Archer, not to mention being Langley's man in Century House. But he had to be moved, he knew that. We had to assume that Aske was persuaded to talk, so, full cauterisation procedure. Of course," he added with barely a pause, "it was the same procedure, after Humphrey's – mmmm – *felo de se* that led us to discover that the files had gone."

Morpurgo had a growing sense of *déjà vu*. "What files?" he asked.

"The Highflyer files. Since it was a PE operation, exclusive to Fish, only he and the Knight had access. The then knight, of course."

"Sir Jason. Did he ever draw them?"

After Philby & Co., Security Directorate had been authorised to rage through SIS like the wrath of God. Epworth was telling him, an ex-Five outsider, things that would endear him even less to those in Century House who still looked upon anyone connected with Security Directorate as the enemy within.

"No," Epworth was saying, "the quality of the product was high. The Knight respected Fish's argument for secrecy. He never drew the files."

"They went in and out of Registry according to the book, but Fish was the one who ran the book."

"You – mmmm – put it so well. He managed a substitution. At least, that's the conclusion we drew from the bonfire."

Morpurgo fought down his emotions. "He had a bonfire before he killed himself. Anything left?"

"Enough to convince forensic that Fish had burned the missing files. Not enough to yield a single word."

Epworth had been head of internal security in SIS before engineering its takeover. He was being told all this, Morpurgo saw, precisely because he was ex-Five, not only vastly experienced in sniffing out treachery but barred by background from any subversive alliance with Fish's former friends among the Century House coordinators.

But why now? It would have puzzled him more, but for Warren Claas's set-piece performance on the Century House roof.

"Before you go on," he said, "what's been happening in Vienna lately?"

As well as the Mona Lisa, Epworth could impersonate the Cheshire Cat, a smile quite separate from his true self.

"Not long ago, Aske came back," he said.

Through the door to the hall, Morpurgo heard the youngest Epworth protesting, "But I want to go in. I want to. I want to see daddy." A woman's voice, soothing but firm, said something inaudible. The child's voice died away, tragic. "But I want to. I want to."

Breaking the following silence, Morpurgo said, "All in one piece?"

Delicately, Epworth picked up his double reed, the vodka long since evaporated. "Virgo intacta, apparently. Showed up late at night asking for his old room. These things can't be kept quiet forever, especially in Vienna. Claas was just making sure we knew that Langley knows."

"What's Aske's story?"

"His story would seem to be that there is no story."

38

"Jesus! Seemingly? Apparently? What is this, a factual account or a bloody fairy story?"

"Whose? Mine? Or Aske's?" Epworth produced a small plastic box. Lined with foam, it held more reeds.

Calm again, Morpurgo said, "You're bringing him home, naturally."

"We'd like to."

So there was more to come, and it would come when Epworth was ready.

Epworth laid his new reed in the box and snapped it shut. "If I'd tried to tell you the story all at once, you would have interrupted far more. Now you have most of the facts, such as they are."

"Like hell I have. What do you mean, Aske's story is that there is no story?"

"He never went to Prague. He knows nothing about Fish, Gossip, Highflyer, not, of course, that they were discussed in those terms. In short, he doesn't know what we're talking about."

One last try, thought Morpurgo. "Genuine amnesia's treatable. Faking's easy to crack."

"So I believe. But he's in Vienna and – "

"I said. You've got to get him back."

"I was about to say that he's very much in the eye of the Austrian authorities."

"I'd have thought they'd be glad to be rid of him. They'd have to be thick not to know what's been going on."

"They have an excellent idea of what's been going on. But being neutral, they can't permit us to harass him. Particularly as he's talking of applying for Austrian citizenship."

"Good God!"

"The ambassador would like to distance himself from SIS by the width of the Atlantic. Everyone knows we must have been running a show from their nice neutral city."

"Can't you tell them that Aske – "

"My dear Johnny, we can tell them nothing about Aske, because we know nothing. Everything was in the files that . . ." Epworth spiralled a finger upward to indicate smoke. "You see the quandary?"

"The man hasn't lived his life in a bloody vacuum. That's the sort of thing raw recruits in Five cut their teeth on." He grinned at Epworth, seeing the quandary only too well. Like any other

Centurion, Epworth wasn't prepared to ask help from Five.

"Department of Employment, even what people like us do counts as work. Inland Revenue, don't tell me he didn't pay taxes. Department of Health and Social Security. General Office of Records, Office of Population and Censuses. Vehicle Licensing Centre unless he's a lifelong pedestrian. Post Office. British Telecom. Electoral Register, General Register Office. Banks, credit card companies, you know all this as well as I do. And that's playing the game. Gloves off and the dirt's there for the asking. The Mount Street computer, for a start. S section would love to help. Put it all together and you'll be amazed how much you'll know about Aske."

"We do know our business," Epworth said patiently. "Fish knew his, too. He wiped the slate clean."

"Are you telling me Fish deleted the man from the public record."

"Short of turning the country upside-down. Which would stir up the kind of publicity Number 10 would have our heads for."

"Even if Fish rubbed him out in the Passport Office, he must still have one, or he couldn't have got back into Austria."

"Oh yes. With lots of Czech visas and border control stamps, dated for every trip he made except the one he says he didn't."

Morpurgo snorted. "Moscow Centre could fake Magna Carta and no one the wiser. I meant revoke it and advise the Austrian authorities. They'd have to do something. Send him home."

"Think about it."

He thought about it. It would turn a private diplomatic incident into a public one. Aske might stay silent. Vienna would not. Claas had proved that.

There was a hearty thump at the door and Amaryllis called, "Cork's out of the bottle, bubbles fizzing away like fury in the you-know-shhh. Another five minutes and the chef will be stinko."

"I didn't bring you over the river" – Epworth ignored the summons – "to turn you into a common or garden spy, not at your age. You also have the advantage of being Sovbloc amber." He meant not necessarily known to the opposition.

"You want me to get Aske out?"

No, damn it, they would have done it themselves but for the Austrian authorities. Now it was too late.

"We must stop that girl knocking back too many G and Ts," Epworth said maddeningly. "They numb the palate and I've put

40

out something rather good in the way of a Hunawihr Riesling. We'll talk again after lunch."

Toward the end of lunch, with Epworth temporarily absent, Amaryllis reached across to take Morpurgo's hand.

"Re what I said about Sylvie. Mum's the word, of course, but I've been thinking. Bound to find out. Nobody's fool, that girl. Best make a clean breast. She'll still be pleased you're going.

"Now," as Epworth reappeared, "another little smackerel of *croûtes aux prunes*. Don't want any left to lead me into temptation. Yes? Super!"

# SIX

Takeoffs, landings and the boredom in between. The gay colours, the soothing music, the padded isolation designed to obscure the fact that passengers were just a troublesome form of freight. The disguised but strict control that required him, a citizen of a free country, to be documented, checked on a manifest, tagged and secretly vetted before he could step outside its boundaries, let along come back. Morpurgo hated flying.

He sulked, not caring who knew it.

Sylvie knew that waiting would only fuel his smouldering fires. "Let's walk through the duty-free shop. You can buy me some toilet water if you feel generous."

"Why don't I buy you some sadistically expensive perfume?"

"Why not? Learn to live first class. You might even get to like it."

That was Sylvie's style: work hard, enjoy the fruits. His mother, though she had criticised Sylvie for never being at home, had secretly approved of her life style. Success, in his mother's book, was not just having money, but being seen to have it. Sylvie was right – his mother would have adjusted to Chelsea, though their lives would have become intolerable in the process.

His sense of guilt punished him instantly, reviving the image of her crumpled at the foot of the stairs, hour upon dark hour, while he had slept untroubled.

"If God had intended some people to travel first class," he said, "he would only have turned one of them out of the Garden of Eden." He walked into a block of concrete.

"Now then, lad" – the concrete had a flat northern accent – "watch where you go, or we shall both of us end up walking

42

wounded." Then, a moment later, "Well I'll be a monkey's uncle! It's yon chap from the dirty tricks department!"

Morpurgo, effete southerner, was more volatile. "Trigger! Fancy seeing you here!"

The other man, fiftyish, chunky, as much prey to emotion as a professional debt collector, had bright, derisive eyes. "Oh aye? Members only, is it?" His gaze switched. "I take it this'll be the missus." He held out a hand like a wicket-keeper's glove.

"Aye, lad" – Sylvie was expert in judging character – "I'm t'little woman." Mutual approval flowed in almost visible waves.

"Now, lass" – the eyes twinkled in that expressionless face – "you must show proper respect. Where I come from a vowel is a vowel, not something the cat brought in."

Rejoicing in the pleasure of hearing A's straight from 'apple', every U out of 'push', Morpurgo was aware that he was grinning idiotically. "Sylvie, this is Mr Trigg, an old friend of mine. Initials E. R., for Eustace Roland, which is . . ."

"Hey up!" Trigg cut in. "What those letters stand for was a bone of contention between me and my mam."

". . . why he's sometimes known to his friends as Trigger," Morpurgo finished hastily.

Prosperous-looking in navy-blue Crombie and a suit of dark pinstripe, Trigg tipped a well brushed bowler. "Happen," he said, "because this chap and me has been close in t'past, he thinks he's the right to presume, Mrs – "

"Sylvie."

"Sylvie, is it? He said nought about you last time round. Is he still in same business, lass, or have you made him respectable?"

Seeing Morpurgo glance instinctively to see who might be listening, he chuckled. "No need to answer that, buttercup. Couldn't be plainer if they'd stamped you OHMS all over."

"Buttercup?" Sylvie's morning was made. "More like a wet lettuce."

"Last time," Morpurgo said, stung, "he called me sunshine."

"Times change," Trigg said. "Us northerners has never been ones for getting stuck in a rut."

"Sunshine!" Sylvie laughed. "He hasn't stopped moaning all morning."

Trigg released her hand at last. "Aye, well, now he's met me, happen he'll mend his manners."

Morpurgo's feelings were mixed. Eustace Roland Trigg, kindred soul but also a law unto himself, had been a tower of

43

strength at the time of the Sattin affair. Few people were aware of the role he had played, and Sylvie was not among them. At any moment, having already sailed perilously close to the wind, he was liable to say something irretrievable.

"What a pity," Morpurgo said, "we had to meet here. I don't know about you, but we're just off. Are you still in Cleethorpes? Still in rock?"

The sooner they parted, the better, but to learn that Trigg was no longer in Cleethorpes, that wildly unfashionable seaside resort and mysterious butt of stand-up comedians, would be like salt losing its savour.

Trigg's features developed the woodenness northerners reserve for questions that tax common politeness. "Am I still in Cleethorpes? Where else is there for a feller of sense and discrimination?"

"Do you" – Sylvie would clearly be uncooperative in any attempt to break off the conversation – "mean seaside rock? The stuff you eat?"

"Some," Trigg informed her, "chomps it, some sucks it. Question of taste, is that. Triggs is renowned for selling rock wherever rock can be sold, nigh on fifty places, all with their name running clear through from one end to t'other. This feller" – another crippling nudge for Morpurgo – "has seen nought more secret than how we get 'Cleethorpes' clear through a twelve-inch stick of peppermint or pineapple. By! Making it for Hove is child's play by comparison."

He produced a card. "Here, lass, this'll give you the idea." It read:

E. R. TRIGG & Son LTD
Quality Confectioners

with an address in Grimsby, South Humberside. On the back was a picture of a modern, single-storey factory of some size.

"Nigh on a hundred lines in spice," Trigg told her, "that being what they called sweets when I was a little lad in Yorkshire. The son on that card, that's me, d'you see? The old dad's dead, my mam too, and since I'm not wed nor likely to be, it'll happen be swallowed by one of the big chaps when I'm gone." He prodded his chest with a great thumb. "Last o' t'line, that's me."

Morpurgo could see that Sylvie was full of questions. Not the least would be how a confectionery manufacturer from Clee-thorpes had ever come together with John Morpurgo.

She began at once. "Are you going on holiday? Or just coming back?"

"Holiday?" The wind of derision was tempered to the shorn lamb. "I've seen a few places in my time and I'll tell you this for nought, not one of 'em was a patch on Cleethorpes. Acapulco of the north-east, is Cleethorpes. If *you'd* been there, like this chap of yours, you'd not want telling twice. However" – he turned his impassive gaze on Morpurgo – "I'm bound to admit I've never been quite the same since buttercup here once took me for a ride in a helicopter."

Oh God! Morpurgo thought. Here it all comes.

But no, it was the same old Trigg. Expert in cat-and-mouse, he went back to his heart's delight. "This business of mine, do you see, was started by my dad. A little hut on the promenade, rock and mint humbugs, nought else. Good wholesome stuff, barring t'risk of broken teeth. Now, what with progress and new lines, things has changed and no mistake.

Emulsifiers, lecithin, glutamate and approved colours. Autoclaves, extruders, enrobers, not forgetting a computer that tells us how much to make of what, and when to say us prayers."

He went so far as to look wistful. "No wrestling with taffee on great hooks. No cheeky lasses wrapping everything by hand. No standing on seafront, rain or shine, telling tales to trippers that made their brass hop in their pockets like fleas on a hedgehog. Space Invaders for engineers and accountants, that's what it is now. By heck, it's nigh on boring."

"So why are you here?" Sylvie asked. "Don't tell me you've bought a helicopter?" Her eyes were brilliant with amusement but also, thought Morpurgo, something more dangerous.

"A helicopter? It'd be summat, would that! Nay, exports, that's why I'm here."

He sensed her doubt. "Oh aye, there's brass in it. Happen you didn't know rock is a British invention? Any road, seeing I was getting a bit restless like, and since that computer has nigh on proved I should be made redundant, I decided it was time the benefits of civilisation was put on offer to deprived foreigners. Export director, that's me."

He spared time from Sylvie to toss Morpurgo another scrap. "I don't mind telling you, buttercup, I've been around a bit since you gave me the taste for flying."

Once again it was getting too warm for comfort. Morpurgo looked at his watch. "We ought to be moving, unfortunately. Time

45

and tide. Maybe we could look you up when we get back?"

"Where are you off to, then?"

"Vienna."

"Nay! Vienna! Is that right? Cheer up, buttercup, you and me is to be fellow travellers."

\*     \*     \*

So there they were, sandwiched halfway between blue infinity and some of the best tank country in Europe, somewhere over Belgium and headed south by east for Vienna. Morpurgo, the loser in some dexterous switching of reservations, decided that no East–West summit could be more difficult than three-way conversation from the wrong side of two high-backed, well-padded, airplane seats.

"Where I come from," Trigg was saying, "and we want to know ought, we ask. What I want to know is what you carry around in that scruffy old bag of yours."

"Cameras. Three cameras and their bits and pieces."

"Three! Get off! And do you chuck 'em away as soon as t'film is used up?"

"If you'll promise to keep it to yourself," she said, "I just might tell you more."

"Oh aye? Well, if you telling me ought is dependent on me making promises, I might end up none the wiser."

Sticking his head uncomfortably over the seat back, Morpurgo said, "Her name isn't Morpurgo, it's Markham."

"Nay! Living in sin, is that it?"

"Sorry to disappoint you," Sylvie said, "but Markham's my professional name."

Trigg opened his smart business case. "Happen you had summat to do with this, then?" He produced a magazine and thumbed through it, his look more wooden than ever.

"You knew!" Sylvie jostled him. "You knew all along." It was a picture feature on the London Festival Ballet that had led directly to the major commission from the Royal Shakespeare Company.

"Right struck by that, I was, me being" – his eyes gleamed sardonically – "a devotee of the ballet as I reckon you'd guess." He foraged once more in his case. "Fair do's, one work of art for another." Hearing Sylvie's exclamation of delight, Morpurgo, cursing under his breath, stood to peer over the top of the seat.

It was a lollipop the size of a small saucer, a translucent purple magnificence with white, embedded letters set around its circumference like figures on the face of a clock. From nine to five they spelled PRATER, from seven to four, WIEN. The splendour was completed by glistening cellophane and a silken bow in the red and white national colours of Austria.

"Here, love." Trigg presented it with a flourish. "Don't suck it now, or we shall be packed off to economy class in disgrace. Trade sample, is that, a few hundred more waiting at Vienna airport. If I said I've a chap works full-time checking the spelling on all this stuff, college feller, but reckons he shall resign if I break into the Japanese market, would you believe me?"

"No," she said, "I wouldn't. How do you get these letters in?"

"Hey up! How do I know you aren't spying for the Japs?"

"Do you know the Prater?"

"No," he said, "but they tell me it's quite a place."

"Oh, it is. The big wheel, the Riesenrad, is famous."

"Then happen you and me will take a turn or two, though we've a wheel on Cleethorpes sands that's not to be sneezed at. Smashing view of the railway one side, and t'other looks out over the sea when tide is in. Which, to be honest, is only now and then. If the world was flat, tide at Cleethorpes'd have dropped over the edge long since."

So Trigg, Morpurgo thought, was on a plane to Vienna to sell lollipops to Austrians after all, and not because the Sattin spy ring business had brought him into the purview of Lawrence Epworth. The fact remained that he, Sylvie and Trigg were bound to spend more time together.

Unlike many a marriage, the Official Secrets Act really was until death did you part, and Trigg had once signed an E74. But he came from a part of the world where people were accustomed to speaking their mind, as well as having small respect for authority. Neither biddable nor a respector of authority himself, as well as being unfashionably moral, it would take more than an E74 to silence him if he had a mind to talk.

One ear tuned, ready to intervene if Trigg should launch on further dangerous reminiscences, Morpurgo stared for a long time at a skyscape in which thin straight lines of diaphanous cloud extended across Germany like a light scattering of snow on a vast ploughed field. Eventually he went forward to the toilet compartments. When he came out, Trigg was in waiting.

"Now, buttercup, time for a word." There were spare seats. He found himself imprisoned by Trigg's marmoreal bulk.

"She tells me, that lass of yours, that yon feller Archer who

47

used to be your errand lad has been made a knight."

Morpurgo nodded. How much had Sylvie said? How much had Trigg inveigled out of her?

"And you and him has parted company. Nay, don't take on. She's not been talking out of turn, not much, anyroad. You didn't like him. He didn't like you. I didn't reckon him at all. So when it comes out you've had a new job nigh on two years, even a pudding-head like me can draw a conclusion."

"Before we go any farther, I hope you haven't forgotten that you signed – "

"When I was about ten," Trigg interrupted with brutal relish, "I signed the temperance pledge. It's not bothered me since. Get the point, do you, buttercup?"

But he lowered his voice as a stewardess went past. "I know why your missus is going to Vienna, because she's told me. She told me why you're going, too. What I must know, if you and me is to stay friends, is whether she was right on both counts."

"That's as good as saying I'm not to be trusted."

"Trust!" The tone and vowels he reserved for statements of unbelievable folly. "I trust none that comes from farther south than Sheffield, and not too many there. Happen I like you, happen not, but trust? It'd want thinking about, would that."

"Sylvie's going on business. I'm keeping her company." He was getting old. His lies, like his legs, were beginning to lose some vitality.

"Is that a fact?" He was being stared at like a spelling mistake in one of Trigg's lollipops.

"It's a fact." He held Trigg's gaze just long enough.

"My word, buttercup," Trigg said affably, "don't take on. I'm willing to trust you any old time. It's your job I don't trust – that and the folk you're in with. How's yon chap Epworth?"

What had Sylvie said about Epworth? Nothing. Sylvie didn't talk out of turn. "Well enough," Morpurgo said.

"Aye, well that's how him and me got on. Well enough. For long enough. I used him and he used me, so well enough was fair enough and that gets shot of that. I never did" – Trigg's Gothic innocence was back – "get it worked out whether you and him was on the same side."

Morpurgo could cope with that. "No," he said. "Neither did I. Sylvie will be wondering what we're up to."

"Your Sylvie" – Trigg hauled himself up – "must spend half her time wondering what you're up to."

48

As they joined her, the plane tilted lazily. On the rim of the horizon was a hint of mountains. Immediately below, as they lost height, the patchwork countryside was fraying into straggling urban threads.

Trigg settled himself back into his seat. "This'll be Vienna then, but what's that great mucky canal?"

"It isn't a canal," Sylvie said. "It's the Danube."

"Nay!" Trigg was dismayed. "Never say that! Why, t'Humber at Clee is a sight bluer than that when tide's in and sun is shining."

Staring down as the plane banked on the approach to Schwechat, he shook his big head. "The blue Danube! I'll tell you summat for nothing, lass. It's not a patch on Cleethorpes. I'm staying at some place called the Bristol. Where're you two putting up?"

"Small world," Sylvie said, "buttercup."

Morpurgo caught Trigg's gaze. It was like looking into thick fog.

# SEVEN

Morpurgo was going to two treffs. The first one was with Mozart.

The very word "treff" was a fossil. An abbreviation of the German for a meeting and with piquant overtones of battle, it commemorated men and women of a dozen nationalities who had fought, and sometimes died, in the cold war's ice age.

Most of the survivors were retired now, yet the word lived on, an antique badge of office. Morpurgo himself had used it when he was still with Five, and heard it again south of the river. With Berlin supplanted by Vienna as the great marketplace for treason he could say in continuance of tradition that he was going to a treff.

He promised himself he would not forget Schubert either, but Mozart came first. Even in the bustle of affluent materialism where the Kärntnerstrasse became a pedestrian precinct, he found himself whistling under his breath, the lingering presence of the bright spirit cascading notes through his head.

He barely knew Vienna. His only other visit had been when he and Eric Pottern were keeping tabs on an Irish terrorist shopping expedition. They had arrived in a chilly dusk, and were whisked through half-seen industrial areas and the twinkling vastness of worker-bee apartment blocks to a small room in a small hotel on the interminable Mariahilferstrasse. A brief photo snatch in the Rathaus gardens and they were on their way home.

This time it was a different Vienna. In the old town the sense of history remained. Across the high rooftops of sidestreets the stone heroes of the Habsburgs postured on the skyline, totem figures in an imperial Disneyland.

Morpurgo remembered Warren Claas's words: *A stage set, just the goddam fancy buildings. The actors have gone someplace else.*

Claas had not just been talking about London but about an entire culture: Europe; the history of the West for two thousand years. But then, he thought, whistling a fragment from the larghetto of the clarinet quintet, Claas had no ear for music.

He was pleasantly tired. He and Sylvie had a large room with a large bed. It might just as well·be a small bed. Sylvie clearly got a kick out of having him with her. He wasn't sure he was up to love in triplicate any more; that kind of tired.

The Stephansplatz was vibrant with sunlight and life. Outside the entrance to the cathedral a yellow squat of Buddhist monks chanted to the rhythmic strokes of a gong. Beyond them the fiacres waited in the midmorning warmth. Surrounded by a crowd at the nearest entrance to the U-bahn, a woman sang *Vilja*. It was both schmaltzy and unreal.

Someone thrust a leaflet at him, non-schmaltzy, very real. *BESUCHEN SIE EUROPA (solange es noch steht)*. The anti-nuclear brigade.

That was what he was doing, visiting Europe while it was still there, shopping in the spies' bazaar that the Austrian government endeavoured to control but made small effort to stop, in case the world stopped with it.

The Buddhists struck their gong, chanted their sutra, stared impassively as he passed. A sudden explosion of bells filled the sky with a winged shrapnel of pigeons. He turned into the narrow Domgasse, saw the Austrian flag hanging limply and walked through the inconspicuous entrance. It was a sensual thrill: a small paved court which was also a stairwell, flight by flight through six floors to the skylight, at each level a balcony, austere sanctity throughout. As he went up he said, the boy from backstreet Wandsworth, *"Wolfgang Amadeus, hier bin ich zuletzt."*

But it was a treff in a tomb. The birthplace of *Figaro* had become a mausoleum. Dutifully inspecting facsimiles, engravings, everything but the smallest echo of the man, he arrived at the stone-framed window overlooking Schulerstrasse.

He checked the time. Spot on. He looked down. In the narrow depths a delivery van forced pedestrians to squeeze past like troops on an obstacle course. Beyond it, a man emerged from a shop. He studied the delivery van carefully, then lit a cigarette. He puffed twice, dropped it in the gutter, turned to glance idly at the window of the Figarohaus and began to saunter. Morpurgo headed for the exit.

They emerged from the old town to cross the Ring and then the Danube canal, green and sedate, by the Aspern bridge. The man Morpurgo was following turned down some steps.

They led to a sparse expanse of grass and gravel. An overgrown path of stone setts followed the water's edge. On the far bank a stream merged beneath a spindly coppice of construction cranes engaged in hauling rentable space out of the ground, floor by floor.

The other man was still strolling, his city suit out of place in this urban isolation. Three boys on bicycles chased each other around a plane tree that spiralled a single leaf into the water.

The man stopped by a slatted seat and sat down with a fastidious hitch of his trousers. After a lingering look at the green glide of the water, Morpurgo walked on, then sat. Without looking, he said, "Toby Farrar, I presume."

"I didn't think we were followed," the other said. "Did you? I rather fancy they've given up."

He was singularly plain, a high-cheeked, bony face with the enviable smoothness of youth, and athlete's shoulders. Morpurgo had heard less monotonous voices making train announcements at Wandsworth Common station, but his suit was in the highest tradition of Savile Row. Morpurgo, his own in the highest tradition of Montague Burton, thought: They still recruit them.

He said, "They being who?"

Legs stretched far before him, hands thrust deep into his pockets, Toby Farrar stared out across the water. Framed between the rising towerblocks and a silvery run of pipeline was a single small building that said Central Europe, one green-tiled, dunce's-cap tower from which Rapunzel might have let down her hair. He nodded at the small confluence across the canal. In that toneless drawl, he said, "That's the River Wien. People think: Vienna, Danube. Half the Viennese never see the Danube from one year to the next."

He bent to pick up a stone. "*If* we'd been followed, Department One, for a bet. That's Austrian internal security."

"I knew that," Morpurgo said, "when you were still at Oxford."

"Cambridge, actually." Toby tossed the stone. It went surprisingly far. Concentric rings drifted towards the Danube, Budapest, the Iron Gates.

"They've been in this a lot. First when Aske didn't come back from Prague. Then when he did. Especially when he complained we were harassing him."

"You? Personally?"

"Not bloody likely. H.E. had a fit when he heard you were coming."

"Anyone else been interested? So far as you know."

Toby gave an ambiguous snort. "This is a United Nations town: come and go as you please so long as you're accredited."

"KGB?"

Another snort. "By the dozen. Here as this or that. Here because they're here."

A second stone plumped into the water. The first leaves of autumn rocked gently in the ripples. "We're supposed to lay off. Lambeth promised H.E. You're here on sufferance: look, don't touch." A train crossed the canal downstream, invisible beyond the silver span of pipeline.

"Funny, really." Not a trace of humour in that deep, toneless drone. "Austrians'd pay gold to get rid of him, terrified he'll put in for Traiskirchen. We mustn't touch, but they wish to God we could disappear him."

"What's Traiskirchen?"

"*Flüchtlingslager*, transit camp for Sovbloc refugees. That's where they'd send him if he claims political asylum. Discussed it with H.E."

A British subject vanishes in Czechoslovakia, comes back denying he ever went, claims political asylum just like a Pole, an East German, a Russian Jew. Morpurgo imagined what the media would make of it.

"What's it like there?"

"Austrian army barracks before the war. Russian occupation troops after. You wouldn't go there for your holidays. Wouldn't put him off. If Czechoslovakia didn't exist, Traiskirchen won't exist."

It was a penetrating comment.

"What does exist?"

"Today," Toby said. "And today and today. To the last syllable of recorded time. Mr Aske doesn't seem to think as far as tomorrow. Incidentally, he's very big on Shakespeare."

One of the construction cranes swung slowly away as if tired. The seat was hard. Morpurgo, too, shifted a little. There was a pervading melancholy about this place that made him think of old, abandoned cemeteries. He stared at the funereal progress of the water. "How far from here to the Danube?"

"Canal's maybe fifteen miles, Nussdorf to Freudenauerhafen. We're about in the middle." For a moment Toby had seemed surprised.

"Suppose you summarise."

"Ants' nest when he vanished. First Department Two, criminal police. Then state security. He had a room in the ninth *Bezirk*. Landlord's an old dodderer name of Stiegelbauer. If you're thinking of calling, watch out for a guy called Mandel."

"Oberpolizeirat Karl-Heinz Mandel, police headquarters on the Schottenring. Top man in Department One."

Toby showed no signs of being impressed. "You've met him?"

"I know the name." He remembered it in connection with the picture snatch outside the Café Sluka.

"Karli to his friends." Toby looked for another stone. "Quite the dandy. Charming, too, off duty. If he ever is off duty. He knows you're here, by the way."

"The hell he does! Anyway, I'm just a bloody tourist."

"Maybe." Toby was bouncing his stone on a large pink palm. "But Karli happened to mention it to head of chancery at some Stadt Wien do last night. Just happened to say he'd heard, via London, you were in town. By the way, I'm to request you not to come anywhere near the embassy."

Who in London had told a high state police official in Vienna that John Morpurgo – remember the Irish job? – was in town? Who had said enough for that same official to warn a senior British diplomat that Morpurgo should watch his step?

"Damn the embassy," Morpurgo said irrationally. This had not been in the script. Epworth apart, only one kind of person would know that John Morpurgo had taken a flight to Vienna. That kind of person – Special Branch, passport and immigration control – reported back to Five. Anything interesting about John Morpurgo could well end up on the desk of Sir Stephen Archer.

"We both agreed we weren't followed."

"But tomorrow? When you see Aske?" Toby lobbed his stone.

"I'm seeing Aske tomorrow?" At least the boy was cool.

"Do you like bookshops, sir?" Sir. Had Toby Farrar decided he was worthy of respect?

"Any particular bookshop?"

"Gerold's, in the Graben."

"What time?"

"Around ten."

"Aske will be there?"

"Odds on. Habit, right back to pre-Prague days. The English section, every Wednesday." On the far side of the canal, where the Wien crept under a bridge to join the canal, a woman and two small children appeared. Their high-pitched chatter spanned the canal, coded by distance.

Toby bent forward for another stone. When he straightened, an envelope lay between them, inconspicuous in the coarse grass. Morpurgo, too, bent for a stone, palmed and pocketed the envelope. "Pics?"

"Will you please . . ."

Morpurgo smiled. ". . . destroy them when I've memorised the face."

Unruffled, Toby waved to the children. "Gerold's English sections's about the best in town, far right as you go in. There's an arcade right by the window, so you – "

"So I can check first. What do you do at the embassy? Theoretically."

"Commercial section. Very humble stuff. Would you believe lollipops?"

Another train crossed the river. Toby said, "Mr Trigg knows what he wants. And when he wants it. We're lunching. Time I was off."

But he stayed. "About Nussdorf and Freudenauerhafen. Was it the lorry park?"

After a hectic but invisible scramble, Morpurgo got it: the junctions of the canal with the Danube. Beyond that he was lost, but he said, "Yes."

"It wasn't there, actually. I'm sorry. I should have thought."

Quickly, a foul blow, Morpurgo said, "Yes, you should, actually." He remembered Toby's earlier surprise. Was this a fence-mending exercise?

"It is on the river bank, though. The city side of the Reichsbridge."

"Go on." What a blessing was authority when it cloaked ignorance!

"Pure rumour, really." For a deadly second Morpurgo thought he was faced with confessing his ignorance, then Toby went on, "Supposed to have gone there the night before his last trip. We don't know why."

"Who uses the lorry park?"

"All sorts, including a few Sovbloc artics, mostly Hungarian.

Come in from Klingenbach – that's the border post for Budapest – and overnight there."

"So what's the theory?" Translation, please explain in words of one syllable what we're talking about.

A reluctant shrug. "Treff" – well, well, even the youngsters used it – "with one of the Hungarians? Something to take to Prague? Drop point when he got there? Recognition system? Raises more questions than it answers."

"Any guesses?"

Toby shuffled his feet. "Not much of a place, Klingenbach. Decent pub at Eisenstadt, though, trout fresh from the lake. No, sir, no guesses."

Something else that was not in the script. Did the many things Epworth had undoubtedly not told Morpurgo include the lorry park? Pure rumour be damned. Department One would have done a lot of digging. Perhaps even before Aske's last trip to Prague. Perhaps out of curiosity over the late Humphrey Fish's numerous visits to Vienna. In this business more questions were left unanswered than otherwise.

Toby shot his cuff to look at an expensive watch. "Lunch with Mr Trigg. Fascinating subject, lollipops." He stood, six-two at least. "Bit like the museums, sir, visitors requested not to touch the exhibits."

"I got the message," Morpurgo said, knowing that Toby must consider it an extraordinary arrangement. But then, Toby hadn't got the same script. He pitched his stone. It fell far short of Toby's languid throws.

He patted the envelope in his pocket. "English section on the far right, I think you said. Pity. I have this deplorable inclination to the left. They probably told you."

Toby smiled. It was like the frog turning into the handsome prince.

"Me too, sir. Upsets H.E. no end. Suspects I'm one of those frightful Labour supporters."

Morpurgo threw another stone before turning just in time to see him disappear up the steps. The boys on bikes sped past in line astern, a scrunch of gravel, a soft whirr of wind and wheels, playing chicken on the very edge of the water. They weren't in the script either.

\*     \*     \*

Sylvie and Trigg were out at their respective business lunches. He looked at the Aske pictures as soon as he was back in the room. One right profile, one semi-left, one full-face, expertly snatched.

An intelligent face, that above all. A humorous face, the full-lipped mouth quirked ready to smile, the nose, fractionally too large, a faintly comical nose. The more appealing for its half-apologetic wistfulness, it was a face that said: Laugh with me. Laugh at me. But like me.

And yet, in a sense that was nothing to do with dark hair, dark brows, dark eyes, it was a dark face.

A flash from his childhood, the circus on Clapham Common. Wild din, exciting smells; candyfloss and stale beer, vinegar and crushed grass. Horses and horse dung, elephants and the Brobdingnagian dung of elephants. Muscular acrobats. Fairy princesses. Bonzo. Bonzo, prince of clowns, keeping his audience in a constant uproar of delight, his painted grin, to a boy of nine, incontrovertible proof of the sheer delight of existence. Better yet, he had seen him in Clapham High Street in broad daylight, and had his recognition recognised. A quick wink, a shy smile, a secret shared in passing.

Two days later it was all about the school. Bonzo had cut his throat. In his caravan, it was. Middle of the night. They said there was blood everywhere.

He went back to the photographs. A face that could make friends and influence people. Especially women, who would sense the sadness behind the smile. But would they sense despair? He thought not, unless, like him, they had known a Bonzo.

He tucked the pictures safely away in his jacket pocket. Before he shredded them he would want to look again at the two faces of Simon Aske. Security Directorate knew more about stripping suspects down to their component parts than the dilettante Centurions, with their Fischer–Karpov minds, were likely to learn in a month of Moscow Sundays. He went out to check the exact whereabouts of the bookshop in the Graben. That had been in the script.

# EIGHT

Sylvie had a call from the publishing house. If the gracious lady permitted, the art director would call upon her at her hotel. Morpurgo arranged to meet her at Gerold's bookshop between ten and half-past. He should already have had his look at Aske. If Sylvie turned up while Aske was there, she would be good cover. After that they had arranged to meet Trigg at the Prater. Morpurgo set out for a new treff.

With time in hand, he still hankered after Mozart. He turned down to the Kärntnerring and walked under limes and planes as far as the Burggarten. Above the leafage the heroic statuary of the Habsburgs crowded the skyline, imperial ninepins long since bowled over by history.

The Mozart memorial, like the Mozart house, was a disappointment, a token nod in the direction of genius. He shared a seat in the sun with a prosperous *Bürgerin* who was working her way through a box of chocolates with the concentration of a chess master.

Someone else joined them, and said in accented English, "We Viennese love a genius only after he has become famous. This usually requires him to be dead."

Handsome in a style that had gone out with Jean Gabin, the man was perhaps ten years Morpurgo's senior, fastidiously dressed; belted raincoat, quality suit, silk shirt and tie. His shoes twinkled, his eyes not. "Mozart lived in Domgasse only a short time, when he had money. In Vienna money makes genius acceptable, if it knows its place. Mozart knew his genius, but not his place. So, his success did not last. Cigarette?" A gold cigarette case, oval Turkish cigarettes, little gold crests. The only other person Morpurgo knew who owned a gold case was Steve Archer. Steve's was monogrammed.

He shook his head. "Thank you." The case clicked shut. It was monogrammed, three elegantly intertwined letters. The lighter, too, was gold, the cigarette holder ivory with a gold band.

"Another Mozart memorial is in Mozartgasse. You know that street?"

"I don't really know Vienna."

"No? Mozartgasse, well, that's not so far from here. Over the Kärntnerring, past Karlskirche in direction Wieden – "

"My name's Morpurgo. John Morpurgo."

"Enchanted." A quick squeeze from a pigskin glove. "As I tell you, a small street, but significant. During the war is there the headquarters of Gestapo. After, in *Besatzungsmächte* time – excuse me, time of liberation – the Soviet liberators have their headquarters in that zone, Hotel Imperial. The building in Mozartgasse becomes most convenient for the KGB."

"I'm sorry," Morpurgo said. "I didn't catch your name."

"There is a section of sidewalk – maybe you will make time to see it? – where the cracks are said to be made by people anxious to end their upstairs business with the Gestapo as quickly as possible. Or perhaps it is with the Russians, one forgets."

Morpurgo smiled. "The more times change . . ."

A flash of white, even teeth, possibly real. "Such souvenirs of history have value. We are a small country. We must protect jealously what is left to us, even cracks in the sidewalk. Poor Mozart! A house in Domgasse, all that stays of eighteen, yes, eighteen houses Mozart once has, moving all the time. An empty tomb in Saint Marxer necropolis, empty because the pauper grave of Mozart is unknown, not even a crack in a sidewalk. But Mozart" – he touched his heart – "lives here in every man, true?"

"It would be nice to think so." As Toby Farrar had said about Karl-Heinz Mandel, 'Charming off duty, if he ever is off duty.'

"For me," Mandel said, "as a good Austrian, this gives a moral." The feather-hatted *Bürgerin*, possibly bored by all this foreign chitchat, took a dignified departure. Mandel raised his snap-brim fedora to her broad rear profile.

"In my country" – if they were to play this game, Morpurgo thought, he would play it in style – "we have a saying: 'Curtsey while you're thinking what to say. It saves time.' "

Mandel was up to it. "The immortal Alice. And the reverend Herr Dodgson, alias Carroll, who has his memorial down the hole of a rabbit. Let us pretend it is you who curtseys. So, what do you think?''

"That you're going to tell me the moral."

Karl-Heinz was equal to that, too. "Take care of the sense, yes? and the sounds will take care of themselves." He didn't even sound smug. "The moral, it is very good sense, is that genius lives longer than statues." The cigarette holder passed across the Hofburg and its rooftop totems dismissively. "We raise high the Habsburgs in order to walk by without seeing them. The genius of Mozart walks with us." He put away the cigarette holder. "Our own little genius, we Viennese, is for survival, and so, like Mozart, we seek always harmony.

"So." He stood. "Visit the house of Schubert before you leave, Herr Morpurgo. Charming. Quite charming. The spirit is there. Take a taxi, or you will go astray in the ninth *Bezirk*. But Gerold is good for books. Those you are permitted to see and also to touch." Leaving, he raised his hat as politely as to any plump *Bürgerin*.

The script had been not so much changed as rewritten. Karl-Heinz Mandel , with no part in the original, had been given good lines and he had spoken them to some effect. With the Iron Curtain no more than a bus ride away, Austria would be more neutral to some than to others.

*       *       *

No Johnny in Gerold's, no Johnny outside. Sylvie had the Pentax with her. She ran through half a spool, then went back into Gerold's.

The English section was in an awkwardly shaped corner, not much room. Two people already occupied most of it. One, short, stocky, was unmistakably Austrian, loden breeches and a green Tyrolean hat with a brush of grouse feathers, his high-cheeked, leathery face the legacy of centuries of Slav and Mongol predation. His stubby forefinger traced the English text under a colour photograph of a ballistic missile.

The other man was in the far corner, where the window looked out on an arcade. His back to Sylvie, he was reading poetry.

Her photographer's eye took him in at a glance. Slightly built; medium height; middle forties. Silky-fine black hair to which isolated threads of silver had come early. Long at the nape, a thick flop at the forehead, it was overdue for cutting. He wore a lightweight tweed jacket, suede-patched at the elbows, shabby

60

cords, an open-neck shirt of navy-blue cotton. He could have been a poet himself, if poets looked poetic.

She took down a book at random. Then the squat Austrian was with her.

*"Entschuldigung, bitte. Sprechen Sie Deutsch, gnädiges Fräulein?"* His forefinger still pressed against the caption under the missile.

Johnny said she picked up the Latin languages like measles. With any of the Germanic tongues she muddled by.

*"Es tut mir leid. Ich spreche Deutsch"* – she held up thumb and forefinger, all but touching – *"nur ein Bisschen."*

No smile in return. His finger stabbed the page. *"Aber Sie können mir, bitte, das in Deutsch lesen?"* He wanted a translation.

It was technical stuff: range, throw weight, TNT equivalent – the vital statistics of annihilation. She shook her head, still smiling, but he was persistent.

Another jab of the finger, anxiety verging on the neurotic. *"Diese Mittelstreckenraketen, sie können Wien von Russland schlagen, nicht wahr?"*

Misinterpreting her helplessness, he patted her arm. *"Sie sind Amerikaner? Horchen Sie, ich bin nie Kommunist nie Kapitalist, verstehen? Ich bin nur für ein atomwaffenfreies Europa, und ich möchte . . ."*

She turned helplessly to the man in the corner. "Excuse me, do you speak English?"

That was when Morpurgo, failing to find her outside, looked in from the arcade. He saw Aske at once. He was talking to Sylvie.

Driven by instinct, he continued towards Stephansplatz. If he went into Gerold's he would be drawn into contact with a man he was not supposed to approach. If it got out, it would be interpreted as typical Morpurgo, the lefty oik stirring things up as usual, too bloody clever by half.

No time for a closer look, but there had been a man behind Sylvie, Austrian, listening almost overtly as she and Aske talked. If Department One knew all about Morpurgo, they would certainly know his wife.

He turned in through the great door of St Stephan's, barely aware of the vaulting grandiosity, the rampaging clash of statuary and styles. If it all came out, Sylvie would learn his true reasons for coming to Vienna. Their marriage had made a comeback, but it still rested on shaky foundations. A revelation of calculated deceit could bring disaster.

The great organ was playing Bach's E flat Prelude and Fugue.

He was hardly more aware of it than of the multilingual parrotings of tour guides, the all-pervading shuffle of feet. He was getting old, brain cells dying off, reflexes the product of panic rather than professional skill. Epworth would not slay him with harsh words, just that devastating *mmmm* to indicate that he was of no further value.

Too late to go back. The conversation between Sylvie and Aske would either be over or dangerously advanced. Sylvie had a genius for drawing strangers into revelations they had had no intention of making.

It occurred to him that he might do a little rewriting of the script himself.

*     *     *

The man turned, book in hand, clearly reluctant to become involved. "I'm sorry, were you speaking to me?" She saw he was reading Sylvia Plath.

"This gentleman has a problem and my German simply isn't up to it." His eyes had already left her for the other.

They returned to her and her smile wavered. Some stray quotation, Johnny without a doubt: *If you stare long enough into the abyss, the abyss will stare back into you.* Almost at once she decided she had imagined it. His own smile was remarkably sweet.

"Of course." His voice had been guarded. Now it was warm, almost intimate. Wow! she thought, this one could be a bit of a heartbreaker.

He asked the other man a question in German. The effect was galvanic. The finger jabbed repeatedly, the voice urgent.

"Excuse me." The Englishman squeezed past, elaborately careful not to make physical contact. He took the book, translated unhesitatingly.

The man in the Tyrolean hat listened as intently as if deciding whether or not to press a red button. His many questions were answered patiently and at length. Finally satisfied, he was profuse in his thanks. After bowing and shaking hands, he left.

"That was kind of you. Poor little man. He obviously appreciated it, though I can't think why."

He smiled again. "The Viennese feel very vulnerable. They know they'll be among the first to go. They don't know they're already dead. I hope you enjoy your holiday." He returned to his book.

Oops! she thought, no intention of socialising with stray Brits.

Feeling oddly let down, she went in search of Johnny.

Eventually she was back outside Gerold's. No Johnny. The Englishman was still in his corner. There was a café across the arcade. She would wait for the time it took to have coffee. She had barely sat down when her Englishman walked in.

"I saw you through the window. I'm terribly sorry, you must have thought me odiously rude."

She laughed. "I did understand. When I see fellow countrymen abroad, I usually sneak off in the opposite direction."

"The least I can do is buy you a coffee or something. Oh God!" Comically exaggerated anxiety. "No sooner do you say that gregarious compatriots are the last thing you want than you've got one forcing himself on you."

"If you offered to buy me coffee," she said, "I'd feel morally obliged to accept."

"Aha! The ploy succeeds! Innocent lady abroad succumbs to wiles of plausible stranger." He called a waitress. She smiled broadly. "Herr Aske! *Wie geht's?*"

*"Danke, es geht mir gut. Und du?"*

Hm, Sylvie thought, not only a charmer when it suits, but well-known.

He said, "You *are* on holiday in this ghost town?"

"Is it a ghost town?"

"A morgue. Can't you smell it?"

"You don't like Vienna."

"All right, a museum. I'm sorry, I shouldn't spoil your holiday."

"Part holiday. Business with pleasure."

"The Viennese motto. That and 'Tomorrow may never come.' "

"Not convinced optimists."

"Did that man in the bookshop strike you as an optimist?"

"Poor little man."

"Poor little world." His finger drew a circle on the table. "Would it be impertinent to ask what sort of business?"

Her least favourite subject. "Photography." Their coffee came.

"Fashion? No! Oh God!" He hid his face. "How appallingly sexist! And unimaginative. Women, clothes, ergo . . ." He peered through his fingers. "He's crawling."

"At least you realised. Anyway, nearly all fashion photographers are men. Now that *is* sexist."

"Would I know you? Sorry, my name's Aske, Simon Aske."

"I gathered that."

His face froze, alarm in his eyes.

"That waitress," she said. "She used it."

A swift recovery. "Thank God! Just for a second the scoundrel thought all was lost. Unmasked, disgraced, his true self laid bare to the world!"

"Are you an actor, by any chance?"

"Exile. Student. *Ausgeflippter*."

"What's *Ausgeflippter*?"

"Dropout." A radiant smile. "You still haven't said your name."

"Sylvie Markham. There, you've never heard of me."

But he had seen some of her exhibitions. He listed things of which she was still proud and he had understood their finer points. "Sorry," he finished, "I haven't seen much of your recent stuff. I don't get home."

She made it over three years since he had been in England.

"Are you really a student?" She ought to be worried about Johnny. From the Stephansplatz a woman's voice soared in *Girls Were Made to Love and Kiss*.

"Meaning he's a bit long in the tooth?" His third person trick should sound twee. Why didn't it? He sketched a bow. "Piotr Sergeyevitch Trofimov, eternal student, *chère madame*." His Russian accent made him convincingly Chekhovian.

"Are you sure you're not an actor?"

"I act the fool, to hide the fact that I am a fool. What are you doing in Vienna?" His combination of near good looks and wistful clowning, she thought, might have rung carillons on box-office cash registers.

She told him about the projected book.

"The Holy Roman Empire! What did Voltaire say? *Ni saint, ni romain, ni empire*. A travel book about Habsburg real estate. About Kakania."

He saw her puzzlement. "K is pronounced *ka* in German, yes? In the days of the Habsburgs everything was K-K, *Kaiserlich-königlich*. King-emperor, if you like. A chap called Musil wrote a marvellous novel about a country called Kakania. Austria-Hungary in its death throes, very unflattering. Do you know Kafka?"

She ought to go. Why didn't she? "I read *The Trial* once."

"Kafka's the *Kaiser-König* of Kakania. King-emperor of a nightmare state. Rational man in an insane world. His name, just

64

right! Ka-ka, an F in the middle for fuck-all." He was speaking quietly, but with a febrile intensity.

"Sorry," he said. "For the language. I'm talking ka-ka. Phonetic French for shit." He stroked his nose. "He was a Jew, you know."

"Musil? Or Kafka?" Actor or not, it was a kind of performance.

He ignored the question. "K-K permitted Jews to exist, so long as they were Germanised. The *Toleranzpatent*. Have you ever thought that if Israel had a population of two hundred million, the rest of the world might be a concentration camp?" His fingers still stroked that slightly oversized nose.

"Are you Jewish?"

"Oy!" He smiled, briefly comical. "What a question! Seriously, why don't you tell them to stuff their book on Kafkaland? You take marvellous pictures of the real world."

"I think you may be right. Except that even if I don't do the unholy non-Romans, I still won't be in the real world." She found herself telling him about the Royal Shakespeare Company.

"But vot" – he was a comic Middle European savant now – "do ve mean py reality? As your Shagspeare puts it, ze vorld is all a stage, ze men and vimmin only agtors." Another lightning switch, this time, though only momentarily, a haunting desolation. " 'We are such stuff as dreams are made on, and our little life is rounded with a sleep.' "

"I don't believe you about not being an actor. You must – "

He cut in almost rudely. "Must? No must in unreality, only might. Go to Stratford and take pictures of unreality. That's real, the only real thing there."

"Don't you ever go back? Home? Or is this – Vienna – really your home?"

"Vienna is unreally my home." He stared at her for so long that she wondered if she had offended him. Abruptly, he said, "Do you know the Czech national anthem?"

"I'm afraid not."

He sang a few words in a tongue that must be Czech. "It translates, 'Where is my homeland?' "

Now she was getting lost, even though there was a curious logic in his nonsense.

"Do you speak Czech? I expect you've been. I'd love to go there, that would be the good thing about taking pictures for that book, going to places like Prague."

"Yes," he said, "you could go to Prague and take pictures of

Slansky's shadow. No, he doesn't speak Czech. And he's never been to Czechoslovakia." He reached to take her wrist. "I'm sorry. I'm a fool. I told you, it's the only disguise for a fool. Will you have lunch with me?"

She was taken aback. "I have to go back to the hotel. I'm expecting a message." Why hadn't she just said no?

"Then afterwards." He sensed her hesitation. "I know an Italian restaurant in the Dorotheergasse, simple but pleasant. One o'clock? You say."

Idiotically, she heard herself saying, "I hardly know you. Or you me."

"*I* hardly know me. Or you you. Who knows anybody? Say yes."

"All right." She hadn't meant to say it.

"Shall we say one? The far end of Dorotheergasse, on the left."

He sat back, smiling. In an accent richer than Trigg's, he said, "Nay, tha niver stood a chance. They don't come stubborner nor more determined than where he's from."

She shook her head ruefully. "Which is the real you?"

Still smiling, he said, "Thinks nought o' me, 'e dunna, not sin' Ah cum south," and, in his normal voice, "Forty years on, and still pushed around by a little lad from Pontefract. Knows what he wants, means to have it, too close to show his hand. I'm just his public image. That leaves him room to move around. That way, he's free."

I have a husband. He'll be wondering where I am. Why hadn't she said that?

She stood abruptly. "I must go, really." Halfway across the Stephansplatz, she halted, turned, went quickly back. Too late to tell him she had changed her mind. He had already gone.

# NINE

Sylvie had the unbiased eye of a camera. In due course, virtually unprompted, she would give him a perceptive sketch of an Englishman she had met by chance, while he himself had avoided all involvement. Epworth, that master of the serendipitous, could not fail to approve.

He also had a satisfactory explanation for his own non-appearance. Crossing the Burggarten, he had bumped into a high-ranking Austrian policeman, a man with whom Five had arranged his previous trip to Vienna. A matter of common courtesy ... blah-blah-blah.

Leaving the cathedral, he found self-approval giving way to a familiar disgust. He was a member of an exclusive club whose sole purpose was conspiracy. Non-members were natural victims, and that included wives.

"Lay Jesuits of the old school, that's us, Johnny," Epworth had once said. "All betrayals for the ultimate good skilfully executed by our dedicated professional staff. No cause too squalid." It was always difficult to tell when Epworth was joking.

Well, thought Morpurgo, heading back towards the hotel, he was still a member in good standing. The proof: he only half-heartedly believed in the cause, hardly at all in the ultimate good.

Kärntnerstrasse, as always, was crowded. He collided with a woman.

"Johnny?"

"Helga!"

The two halves of his existence, public and secret, came together like the core of a nuclear device. It was a silent explosion, the air full of devastation; past events, present emotions, reawakened guilt.

She had always been waiflike, little girl lost. War refugee, Russian-raped, a lifetime of suffering before she was twenty. An appalling odyssey, east to west of the old Germany before it was divided. In Berlin she had met Steve Archer, years older, still working at that time for SIS. She had snatched gratefully at his eventual offer of marriage.

More than twenty years later, both of their children launched on their respective careers, she had become Steve's chattel, a Valium housewife, just as Morpurgo, after inflicting half a lifetime of unsocial hours on Sylvie, found himself on the receiving end as Sylvie's new career rocketed her to success. The affair with Helga had been almost inevitable.

In the wake of the Sattin affair it had all come out. Faced with Steve's implacably male and self-righteous wrath, Helga had tried to kill herself, but miscalculated in that as in everything else. Failed suicide, divorced, her family scattered, she had quietly renounced Steve's coldly proper financial provisions. It had eventually filtered through that Helga Archer, *née* Schlegel, no known relatives after Götterdämmerung, had returned to Germany.

Instinctively he drew her aside from the flow of the crowd. Always ethereal, in two years she had undergone a kind of spiritual distillation. What remained had the pale, refractory glitter of a diamond.

Each said, "What are you doing here?" Both laughed. Helga's laugh, once attractively childlike, had a tubercular aridity.

"Holiday," he said. "Just a day or so. What about you?"

"With Sylvie?" Her small triangular face had always been secretive. Now it was a sculpture, lifelike, lifeless.

"Yes. I'm just off to find her." His mind was already checking the exits. The oddest feature of their affair, two lonely people consoling themselves rather than each other, had been Helga's unfeigned admiration for Sylvie. He thought it was a product of her war's-end nightmare, an ability to wall off deeds from their moral consequences.

"She is well?" She clearly no longer spoke English habitually.

"She's fine. What about you?" The only path for the conversation led backward, making him cowardly in anticipation.

"Me? Oh. I'm fine. You are here how long, in Wien?"

"Only a day or so." Be vague, cold, heartless as a bloody psychopath. "Sylvie has business. After that . . ." He shrugged, smiled, despised himself.

"Really? Not you? Your own business?" Helga knew only too painfully the general nature of his business. The general nature of his – and Steve's – business had wrecked her life.

"Really. Her business, not mine." His business, the living lie. A silence would come and he would not know how to fill it.

"Me also, a little business. Then back to Germany." She laid a thin hand on his forearm. "To speak is not easy, yes? Perhaps we should go to bed, no need there for talking." She had escaped from violence and depravity with her childlike nature no more than bruised. The last two years, he could see, might have changed all that. She smiled. "I think this meeting must not continue, do you agree?"

A tourist, male, fat, clumsy, camera aimed toward the Stephansdom, stepped back, colliding heavily with them. "*Entschuldigung!*" He moved a little away.

Helga said, "Kiss me, Johnny, and goodbye." Her pale face tilted.

He hesitated momentarily before bending his head. Her lips, cold and hard, pressed themselves on his. Through the soft redgold of her crown he saw a camera swing towards them, a model Sylvie used for what she called 'quick stuff'.

Quick stuff it was. The automatic wind-on fizzed three or four times. The man melted into the crowd. "*Wiedersehen*, Johnny." Helga too moved quickly, the U-bahn only yards away. At the top of the steps she waved. "*Tschüss!*"

Bye-bye!

He made no attempt to follow. It was his true punishment, a time-bomb much delayed.

He had been set up, a classically neat operation, perfectly exploiting a wronged and bitter woman's revenge if she were persuaded to hold not only her husband and her lover but their country – which was not her country – responsible for ruining her life.

How, they would ask, could he explain away meeting her again after two years? In Vienna, that marketplace of spies? Perhaps, they might suggest, there had been other times and other places. His image of 'them' was vague, but undoubtedly hostile.

While he waited for the lights to change at the junction with Operngasse, doubt fell on him like the sudden darkness of an eclipse. The London security community, American as well as

British, had thought him bloody lucky to find his feet last time. What if the purpose, plain and simple, was to make sure, this time, that he went down and stayed down?

In that case there could only be one 'they', and nothing so subtle as blackmail.

He had no intention at all of yielding without a fight. Reaching Walfischgasse, the Bristol in sight, he had already made his decision. He would tell Sylvie first, the sooner the better. After that, Epworth. Epworth would see to the rest.

There was a message for him at the Bristol. Sylvie had got herself tied up with her publishers after all. She would see him when he and Trigg came back from the Prater. He put in a call to Epworth. After an hour and three attempts he accepted the fact that the Epworths must be out. Picking bloody reeds, he thought sourly, and went to meet Trigg.

\*　　　\*　　　\*

There was little to be seen of the restaurant from Dorotheergasse: a leaded window, opaque glass, a hand-written menu. Inside, busy, no Simon Aske as yet.

A waiter appeared. *"Buon giorno, signorina. Una? Für ein?"*

She smiled, suspecting that Italian accent. *"Aspetto qualcuno. Saremo due."* The place was busy, not too many tourists, a lot of young business types in sharp three-piece suits. At the far end, flying fingers traced out savoury patterns on pizza pastry.

She was wrong. The waiter was a Tyroler, Italian- as well as German-speaking. Installed with the panache due to minor royalty, persuaded to an aperitivo, she resigned herself to being ingratiatingly harassed until the arrival of Simon Aske.

\*　　　\*　　　\*

*"Vom Fass,"* Trigg finally set aside his disappointment at Sylvie's absence. *"It means straight from the barrel, does that, and right good ale it is."* His breath, too, was *vom Fass.* Any attempt Toby Farrar might have made at luring him to wine over lunch had clearly failed.

He looked about him approvingly. *"By! Takes me back years, does a place like this. Take deep breaths, buttercup. This is the smell of simple folk enjoying themselves."*

It was the smell of the Prater, cooking fat, onions, wurst, vanilla, all borne on the stale breath of the internal combustion engine. With it came a cacophony of pop music, the amplified rasp of barkers.

"By heck!" Trigg returned his attention to the giant wheel. "It's a big 'un, is that. Right, are you on then?"

"On?" Morpurgo was finding it hard to forget the possible consequences of his meeting with Helga. Things were moving still farther away from the script.

"Yon wheel, you dozy ha'poth! By, you're that thick sometimes!" Giving a decisive slap to what he called his billycock hat, he propelled Morpurgo towards the queue.

Once inside a car he continued to the farther end. Behind them were a party of Japanese, cameras already at work, and an elderly couple, Austrian as Kaiserschmarrn. As the wheel resumed its halting progress, girders and crossbeams changed their relative positions with the stately precision of a Newtonian universe.

A tree-thick axle ran the length of the car. Studying its barely perceptible movement impassively as they slowly ascended, Trigg said, "Not much of a life, is it, buttercup, spending all your time looking over your shoulder?" The movement stopped while the car behind them loaded.

"I didn't know I was."

"Come off it. You've never stopped."

"Can we talk about something else?"

"That feller Sattin, for instance?"

Morpurgo checked himself in the act of looking behind. "You wanted to come on this thing. Why don't you admire the bloody view?"

The city had expanded to fill half of the horizon, pink and buff between the misty heights of the Leopoldsberg and the Wienerwald. At the foot of the wheel children, small, active dots, played on a great model of the world, quarrelling as to which way it should be turned, spinning it this way and that. Life could be very corny.

"Back before the Hitler war," Trigg said, "Grimsby and Cleethorpes – happen I've told you this before – was mainly fish. Biggest fishing port in t'world, was Grimsby in those days, thousands relying on it for a living." His eyes had a sardonic gleam.

"If you had cause," he went on, "to catch a bus around knocking-off time, you could always tell which was ones that actually handled fish. You could tell it yards away. First thing they did when they got home was change out of their clothes and boots."

71

Morpurgo grinned reluctantly. "I get the message."

"Nay, lad, you only get half the message. I don't mind letting on I took a bit of a fancy to you first time we met. Not lost, I said to myself, nor even gone before, but he'll have to change more than his clothes before he's fit for decent company. He'll have to change his trade."

He prodded Morpurgo. "It's one thing for you to be mixed up with stinking fish. It's another for that lass of yours. I reckon nought of that."

The wheel turned with the slow dignity of a waltzing dowager, each silver car in turn catching the sun in a silent flare of light. They were almost at the summit, Vienna diminished to a hazy sprawl, golden with autumn. In the east the suburbs, scored by the brown gash of the Danube, dwindled away into the marshy Lobau.

Making the obligatory response, he said, "Sylvie does her job. I do mine. At the moment, I'm on holiday."

"Here's Billy Muggins," Trigg said after a weighty pause, "who's always thought Danube was blue and ran through the middle of Vienna like letters in a stick of rock, while all folk waltzed on both banks."

They were on the way down. "It's a lesson to me," Trigg said, "not to believe everything I'm told." They finished the halting descent in silence.

As they walked away, Trigg, surprised, said, "Hey up! Here's yon chap Farrar. Judging by t'look on his face, lollipops has run into a bear market." At last they were back with the script.

Managing to look as if the entire Prater were no more than a mirage, Toby produced his most boringly matter-of-fact voice. "Bit of luck finding you so easily, Mr Trigg. Would this be Mr Morpurgo?"

Morpurgo took his cue gratefully. "I'm Morpurgo."

"Personal matter, sir. They'd be grateful if you'd call in at the embassy. I've a car waiting."

He turned back to Trigg. "Perhaps you'll want to stay on, sir. If not, my chap will be glad to lay on a taxi. H.M.G. will take care of the fare."

"When Her Majesty's Government," Trigg said, "has earned one honest penny on its own account, I'll say thanks."

Eloquent in his biddable silence, he allowed himself to be dispatched. Toby's driver, his wooden face and aggressively correct bearing underscored by a knowingness common among ex-N.C.O.s in almost any service, swept Farrar and Morpurgo around the Praterstern without further orders. Instead of crossing the Ring, they took the slip road to the autobahn, where the signs said Bratislava, Budapest.

Morpurgo looked at Toby. "Which embassy did you have in mind?"

"H.E." – Toby was giving his sprawling imitation of gilded youth – "would have kittens if I brought you within a kilometre of the embassy."

The driver, in gentrified Glaswegian, said, "Will I put my foot down, Mr Farrar? We're not over-blessed with time."

"Yes, best put your wee bit footie down, Mac," Toby said in his unrevealing monotone, but he winked at Morpurgo. The car leaped forward like a predator to a kill. They passed a junction, the goblin castles of a petrochemical plant silver-pale in the distance. A sign for entering traffic said SCHWECHAT above an airport symbol.

"My instructions," Toby said, "were to get you on the first plane out, sir."

Morpurgo sat up. "First plane out to where, for Christ's sake?" Once again the script was being rewritten.

"London." Toby gestured warningly at the driver's back. "All I know, I'm afraid."

"What about my wife?"

"My instructions don't cover Mrs Morpurgo, sir. I'm sure Fawcett, he's head of chancery, will take care she's informed."

"And my gear?" He was like a child working routinely through all the unacceptable reasons for not being sent to bed.

"I'm sure," Toby said confidently, "Mrs Morpurgo will cope."

Morpurgo had a vision of the day as some great baroque edifice on which an expert demolition squad had worked, one of those perfect jobs that squats in massive slow motion before being swallowed by billowing dust. Except that this was a one-man effort. Epworth, you bastard!

"I'll put myself on a plane. Just drop me at the bloody terminal." If only he could get to a phone. He had no real hopes.

"Made the same point myself to Fawcett." Toby whistled and rolled his eyes to illustrate official reaction. "Orders is orders, see you aboard."

"Anybody meeting me at Heathrow?"

"Haven't the foggiest, sir. Mind, meet you at Heathrow! Whoever would find you?"

# TEN

He gave up trying to reach Sylvie around midnight. If she were so angry as to remain incommunicado, let her enjoy her sleep.

No such compunction about Epworth: only repeated failure to raise any of the daunting brood finally drove him to bed. Tomorrow would be another day. But it was already tomorrow. That was enough to keep him awake.

He could retreat from Sylvie behind the blank, impregnable barrier of the Act, no need after all to mention even Helga Archer. He had gone to Vienna in good faith, the blame for his recall automatically transferred to Epworth. If he played it right, he might even win sympathy, a minor martyr, holiday wrecked, marital relations jeopardised by the unspeakable Epworth. She knew better than to look for either explanation or apology in that quarter.

But he had been summarily recalled, and they would all know. He was ex-Five, Morpurgo the lefty outsider, cuckolder of his better. From their point of view, it would be sufficient that there was smoke. They would be happy to heap on coals of fire in the hope that the resulting flames might also consume Lawrence Epworth.

Yet even that was not his biggest problem. The biggest was that until someone told him why he had been snatched back and left in limbo, he didn't know what the rest of his problems were. Rather than wait to see what might happen next, he walked toward the sound of silence.

The Century House lobby has all the sensuous comfort of an undertaker's delivery bay. "Dancer" Hallett, a promising welterweight renowned, in his army days, for a shuffle modelled on

Mohammed Ali's, was Morpurgo's favourite among the security guards.

He took Morpurgo's pass. "American Express? That'll do nicely, Mr Morpurgo." An old joke, and the usual old twist. "Random check, sir. First prize, a week in Brixton. Second prize two weeks in Brixton. Back to you inside the hour, sir."

Random checks were frequent, but this time, going on up, he knew his pass would not come back. Betty Pringle was not there, though her usual territorial markings – library book, knitting, private flask of coffee – were on display. They would have concocted some tale for her benefit.

Playing the farce to its finish, he tried the door of his office. Double-locked, his own key useless. Behind him, the voice he had expected to hear said, "Spare a minute, Johnny? Couple of things to settle before life goes on its merry way."

Wriothsley's mane of silky blond hair, just beginning to silver at the temples, gave him an air of lordly raffishness. Senior operational officer after Epworth, he was also Winchester and Balliol – *sum, ergo cogito* – and coordinator, Middle East.

Elsenham, next in seniority, was waiting in Wriothsley's office. They were doing it by the book. Elsenham, assassin's eyes in the superficially indulgent face of a paterfamilias, was coordinator, Western Europe. As SIS representative on the Northern Ireland Joint Security Committee, and himself a Catholic, being unofficially known as the Anti-Pope taxed his brittle humour.

Wriothsley and Elsenham had three things in common. They represented the old school, which was to say the way things had been before Epworth's *coup d'état*. They deplored the diminished world role of SIS, and blamed it on people whose class, broadly speaking, was nearer Morpurgo's than their own. And both were clubland cronies of ex-SIS field man Sir Stephen Archer. Epworth, Morpurgo's ears only, referred to them as the leaders of the – mmmm – Century House cabal.

The couple of things Wriothsley had it in mind to settle occupied a suave but notably unsentimental five minutes.

"In other words," Morpurgo said, "suspended."

Wriothsley was at his blandest. "Profit-and-loss, old boy. Indefinite leave, I'm afraid." He concealed his fear like a man. Elsenham was all but licking his thin lips.

Profit-and-loss; a committee of enquiry, three or four hand-picked assessors like these two. It would examine the career of John Morpurgo from A to whatever letter of the alphabet it had reached, every operation with which he had had the smallest connection. If, when a balance was struck, there was the smallest suggestion that his overall contribution had been negative, the investigation had only just begun.

"It's barely two years," he said, "since I came over the river. For most of that time I've been sharpening other people's pencils. You can't run a profit-and-loss on bugger all."

"All depends, old chap" – Wriothsley's pseudo-boyish charm had gone into retreat – "on how far back one goes."

"How far back did you have in mind?"

"Not us." Elsenham was brisk. "You know the drill. You have the right to make the usual representations." The trap sprung, he had no more time to waste. "Leave anything else to you, David. If there is anything else." He left without so much as a nod.

Morpurgo pulled himself together. Script or no, it was hard to take. "Do you mean this will be a joint enquiry? Six and Five?"

Left on his own, Wriothsley, ever the trimmer, switched to prisoner's friend. "Sorry, old boy, but you know how it is. You could go to the D-G, of course, but he'll only pass the buck. He knows it's out of his hands."

"Whose hands is it in? Steve Archer's?" Could Epworth conceivably have been outsmarted at last?

Wriothsley laughed through his nose. "That'll be the day! Look, you'll learn soon enough when your lord and master comes back from leave, so you might as well know now. He's the one who pulled you out before you did any more damage."

He smiled the thin smile of the morally superior. "Know what the Book of Common Prayer says? Put not your trust in princes, for there is no help in them. Now, tiresome and all that, but I must ask you for your keys."

He was about to close the door behind him when Wriothsley spoke again.

"Morpurgo."

He turned, Wriothsley was staring at him like a puzzled child. "Why the devil did you come here? When they turfed you out last time, why the devil didn't you stay out? You can't possibly imagine you'll ever belong."

*       *       *

The church stood in its own square-within-a-square, railinged, ringed with trees, classically porticoed, but for all its elegance it had the standard festooning of parked cars. The old Volvo child

76

transporter was parked on a meter that wore a plastic glove: OUT OF ORDER.

He bent to the open window. "People go mad looking for parking space round here. What makes you so special?"

Epworth flipped open the glove compartment. It held a neat stack of plastic gloves. "When you – mmmm – name a trysting place, make sure you can keep the tryst. How was the show so far?"

"You didn't warn me you were changing the plot."

"The essence of good theatre is surprise. Besides" – Epworth was driving, stationary at the meter, hands at a quarter to three – "it was essential to ensure your pristine response to – mmmm – Cassius and the envious Casca."

"Et tu, Brute," Morpurgo said. "Et bloody tu."

"Tell me about Acts One and Two."

Morpurgo got in, pushing aside empty potato crisp packets with his foot. "Toby Farrar's a good man."

"Nothing like believing in the part."

"Meaning that he didn't know it was a part, yes, I realised that."

Epworth's hands dropped to his lap, as hands do when traffic gels and the wait is going to be a long one. "What about the rest of the second act?"

Just wait, Morpurgo thought with grim relish, until you hear the rest of the first act. Especially the surprise guest star. "What did you do? Take the family into the priest-hole for the night?"

"How many times did you ring?"

"Enough to be convincing. In case Tinkerbell paid a visit while we were away."

"She didn't."

"No," Morpurgo said, "and since you ask, I owe the information to Sid. Bit part, salt-of-the-earth working-class stereotype, but then, not exactly into social realism, are we?"

"Painter and decorator," Epworth said. "Working nights to please Sylvie. He won't be pleased you're back early. You distract him." He did his Mona Lisa. "Not the type to see you as a class enemy, but you're definitely – mmmm – posh. One of Them."

Momentarily distracted, Morpurgo said, "How much longer do we have to sit in this bloody car? All right, you know all about Sid. Are you sure about the phone fairies?"

Epworth was already opening his door. "Come to church.

77

Confession is good for the soul." He headed for the columned portico.

Morpurgo made one last attempt as they went up the steps towards the massive doors. "When we discussed all this after lunch last week, you didn't tell me that Trigg – "

'That Hunawihr Clos Sainte-Hune we had with lunch" – Epworth held open the door for him – "was a disappointment. Keep your voice down. The red light may be on."

They were in a roomy vestibule. Ahead of them was another pair of doors, heavily padded. A sign in cut-out letters said, RECORDING IN PROGRESS, but the red light was not on. Epworth steered him down a flight of steps. "A crypt," he said, "is an excellent place for conspiracy."

The crypt, vaulted, honey-brown stonework running the full width of the edifice, had been turned into a refectory; long, gleaming tables, ancient and massive, seats that were obviously the highbacked former pews. It was soft, intimate, a company of gentle shadows, an air of austerely civilised comfort.

The tables nearest the servery were occupied by several small groups of people, both sexes, informally dressed, the age group that made Morpurgo most aware of his own. One of the men waved.

"Hello, Lawrie. Come to pick up some tips?" Morpurgo found it a kind of cheerful blasphemy, like addressing God as Pop.

"Something like that." Epworth had undergone one of his metamorphoses, indulgent tutor, academic brood. He motioned Morpurgo to the nearest unoccupied table. "How goes Gesualdo?"

A girl with red-gold hair and the face of a Rossetti damsel said, "*Bella, bella, bellissima.*"

"*'Bello,*" someone corrected. "I mean, Gesualdo was a feller, for Christ's sake!"

The Rossetti maiden was contemptuous. "*Bella*, do you mind? *E bella, la musica, vero?*"

Still nursing assorted grievances, Morpurgo said, "Not even in Vienna long enough to hear any music, I resent that, too."

"More good music in London in a week than Vienna in a month." Epworth seemed to have abandoned the topic that had brought them together.

A man at the next table looked up from a copy of *The Gramophone*. "How's the old Cornysh, then? I hear you're going to cut some wax."

78

"The Cornysh Consort" – Epworth was looking amiably ineffectual – "is in – mmmm – good fettle. Like the small fowle, we maken melody. That object," bringing Morpurgo into the conversation at last with an indolent wave at *The Gramophone*, "calls itself a recording engineer, as do its fellow layabouts. And these" – he indicated the others – "are the Early Musicke Group with a *cke*. They're recording some Gesualdo madrigals. If you're ready to eat, I can recommend the quiche and salad, and the white wine is drinkable."

"Are you," the Rossetti girl asked Morpurgo, "some sort of musician?" and by the time Epworth brought the quiche he had gathered that it was his musical skills that had earned Lawrence Epworth, effective head of Her Majesty's Secret Intelligence Service, the cheerfully irreverent but unmistakable respect of the present company. He also learned that Epworth and the Cornysh Consort would shortly record an album of sixteenth-century English court music.

This was, Morpurgo had to admit, a very safe house.

When the conversation turned elsewhere, Epworth returned to their own. "You mentioned your friend Trigg."

"Your friend, too. He seems to think so, anyway, though God knows why."

"Really?" Epworth looked pleased. "Did I know he would be on that flight? I think that would be your next question."

"Did you?"

"I knew he was with you when Toby Farrar told me. Not before." Epworth munched lettuce enthusiastically, but his air was expectant.

"And Karl-Heinz Mandel?" At the next table a woman with fair frizzy hair was settling a nice point of pronunciation in cinquecento Italian.

Dabbing his lips with his paper napkin, Epworth turned a look of polite interest on Morpurgo. "Suppose you give me a summary of – mmmm – Act One?"

Perhaps, after all, Toby Farrar had not told Epworth everything. Perhaps, Morpurgo thought, he might not be the only one for whom those last hours had been crowded.

"Did Toby tell you how Sylvie met Aske? Or how I met Helga Archer?"

All around them people were getting to their feet. The man who had spoken to them first – his name, Morpurgo succeeded in remembering, was Tony – came across.

"Coming up? You could listen to the takes and tell us what you think."

"Or alternatively," said *The Gramophone*, "pick up a few tips."

Epworth smiled vaguely. "When the Cornysh – mmmm – cuts its own wax, you may all come to jeer and stay to cheer. In the meantime we would feel *de trop*." But he was already rising.

It was a large hall in the Palladian style, the high, moulded ceiling with its stucco frieze a distant echo of baroque Vienna. It was lit by tall leaded windows through which little could be seen but treetops. Soundproofing conferred a near-total silence.

Where the altar had been was a low platform on which timpani and side drums in their padded transporter bags huddled with a wry-necked gaggle of music stands. At the opposite end, the gallery wore a silvery tiara of organ pipes.

The singers had a semicircle of chairs toward the centre, a small thicket of microphones bending their necks to eavesdrop. A disembodied voice said, "Ready when you are, boys and girls." Morpurgo followed Epworth up to the balcony.

A disembodied voice said, "Okay then? Right. Take 42. Here we go." Another instant and the room was drenched in glory: soprano, contralto, tenor, baritone and bass interthreaded like larksong. Morpurgo found his mind purged by the languorous sensuality of the music.

Gesualdo, Renaissance prince, dispenser of condign vengeance, neurotic penitent, as inextricably entangled in the welter of his passions as were his passions in his music. That, Morpurgo thought, he could understand.

But Epworth, bloodless, yet loving with shawm, crumhorn and early music, Epworth, epicene, yet father of four from a jolly earth mother, Epworth, equally expert in plot, trap and, if necessary, sudden death, all with the unshakable serenity of clear conscience or none. No, he thought, he would never understand him.

Epworth leaned close. "Utterly ravishing. Tell me about Helga Archer."

Afterwards it was to come back to him repeatedly, a kind of exotic dream: the frequent breaks while five ardent perfectionists anatomised and reconstituted apparent flawlessness, the ambient stillness in the heart of a metropolis, above all, that seemingly endless outpouring of sensual enchantment.

Except that it did end.

One of the girls, exaggerating the accent, said, "*Arrivederci,*

Gesualdo!" On the producer's speaker the disembodied voice said, "Who's for a jar when we've stowed the gear?" People appeared, disconnecting leads, packing up accessories. Their privacy was gone.

Tony said, "We're off for a quickie before we break up. Join us?"

"Time, Tony, the eternal enemy." Epworth held up a palm as if to stop time.

"What did you think?"

"Oh." Epworth gestured again, both hands this time. "*Molto squisito!* So – mmmm – deliciously anguished."

"Yes," Tony said, "Don't see you putting the same charge into Lawes and Tomkins, but best of luck anyway."

Epworth looked at Morpurgo. "Give you a lift?"

"Where to? Home?"

Epworth giggled. "You won't catch me near your place until this has blown over." He started toward his car. "You'd better accept the lift."

Morpurgo waited while Epworth unlocked the car. They both got in.

"On the other hand" – Epworth put the key in the ignition without switching on – "where more private than this? When's Sylvie due back?"

"I don't know. If she knew I went to Vienna for you, she might not come back."

"We agreed," Epworth said, "that no one is going to believe you went just for her."

"No one's going to believe I went just to look at Aske. I told you that was daft. Toby Farrar thought it was daft."

"You're not in trouble because I sent you. No one knows I did. You're in trouble because you used Sylvie as an excuse to go, and then did something – mmmm – daft. Of course, Sylvie will testify that you had nothing to do with her meeting Aske. No one will believe that, either."

"Sylvie's not going to testify to anyone."

"In a profit-and-loss," Epworth said, "enquiries are not restricted to the – mmmm – ledger clerk."

"Thank you very bloody much! Still, you rank me higher than Wriothsley. He wouldn't even trust me with the petty cash."

"Nailed his colours to the mast, did he?" Epworth showed pleasure. "Splendid!" He laid an earnest hand on Morpurgo's arm. "Look, we can't have you and Sylvie quarrelling. I mean not before we know what she learned about Aske."

"Sod you!" Morpurgo felt for the door release. "You probably care more about Helga."

"How did she look?"

"Why don't you wait for the pictures?"

"The question was serious." Epworth started the car.

"That's how she looked. Serious."

"Calm and serious? Neurotically serious? Determinedly serious?"

Morpurgo opened the door. Through the gap, traffic in Borough High Street snarled at them like a beast behind bars.

"Calm but taut, almost see the light through her."

"In that case" – Epworth's giggle jarred more than usual – "she may not come out in the snaps."

"Very funny. What happens when they put the bite on?" Epworth was gently revving the engine. Morpurgo said, "Do you have the faintest idea who they are?"

"Not the smallest." Epworth revved a little louder. "The only way to find out is to continue as we began."

"I love that 'we'. *Will* there be a profit-and-loss?"

"Possibly. Probably. It depends."

"On what, for Christ's sake?"

"On what Sylvie can tell you." Epworth revved up again. The engine was rough. "On what Mandel knows, and whether he keeps it to himself. On how much of Aske's past you can uncover before they guess what you're up to."

"I thought the whole idea was that they shouldn't." Morpurgo opened the door wide. "I shall tell Sylvie you recalled me. I shan't tell her you're sorry. She wouldn't believe me. Perhaps Amaryllis will say sorry for you. By the way, your big end's going." He got out and began to walk.

*　　*　　*

"Message, Mr Morpurgo. From the lady." Sid fished in his coveralls to produce a neatly folded sheet of paper, found a pair of half-moon glasses. "She's left Vienna by now, back nineish."

"At Heathrow?"

"No, not Heathrow, sir. Here." Sid consulted his notes. "Said not to meet her, she'll take a cab."

Morpurgo wandered towards his piano. Sylvie wouldn't know where he was. Naturally she would take a cab rather than let him meet her. He knew he was kidding himself.

He picked out the opening of *La ci darem la mano* with one hand. The last note dwindled, dying abruptly as he lifted his finger. He had an image of Vienna, forlorn, moribund.

"Like to finish this coat," Sid said, "if it won't disturb you."

"What?" His mind was adrift.

"The painting. Promised the lady I'd finish this room tonight. Being you wasn't supposed to be back, see, Mr Morpurgo?"

"I'm sorry. You carry on. I'm going out anyway." He closed the lid of the piano: no more music.

Sid decided to be generous. "I mean, it don't bother me if I don't bother you. If you was feeling like playing something."

"I wasn't really playing. Just messing about." He smiled. "That's what my mum used to say. 'Why don't you play properly? You're just messing about.' Where are you from, Sid?"

Sid had already gone to pick up his brush. "Me? Here, Mr Morpurgo. London born, London bred, that's me."

"I meant, which part?"

"Wandsworth. Wandsworth proper, not Putney or Streatham or that. Never more'n a stone's throw from Lavender Hill." He loaded his brush expertly.

"Trinity Road," Morpurgo said. "That was me. Well, just off Trinity Road. My mum lived there till she died."

Sid began to lay off paint. "Reckon that'd be a tidy while ago, Mr Morpurgo."

It was barely two months since they had found her at the foot of the stairs. Up to then it had still been home, the home of that other and in some ways more real Morpurgo. He could barely remember his father, the elementary school teacher, so self-effacing as to be all but a ghost before his early death. It was she, the backstreet greengrocer's daughter with her grimly held belief that the only reason for being in the world was to get on and do well, who had made him.

He had got on. He had not done well. She had made that plain right to the end.

"Reckon you wouldn't find it your style these days." Sid broke through the fog of memory. The idea of Morpurgo, owner of a posh house in Chelsea, as a Wandsworth boy was something just this side of fantasy. "Gone downhill something shocking over the years, Mr Morpurgo."

He had been put in his place. No, he had been put in his class. He thought: Thanks for nothing, mum. He went out until Sylvie should be back.

# ELEVEN

Sid had gone. Sylvie was in the bedroom, still unpacking. She said, "Hello." He knew at once that it was going to be difficult.

"I went out to the pub. Sid wanted to get on. Good flight?"

"Up, over, down."

"I'm sorry about leaving in such a hurry. I hadn't the smallest chance to get in touch with you."

"So I gathered." She moved through his airspace as if he didn't exist.

"Have you eaten?"

"There was food on the plane but I wasn't hungry."

"Would you like – "

"Was it important?" She slid the question in almost indifferently.

He was not deceived. "Not very, as it turned out. I told Epworth what I thought."

"You can take those away." She indicated the bags. She had unpacked for him too.

"I'm sorry you were stuck with my things." They were both circling the combat zone.

He said, "I hope they were suitably apologetic."

"A man called Farrar. He did his best. Eustace Roland told me you'd gone to the embassy, but you hadn't, had you?"

"I tried phoning you once I was back. I gave up when it got late. I've been out all day. Sid gave me your message when I got back."

She turned in the doorway. "Bring my bag. There's something in it for you."

Three photographs of Simon Aske.

Years of experience, yet instead of destroying the photographs he had left them for Sylvie to find when she packed. He went down.

She was pouring herself a drink. She took it to a chair, lit a cigarette, looked at him impassively.

He said, "Am I allowed to explain?"

"Can you?"

"What did Farrar tell you?"

"Recalled. No choice. Rigours of the service. Couldn't have told me why even if he'd known, and of course, he didn't." She perfectly recaptured Toby's toneless brevities.

He sat, a stranger in his own house. "The flight was due out almost immediately. I only just caught it. We didn't go to the embassy. That was just to put Trigg off the scent."

"You're not doing very well. Perhaps you're getting too old for the job." That made him wince inwardly.

"I mean," she said, "I've never been sure when you were lying, not even after years of practice. I used to tell myself it wasn't my business anyway. That secrets were secrets, so long as they were things I had no right to know."

"Concealing the truth isn't necessarily lying." He knew she was talking about his affair with Helga.

She went on as if he had said nothing. "I suppose I stopped bothering. I suppose that gives you some sort of excuse."

"I'm not looking for excuses, Sylvie." There was still the meeting with Helga to come, but the pictures of Aske in his hand had power over his tongue.

She downed half of her drink at a gulp. "Better say something, even if it's that you're not allowed to say anything. The standard cop-out."

He ripped up the photographs methodically. "I'm sorry you saw these. I agreed to go to Vienna because I thought it would please you. Amaryllis warned me of the risk."

"Truth will out?" She had regained self-control. "Not often. Your kind of business is to see that it won't."

She put out her cigarette. "All right. The eleventh commandment, thou shalt not expect others to be more moral than thyself. I met him, the man in those pictures. I even talked to him. I expect you know."

"Yes," he said, "I know. That's probably where things started to go wrong."

Before he had finished the story she had kicked off her shoes and tucked her feet under her. It marked a change in their

85

relationship. He dared to hope it was progress.

Her first question was typical. "How did Helga look?"

She had never borne Helga any grudge. Only Steve Archer's Old Testamental rectitude had prevented her from trying to help when Helga, after her attempted suicide, plunged headlong into breakdown.

How, he wanted to say, did Simon Aske look? How did he sound, and what did he say? But she had shamed him and he must do penance.

He repeated what he had said to Epworth about Helga. He saw that she was wryly amused. "Well," she said, "she must have got some kind of a kick out of it, no matter what happens. Hell hath no fury, but revenge is sweet."

"What happens may not be so funny." He had to keep some kind of faith with Epworth. "I'm in trouble up to my neck." How long before he could decently bring the conversation back to Simon Aske?

She listened again while he told her how Wriothsley had been waiting for him at Century House. On his meeting with Epworth he would have to be altogether more selective.

"Is that why you were recalled? Because of Simon Aske? It doesn't make sense. If Epworth sent you to Vienna, why should he bring you back in disgrace?"

"This is where it gets difficult."

She waggled her fingers. "Bye-bye, truth."

"I've already told you far more than I should."

"Very little option, my boy. And you aren't out of the wood yet."

"I'm still a servant of the Crown."

"Suspended."

"Not quite. But from now on, the smallest step out of line would be wilful breach."

"Of what?"

"The Act."

"Stuff the Act! What about wilful breach of our marriage vows?"

He preferred to stick with the Act. "Unlawful use of information given to me in confidence, as someone in a position of special trust."

"Stuff that too. They don't trust you, or you wouldn't be where you are."

"Makes no difference. The Act binds me for life. If they send

86

me to prison, I'm still bound. And still bound when I get out."

"I'm not bound. And what passes between husband and wife is privileged, too."

"You are bound. The fact that you've signed nothing makes no difference. You're asking me to break the law by telling you things covered by the Act. I'm not being evasive, Sylvie. You're breaking the law just by asking."

"My husband's in trouble and I can't ask him why. Is that what we've been living with all these years?"

"You've always known that."

"Are you in trouble? Really in trouble?" The fencing was over.

"I've done nothing wrong, if that's what you're wondering. In this game you're in trouble the minute you step out of line."

"But you didn't. Quite the opposite. The minute you saw me with Simon Aske, you walked away."

"I know that. You know that. It may not look that way in a profit-and-loss."

He could see now, more clearly than ever before, just how far his world was from hers, from any world populated by normal, halfway decent people. It was one thing to recognise the existence of deceit. It was quite another to work for people who saw no one and nothing as being beyond question, who never gave the benefit of the doubt.

"If Epworth doesn't believe you," she said, "then no one believes you. He sent you. He *knows* what happened."

"He knows what I told him, nothing more." There was so much she could say that might help, and they were almost upon it.

He said, "Tell me about Simon Aske. If you tell me, it's just possible they might not ask you."

Her face hardened. "Oh, another one like that." They were both remembering the Sattin affair. Correction, the Helga Archer affair.

She said, "Last time it was the Punch and Judy man who was asking the questions. Who will it be this time?" Epworth was her Punch and Judy man, for reasons not very flattering to John Morpurgo.

"Let's hope it will still be Epworth."

"Oh my God!" she said, making some kind of joke of it. "As bad as that?"

No point in minimising things now. "That could be a best case situation. They winged me last time. This time they'll try to finish me off."

"Who, for God's sake?"

"At Century House they're so far to the right they make Five look like the Salvation Army. Some of them think Five *is* the Salvation Army." He grinned crookedly. "I know. A case of class consciousness that's practically in the category of self-inflicted wound. True, all the same."

She made the big jump. "SIS man, not many friends, in trouble once already, goes to Vienna on secret mission. Not supposed to break cover so he talks his wife into doing what he can't do himself. Everything's fine until he's tricked into being photographed in compromising circumstances. With the same woman he compromised himself with once before. The divorced wife of a man who's now head of Five. A woman who's only British by marriage."

She looked at him in disbelief and not a little disgust. "They'd try to make a tale like that stick, just to get rid of you?"

"You missed something out. The Punch and Judy man."

"You went because he sent you."

He nodded. "At a time when Aske's the cause of a very delicate diplomatic situation. Potentially embarrassing both to us and to the Austrians."

"So it's not you they're after. It's him. Epworth."

"Let's say two birds with one stone."

"Don't tell me the mastermind's been given a dose of his own medicine." She said it lightly, but her eyes were full of pain.

Yes, he thought, this is what we've lived with all these years. If only he could tell her, but it was more than a question of trust.

"Sylvie, you know why I've stayed in this business."

"Because if you left they'd put someone in your place who *did* believe everything's either black or white." She said it with weary familiarity.

"Yes," he said. "Someone like Steve Archer. It's also why, on the whole, I put up with Epworth. Because of the rest."

"Epworth as the best of a bad lot." She shook her head. "It's a man's reason."

"There are worse. I could make it much clearer. But if I did, and they found out, life could become very unpleasant. For both of us."

For a moment, watching her nibble her lip, he hoped he had frightened her off. Instead, she said, "I wonder where I stand under the Act if I tell you that Pierre Weber warned me days ago you might catch it in the neck if you went to Vienna? I wonder where he stands under the Act for telling me?"

"Well at least you're safe there," he said. "You didn't tell me." Outside, Chelsea was going about its business, which was mainly pleasure.

"I'll tell you this," she said eventually. "I'm hungry. You can pay."

\*     \*     \*

It was one of those uninhibitedly upmarket bistros which are Chelsea's answer to convenience foods. He told her more of his side, up to a point. She sketched out hers, without warmth. It was a kind of border skirmishing.

"Why couldn't Weber tell me?" He liked Pierre Weber, had always felt that Weber liked him. Claas now, Claas wouldn't have handed out private warnings to help a man who – Claas's words – was always in two minds but seldom the right one at the right time.

She dealt brusquely with the question. "You'd already told me you wouldn't go to Vienna. That's all he wanted to know."

"But if he knew . . ." He stopped. If he told her what Weber must have known, he might as well tell her everything.

She had anticipated him. "He knew they had plans for you. What he called the anti-Epworth club."

What Epworth called the cabal. "Did he say who they were?"

"Maybe. Maybe not."

"So you knew I had enemies, but you weren't going to tell me."

She laughed derisively. "You've always had enemies. And I was going to tell you. I was going to tell you while we were in Vienna. It meant something to me, Johnny, going to Vienna together." She bit her lip. "This is what it's brought us to, your damned job! You're two people. One I love. The other lies, cheats, spies. What am I supposed to fight back with? Sweet reason?" Her eyes glittering, she looked away.

He stretched out a hand, withdrew it.

She took a deep breath, once more herself. "Isn't almost anything better than this? Anyway, they can't make wives testify against husbands."

"Not in court. With our lot, it doesn't matter by then."

He looked over each shoulder, the reflex action Trigg had been quick to spot. "Anyway, what Pierre Weber told you isn't news to Epworth. That's why he wanted me to go to Vienna. So I could be sent back. Officially, no one's supposed to go anywhere near Aske. I can't tell you why."

"You couldn't be sent officially. But if you just happened to be there, just happened" – she made no attempt to conceal her bitterness – "to be on holiday with your wife . . ."

He made himself look at her. "Exactly. And someone tipped off the Austrian authorities."

"Someone who knows you well enough not to believe you were going just to keep me company. Steve, for instance?" She saw him react. "Well, he was right, wasn't he?"

He grimaced. "I'm sorry. Oh, Christ! Really! Very sorry."

She waved the apology away. "Sorry now you've been found out. Not sorry then. So from the minute we arrived in Vienna, we were watched. Waiting for you to make some sort of contact with Aske."

"Is that what Pierre said would happen?"

She ignored the question. "Steve Archer. Pierre said as much. Steve doesn't see why his people should have to put up with lie detectors and stuff while raving reds in SIS go unchallenged. Quote, not even joint vetting with Langley, unquote. Stop looking over your shoulder. It's very unprofessional."

"If you end up at the Bailey," he said, "it's Pierre you'll have to thank. But since we've gone this far, the surveillance was laid on by an Austrian policeman called Mandel. And he wasn't tipped off by Steve. He was tipped off by Epworth, though I've only just worked that out."

"Pierre said it would be Steve and some of his pals at Century House."

"He got that one wrong. I tried Steve's name on Mandel. He looked surprised. Now I know why." He sensed a betterment of the climate. "Otherwise, Pierre wasn't far out. Steve would give a lot to make trouble for Epworth. I'm just the means to the end."

She was back to being Sylvie Markham, emotional crises professionally counterproductive. "If you're right, then Steve must have been in on the business of setting you up. Procuring his ex-wife for immoral purposes? That doesn't sound like Steve." She was right. Steve might make the average Thames Valley Tory look deliquescent when it came to the enemy within, but he had his code. He had discarded Helga for offending against it. That would automatically rule out his using her.

"No," he said, "give the devil his due, he couldn't have known."

"But somebody did it, and not for a joke."

"Don't worry. Epworth's working on it. And it would put me under deeper suspicion without actually proving a thing."

"Why was Epworth so anxious to put you under suspicion?"

"Aske is political dynamite. I've already said, I can't tell you why. Steve and his pals in Six want to keep the lid on."

"And Epworth wants to take it off. That goes without saying."

He would have to go just a little farther.

"Look, it's Epworth who got me kicked out of Vienna. It's Epworth who's ordered a profit-and-loss. It leaves the opposition thinking they've stymied any further attempt to dig into the Aske business. Finish your mushrooms. Your handsome young waiter's longing to come and look down your dress again."

"That beautiful boy," Sylvie said, "is about as interested in me as you'd be in Mister Universe."

He had succeeded at last in getting her away from a growingly dangerous topic. "Then it must be me," he said.

"Only if he thinks you're some West End producer. They're all resting actors in this place."

He found himself saying, "I love you. I think you're entitled to know."

"Why don't they want you to dig into the Aske business?"

He might have known. Sylvie could be a human burr. "Someone could be compromised. That's the last I'm saying."

"I liked him," she said. "Simon Aske. Did I tell you that? I think you're entitled to know, since you're obviously going to go on digging."

The waiter brought their second course.

When they were alone again, she said, "You must be planning to dig deep. He hasn't been home for years. He told me. Have you heard of Kakania?"

"Some Austrian novelist. A book about cultural collapse in an empire that's dead but won't lie down."

"He thinks this country's the new Kakania."

"He may have a point. Is that what you were talking about in the bookshop?"

"I told you. Range, throw weight, TNT equivalent, mere idle chitchat. All in German, of course."

"Yes," he said, "you did tell me. Quite a lot. But you know more. More than you think." Their relationship was no longer that of husband and wife, no longer intimate, though they sat intimately at their little table with its intimate little lamp. She

91

could see how he might be alarming. It made her tense, wary.

He was clever, too, getting at her through unguarded doors. "You're a photographer, Sylvie. No, that's not what I mean. An artist. You see things more clearly than people like me. You liked him. Straight off, or little by little?"

Involuntarily, she said, " 'If you stare long enough into the abyss, the abyss will stare back into you'. Something like that?"

"Nietzsche. Was he? Staring into the abyss?"

"First impression. Afterwards, I thought I was wrong."

"Bit of a chameleon, your Simon Aske. Isn't he?"

She realised he was checking a list she was barely aware of having given him. "Not mine, damn you. And not yours. I'm not sure he's anyone's."

"Personable," he said. "I think that was your first impression."

"Yes." She had acquired a guardedness, as if what she was saying might be taken down and used against her.

"Casually dressed, I saw that myself. Made you think of a poet, might equally pass for an actor."

"I told you. He said – "

"I know what you told me. Perfect German. No mention of any other languages?"

"I don't think so." He would be formidable in his job, and, in her case anyway, somehow hypnotic, even against her will. "Except . . ."

"Except what?"

"Accents." She dealt with him coolly, but she was becoming interested in spite of herself. "He was good at accents. When he was doing his little imitations, I mean. Even when he did his comic Chekhov, it sounded . . . well, real. And French, only little bits, but a very good accent."

"Keep thinking." He was leaning on her now, driving her mind into the past like a kind of road drill. "Any mention of Czech?"

"He sang the first line of the Czech national anthem in Czech. At least, I suppose it was Czech."

A party, three tables pushed together on the far side of the room, was becoming uproarious, Sloane Rangers whooping in free fall. He scowled. She knew it was less the noise than those untrammelled patrician accents.

She said, "He doesn't speak Czech, he's never been to Czechoslovakia, quote, unquote. He said I could go to Prague and take pictures of Slansky's shadow. He lost me with that."

"Secretary of the Czech Communist Party under Stalin. Trotskyist-Zionist tool of American imperialism, hung by the neck until dead in '52. Must be Aske's idea of a joke." The upper-class tools of capitalist imperialism still distracting him, he had no time for jokes. "His trick of speaking in the third person, what did you make of it?"

"A bit precious, at first. Then I decided it might be shyness. A way of talking about himself without being embarrassed."

"Shy, yet always performing, always putting on an act. It sounds a bit contradictory."

"Not necessarily," she said. "Some actors can only be themselves when they're someone else."

"I wouldn't know. I don't know much about actors." He glanced at their waiter.

Misinterpreting Morpurgo's glance, the waiter came to clear. "Something from the trolley, or just coffee?" He dropped a knife, bent to pick it up. "Oh, Gawd!" he said, camping it up. "*Now* look what she's done, silly cow!" and then, in his normal voice, "Terribly sorry, madam."

Morpurgo watched the man depart. "Out-of-work actors! Sorry, resting. But Aske said he wasn't."

"He said we're all actors."

"Of course, there's another explanation. Isn't there?"

She remembered how careful Aske had been not to come into contact with her as he squeezed past in Gerold's. "Is there?" Why should she suddenly feel protective of Aske.

"Come on, Sylvie," he said. "What do you think?"

"Homosexual? Could be, I suppose. Yet somehow . . ."

"You didn't think so."

"I still don't."

"All right. What about being a Jew? Did you believe that?"

"He didn't say he was a Jew. You could just as easily call what he said antisemitic."

"If there were two hundred million Israelis, the rest of us might all be in concentration camps." He knew people in Mossad and Shin Beth who would make the Centurions look like the Salvation Army. "Then, when he saw you might be thinking he was antisemitic, he said – "

"I said, outright, 'Are you Jewish?' And he touched his nose and said, oh, something like, 'Oy, what a question!' Not very funny, really."

"Could he be Jewish?"

She squinted, looking through an imaginary view-finder. "You might say he looked Jewish. But not very."

"A possible Yorkshire Jew. What about Yorkshire?"

"I told you, good at accents."

"Forty years being shoved around by a little lad from Ponte-fract. Meaning himself."

"Same old trick, using the third person to say something about himself."

"You believed him that time?"

"That time, yes." She was tired after the flight, tired of being questioned, still angry and hurt. Time, she decided, to fight back. "Would you like some more facts?"

He shared the last of the wine between them. "Good girl. That's why it all takes time."

"Yes," she said, "I do know this is the way skilled interrogation goes. I've experienced it before, remember." At Epworth's hands, when Epworth was mole-hunting and simultaneously undermining his Director-General. "Don't flatter yourself. This is something I've been holding back. I didn't get tied up with the publishers as I said. He invited me to lunch. Aske."

She said it with mild malice. She could have forgiven him if he had shown emotion. He showed none.

"Did you accept?"

"Yes. Some men would be angry."

"You're right. I'm sorry."

"You will be. He never turned up."

She watched his feelings shift: disappointment, calculation, suspicion. "Sometimes," she said. "I'm not sure whether I love you. I think you're entitled to know."

He considered. "If he'd suspected anything, he wouldn't have come after you in the first place. What made you accept?"

She was in no mood to mention her last-minute attempt to back out. "Didn't I tell you? I fancied him."

He didn't even take it seriously. "Not much to go on, all in all."

"No," she said, "not much. But then, I didn't know I was working for your lot, did I? I think I'd like to go home."

On the short walk back, he broached the other topic. "Eustace Roland must have guessed something was wrong."

"Not guessed. Knew." She stopped in the street. "Look, innocent people behave innocently. If you'd shown up in the morning, I would never have met Simon Aske. If you'd turned up in the afternoon, I'd have told you about this rather odd

Englishman I ran into. You didn't show up at all. Eustace Roland did, so I told him instead."

"What did he say?" It had jolted him. She was glad.

"About what?" They began walking again, she with a taut, straight-ahead gaze.

"Everything. Toby showing up at the Prater. Me being flown back to London. Your little adventure with Aske."

"He knows quite a bit about you, doesn't he? Things I didn't know myself. He didn't say much, but he's not stupid."

Only as he was feeling for his key did her last words penetrate. "What do you mean, he knows things you didn't know?"

She switched on lights, but didn't sit down. "We spent the evening together. You weren't there, remember? Do you think he gives a damn for your bloody Act?"

"You spent the evening together. What did you talk about?"

"Ships," she said. "Sealing wax. Sattin. His one and only public performance, Bow Street magistrates' court, wasn't it? A walking-on part at a remand hearing? I gather one of your tame thugs in Five had worked Sattin over. I gather there'd have been a public scandal if he'd been put up in person. I gather he and Eustace Roland were enough alike to fool all of the people for enough of the time."

He sat down heavily, his worst fears confirmed. "Do you know that's enough to put the pair of you away?"

It was all true. Eustace Roland Trigg bore a remarkable resemblance to the late Josef Sattin. A visit to London when the Sattin ring was still under surveillance had led a Special Branch man who happened to see him into making a misidentification.

Once cleared up, the matter might have been forgotten. But Sattin, after his later arrest and transfer to Five's country interrogation centre, had unintentionally received rough treatment just before he was due to return to Bow Street for a renewal of the remand order.

Sattin's appearance in the dock with a marked face would have had the Sovs shouting torture from the world's rooftops. There was only one thing Moscow Centre would have liked even better: sensational, orchestrated and highly publicised speculation over his failure to appear at all as required by British law.

Luckily, Morpurgo had remembered the mistaken identification. Tracing Trigg back to Cleethorpes, he had persuaded him, not without difficulty, to play the leading role in a deception that had saved a shaky government at a time when scandal might have brought it down.

"Will you help?" Sylvie asked, interrupting a disturbing reverie.

"What do you mean, help?"

"If they find out, will you help to put us away? Will they put *you* away if you don't?"

He pulled himself together. "Sylvie, do you know what you're saying? It's no joke. The way things are in this country today, it's less of a joke than ever."

"Yes," she said. "I've been coming to that conclusion. Keep as much as possible from the public at large. Pity they *are* at large, really. Eustace Roland says it's little dogs with little bones as buries them deepest. Do you remember Uncle Norman?"

That brought him back sharply enough. He had met Uncle Norman on that first trip to Cleethorpes, when his arrival had coincided with Trigg's mother's funeral and a gathering of the clan. A massively built Yorkshireman, large where Trigg himself gave only an impression of largeness. Less a walk than a waddle, vowels with a pile-driving power that made Trigg's seem almost effete, a capacity for alcohol that inspired awe and disbelief.

She nodded. "I see you do. Lives in Pontefract, does Uncle Norman, only they call it Pomfret up there. A bit of a queer fish that claims to come from Pomfret? A personal challenge, is that, nought Uncle Norman doesn't know about folk in Pomfret, past, present and nine months to come."

"Trigg's going to tell Uncle Norman about Simon Aske? Jesus Christ!"

"I'm going to bed. Goodnight." Revenge, she thought, *was* sweet.

# TWELVE

At breakfast the next day, he and Sylvie were business acquaintances; a degree of commonality in background and purpose,
only superficial intimacy. He knew better than to force the issue.
He knew she was going north, a preliminary to her ICI commission. Slough, Welwyn, the Midlands, Teesside. He had no idea
how long she would be in any given place; nor did she tell him.

Two days later he had heard nothing. When she had first
learned about his affair with Helga Archer, Sylvie had simply
walked out; no reason to expect she would ever come back. He
didn't think this was a repeat performance, but when she was on
her travels she normally left him a copy of her schedule. Not this
time.

He could ring her agent. He did not. To have to ask where
Sylvie was might make her agent wonder what was going on. He
knew what was going on. He was being punished. At least, he
hoped that was all it was.

Sid had come back, this time to work in the kitchen. His
presence should have taken away some of the feeling of
emptiness, yet somehow it reinforced it. Feeling unwanted in his
own house, he made a start on Epworth's plan, beginning with a
call at the Public Records Office to enquire about one Simon Aske.

There must have been a standing instruction on what to do in
the event of such enquiries. He left his telephone number as
requested and went on without haste to the Department of
Employment, the Census Office, the Inland Revenue. Each time
the sight of his ID card produced politeness and a similar
response.

He was about to cross the Brompton Road on his way home

when a car drew up. It was black, lustrous, chauffeur-driven by a man who was not a chauffeur.

The rear window was already down. "Johnny."

His mind came swiftly back from the traffic hazards.

"Spare me a little time?" Steve Archer was invariably at his most charming when confident that what he wanted was what he would get. He was almost always most charming.

"Before you ask, no, we weren't tailing you," Steve said, as Morpurgo got in. "Just a happy chance." He made it clear that he didn't give a damn whether Morpurgo believed him or not.

A darkly handsome man with a deeply cleft chin, his manner lazy but for the alertness of his eyes, Sir Stephen Archer had the social graces of one born to rule, and a polished thuggishness to match.

He had acquired some weight, a touch of *de rigueur* silver at the temples, the ruddiness of his cheeks no longer wholly ascribable to fresh air and field sports.

"Now, this suspension of yours." He might have been an ex-public school car salesman about to recommend turning in the Granada estate for a Range Rover. "I thought we might talk. My club?"

"Why not?" Morpurgo had no clubs, only pubs. Steve's principal club was the Establishment inner circle, the right to know almost everything about almost everyone. He had several others, all of them with rules made by people used to making rules and equally skilled in breaking them. As the car took them back towards the West End without, Morpurgo noted, any need for instructions to the bodyguard-driver, Steve displayed a seeming wish to engage in the customary niceties.

"How's Sylvie?"

"Fine, thanks."

"I think I may be going to remarry." Steve said it as if it were faintly amusing, utterly inconsequential, but its purpose, Morpurgo knew, was to put him on the defensive by reminding him of an unforgiven past. Steve Archer was no genius, not even particularly quick-witted, but it didn't do to underestimate his shrewdness.

"I hope you'll be very happy." With Steve it was always safe to fall back on the conventional.

"Fiona Cloudesley. Kildennis's eldest. We seem to fit. I gather you've just moved house."

Targets of opportunity. "Yes. Still settling in. It takes time," he said.

"Pleasant area. Some fancy neighbours, too." Steve lolled, one hand hooked through the passenger strap though the ride was as smooth as a swan on a lake.

Fast footwork, Steve's way of saying that Chelsea was a long way from Wandsworth and the ideological home ground of John Morpurgo.

"I wouldn't know. Anyway, moving house is hell, even when it's well organised." He had to play every ball if he were to get the measure of Steve's skill and purpose.

"Knowing Sylvie," Steve said, "it would be well organised."

"Oh yes. She took time off. Now she's gone on her travels again."

"Out of the country?" A googly, packed with disguised and tricky spin.

"No, just out of town." Not chitchat between old friends; the warm-up for a needle match.

Steve switched abruptly. "Sorry to hear about your mother. Must have come as a blow."

"It was, rather." With Steve you tended to talk like Steve. Emotion, like Victorian sex, was something whose existence was recognised but never discussed.

"Gather" – Steve appeared to be interested in Green Park, where the trees were grudgingly doling out the first gold of autumn – "she'd only just been given a clean bill of health."

Another sharp but subtle nudge; Steve was in a position to gather a great deal. In his own days with Five, Morpurgo had gathered a great deal himself, and by the same means.

"Yes," he said. "She had." Steve was ruthless, but not sadistic. This must be endured as unintentional torment.

"Old age," Steve said. "Rather sad. Sooner be put down, personally. Anyway, I'm sorry."

They had arrived. Morpurgo followed him into the dark lobby where a porter was suitably respectful: no, no messages, Sir Stephen, three bags full, Sir Stephen, good evening, sir.

Give him for preference, sir thought, the seediest pub in town. There, life would be thrusting, natural and, above all, noisy. Having experienced the overpowering opulence of American clubs, he had some sympathy with Warren Claas's thinly disguised contempt for shabby British dignity.

He took a casually indicated seat, knowing that there was nothing casual about it. It was in an alcove in a corner, and so free

99

from intrusion. He watched Steve nod a greeting to a man with cheeks like purple pincushions, exchange a brief word with two gilt-edged securities, then join him.

Steve found his monogrammed gold cigarette case, selected a cigarette, tapped it – nothing changed there – pointlessly on the burnished surface. Morpurgo thought of Karl-Heinz Mandel. These were the only two people he knew who carried their cigarettes in a case, let alone monogrammed. Was there a significance? If there was, did it matter?

Steve lit the cigarette with his monogrammed gold lighter. "Supposed to be giving them up." He inhaled like a man on whom sharp pain is being inflicted. "Least, Fiona's doing her best to make me. Down to twenty a day, bet that surprises you."

"I'm impressed." What impressed him was the subtlety with which their former relationship was being invoked. Steve Archer, no genius, but still less a fool, was learning top people's tricks.

"Bloody well should be, old boy." Another switch in tactics; Steve informal was Steve coolly arrogant, life a black joke devised by God for his personal entertainment. The steward brought double Scotches, a little of his deference spreading to Morpurgo as the weed is watered with the rose. There was a murmur of voices from the bar, the distant chink of cutlery where tables were being laid for early diners.

"Cheers." Steve waved his glass perfunctorily. "As I was saying." To himself Morpurgo said: Here we go.

"Profit-and-loss." Steve watched cigarette smoke wobble towards a stucco ceiling. "God, what a dreary bore!"

Morpurgo said nothing. The security community was like any other small village, but this was more than local gossip. Steve expelled smoke and amusement. "Don't blame you. Wouldn't feel chatty myself." He put out his cigarette. "There, how's that for willpower?"

He stretched out his legs, four fingers thrust deep into each jacket pocket. "Okay. Brass tacks. Thing is, old son, you have more than me for enemies." He shook his head. "Sorry. Didn't mean it quite like that." But you did, Morpurgo thought, impressed.

"What passed between you and me" – if Steve really was sorry, he was concealing it well – "well, time may not heal all things, sometimes clarifies them. Helga . . ."

He put down most of his drink. "Never mind about Helga,

water under the bridge." It was the first time in their rare post-Five encounters that he had even mentioned Helga's name. "When we were working together, you and I, we had our little differences. I called you a bloody commie. You called me a fascist bastard. Nothing serious, wasn't taken seriously. We rubbed along."

True, Morpurgo thought reluctantly. Never mind about Helga, but until she opened her legs to spite Steve and pander to nobody-loves-me Morpurgo, we rubbed along.

"What I mean" – if Archer had chosen his words carefully this far, he was hand-picking them now – "is that when I used to call you comrade, it was a joke." When you said it to my face, Morpurgo thought, yes. "But things have changed in Five. Things are being said that aren't meant to be funny, and some people are only too happy to hear them."

"What sort of things?"

Steve was not one for answering questions when he was doing the talking. "Things have changed," he repeated. "Never the same since that damned jury flew in the face of the judge's summing up. Bloody morons! Matter of common sense that the only people who know what is or isn't in the interest of the state are the people who run it."

There, Morpurgo told himself, was the real Steve, one of the people who ran the state.

"If the jury hadn't made the distinction, mightn't you be out of a job?" he asked.

"Don't get you." Familiar grooves had appeared above Steve's nose, instinctive disapproval of a point his mind had not yet grasped.

Tempted by the recollection of the rooftop set-piece on the day of Warren Claas's departure, Morpurgo made the mistake of continuing.

"A government is simply the party in power, and it's in power to carry out its own party policies. If the national interest is whatever the party in power says it is, then the national interest will always be the interest of the party in power."

For once, now he knew what it was he had instinctively disapproved of, Steve's easy manner failed him. "Nothing wrong with that, comrade, so long as it's the right party."

"Remember the American corporation chairman who got himself in shtuck by saying, 'What's good for General Motors is good for the country'?"

"It's a point of view."

Morpurgo smiled. "When he'd just gone to Washington from General Motors to serve as Defense Secretary? All those billion dollar contracts?"

He had gone too far. He waited for Steve to cut loose. Instead, Steve said, "What's it got to do with my being out of a job?"

Nothing for it. "Well, if the interests of the state are what the government says they are and the government is the party in power, I could be seen as a threat to the state just by happening to be opposed to the party in power."

"And vice versa, my lad! And vice versa!"

"Of course. So, no need for Five. Those who aren't for us are against us. All you need is Special Branch and the Prison Service. Oh, and a big enough majority in the House."

Steve's face had begun to show something more than the ruddy colour of well-nourished middle age and ego. "Fortunately, we have a judiciary that knows the difference between a real threat and a spurious one." He saw his mistake an instant too late. "All right, and we have juries that are prepared to ignore a judge when they're not happy with the outcome."

It was handsome enough in the circumstances. It was the circumstances that worried Morpurgo, especially when Steve said, "Damn it, Johnny, stop being so bloody clever-clever. What I brought you here for was to tell you that so far as I'm concerned they can go through the old firm's books from start to finish, and they won't find a wrong entry."

Now that was very handsome indeed, so why wasn't he grateful? Answer: He was sitting in Steve's club, drinking whisky at Steve's expense because he had made a perfectly legitimate enquiry at the Public Records Office.

"A clean bill of health in the profit-and-loss?"

Steve had recovered. "Never denied your professional ability. The way you handled the Sattin business was brilliant. Said so at the time."

Suspected me of being a mole at the time, Morpurgo remembered, and you certainly had Trigg down as a lumpen prole who would blow the whistle at the first opportunity.

"Of course" – Steve let it hang while he savoured his Scotch – "other people may say other things." It took him a little while to realise that Morpurgo was not going to help him. His hand strayed towards his cigarette case, hesitated, came away. Elaborately nonchalant, he said, "Friend Epworth will declare public

102

support, no doubt?"

"Friend Epworth isn't given to public declarations."

"Well, that's true enough, God knows." Steve's hand again ventured cigarette-wards before losing its resolution. "Can't claim to know what you've been doing over there in Lambeth, of course."

"Bugger all. I'm not sure whether that'll count as credit or debit."

Steve succumbed to his vice. Going through the meaningless ritual of choosing and tapping, he said, "In present circs, good thing to do."

Well, well, Morpurgo thought. The lad's getting crafty in his old age.

"Shame about your holiday. Imagine Sylvie was disappointed, too. How's brother Trigg?"

Not just crafty; positively Machiavellian. "Trigg?" He thought of what Trigg knew now, and of what Steve would say if he knew. "I literally bumped into him at Heathrow. Off to to sell lollipops to the Austrians, would you believe?"

"Really? Still, if you say so." Sighing out a feather of smoke, Steve waved his cigarette in mock guilt. "Promise you won't tell? Women can make life damned uncomfortable at times." He shot a heavy-browed glance. "As I'm sure you'll agree."

Now they were coming to the little matter of Helga. Morpurgo found himself repelled yet once again impressed by the fact that Steve must have helped set it up after all.

But no. Steve looked at his cigarette, then at Morpurgo. "All right, better spell it out, yes? Don't exactly owe you anything, comrade of former days, but I do rather care for fair play."

He did, too, but then, he was one of those who wrote the rules.

"I mean," Steve said, "it would be a pretty poor show if you copped it just for being in Vienna at the wrong time. Pure poison for a chap in your present unhappy position. Of course, friend Lawrence is on leave, isn't he? Couldn't possibly have told you about a chap called Aske."

How much, Morpurgo asked himself, savage in the knowledge that he was being outsmarted by a man who had never been smart, did Steve Archer really know of what Epworth was up to? How much was he hoping to find out?

"Am I supposed to know what you're talking about?"

Steve refused to play. "Something you should remember about Epworth, old son. Quote me, if you like. Won't come as news."

He flicked ash from his cigarette, reminding Morpurgo of Humphrey Fish, who had never quite made it to the ashtray. Now Fish stood behind Steve like the ghost of Banquo.

"Altogether cleverer than me, friend Lawrence," Steve said. "Everything worked out while other chaps are stuck with donkey-work and hunches. But he still has to make his landfall, get me? I'm home and dry."

Morpurgo got him all right, well and truly got Sir Stephen Archer, Director-General of Five, home, dry, settled in the clubhouse for the next decade or so.

Lawrence Epworth might be some kind of offbeat genius. He might have a Director-General who, as well as being new to the game, could be kept happy in the role of front man. The fact remained that he was perched precariously at the top of a human pyramid. At least half its members, their memory of Epworth's swift and ruthless takeover and its consequences for Humphrey Fish still fresh and vengeful, would walk away without warning if the price were right.

"Of course" – Steve, wonderfully relaxed and masterful now, was enjoying his metaphor – "friend Lawrence might decide his chances could be improved by lightening the boat." He studied his cigarette and, reminded of the absent Fiona, reluctantly put it out. "In which case, a wise passenger might do well to ponder the idea of abandoning ship. Same again?"

"Don't think I ought," Morpurgo said. "Have another drink, I mean. Don't let me stop you, though."

"Oh, you won't stop me, old son. As I tell Fiona, I'm not the biddable type. Talking about smoking, of course," and he ordered another round.

"Let's talk," Steve said when they were alone again, "about bugger all, since that's what you say you've been doing."

He narrowed his eyes, staring at a murky eighteenth-century portrait on the far wall as if it were an enemy in disguise.

"Ours is a messy business. Has to be. Treachery" – he raised his voice easily as Morpurgo stirred – "is also a messy business. No, not you, old son. No one's calling you a traitor. But why did friend Lawrence take you on when everyone in the business, including you, thought you were through? Ever asked yourself that one? Course you have, often."

His last cigarette still smouldering in the ashtray, he dealt with it methodically. "Secrets," he said. "That's what keeps us in business, not bloody governments. No secrets, no jobs for the likes of you and me. But life's a mystery, and mysteries breed secrets. Eve had the first secret, Adam told the first lie and – bingo! – we were in business."

He paused to drink, confident that he would not be interrupted. Morpurgo thought of days, not long gone, when Steve Archer had been his efficient but not over-bright 2 i/c.

"Yes," Steve said comfortably, "life's a mystery. Keep 'em guessing. Stop 'em finding out. Your left-wing friends are no different; don't kid yourself, comrade. Difference is, my side's more honest. We say straight out, 'None of your bloody business!' Your crowd look pious and mumble, 'Least said, soonest mended.' But the secrets are there. Can't have power without secrets. Can't keep it without trying to ferret out the other chap's secrets, either. Get theirs, stop 'em getting yours, right?" He turned himself toward Morpurgo as if all preliminaries to trade had been disposed of.

Morpurgo, his drink untouched, said nothing.

"Why did he snap you up?" Archer repeated. "Not for your know-how, old son. For your know-nothing. None of your business, so less said the better, yes?"

"I think I'd better be going." Morpurgo pushed back his chair. "Sylvie might – "

"Sylvie" – Steve had never been more relaxed, the ease of unchallengeable power – "is in Cleethorpes, helping brother Trigg with his lollipops. Surprised at you, Johnny. Never thought you'd do anything that might get Sylvie into trouble." He sipped Scotch without removing his gaze.

"Friend Epworth is a clever devil. Who was it who said that the really clever chap is the one who hides his cleverness? Never mind. Going to tell you something. Probably know it already. No matter.

"Humphrey Fish was a pal of mine. More than a pal. A mentor. He was my prefect, I was his fag. Don't take that literally.

"Taught me a lot, Humphrey, especially when we were both in Berlin. Wasn't perfect – which of us is? – but a smart operator, a very smart operator, ferreted out more secrets from Ivan than you'd ever believe.

"We deal in dirt, right? Most secrets are grubby, or they come in grubby wrappers. Humphrey got his fingers dirty. We all do, you included. You" – he gave Morpurgo a look of pure ice – "may point in one direction and march in another, but both paths go through the mire, and comrade, believe me, your betters have walked them before you.

"So if Humphrey made the odd mistake, if he did the odd thing that some people might consider to be to his discredit, well, that's the way it goes. As you know better than most. We all have to eat our peck of dirt, as my dear mama used to say when we were kids."

He quirked his lips, all friendliness, if it had ever existed, a thing of the past, and leaned to prod Morpurgo lightly with an immaculately manicured fingertip that was nevertheless nicotine-stained.

"All that matters in our game, brother, is results. Morality's a luxury you can't afford when it's a case of you or them. And those who aren't for us are against. Woolly hats and woolly minds, people who think all you need to deal with Ivan, subversion, terrorism, is clean hands and good intentions; they owe their clean hands to our dirty ones."

He paused. "Tell me I'm wrong."

Morpurgo examined his own stubby fingernails.

"So" – Steve's voice was low, but harsh now – "no fingernail inspection. Do you get me, Johnny? I don't know what Humphrey Fish did that was wrong. I don't even know for certain that he did anything wrong, or any more wrong than is par for our particular course. I only know what he did that wasn't. That's enough for me, enough for his friends in Five *and* Six. He used to say that in our business we all need a little private place, a little zone of silence, where we can confess our sins to ourselves because the Act doesn't allow us to confess them to anyone else.

"I go for that. I don't go for attempts to dig up the past that do nothing except stir up scandal, bring discredit on the security services and give comfort to our enemies, without and within. Now drink up and have one for the road. Give you time to decide if I've said anything you disagree with."

"No, thanks." This time Morpurgo did get up. "My shout next time. If there is a next time."

No overt tension, no further signs of hostility, yet, somehow, no handshake. As they parted, Steve said, "Hope it all comes out in the wash, Johnny. In the clear, I mean. Employable. Pensionable. Left-aloneable. After all, we all know you're a sensible sort of chap. Love to Sylvie."

As he left, the porter, knowing the enemy, gave him a distant nod.

Left-aloneable. In the security services that was code for a threat in a class of its own. Where disloyalty was suspected, Five and Six both had a cold lust for retribution that would have inspired the Eumenides.

He went towards Piccadilly in the knowledge that he had been both warned off and urged to leave Epworth to whatever fate the cabal had in store for him. In return, they were saying, he just might walk away without a scratch.

They were all stark, raving mad. He, since he would stick to his bargain with Epworth, was the maddest.

# THIRTEEN

He went up a path heavily defended with laurel and privet, and rang the doorbell. There was a long silence, then a blurred shape on the glass. The door opened.

"Hey up, look what tide's washed up." The gap widened. "Well, since you're here," Trigg said, "you'd best step inside."

In the hall the walls, brown lincrusta topped with porridge-hued paper, were hung with engravings of mountains and Gothic castles, photographs, foggy and faded in oval mounts, of trilbies, cloches and high collars, winged or lace according to sex.

A barometer, a hat rack devoted to the support of Trigg's raincoat and billycock hat, a tall grandfather clock with a slow and ponderous tick hinting at eternity and a better life to come. On his previous visit, in search of help from a man who bore a respectable likeness to Josef Sattin, he had arrived on the day of Trigg's mother's funeral. Little in these surroundings, he guessed, had changed since then.

Hands on hips, Trigg continued his unrevealing stare, but there was the sardonic gleam with which Morpurgo was only too familiar.

"And what might you be wanting, buttercup?"

Morpurgo said, "Is she here?"

"Is who here, lad?"

"Sylvie."

"Sylvie? Your Sylvie? Now whatever gave you a daft idea like that?"

"Oh, for God's sake, Trigger!" That was the second time he had used Trigg's nickname. He was running risks. "Is she still here?" Somehow or other, he proposed to get round the fact that

108

he had learned of her visit from Steve Archer. He had not been followed, that was certain, nor were there any innocently occupied cars or plain vans parked near Trigg's house.

"Now, let's see," Trigg said, "if I've got this right. You fancy there's someone in this house you'd like to see, is that about it?"

"That's it. Now tell me I'm daft."

"Nay, lad" – Trigg's big hand applied itself to the small of his back – "you're not daft. What's more, though it beats me why, that same somebody wants to see you, so no sense in hanging about."

Pausing only to put down a pewter tankard and wipe his mouth with the back of one huge hand, Uncle Norman, two hundred and fifty pounds of prime Yorkshire beef in a check suit after Bridget Riley, rose from his chair as awesomely as any Cape Kennedy lift-off.

"By heck!" he said. "It's just like old times, is this, lad. All we need now is a burying."

The last time Morpurgo had seen Uncle Norman had been at the funeral of the late Mrs Trigg. Seventeen years younger than his sister and perhaps ten older than Trigg, he had never, Uncle Norman had explained with relish, been meant to come into the world. If Trigg was Yorkshire by background, Uncle Norman was the bedrock from which he had been hewn.

Allowing his hand to be crushed, Morpurgo looked around. "Where is she?"

"Where is she?" Trigg repeated. "Gone, buttercup, that's where. Give the lad his hand back, Uncle Norman. Happen he'll need it again. Oh, she's been here. And before you ask why, she came because she wanted to, isn't that right, Uncle Norman?"

"Your Sylvie," Uncle Norman said, "is a right bonny lass. I could almost forgive 'er for not being born i' Yorkshire."

"Sit down, lad," Trigg said, still not asking how Morpurgo had acquired his knowledge. "You're giving me the fidgets."

They placed him between them in the large, overfurnished room. Through a big bay window, brilliant sunlight poured into his eyes. Uncle Norman resettled himself on a sofa his bulk reduced to a chair.

"She was here last night, buttercup. Been up north and couldn't deny herself the chance of seeing the Marbella of South Humberside."

"Nor," said Uncle Norman, "the uncrowned king of t'international spice trade. I'd not say no to another drop, our Roly."

"Then you must wait or fetch it yourself," Trigg said. "Arrived pretty nigh simultaneously, did your Sylvie and Uncle Norman."

Uncle Norman sighed. "There was a time when his ma used to send our Roly by train to Pomfret wi' a label round his neck. When I'd had enough of his cheek I used to put him o'er my knee and tan his backside. I reckon he's done a bit of catching up sin' then."

"Aye, Uncle Norman." Trigg was unmoved. "I reckon I have."

"Eh, well," Uncle Norman said, "then if I must wait, I must wait. Though I'm bound to remark it's downright discouraging to come down hotfoot from Pomfret and be denied t'milk of human kindness."

"If it's milk you want, fridge is full of it." Trigg stood purposefully.

"Are we off t'pub then?" Uncle Norman was suddenly hopeful. "It's thirsty work, is digging up t'past, even if there's a round or two to be stood in the process. This chap Aske – "

"Uncle Norman," Trigg said firmly, "Morpurgo here didn't drive all this way to hark to your wamblings." He turned to Morpurgo. "Right, lad, are you set?"

Morpurgo knew when he was beaten. "Where are we going?"

"Where?" Trigg looked incredulous. "Finest stretch of coast this side of the Pearly Gates? We're going for a walk, buttercup. Uncle Norman can meet us in t'pub if he's a mind, but before that, you and me's got things to discuss."

\*     \*     \*

The sea was as he remembered it, no more than a distant, glimmering presence far out towards the edge of the world. Above it the sky arched hugely, a great bowl of faded blue on which puffy white clouds grazed like sheep. Seven miles away across the tidal channel, the Yorkshire coast ended in a pale thread of dune and the white dot of a lighthouse.

The promenade turned into little more than a raised path alongside a concrete-edged boating lake. Between them and the distant water lay a Saharan expanse of flat, pool-speckled sand. Nearer at hand the winds had breathed life into it so that it threatened to engulf everything in drifts of pale buff, tufts of marram grass poking through to bend and quiver in a light breeze.

Longing to know about Sylvie, and about Simon Aske, Morpurgo tentatively breached the long silence. "What does

110

Uncle Norman do?"

"Do?" Trigg crammed on his bowler against a sudden stronger gust. "Nought, in a manner of speaking, being long since retired. And then again, everything, since he does what he's always done. Betting and boozing, that's Uncle Norman's life and always has been."

It apparently suited him to continue. "He was a bookie, do you see? Street corners in Brighouse, where the family hails from, worked himself up to respectability and a nice little chain of betting shops. Sold out to the big boys a while back. Not stuck for brass, isn't Uncle Norman, nor for pals neither."

"And now he lives in Pontefract."

"Nigh on forty year. What with Masonic, cricket, horses, pigeons, all t'things that's part and parcel of being a proper Yorkshireman, there's not much goes on Uncle Norman doesn't know about."

Ahead, the huge, flat sweep of the coast stretched away to vanish in fine weather haze, virtually treeless. The incoming tide was little more than a white, endlessly changing line, an occasional wink of diamond, a whisper on the breeze. Beyond the raised earth wall, where grass and sand grappled stubbornly, broken crates, bleached logs and the plastic detritus of consumerism marked the changing frontier. Somewhere above them was birdsong. Larks, Morpurgo thought vaguely.

"Aye." Trigg favoured him with a basilisk stare. "Like your lot, is Uncle Norman, not much going on he doesn't know about." It was the nearest they had come to Morpurgo's knowledge of Sylvie's visit.

He took a gargantuan breath. "Get this in your lungs, buttercup. Your Sylvie said it was worth t'trip on its own."

It was an invitation and a challenge.

Trigg's pace increased. After a while he said, "You'll have been doing some thinking."

"Happen," Morpurgo said.

It produced a grim chuckle. "Aye, happen. And happen so has she."

They passed two or three rows of beach huts, a clump of wind-combed shrubbery. Far to the west, a row of hills rode the horizon like green whales. It was a coast that would wear another face given a change of season. Eastwards, nothing stood between them and Siberia.

111

Trigg stopped abruptly. "Now then, buttercup. Take a look at this."

A metal strip ran diagonally across the tarmac under their feet. Morpurgo bent to look. It marked the Greenwich meridian, longitude 0 degrees, 0 minutes, 0 seconds. Instinctively, he stood astride it.

Trigg straddled it too, a curious glint in his eyes. "When I was a little lad and used to come out here to stop being moithered by folk, I used to stand like this, one foot in the east, one in t'west, and think I was like that feller in Shakespeare, bestriding the world like a colossus."

He stepped back into the western hemisphere. "Mind, those was the days when the war was supposed to be settling all that."

Ahead of them on the sea-wall was a seat. Walking on, he settled himself.

"Being only a little lad, it never occurred to me there'd be two colossuses when it was all over. Nor a bunch of midgets to do their dirty work. Oh aye, she talked, did that lass of yours. There's nought much we didn't talk about, her and me."

Moments previously, Morpurgo had straddled a notional divide. Now he sensed himself poised over another. If he were to get up from this seat and go back to London without another word, he would stay in a world where risks were calculable. If he were to remain until Trigg spoke again, he and Simon Aske would be inextricably linked, for better or for worse. He took no decision.

"What we were wondering, her and me" – Trigg stared towards the distant hills – "is which midgets are you dancing for this time round?"

"None." He felt he could say that. His ultimate fate was in the hands of midgets, but for the time being, here where the world was divided by nothing more complicated than a line on the ground, he was his own man for as long as he chose. No, he thought seconds later, he had already chosen.

"None?" Trigg's blunt vowel gave the word a brutal sound. "Nay, is that right?" He turned to stare. "Yon feller Epworth, you wouldn't call him a midget?"

"Not in the sense I thought you meant."

Trigg chuckled. "You want to watch out, buttercup, trying to make sense of what I mean." He cocked his big head sideways, tendrils of sparse hair waving like the marram grass.

"There's more larks in this part of world" – he stared up at the

112

blue grazing ground of the clouds – "than any other place I know. I reckon Cleethorpes is where tired larks and old larks and larks that's just fed up with things comes to be done good to. You've only to hark to know it works. It's a great place to come to, is Cleethorpes, for being done good to."

A man with a dog went past, the dog pulling so hard at its leash that it wheezed chokingly. "Them that helps your lot," Trigg said, watching the dog, "is apt to end up like yon hound. For larks it'd have to be cages, so" – like the lark descending, his gaze came swiftly back to Morpurgo – "just you tell me this. Which matters most, her or Aske?"

"She does, of course." It was what he had to say, but was that why he had said it?

Trigg took off his hat, brushed it with his sleeve, rapped it on his knuckles. "So if she comes here, finds Uncle Norman has a bit of information to impart and says she'd rather it was kept quiet, it'd be the end of the matter?"

Morpurgo listened for a while to the larks. "Yes," he said eventually. "That would be the end of it."

"By!" Trigg shook his head, but he had something not unlike a smile. "You were quick off the mark first time round. If you'd been as quick again I'd have told you to get on your bike."

"Yes." Morpurgo smiled too. "I expect you would."

"This chap Aske," Trigg said, and if there had been any means of telling, he might have been pleased, "what's he reckoned to have done?"

"You know I can't tell you that."

Trigg went back to listening to larks. The sound of the sea was louder, the breeze stronger and more persistent. Morpurgo looked behind him. After lurking endlessly on the rim of the world, it had come in without fuss or warning. Now it crawled, ripple upon glittering ripple, up the flat, flotsam-fringed beach.

"Is there anything you two haven't told each other? Or Uncle Norman?"

"Uncle Norman," Trigg said, "is only here for the beer. As for your Sylvie, she's of the opinion that secrets shared is secrets halved. Safety in numbers, d'you see? It wouldn't surprise me if your Sylvie hadn't a mind to put your lot out of business."

"My Sylvie" – he felt fiercely protective – "shouldn't need telling that my lot don't lose much sleep over caged skylarks. Damn it, she knows more about Aske than I do."

"In Vienna," Trigg said, "she told me she liked him. A rum

113

chap, but she liked him. It counts a lot with me, does that."

"A lot of people," Morpurgo said, "liked Philby. And the Queen made Blunt a knight. But for my lot the Queen would probably have made Philby a knight too."

Trigg snorted. "She does as she's told, does Queen, just as the rest of us is supposed to. If like had ought to do with it, there's a lot she'd happen as soon run through with that sword of hers as knight 'em to please politicians. Are you telling me this Aske is some sort of a spy?"

"I'm not telling you anything."

"That's right, nor me you, so let's just shake hands and go our separate ways."

"I have a wife," Morpurgo said. "And I have a job. I'd like to keep them both."

"The way I heard tell, you could. Leastways, your wife and a better job than playing Peeping Tom for folks that'd sell you for tuppence and a place in the sun."

"Her job, on her terms. She doesn't realise it, but that's how it would be." These skylarks, Morpurgo thought, had been singing duets.

"Oh, she sees t'risk," Trigg said. "But she reckons she wouldn't make that mistake. I told her she'd best think on."

He looked sideways at Morpurgo. "Now then, buttercup, don't look so surprised. Long after I was a grown man, my mam chased me about as if I was still in short pants instead of running the firm. I'm not saying your Sylvie'd do the same, but by heck, she'd be tempted. Where's yon chap Archer stand in all this?"

"Not where I stand, you old bugger," Morpurgo said. "Are you going to tell me about Aske or aren't you?" Archer had not only made the mistake of questioning whether Trigg could be trusted in the Sattin affair, he had called Cleethorpes the back of beyond.

But he wasn't home yet. He should have known.

"When I stood in for Sattin that time" – Trigg, too, was recollecting times past – "I was at risk, not that anyone told me. What about Aske? Is he at risk?"

"Not if he's done nothing wrong."

"He's done summat, or you'd not be bothered about him. Who's to say whether it was wrong or not?"

"Epworth."

"Eh, lad, I wasn't born yesterday. Me and Epworth got on because I didn't trust him and he counted on it. You and me gets

114

on because I do trust you and you don't count on it. Do you trust Epworth?''

It was the question he seemed unable to avoid. ''Up to a point,'' he said.

''Up to a point! And how do you tell when you've reached the point? Is he marked with it like a Plimsoll line? And who's sunk when you go past it, him or you?''

He shifted his broad beam on the weather-scoured seat. ''You can find out easy enough where your Sylvie's been, but the only way you can discover ought about this feller Aske is by way of me and Uncle Norman. It's rum, is that.''

He read Morpurgo's hesitation expertly. ''Because there's things you're told and things you're not, is that it? Did nobody ever tell you that them that plays pig in the middle is liable to end up as sausage meat?''

He put back his bowler and clapped it into place. ''And what if Epworth doesn't care whether Aske is innocent or not?''

''Is that what's bothering Sylvie? Just because she liked him?''

''If you're asking me what's bothering your Sylvie, it's how much what you're mixed up in is going to bother you.'' Trigg was on his feet and facing homeward. The tide had reached the flotsam, dying among plastic bottles, driftwood and used condoms. In the hazy distance, Cleethorpes glimmered like the celestial city.

They reached the meridian again. Once again Trigg straddled it. ''East, west,'' he said, ''home's best. Which is the opinion of most folk if only politicians'd leave 'em alone to get on with it. I sometimes wonder, what if Chinese had been the first to invent longitude? If it was the Peking meridian, Cleethorpes'd be the Pearl of the Orient.''

He nudged Morpurgo, not unfriendly. ''Come on, lad. We'd best find Uncle Norman while he's still in a fit state to talk.''

Uncle Norman was in the first pub they came to. ''Right, then,'' he greeted them. ''Shall we be having another one 'ere, or are we off to do some serious supping?'' His awe-inspiring endowment of red blood corpuscles had begun to congregate in his face.

''If Uncle Norman'' – Trigg settled himself – ''was to sign the pledge, you'd be hard put to hear yourself speak in Pomfret for the wailing and gnashing of teeth.''

He moved a quantity of empty glasses to the next table. ''Uncle Norman, tell this chap the results of your enquiries in the matter of Aske.''

"Nay, our Roly," Uncle Norman protested, "don't ask me to tell t'yarn wi' an empty glass. Get t'next ones in and I'm your man."

Trigg moved the last glasses into check. "By heck, man, why don't you just tell the lad they're both dead?"

Uncle Norman, about to fight on, found the war was already over. "Eeeeh!" he said. "You've spoiled my yarn, our Roly."

An instant later he saw the advantage. "But seeing as that nigh on completes it . . ." The table walked toward them as he stood up. Moments later, he was at the bar.

"Uncle Norman," Trigg said, "did the drinking and I did the thinking." He took out his wallet and produced a photograph.

It was a white marble headstone, the inscription starkly legible.

THOMAS ASKE
b. July 21, 1899 A.D.
and his beloved wife
WINIFRED MARY
b. November 2, 1919 A.D.
called untimely
to their eternal rest
April 22, 1953

Thy will be done

# FOURTEEN

The lights were on. He opened the door to be greeted by the slow movement of the Twenty-third Piano Concerto. Sylvie was checking cameras, lenses, filters, a sure sign that she would not be around for long.

He stood there, not certain of his greeting. "Do you mind if I turn that thing off?"

She looked up, astonished.

"I know," he said. "Mozart. All the same." He went to switch off.

"Are you well?" The tone was not unfriendly.

He flopped wearily. "No."

She put down the puffer brush and the Nikon.

"If you must know," he said, "I've got a bloody hangover. If you must know, I've probably got a terminal bloody hangover. All right, laugh. Did they take *you* out drinking while you were there? Correction. Boozing." He winced. "By God, there's a difference."

"Would you like some coffee?"

"Hemlock. Probably the only thing we didn't drink. Second thoughts, we probably did."

"At least," she said as she brought him the coffee, "they made sure you were fit to drive. Eustace Roland will be ringing again any time now, to see if you're back."

"Again?"

"They have your best interests at heart. Uncle Norman said he wouldn't be ashamed to take you out in Pomfret."

He sipped coffee gratefully. "*And* I got done for speeding. Three miles an hour over the limit, would you believe? Must be

117

hard up for business."

"Were you breathalysed?"

"I was. I passed. Just. Probably stupefied the thing." He opened his case, grimacing at the din of the zip, and took out the photograph of the Aske tombstone. "I expect they showed you this."

"I didn't know about it when I went there."

"Steve Archer told me you were there. Before you ask. A bit of cheap showmanship."

"Steve." She picked up the puffer brush once more.

Watching her, he said, "What made you go there?"

"I'd been invited, remember? And I was passing by."

"Is that all?"

"No."

"Go on."

"I needed a touchstone."

In spite of his hangover, he understood that. "Trigg."

"Well, isn't he?"

"You started something in Vienna. Now you can't let it drop."

"You left something in Vienna," she said. "I decided to pick it up. It was nice to talk to someone refreshingly sane."

"But what good do you imagine it will do?"

"I told you before, you live two lives. I decided it was time I was in both of them. It's what marriage is supposed to be about."

"We both live two lives," he said. "Neither of yours is dangerous."

"You've already been invited into mine. Now I've invited me into yours."

"You do realise what they could do to you and Trigg if they found out about your heart-to-hearts?"

"I don't give a damn." She smiled faintly. "And I'm sure Trigg doesn't." She squeezed the puffer several times against her cheek. Its small noise punctuated a silence that grew.

"A few little secrets," she said. "I know. You'll say they're not. That's because they're the only ones you've got. I don't mean you personally. I mean the collective you. The firm."

His head throbbed. "Little secrets add up to big ones. You're getting yourself involved in something you don't understand. Something it's best you shouldn't."

She looked again at the photograph of the headstone. "Simon Benjamin Aske. A collection of little mysteries that might add up to a big one. Well, now you've got another, haven't you?"

He looked at her with respect. "You spotted it."

He shook his head ruefully, winced again. "Didn't strike me until I was nearly home. Jewish cemeteries don't go in for crosses. Or quotations from the Lord's Prayer."

"He didn't say he was Jewish, not in so many words. More coffee?"

"There's a lot of things he didn't say in so many words." He looked at her scattered gear. "When are you off again?"

"Day after tomorrow. Stratford. I want to catch a rehearsal. One or two things here in town first. After that I may have to do the New York trip before anything else. Why?"

He tried to sound casual. "It does matter to me whether you're around."

She threw the puffer at him, but gently. "If you want my help, you'll have to tell me more." He found himself unbearably tempted.

The phone rang, making him feel he had run his head into a circular saw. She said, "That'll be Eustace Roland for you," but she took it herself. She said, "Yes, he is," then listened for a long time. Morpurgo drank his second cup of coffee, trying not to strain to overhear.

She said, "I see," and gave him a glance. She said, "Yes, he has," and then, "No, not yet."

He pretended not to be trying to fill in the gaps.

She said, "He was breathalysed. They're charging him with damaging police property. Hold on. He'd like you to hear his dying words."

Morpurgo took the phone. "Hello."

Trigg was not the man for hellos. He said, "Tell her the lot, buttercup, or I will. No more secrets." The dialling tone made Morpurgo wince. He replaced the receiver, very gently.

Sylvie said, "I gather there's more. He'll tell me if you don't."

She aimed the Nikon at him, pressed the button. The motor fizzed away for several seconds while she listened critically. When it stopped, she said, "That bit on the headstone about 'untimely to their eternal rest'. A bit sinister?"

"Car smash, both killed outright." He said it reluctantly. It was not earth-shaking, but other things might be and a precedent had been set.

"1953. That would make Simon Benjamin — what? Eleven? Twelve?"

"Something like that." He groaned over the battlefield in his

119

head. "Aske senior – nobody seems to remember much about them – had some kind of engineering business. Not Yorkshire-born, moved north and set up on his own early in the war, maybe '41. Newly wed, Uncle Norman fancies. Made a packet in the war, retired in the '50s – "

She flagged him down. "Hold on. Early 1940s. So Simon Benjamin, poor little mite, was – "

"Are you sure", Morpurgo asked, "you didn't fall for the poor little mite?"

"Poor little mite because he lost his mum and dad when he was only eleven, you heartless oaf. So he'd barely been born when they came north."

"I suppose so. After all, it's a long time ago."

"You mean you didn't want Uncle Norman going around asking too many questions. Go on."

"Poor little beggar was sent away to school practically as soon as he could walk. Some place near Trowbridge. That's in wurzel land, isn't it? Wilts? Somerset?"

"Anything bigger than Richmond Park is wurzel land as far as you're concerned. It's in Wiltshire. Was it definitely Trowbridge? Wilts is quite an area for public schools."

He made a brave attempt at Uncle Norman's accent. "This feller said it were Trowbridge. Happened to know that part of t'world. Summat to do wi' t'Royals, it were, though he couldn't rightly say what."

"Then it was King's Ashton. I suppose that's where you'll start. There must be a quicker way."

"Of course there is, if I want to draw attention to myself."

"Who in particular? Steve?"

He might have known she would go back to Steve. "Steve just happened to run into me while you were away. Far too much of a gent to count out the thirty pieces of silver, but every time he moved, he jingled." He had no intention of mentioning the veiled threats.

"Steve hasn't learned much if he thinks you'd sell out."

"He's learned more than you might think."

"In that case he probably threatened you too, knowing Steve."

"After twenty years, I'm not exactly a beginner at the game."

"Oh, the game! Well, you play yours and I'll play mine. That trip to Vienna's changed a lot of things, for me, if not for you."

"What you did there was accidental. Going to Cleethorpes wasn't. I couldn't save you now, if things went wrong."

120

"I wouldn't *want* to be bloody well saved!" She recovered almost instantly. "All right. Just as long as we know where we are. I'm not giving up my work, not for you, not for anybody. And you're obviously not giving up yours. I thought we might find a bit of common ground and be damned to the Act. Well, I was wrong, so all we have to decide is whether to go on working out of the same premises."

He spoke gently. "Nobody's asking you to give up your work. But I don't want you mixed up in mine. I may not have it much longer."

He made her sit, and sat next to her, taking his time. He knew he had committed himself now.

"There are three kinds of people in our business. The rank and file think they know who the enemy is, half gut feeling, half received wisdom, but with them it's just a job." He grinned crookedly. "I wasn't so very different when I first joined Five."

She said nothing, but he felt some of her hostility depart.

"Then there's the conviction boys. Not necessarily political geniuses, just the broad brush strokes, all the facts handpicked to dovetail with their prejudices. God is a Tory, must be, since he made them in his likeness. They're the zealots. If you're not with them, you're against them. That makes you a communist, a terrorist or a dupe."

"No wonder a lot of people in Five didn't like you."

"Didn't and don't. Listen, I'm telling you something because it's the only way you'll ever understand, and I haven't finished."

"Yes, Johnny."

"The third kind are the clever ones. Not just clever. Intellectual. Subtle. They believe all the right things, of course, but most of all they believe in themselves. For them – Six even more than Five – it's both an ego trip and a game. Very simple rules: anything goes, winner takes all. Oh, I nearly forgot. If you get hooked, really hooked, and some of them do, winning can get to be more important than which side you're on."

Twenty years, she thought, and he thinks this is all news.

"I don't mean they'd change sides just to win," he was saying. "That would be far too crude. The secret of being one of the elite is to be able to convince yourself you're right even when you're wrong. And since there's no such thing as thinking you're too right, when you go wrong, you go very wrong."

She saw suddenly that it was news after all. "You mean someone has. Not Simon Aske. Someone much higher."

121

"I think so. Someone very much higher."

"One of the top people in Six?"

"Oh yes," he said. "Definitely one of the elite."

"A mole. Is that what we're talking about? Another mole?"

"Yes," he said cheerfully. "Bloody presumptuous of someone with my background, I suppose, but that's what we're talking about."

"But you said it was some kind of power struggle between Epworth and the old guard. Steve and his pals in the SIS old guard."

"I did. It is. Aske is the key, something about Aske it's more than my life's worth to tell you. If Epworth can crack it, he'll be able to rout the old guard and Steve. He'll be king of the castle, Downing Street's blue-eyed boy."

"Yes," she said. "I see that. Only I don't. Because if one of the old guard is a mole . . . and all this Aske business is Epworth versus Steve, and his pals in SIS . . ."

"Go on." It had gone much too far but it was the first time he had heard it spelled out by someone else.

Her face the very image of disbelief, she said, "Steve Archer as a mole? Or connected with a mole. . . ?" Her brow cleared. "Or the dupe of a mole. Of course!"

She was both shocked and titillated. He knew she had never forgiven Steve for his treatment of Helga. "That's it, isn't it? If Epworth dug up the mole and the mole turned out to be one of Steve's bosom pals from his days with SIS, someone he's still cosy with, he'd – "

"No one's going to accuse Steve himself of being a traitor," he said. "But the mere idea of the head of Five consorting with a traitor! The media would go beserk. If it got out, it could rock the government."

"By!" Sylvie said. "It wants some thinking about, does that. But why did you say you might not have a job much longer? I can see why you wouldn't be popular with all the people who think you aren't fit to lick Steve's shoes. But if Epworth came out top dog . . ."

". . . I'd have even more of a dog's life than I have now. So the idea would be to quit while I was winning."

Still smiling, he said, "Since you're not off on your professional travels for a couple of days, I thought we might have a little outing. To wurzel land."

"You bastard!" Sylvie said. "I knew you were after something." She wondered why, having penetrated so close to the heart of silence, she should feel less triumphant than apprehensive. A little later she saw it was because a man like Steve Archer, given the smallest inkling of what was going on, was unlikely to sit back and wait for it to happen.

# THE
# INNER
# ZONE

# FIFTEEN

Morpurgo took an instant dislike to Headmaster. To begin with, he was the younger man yet behaved as if he were the older. Clean-cut, firm-chinned, manly, he was also smugly aware that he possessed a voice like the sound of a great amen. He deployed a bark – hah! hah! – in place of a sense of humour, and sealed his fate with Morpurgo by conferring a brisk, manly handshake before concentrating wholly on Sylvie.

Sylvie played up shamelessly, a woman who knew her place in the presence of the dominant male. She also displayed bravura talent during a prolonged discussion of a fictitious nephew currently in the Gilbert Islands but due shortly to begin an English public school education. Morpurgo even found himself beginning to detest Sylvie's non-existent relatives.

After such preliminaries they were delivered to a much older man, white-haired, rosy-cheeked, adolescence in aspic. Mr Porteous was senior master and senior housemaster. If anyone could show them the school and answer their questions, it was Mr Porteous. Mr Porteous – hah! hah! – knew more about School than Headmaster himself.

Mr Porteous was eager, jocular and a born salesman. When Morpurgo, after tramping around Dickensian dormitories, horse-box study cubicles and a refectory that smelled of stale food and boys in the rough, asked him how long he had been – the arrogant simplicity was unavoidable – at School, he was away like an old hack heading for home.

"Oh, lord, time passes so quickly that one – well, let's see – yes, of course, just before the opening of the Aubrey Wing, new then, old now. So-o-o, that would make it – but wait. No. That was Her Majesty and I'm thinking of Her Royal Highness, which means –

aha! – the dedication of the Chapel of Ease. This place, Mrs Morpurgo, burgeons, the *mot juste*, like a garden city. Though of course, one calls them New Towns these days."

They had arrived in the gym. He stopped abruptly in front of a vaulting horse as if contemplating a standing leap. "Twenty-six years, Michaelmas ultimo. And it don't, as the old song has it, seem a day too much." A bunch of juniors were doing running somersaults in a pungent atmosphere of sweat and gym shoes.

Morpurgo did mental arithmetic. If Aske had been sent barbarously away to school – sorry, School – while still a child, he must have spent approximately the decade of the fifties at this place.

"All that long?" Porteous was saying to Sylvie. "Well, no, can't truly say it seems so. A thousand ages in His sight are like an evening gone, so-o-o, you might say that twenty-six years barely gives one time to doff one's coat. You look pensive, Mr – ah – Morpurgo."

"Just curiosity. I happen to have had an old friend here years ago. I think it must have been just before your time."

"What was his name, your Achates? Or perhaps he was not *quite* that close." Porteous laughed roguishly.

"Let's say an acquaintance." Morpurgo tried not to be brusque. "His name was Aske. Simon Aske." Not yet flesh on the bones, not even bones, but an evocation.

"Aske?" Porteous stared into space, humming on two or three ill-matched notes. "Hm. Aske." He hitched his gown about his plumply padded shoulders. "Hm," he said again. "Somewhere. Ssssomewhere. Yesss. Come, let us pursue."

They followed him around three sides of a quadrangle with a sundial and a view of the distant Avon, dots and dashes of silver among trees and water meadows. "Hall," he said, "is our pantheon, the dwelling place of our immortals. *Sunt hic etiam sua praemia laudi*, and I *rather* think . . ." Across his busy back, Sylvie winked at Morpurgo.

Hall – Morpurgo wondered how far this imperial proscription of the definite article had been taken – was a great mock-Tudor conceit with hammerbeam roof, oak-panelled walls and leaded windows. In Hall the polished pine-strip floor glowed religiously. In Hall dense rows of shiny yellow chairs paraded like limbless veterans in wheelchairs. On a wide rostrum a double row of superior chairs respectfully attended a lectern, tall and stern.

It was not difficult to imagine Headmaster, similarly tall and

128

stern, with his evangelical chin and challenging evangelical eyes, projecting his just short of sinfully euphonious voice at School in Hall assembled, Boy by Boy.

Mr Porteous trotted down the side of Hall, scrutinising the panelling as if for woodworm. Those nearest the rostrum were inscribed in gold with the names of boys who, academically or sportingly, had conjured dividends from the investments of affluent or self-sacrificing parents.

"Ah-*hah!*" Porteous halted again, one foot forward, perky little nose elevated, a chubby, aged pointer. Morpurgo, following the unspoken invitation, searched and in due course found in a list of scholastic achievers:

Simon Aske    Oxford    1959

"Thought I recalled." Porteous was complacent. "One doesn't sit in Hall every morning for years without absorbing, even if subliminally, the minor details of environment. Yes. Oxford then, exhibitioner, one fancies, though the name of the college evades. But then" – he looked at Morpurgo, mildly curious – "you doubtless know it, Mr – ah – Morpurgo?"

Morpurgo came back with a lurch. "Been out of touch for years, almost forgotten old Simon until we arranged to come down here." He embroidered a little. "Could be dead by now, I suppose."

Porteous indicated the honours roll. "*Dignum laude virum, Musa vetat mori*, as Horace has it." His glance at Morpurgo was sly. "Or if not the Muse, most certainly by School, mm?"

Buggered, Morpurgo told himself, if he would ask for a translation.

Sylvie said, "Translation, please."

Porteous flicked Morpurgo the smallest of wicked smiles. "Of course. Do forgive me. The man worthy of praise, says Horace, is forbidden by the Muse to die. Was Simon Aske worthy of praise, Mr – ah – Morpurgo?"

"I didn't really know him all that well. As I said, more of an acquaintance."

"So it doesn't greatly matter?" Did Porteous scent improbability in this story of a long-lost friend?

"Not very much," Morpurgo said. "I do remember Oxford now. Though not the college." Knowing the college would have saved time.

"Headmaster has been thinning the ranks of age," Porteous

129

said. "I alone remain, a token presence of white hairs and wisdom, but alas, post-Aske. Bursar would know the college – gone up to Town, unfortunately." He was blossoming extravagantly for Sylvie's benefit. Most men did.

Headmaster, dispensing tea, seized the referred enquiry as a text for urbane sales talk.

"Of course, we do try to follow our boys in afterlife, but though we have a goodly collection of achievers some – hah! hah! – are less equal than others. Mrs Morpurgo, more tea. No? Perhaps another langue de chat?"

Hands laced behind a head tilted to display the profile, he began a use-polished litany. "Ministers, in and out of Cabinet. High mandarins of Whitehall. Captains of industry. As for bishops . . . But there!" He too having taken to performing for Sylvie, he left them to imagine an entire convocation of bishops.

"Still, icing on the cake. What's more important to us, and doubtless to the boys' parents, is the quality of the cake itself. We do pride ourselves on turning out something – hah! – better than stodge.

"Which is not to say that your friend might not have made his mark. What was his line?"

By now Morpurgo was in the mood for mischief. "Oh, something or other in the Foreign Office. I forget what exactly."

"Indeed?" Headmaster perked up, less evangelical now than redemptive. "In the Dip, perhaps?"

Another name for a possible tally of ambassadors, Morpurgo saw. "Small beer if he was, nothing to write home about."

"Hah! Nicely put. An honest man sent to lie abroad for his country, but nothing to write home about. Hah! Hah! Did Porteous happen to mention which house?"

"Bath," Sylvie said, and Morpurgo remembered that that too had been on the honours board.

"Bath, Bath, Bath." Headmaster gave her a second dose of profile, this time closing his eyes flutteringly. "A Lilywhite. In 1959. That would be Haystock."

Morpurgo caught Sylvie's eye. It was she who looked hastily away; he was wearing his occupational mask.

Headmaster barked his "Hah!" then, "Let me disentangle. School has four houses, all episcopal as it were. Bath, Wells, Salisbury and Gloucester. Bit of a swizzle really, Bath and Wells being a single diocese. Aske was in Bath. That makes him a Lilywhite. Lily-white boys, do you see? Must be if they spend

130

nine or ten years in Bath. That's the way our chaps have always seen it, anyway, Hah! Hah! Hah! Well, there you are.

"And one Peter Haystock, master of Bath House in the days of your friend Aske." His hands twirled. "Hair *and* manner, shall we say exuberant? An explosion in a mattress factory, yes? Yes. As for the nickname, well, need you ask? Hardly imaginative – boys' nicknames seldom are – but naughtily close to the mark. The Haystack. Hah! Hah! Yes.

"But well-loved, well-loved, Peter Haystock and his wife, a veritable Baucis and Philemon, Mr Chips with a happy ending. Henley-in-Arden, I believe, delightfully pastoral setting for a couple of Haystacks, one's obliged to think? Hah! Hah! Yes indeed." He flashed his white and mirthless teeth and no more was said on the subject of Aske's college.

\* \* \*

"Bath!" Morpurgo drove fast as they headed for home. "The only house we had at my school was outside. We called it the shit-house."

"Your Simon Aske" – Sylvie was used to this mood – "was privileged. Better face it, digging up his past is going to jangle every nerve in your pathetically proletarian body."

All right for you, he thought, instantly identified by Porteous and Headmaster as one of Us. Aloud, he said, "Incidentally, what price a little Jewish boy at a Protestant evangelical school?"

"So he's obviously not Jewish after all, not that I can see that it matters. I'm going to Stratford mid-week, remember? You could go on to Henley and pay a call on the Haystack if you can bear another stroll through the groves of Academe."

"Everything matters. Nothing to do with race or privilege, a question of motivation. I accept your offer, but why make it if you aren't curious in spite of everything?"

Sylvie smiled a cold little smile. "Those whom the gods wish to destroy. You'll do it anyway. I might as well be around to pick up the bits."

\* \* \*

It was one of the small roads that run off the larger roads that run off Hampstead Heath: not grand, but pleasant, with a tentacle of the Heath just behind.

Pierre Weber opened the door. "Hi. Long time. Come on in." A room full of books and cosily shabby furniture looked out to a distant, tree-crowned rise. Morpurgo knew at once that he would like the people who owned the house; nothing new, no priceless antiques either, just atmosphere at pounds per square inch.

"Coffee's perked. Rest the feet. Be right with you." Weber went out, and Morpurgo could hear his methodical movements in the kitchen. He returned with a tray. "Cookies, too. No Warren Claas, so we both get to eat more than one." That was another part of the strangeness: in the past, events had almost always involved Pierre Weber and Warren Claas.

"How's Sylvie?" Weber busied himself with pouring.

"As well as the last time you saw her. Maybe better."

Weber smiled his pothook smile, wistful enough to melt the hearts of people with hearts to melt. His spaniel look made some women want to pat him. Some but not all of them: Weber's wife had left him years ago, for reasons unknown and never discussed. "Told you I visited with her, huh? Sure she did. Help yourself to cookies." He sat facing, the up side of his smile extending a little farther.

There was a feeling of companionship in the air – old friends, meeting only occasionally, who could resume a relationship as comfortably as the coming together of foot and favourite shoe. But this shoe might prove to pinch. Morpurgo took a cookie. "How's Barzelian?"

It was an interesting situation. Weber was big in the CIA. He had been Claas's boss, might still be, even though Claas was now back in Langley. More to the point, he was Barzelian's troubleshooter and Barzelian, as the CIA's Head of Operations, made much of the trouble that later had to be shot.

"Sends you his regards, what else?" Morpurgo and Barzelian had never met, but Morpurgo had walked in his shadow. Barzelian, an unlikely blend of Missouri farming stock and Armenian ancestry, was not, in his own words, a man to buy a second-hand carpet from.

Weber patted the air soothingly. "Okay, you're wondering what the Cousins have in store. Why do you think I arranged a clandestine meet instead of inviting you to drop by the embassy? This is strictly a solo flight. Have another cookie. I hear you were in Vienna."

"Couldn't resist it." Somebody, somewhere, was taking a close interest in his activities, and it sounded less and less like the profit-and-loss brigade. "Claas gave Vienna a terrific build-up just before he left. On the Century House rooftop, admiring the panorama of power. Or didn't he tell you?"

"Now why ever," Weber said, "would Warren do a thing like that?"

"I thought you might tell me."

Weber pulled his sharp nose. "Maybe Warren was rehearsing a new role: here's the great expert on European affairs come back to put Langley straight. How was Vienna?"

"Baroque. Very."

"You sound like something out of Noël Coward. But then," Weber said, "to a whole lot of Yanks a whole lot of Brits sound like something out of Noël Coward." He pushed the plate. "Have another cookie." He took one himself. "Very baroque, huh? Like, twisty?"

"Very twisty. You might say rococo." Playing poker with a man who might know your hand when you could only guess at his was a risky business. Morpurgo had never underestimated Weber as he had Claas.

Weber waved half a cookie, munching furiously. "Rococo. Meaning excessively twisty. Would you say excessively?"

"Let's say, not to my taste."

"A man," Weber said sadly, "who could leave behind a woman like Sylvie has to be a bit of a dog. Have that last cookie. Did brother Lawrence ever tell you Fish used to be our man in Century House?"

Morpurgo, remembering that Epworth had, shook his head. A twitch of the lips told him Weber had not been deceived. He said, "Does Epworth know you're in town, Pierre?"

"He knows I'm in town. He doesn't know I'm here with you. Unless you told him."

Let him stew on that one. "Why are you in town?"

Weber, too, was an expert in letting things stew. "About Fish. Don't get me wrong. No money. No top secret stuff in dead drops, nothing like that. Fish was just one of the SIS guys who happen to think the road to the future runs through Langley."

Morpurgo, noting the present tense, doubted that it was accidental.

"You know how it is," Weber said, "Joint Intelligence Agreement, the daily call, the once-a-weeker in Gower Street where we tell each other every last little thing except what matters. Fish filled in gaps."

"Who fills them in now?"

"You wouldn't believe me if I said no one."

"Was Fish filling in gaps while I was rounding up the Sattin ring?"

Weber nodded. "Uh-huh."

"What sort of gaps?" They were drawing closer to Gossip, Aske and Operation Highflyer. He suspected Weber knew that.

"As soon as you broke the ring," Weber said, "Moscow Centre offered to swap Sattin for an SIS fieldman they'd picked up in the DDR, right? Nothing secret about that, we got it through channels. But we got it through Fish, too. Fish worked hard on Warren to have Langley back the swap. To pressure SIS."

"He worked hard on us, too. I mean SIS was pushing Five. We had a meeting; me, Fish, Epworth and the Directors-General."

Weber was nodding again. "I know it. Fish told Warren that Epworth was against the swap. That Epworth was the main obstacle, not Five. He was kind of hinting" – nothing had lightened Weber's outward melancholy, but Morpurgo knew they had reached some kind of crux – "that Epworth had his private reasons for not wanting the exchange to take place."

For Fish to tell Langley that Epworth was opposing an exchange was more than a breach of security. It could have laid Epworth open to suspicion.

Morpurgo had been present at the meeting held to consider the exchange of Sattin for a captured SIS agent. During the recent discussion in Epworth's music room he had learned for the first time that the agent in question had been Gossip, the top-quality source in Fish's own personal operation, Highflyer.

Fish had pressed hard for the earliest possible exchange. But so had Epworth. At least, Morpurgo thought, so far as you could be sure that Epworth was pressing hard for anything.

So why had Fish said otherwise to Langley? And why was Weber going to all this trouble to tell him about it now?

He feigned only mild interest, aware that Weber was watching him discreetly. "Did Warren have any views?"

"Warren just said that Fish was willing to try anything to get his man back. Warren kind of admired it. He said Fish was like one of these guys who marries a Russian girl and then finds the Sovs won't let her out of the country."

He stopped laughing. "Let's face it, John, they shipped that poor guy from Karlshorst to Lefortovo. People who stay in that place too long leave their brains behind."

Beyond the garden a straggle of riders went by, five bobbing nymphets in hard hats. Their voices carried as a series of fading squeals above the canter and snort of the horses. "Of course," Weber said, "Sattin dying before he even came to trial hit Fish hard. Didn't he know the guy had cancer or whatever it was?"

"Knew he was ill," Morpurgo said. He was sure Langley knew exactly what had killed Sattin. "That's as far as it went."

Weber was giving him too many things to think about. He would have to sift through them later.

Weber stacked the coffee things. "Come on through to the kitchen. I have to leave this place fit for me to come back to." He might have finished with the subject of Humphrey Fish, but Morpurgo doubted it.

"Nice place. Should I ask whose it is?"

"Why not?" Weber leaned against the sink unit. Its stainless steel bounced light from outside, throwing him into slim semi-silhouette. "Nice safe house. Meaning nothing to do with Langley, the embassy or dressed-up garbage like you and me. Belongs to nice, safe folk who happen to be friends of mine."

"Doctors," Morpurgo said. "One of them, at least. Psychologist? Psychiatrist? Something like that."

"You've been snooping," Weber accused, but with no heat.

"The place is full of medical books. One whole side of the fireplace is shrink stuff."

"Doctors both," Weber said. "She's the shrink. You know anything about houseplants?"

"Not a thing." Morpurgo waited.

"No, well." Weber glanced out at the garden. "There's this old guy who comes to take care of the yard and stuff. I'll fix with him to adopt the houseplants too. So you and Fish had no soulful heart-to-heart at Sattin's funeral? Or did Sattin have a funeral? I forget."

Morpurgo pretended to look at his watch. "No offence, Pierre, but I have things to do." He came to inspect the potplants as Weber went walkabout. Weber ended up back at the sink. They both looked out of the window.

Weber said, "Lawrence Epworth never gives up, does he?"

"I hope not. Not so long as he does what he does and I work for him." Morpurgo prodded a potted geranium. "This needs watering, I think."

"I told you, I'll fix it with the old guy who leans on his spade. He really is a gardener. I had him checked out." He gave Morpurgo a quick look. "My friends – did I say? – travel around. Collect conferences the way I collect tough assignments.

135

Where've you been since they pulled you out of the city of waltz, schmaltz and *Weltschmerz*? I guess you know I'm some kind of an expert on *Weltschmerz*."

They were looking at each other with only a foot or so between them. Weber, staring straight back, said, "If you have a cool, manly, unblinking stare everybody knows you're not to be trusted, so you put on this shifty look and everybody says, 'This guy knows cool, unblinking looks are not to be trusted, so what's with this shifty look? I guess we'd better not trust him.' " He put on a shifty look and leered. What he looked most was anxious.

"Just why," Morpurgo said, "did Warren Claas come out with that set-piece rubbishing of everything British when he took his leave of dear old Century House?"

"You say rubbishing and I say trashing," Weber sang in a voice like a parrot with psittacosis, "I say terrific and you say smashing, so let's call the whole thing off." He danced a brief buck-and-wing.

"He did it because he was struck, as a thinking, caring, red-blooded, apple-pie-loving American, by the unmistakable resemblance between London, Vienna and the Holy Roman Empire. Also because we figured it was time to let Lawrence Epworth know the word was out. Shall we dance?"

"What word?"

"Aske." Humming the Emperor Waltz to himself, Weber whirled an invisible partner lightly around the table. "I mean, things like that don't stay secret. Langley reckons there are around ten thousand people in Vienna who work for some security service or other. Or was that just for the Sovbloc? I forget. I guess I'm getting old."

He spun in a final circle, bowed gracefully, and turned back to Morpurgo. "Brother Lawrence is like an old, smart fly, always one wall ahead of the swatter. I should have known when I heard he was on vacation. Brother Lawrence takes vacations the way Moscow Centre does conducted tours."

He switched on the dishwasher and shooed Morpurgo through the door.

"Fish ran a little something that fell apart. Now it's kind of coming together again. There must be people at Century House who aren't too wild about that. Still, I guess it's all in hand. Win a few, lose a few, it's the last one that counts, as my old mom used to say as she cleaned them out at gin rummy."

At the street door he said, "On the other hand, I imagine there are people at Century House who could use it all to do one hell of a job of destabilisation." He tsked. "Damned spook jargon! Has the darndest habit of coming out back to front. For destabilise read consolidate."

He patted Morpurgo's shoulder, his pothook smile more lopsided than ever. "Hell, you know old Pierre. May not get there in the end, but he sure louses up a few things on the way."

"Thanks for the coffee and cookies. Come and see Sylvie and me when we're both at home."

"What coffee and cookies?" Weber said. "I never saw you in my life before."

Watching Morpurgo open the gate from the flagged front garden to the street, he called. "Hey! Say hello to – what did you say her name was?" He looked tired now, tired and wistful, but above all, anxious.

Morpurgo nodded, closing the gate. "I will."

"Hey!" He looked back.

"I forgot. Too bad about your mom."

"Thanks." He started down the street.

"Hey!" He stopped.

Weber's anxiety had become a force, telekinetic. "You just take care now. These days it's hard to tell enemies from friends."

Walking away, Morpurgo began sifting through the facts. One of them was that if he, John Morpurgo, succeeding in bridging the gap between Pontefract, School, Vienna and Prague, Epworth might become king of the new Kakania. It made him walk very slowly.

In due course, he found himself puzzling, even more bafflingly, over Simon Aske's suggestion that Sylvie might go to Prague to photograph Slansky's shadow. It made him abandon the whole thing in favour of a drink.

# SIXTEEN

The countryside, warm and golden in what Sylvie liked to call Saint Luke's Little Summer, was tranquilly beautiful. He knew that he should be enjoying the drive to Stratford. Epworth might have been less than enthusiastic about exchanging Sattin for Gossip. It was a long way from saying that he had been opposed.

But there had been other circumstances. Lawrence Epworth, already planning the coup that would oust Fish and the then Director-General of SIS, might well have classed the repatriation of a captured agent – probably recoverable later if Sattin had not died – as a temporarily unnecessary hindrance.

Especially as Fish was yet to kill himself and there was no great mystery.

"I suppose," Sylvie said, "if I said 'Penny for your thoughts' you could get me under the Act."

"What?" He discovered that they were on the outskirts of Stratford.

"It comes to something when you daren't ask your old man what he's thinking about, in case you're committing an offence."

"I wasn't thinking about anything in particular." Slansky's shadow?

"Not even Haystacks?"

"Not even Haystacks. Just things in general." *Slansky's shadow?*

"Come off it! You've scarcely said a word all the way up. Is it Steve?"

He hadn't told her about the meeting with Weber. If she had known, it would still have been a good guess. He had thought, off and on, that Weber's renewed warning might indeed have been about Steve.

So long as Epworth was allowed to trace the relationship between Fish and Aske without interference, Steve would consider himself, his friends, his whole world under threat.

"No," he said reluctantly, "not Steve. Why should it be?"

"Well," she said, "maybe you're right. After all, if the Punch and Judy man gets what he wants, he'll be God Almighty, won't he? Nobody to say him nay in Five or Six, least of all Steve."

He would have been prepared to swear, up to the instant of seeing Simon Aske's name in the gold-leaf ranks of privilege at School, that it was all a question of principle. Until his realisation that Aske and Archer were both products of a system to which he was instinctively hostile, he would have sworn that he had not been influenced by a temptation to see Steve Archer and his pals swept away in any débâcle Epworth might engineer.

Now he wondered if Epworth had read him better than he had read himself.

He said, "Steve could make life difficult if he knew I was ferreting, but I doubt he'd dare."

She came off the bridge, turning towards the theatre. "It's against the law to visit retired schoolmasters?"

"It's the end they look at, not the means."

"Oh, lord," she said, "I never knew that Steve was into philosophy."

He took the car from her at the side of the theatre. Boats pottered about the river. White smoke-puffs of cloud trundled overhead. Discharged coachloads of day-trippers drifted aimlessly over the parched and tired grass as if the theatre were some cultural ossuary, conferring grace by proximity.

"The stage door's there." She pointed. "Behind the redbrick Gothic. I'll make sure they know where I am."

He shortcut by a bed-and-breakfast route that revealed the real Stratford, a minor market town, streets small, even drab, hauled from obscurity by one man and his works.

He could take Shakespeare or leave him. He had mostly left him. Sylvie's eye would conjure up some complex, kaleidoscopic image to summarise the man and all those who celebrated his august dust. Morpurgo was, as always, proud of Sylvie yet envious. His work consisted in rummaging though the lives of lesser folk, as glamorous as scavenging, creative as making rugs from rags.

A surprise awaited in olde worlde Henley-in-Arden. He drove

139

down the picturesque main street, everything from Tudor to Regency, and continued on. No glamour in the Haystock home, no thatched cottage or rural idyll, but a bungalow on the far outskirts, not old, not new, some thirties builder's speculative hit-and-miss.

It had timbers, but they were Euclidian fake, cemented in off-white pebble dash. There was thatch, but it was over a rickety birdtable only a cat's leap above a lawn hemmed about by more and kitschier dahlias than were proper outside the poorer kind of municipal park.

The dahlias sheltered a luxurious undergrowth of weeds. The tarmac drive was crumbling, grass in its cracks. The paintwork on the house and a garage with its own nailed-on timbering was dull and flaking. Even the bright orange curtains of a caravan at the side of the garage offered evidence of the universal entropy: faded, a hem adrift, sagging unevenly where plastic hooks had snapped.

Then Haystock was upon him. He was Struwelpeter, all hair, nose and elbows, a continuous spiky explosion ricocheting around the corner of the garage to assault him from every direction at once.

"Morpurgo, yes?" His hand was grasped, his shoulder thumped, his not inconsiderable weight propelled bodily around the side of the garage by a palm in the small of the back.

Peter Haystock, he supposed, would be in his late sixties, a compressed spring of a man whose pure white hair sprang bristling from his head as if charged with static electricity. Of medium height, he wore a faded blue sleeveless shirt, a shapeless pair of khaki shorts, plastic beach sandals from which yellowing toes protruded.

"Must be weary, come a long way. London? Pushed it too, dare say. Know your sort of chap, no offence. Don't care for the fast roads personally, more haste, more risk. Smart boys doing the ton in the outside lane, nose up your tail, lights flashing, God Almighty in a hurry."

They debouched into the back garden. "Ellie, here's Mr Morpurgo, just arrived, panting for a goblet of vino. Sit, dear boy. Sit, sit, sit."

Mrs Haystock, a little her husband's junior, unfolded herself from a dilapidated camping chair, getting her feet caught in the frame and almost toppling in the process. She was well over six feet, a head taller than her husband, with the awkward angularity of a giraffe. She wore a red striped dress, years too young for her, that conjured up barbers' poles.

The Haystocks had been eating al fresco, a folding table with tubular legs at some time bent and ineptly straightened to give it a crouched and lurching look. There were the limp remains of a salad and enough crumbs to have feasted the five thousand. There were also two unmatched tumblers, one half-filled, the empty one Ellie Haystock's. Haystock, in a lightning swoop, came back from the garage with an old deckchair, dangerously assembling it on the run.

Ellie Haystock jerked Morpurgo's hand once, hard, as if confident it would come off. "No more plonk," she said in a high, humorously complaining voice. "Off to the cellar, Peterkins, there's a lamb." She flapped at Morpurgo and, echoing Haystock, said, "Sit, sit, sit."

Morpurgo lowered himself gingerly, while Haystock vanished indoors. Here at the back of the house creeping disorder was yet more evident, a flagged terrace crisscrossed with mini-hedges of moss and weed, a herbaceous border far gone, a lawn as diseased as the fur of an old cat.

"He remembers them all, you know," Ellie Haystock announced in her high whoop of a voice. "Aske and it shall be given you; seek and ye shall find." Morpurgo wondered how many more times he was doomed to hear the over-apt quotation, but Haystock was back with a Sainsbury's box wine and yet another incompatible glass.

Flinging himself into his chair, he concentrated on Morpurgo. "Aske, right? Young Simon. Well, well, sad, sad, sad." He shook his head violently over the sadness of it.

Morpurgo had a story this time. "Yes, it is, rather, but they're hopeful. In the meantime, anything you can remember."

"Just like him to lose his memory, right, Ellie? Anything to make a drama." Haystock flung himself towards Morpurgo. "Sure it's not a put-on? Steady, old girl." The second remark, whiplash, was to his wife, whose glass was now aflood.

"Ooops!" she said, high-pitched and clarion with just a trace of slur. "*Scusi*, everyone, better safe than whatsit." Bending her equine, good-natured face over her glass, she sucked off a little wine noisily.

"Very fond of put-ons, young Simon." As Haystock turned back from his wife, murder showed momentarily in his face. Hello, Morpurgo thought, not necessarily Baucis and Philemon.

141

*"Puts-on*, Peterkins." Ellie Haystock made it sound trattoria Italian, like her *scusi*. She gave a great uninhibited whoop. "No, *can't* be right, can it?" She honked, snorted, said, "Cheers, *tout le monde*," and sank much of her wine. "Very fond of her plonk, Ellie is. Tray, tray fond of her vino."

Morpurgo plunged on. "Genuine amnesia, that's what the doctors say. Pressure of work, nervous stress, these things do happen."

"Don't forget 'em, you know," Haystock said tautly. "Never. Well, not often. Still, mustn't ramble on. Right. Questions? Fire away."

"You obviously remember Aske."

"Odd boy," Haystock said. "Mass of contradictions." Ellie Haystock, toying with her recently refilled glass, suddenly drank noisily.

Mustn't be too much the interrogator. "I don't want to take up much of your time. I've a good many other enquiries to make. A vignette?"

Once again, as at School, he was irritated to find himself putting on the posh.

*"Multum in parvo?"* Haystock laughed, a shrill yelp. Morpurgo could imagine it as a cornerstone in the mimickry of countless boys. Was he going to be another scatterer of Latin tags and quotations?

"Meaning which young Aske. Which young Simon Aske in particular. Polarised, that boy. Yes. Problem. Quite a problem. Jekyll and Hyde." He scrubbed his chin ferociously.

"Hide and seek," Ellie Haystock said obscurely, and produced her snort of inward amusement.

Haystock ignored her. "Timid little chap when he came. Introspective, very. Out of his way not to be noticed. Odd, when one thinks of later."

The pair of them seemed unable to get their act together. Lines from the old song came to Morpurgo's mind: 'How happy could I be with either, were t'other dear charmer away. But while ye thus tease me together . . .' Tarumty-tarumty-tarum.

He watched Ellie Haystock run herself off more wine. "To be," she pronounced, staring at a border where even the weeds looked neglected, "or not to be, that was his question."

Her enigmatic remark had an effect. "Hamlet!" Haystock said. "Other boys took it out on him to begin with, instincts of the pack. But hawk from a handsaw? Oh dear, yes!" He was trying to

142

work something out.

"Toads," Ellie said, glass to lips. "Natural to-o-o-ads."

"Discovered the knack of making 'em laugh, do you see?" Haystock had decided on a line. "Extraordinary thing, sometimes happens. Quiet chap, not tough enough to slog it out, uses wits, natural talent. Clown, get me? No, more than that. Real wit, touch of slyness: other chaps think he's acting the fool, actually making fools of them. Absurdly sensitive about his name, too – used to make sort of preemptive puns, but always at *their* expense."

"He had a dream," Ellie Haystock announced like the beginning of a funeral oration for Martin Luther King. She took an audible gulp of wine. "He used to have *spells* from time to time in the early days, did young Simon. Nothing to put a finger on, just" – she laughed her dreadful laugh – "*dumps*. Bit of a fever, into the san" – sanatorium, Morpurgo translated for himself – "for a day or so, back to normal and no harm done."

"Pubescence." Haystock said it impatiently. "Not unusual, especially in the more delicate chaps. I really don't see, Ellie – "

She cut him off. "I went to see the poor little toad. 'Oh,' he said, 'an awful dream, Mrs Haystock, such an awful dream.' " Her voice took on the shrillness and exaggerated inflection of a child.

" 'They were sandcastles. All sandcastles on the beach, and the sea was coming in. Each time there was a wave they melted a bit more. And at last' " – she waved both arms for emphasis; wine flew from her glass to blotch her dress – " 'they were *all* washed away.' "

She paused, eyes rounded, her high, belling voice full of a tragedy both gripping and absurd. " '*All* washed away,' " she repeated. "He tried to save them but they wouldn't let him."

"Ellie," Haystock said, "what's this got to do with a man who's lost his memory?" but his annoyance was half-hearted.

Ellie Haystock, hugging herself under limp, hidden breasts, whooped, suddenly delighted. "Isn't that *super*?"

She emptied her glass with that toss of the head which comes when drink is no longer drink but abdication.

"*I* said," she went on, " 'but they were only *sand*castles, Simon. Sandcastles *do* get washed away by the tide.' He said" – she turned her glass upside-down, watching drops gather like blood and fall from its rim – " 'No,' he said, 'you don't understand. They were people, too.' He tried to save them, but they melted themselves away."

She extended a finger to catch the last drop of wine. Her nails had been lacquered at some time. Now they were chipped, worn, not very clean. "And then" – she produced her incongruous hoot of mirth – "he said, 'I'm tired now,' and blow me if he didn't go sleep."

When she had finished there was only the distant sound of someone mowing a lawn. Haystock broke in peremptorily. "More wine, dear chap. Have some more wine." His hair seemed spikier, his face sharper. There was a feverish flush in his cheeks.

When Morpurgo refused he snapped, "Ellie, we'd all like coffee. Go and make us some coffee, there's a good girl."

Getting up with movements not unlike the earlier unfolding of the deckchair, she wobbled, steadied herself, began a gawky progress towards the bungalow. As she went she hooted, snorted, then said, "*Good* old Ellie, always making bishes."

"Gets carried away." Haystock was drained of some of his explosive energy. "No young ourselves. Wouldn't be young now anyway. Liked playing the mother; never saw how the little devils mocked her."

Hands on his bare, bony knees, head bent, he stared at the unkempt terrace. "Or perhaps," he said, "she did."

He flung himself perilously back in his chair. "Nothing so" – he searched for a word – "pathetic as your retired pedagogue. How's that fool of a headmaster? Don't answer that. Shouldn't have asked."

Something of his original fire returned. "Must be important, young Aske, people like you going round looking for his past like lost baggage." From the house there came a furious bang and clatter.

"Not really," Morpurgo said. Something Ellie Haystock had said was bothering him. Yes. '*He* tried to save them. They wouldn't let *him* near.' "Did you ever meet his parents?"

Haystock had built up a fresh head of steam. "Hard, domineering chap, something in industry. Silly little birdy wife, much younger, all tweets and flutters. Came once a year, speech day, never stayed long afterwards. She would have liked to, pretty sure. Not him. Waste of time, high-faluting nonsense. Rather fancy he was *sui generis*, time's money, that sort of thing."

"I believe there was a tragedy."

Haystock snapped his fingers. "Course! Course! Car smash, remember what I said about cut-and-thrust drivers? Some drunken fool driver, fancy forgetting! Poor little beast, a trust fund, no living relatives, suppose that's what's causing you these problems now. Although . . ."

Again he lost his way briefly in the past, returning to say, "Funny thing was, now I remember, didn't seem to make much odds to the little beggar, kept it bottled up. Wasn't even – Yes! Fancy forgetting! – Wasn't even averse to trading on the sympathy when other lads leaned too hard."

He shook his head, over Aske, over his own failing memory. "Funny, young Aske in the Foreign Office. Father wouldn't have approved, sure of that. Still, he'd have approved even less if the boy had done what we all expected."

"What was that?"

Haystock looked surprised. "Don't know much, do you? Relatives or no, should have thought the FO would have a pretty comprehensive curriculum vitae."

Things were taking a tricky turn. "Sorry," Morpurgo said, "not them, me. No point in reading everything up if you're sent out to dig."

From the house there was a sudden splintering crash of dropped crockery.

Haystock looked towards it, every muscle briefly locked. He sighed. It was a desperate sound.

" 'To be, or not to be,' " he said. "That's Ellie for you: nips through to the point, waits for you to catch up if you can find her. The stage, Mr Morpurgo, the stage. We all thought he was a natural."

He was willing himself to ignore whatever might be happening in the kitchen. "Told you, I believe, lad found a way of coming out on top by playing the fool, sort of sharp-edged mockery. Quite unpredictable, too. Most of the time, so quiet you would forget he was there. Every so often" – he punched a fist at the air – "break out, acting the clown with a kind of genius. Anything! Girlish, Jewish, Yorkshire bumpkin, anything at all. Made *them* act too, fantastic roles of his own invention. Extraordinary!"

Morpurgo had a vision of himself being made to act the clown by an outwardly shy yet mocking-eyed man he had never even met. He was in pursuit of a Proteus.

"I suppose there was a school drama society?"

"Oh yes. To be or not to be! Some of the time he wasn't. More or less bullied into acting the first time, sick, almost literally, until the curtain went up but then . . ." Haystock held up his hands, miming amazement. "Brilliant! Over the top, perhaps, but brilliant."

"He actually played Hamlet? Is that what Mrs Haystock meant?"

"Oh, lord, no! End-of-term entertainment, just the soliloquy. Extraordinary! Over the top, but extraordinary. Just as if the boy were thinking it out for himself."

"What did he read when he went up to Oxford? English?"

Caught in a distraught look towards the house, Haystock came back with a start. "No. That was the point. Baxter, senior English, ran the drama group, took it for granted the boy would read English, convinced the stage had lost a budding genius when he switched. Though one did hear that when he went up . . ." His gaze drifted back toward the ominously silent kitchen.

"Trinity." The first college that came into Morpurgo's head.

"Wadham," Haystock corrected automatically. "Ability? Bursting with it. Question was, what would he do with it? My own theory, still believe it, question of influence."

He had lost Morpurgo. "I'm sorry. Whose influence?"

"Exactly! Whose influence! Well now, who was the showman? Donne, modern languages. *And* who had the pretty daughter? Donne again, young Serena, lust object for every boy whose voice had broken. Gave promise of pneumatic bliss, young Serena. And Donne gave out-of-hours tutorials for promising young linguists."

"Aske switched to languages because he was in love with the language master's daughter?"

"Might have been, I suppose. She went to Oxford in the same year, art at the Ruskin; no real talent, mind. Not what I meant, though. The lad was extraordinarily susceptible to influence: fancied I'd snared him myself at one stage. But Donne – bit of an exhibitionist, between ourselves – was the chap who captivated him at the crucial time. Charismatic. Worked on the susceptible like a snake charmer.

"So what did the boy do? Chuck up English, go for German and French. Got his Oxford entry on modern languages. Poor Baxter was convinced he'd ruined his career."

"You were saying something about his time at Oxford."

"Was I?" Haystock managed to retrieve his mind from Ellie and the kitchen. "Ah! Yes! There was the Shylock furore, of course, but then one heard that after his finals he went on to . . ."

The reminiscences ended abruptly. Ellie Haystock reappeared with a loaded tray. "Sorry, chaps. Another bish from Ellie, dropped half the china. Cheap Spanish muck, thank Gawd, plenty more where that came from."

"Three or four months a year abroad," Haystock said distractedly. "See the caravan? Yes. Spain, Portugal. France getting a trifle pricey now." Ellie Haystock was descending to the terrace.

He got up just too late. She put a foot out like some ancient Naiad testing the water, lost her balance, and pitched forward with a loud hoot of dismay.

Making a brief, indescribable sound, Haystock reached her in two or three strides, but not to help. In an ecstasy of rage he began kicking out at cups, saucers, broken and whole, while Ellie threshed and snorted in spilled milk and coffee.

"Idiot woman!" Haystock lashed out at the teapot, missed, scattered the shards of a cup. "Stupid idiot woman!" His foot connected with the milk jug. It arced toward Morpurgo, struck a leg of the table, spawned china meteorites. Haystock was hopping with fury. "Fool! Clumsy, drunken, idiot fool!"

Morpurgo went to help, dismally aware that he would have preferred to slip quietly away; determined to do so, quietly or otherwise, as soon as he had got Ellie Haystock back on her large and uncontrollable feet.

Somewhat later, Haystock, still blotched red and white, made a token attempt to see him off. "My dear chap, what can I say? Unforgivable lapse. Pressures. Are you a married man? Yes. Pressure sometimes becomes too much, you know, especially in retirement. Can't live with, can't live without."

He found a focus for barely controlled emotions. "Damn fool headmaster! Used to call Ellie and me Baucis and Philemon, farewell speech about Mr and Mrs Chips. Didn't know there were times when I could have committed murder, Ellie, boys, whole damn school. Young Aske wasn't the only one with a talent for acting."

He fumbled Morpurgo's arm in clumsy anguish. "It passes. Don't know what I'd do without the old thing, wouldn't have you think otherwise."

\*       \*       \*

In the stage door office the girl on the swivel chair was expecting him, or almost.

"Morpurgo? Oh, Sylvie Markham's husband, sorry. They're in the rehearsal room. Hang on. Gerry'll show you." She signalled a passing technician.

"Gerry, take this gentleman through to the rehearsal room, will you? Ta!" She smiled at Morpurgo perkily from her swivel chair. "There you go." He went meekly, Sylvie Markham's husband, couldn't live without.

There was no glamour beyond the stage door, no glamour in the rehearsal room, only a scatter of chairs and benches, a wooden throne, gilt faded and chipped, over which someone had tossed a faded crimson cloak. Extractor fans whispered. Exposed ducts ran across one high wall. Circular skylights and a scatter of fluorescents far above emphasised size, emptiness, dead space.

At one end, where a double staircase climbed to a balcony and a hanging drape, were two men and two women. The only one of them not in jeans and sweater was Sylvie.

One of the men, beard and steel-rimmed glasses, squatting a little apart, turned to see who had come in. The other pair faced each other, the man slight, lithe, dark, the woman a little younger than Sylvie, with a shock of tawny hair and a face that occupied the middle ground between attractiveness and beauty.

Sylvie, armed with a camera, said something to the crouching man. He nodded. "Grab a pew, Mr Markham. Shan't be long." Sylvie smiled apologetically. He took himself well out of the way.

"Right," said the bearded man. "Let's try again, from 'O Hamlet.' Okay, Lotta? Get this right and we'll take a break."

"All right," said the woman with the lion's mane. "But I'm still not happy. The emotion. I'm not happy about the bloody emotion, Hugh."

Hugh sank to the grubby floor. "Look, love, I'm not asking you to play it like Sarah. I mean I'm not asking you to be Sarah. I want you to be you, Lotta, right? But Lotta as Gertrude. I mean we can't change the whole bloody emphasis or we'll end up rewriting *Hamlet*."

"I know that, for God's sake," Lotta said while Morpurgo tried to remember whether her name should mean anything to him. "I don't want to change the emphasis. But Sarah plays her more" – she snapped her fingers, seeking a word – "fearfully, yes, fearfully, than I feel it. Okay, I'm Hamlet's mum, old enough to know better, and I'm shacked up with his uncle. Sarah plays it as if she knows it's outrageous. All right, that's the way she feels it. I don't feel that. Wrong, but not outrageous, and I don't want to be reminded, right? The old bugger's giving me a good time, first decent bit of bed I've had for ages, probably sick of my first old man anyway. Life's started all over again, but now this creep" –

she patted the cheek of the dark young man – "only has to show his puky face to make it plain he thinks I didn't ought to do it."

They were laughing now, while Sylvie, unobtrusive and intent, circled with no more sound than the zip-click of her camera.

Lotta was laughing too, but unwilling to yield. "Wo' I mean *is*" – she switched to the South Londonese of Morpurgo's home ground – "he's gettin' to me, see? Gettin' on me wick. Sarah begins to worry about her immortal soul. I don't give a tinker's about me immortal soul. It's me body that matters, on account it's having some fun for the first time in years, right? So I don't want no snotty-nosed kid I'd like to think I wasn't old enough to be mum to forever remindin' me I didn't ought to be at it, okay, Hugh?"

Hugh held up his hands in mock despair. "I don't know, but let's try it both ways, then we'll see. Now, first time, Sarah's way. You're not the brightest woman that ever queened around, but after the play within the play, even you might have begun to wonder exactly what *kind* of snake it was that did for your old man in the orchard."

"Well, if I have, I'm not exactly busting to know the answer," Lotta said. "Especially from this wimp," and she gave Hamlet a hearty shove.

Morpurgo found himself faintly shocked at the levity of the thing, not at all the way he had imagined Shakespeare being rehearsed. It occurred to him that he had never thought much about how any play was rehearsed.

"You'd rather not know," Hugh was saying, "because once you know, you're doubly damned. Marriage of brother-in-law and widow was as much incest in those days as anything you lap up in the *News of the World* today, and incest was a mortal sin. Okay, let's try it. 'O Hamlet . . .' "

Lotta bowed her head briefly, then began.

> "O Hamlet, speak no more:
> Thou turnst my eyes into my very soul;
> And there I see such black and grained spots
> As will not leave their tint."

They played it as far as Hamlet's accusation that the new king had stolen the crown. Lotta's hands flew to her ears, her voice lifted and when she cried " 'No more!' " the sound was pure terror.

The two of them stopped. With mock complacency Lotta said, "Bit of all right, wonnit?" and in her own voice, "But not my style, Hugh love."

Hugh nodded. "All right. Now your way."

They played the scene again. This time Lotta as Gertrude was a woman moved by more complex feelings. Fear, certainly, but also a weakly desperate rage. And the rage itself was divided, part against the presumption of a son daring to speak of things not seen as his concern, part that of a woman compelled to listen to what she had conditioned herself not to hear.

For Morpurgo, denizen of a world in which emotion was a thing to be concealed, it was a kind of miracle that they could switch so swiftly and convincingly from persona to persona. If Simon Aske had the same facility . . .

Simon Aske, he reminded himself, did have the same facility.

Hugh looked at Hamlet. "Tim? Did that Gertrude feel right?"

"Yes, I think it did. I think Lotta's got something."

"Lotta, you really feel that's it?"

"Of course I think that's it," she said. "That's why I did it. Bloody men, asking each other whether the way a woman plays a woman's part is right! Stuff the lot of you, that's what I say!"

Stroking his beard, Hugh rocked back and forth on his shabby trainers. "Let me think about it. From Hamlet's side. After all, the play's about Hamlet."

"No Gertrude," Lotta said, "no Hamlet. It's her world too."

Hugh started to speak but changed his mind. "Let's go and have a cuppa."

Sylvie came over. "Sorry, Johnny. It's your world too. Morpurgo in yours, Markham in mine. How were the Haystacks?"

"Straws in their hair," he said. "Tell you later." Lotta was coming across.

"This it, Sylv?" She looked at Morpurgo very directly, mingled mockery and sexual challenge.

"This is him," Sylvie corrected gently. "My old man. Johnny, you know Lotta Boyle."

He said, "No," an instinctive response to that look, though he was not actually sure whether or not he had heard of her.

He got no second chance. Her narrow, triangular face, eyes heavy-lidded, bones only just under the chin, the mouth thin and mobile, gave her a strange, almost fey appearance, but her laugh, real or feigned, was loud, husky, close to raucous.

"Too-shay!" She tucked her arm in his, drawing him after the others. "Fly with me to the greenroom. What's he do, Sylv?"

"Civil servant." Sylvie unslung the Nikon and scooped up her camera bag as they passed it. "Sort of. Corridors of power." They emerged backstage and turned towards the river.

"I like it!" Lotta shook his arm provocatively. "You the glam, him the grind, way it bloody should be." She smiled at him. "Don't mind us, sweety, we're not people, not really, just bloody *ac*-tors."

She brought three teas in plastic cups to a table in the corner and settled herself heavily against Morpurgo. "Well? Tell. What do you do in the corridors of power? Peek through the keyholes?" She laughed delightedly. "I'm right, aren't I, Sylv? A nark! He's a nark, man in a man's world, written all over his guilty face."

He said, "FCO, Foreign and Commonwealth. Just up for the ride."

"Oooooh!" she said. "Foreign *and* Commonwealth! You must be in the common bit. Not foreign, is he, Sylv?"

He said, "Don't you even take a break in the break?" Meant to float like a soufflé, it fell like soggy dough.

She brought her face close to his. She had jade green eyes. "*Ac*-tor, daahling. Actors act. Actors always act."

He got a grip on himself. "Really? Always?"

"Always." Her face was still very close. He could smell her spicy perfume. He felt about seventeen years old, all hands and shuffle.

She said, "What else would we do, sweety? No real identity of our own, everyone else's tucked away in our little insides. That's acting."

"Of course." He smiled. "Silly of me. Must be a bit like being the vacuum nature's supposed to abhor."

"Hm," she said, "not sure I like that. *Cet animal est méchant. Quand on l'attaque, il se défend.*" She sipped tea, still studying him. No mock Cockney, purest patrician Shires, she said, "I've got your number, Markham my boy. Foreign Office? Hmmmm, maybe, but still, oh, still a nark."

Sylvie, trying not to laugh, said, "His name's Morpurgo, actually. So's mine." She gave Morpurgo's wrist a squeeze.

# SEVENTEEN

Of course he was prejudiced against Oxford. The London School of Economics had virtually run courses in prejudice against Oxford, with Cambridge as an optional extra. Two years in Century House had qualified him for his master's degree.

Edmund Dukinfield; there was a name for an Oxford don! A man, said his prejudice as he cruised North Oxford through tree-lined streets rich in the domestic architecture of Victorian certitude, who would probably read Montaigne in the French, Goethe in the German, do the *Times* crossword in five minutes. He would have silver for his Queen Anne table, a cellar lined with *crus bourgeois* and *petits châteaux*.

He would, in short, be close kin to a great many aloof and clever people at Century House, and politely patronising to John Morpurgo.

The house was big, red brick with stone facings, a vast bay window of crimson and buff behind a privet hedge, a monkey puzzle tree, funereal clumps of mauve Michaelmas daisies. Dukinfield had the ground floor.

"Mr Morpurgo? Pray come in. Unexpectedly felicitous to find someone with an old-fashioned regard for punctuality."

Here we go! thought Morpurgo.

Sixtyish, which would make Dukinfield relatively young when Aske was up. A tall, thin man with a cold, dry hand, a light dry voice hovering on the brink of petulance. Hair pewter, an El Greco elongation of the face, mouth thin-lipped, waspish, eyes black and agnostic.

Overall, Morpurgo decided, no pushover.

Following Dukinfield down a corridor with prints of old

Oxford, he noted another idiosyncrasy. The man loped, steps exaggeratedly long, arms a little spread, as if picking his way over widely spaced stepping stones. The hint of caricature bolstered Morpurgo's confidence.

The room was equally reassuring: decent taste but nothing dauntingly old or valuable, a plentiful furnishing of books, little in the way of gilt or leather bindings.

"Sorry about the higgle." The apology was perfunctory. Dukinfield removed a stack of books from a chair upholstered in faded green velveteen. "Pray be seated." There was no self-mockery in the repeated use of the archaism.

"Positive vetting, you said. Intriguing. What has the gentleman been up to, or mayn't one enquire?"

"Oh, he hasn't been up to anything. These things are a matter of routine nowadays." Would it be too much to think that Dukinfield was disappointed?

"I see. Ye-e-es." The word slid down a slow cadence of conjecture. "Twenty years and more. Isn't that excessively positive?"

"Exhaustive. Not excessive."

"The changing times." Dukinfield was lofty now. "Aske, a Foreign Office panjandrum. Well, well!" His every word was articulated with the absolute precision of an elocutionist.

"Oh," Morpurgo said, "hardly a panjandrum."

Dukinfield stretched out long shanks. He had socks of pale blue silk that matched his high-necked sweater. "How's Spencer? Still in the business? Perhaps he sent you here?"

As a hook with which to fish for information it was triple-barbed. Make a connection, appear to be knowing, attempt a social and professional put-down.

"Positive vetting," Morpurgo said equably, "has to be repeated every so many years. They send someone with no previous knowledge."

"Delightfully ambiguous. And doubtless intended to be." Dukinfield's slender fingers strummed on the arm of his chair.

Morpurgo, smiling politely, thought: Damn right! He had no idea who or what Spencer was, but had every intention of finding out. "You surely don't remember all your students?"

"Tutees," Dukinfield corrected. "Horrid word. Horrid creatures sometimes." The squeezed smile had become a fixture. He would love to know, Morpurgo concluded, how much I already know; but about what?

153

"Twenty years," Dukinfield said. "More. Nearer twenty-five. But you, no doubt, thought, reclusive Oxford don, a quarter of a century no more than the day before yesterday."

He patted his pewter hair. " 'Men of great learning, fruitful to the church of God and – ha! – to the king and realm.' "

The smile, acid, puckered his lips. "Pray tell that to the present breed of young gentlemen *in statu pupillari*." Pick up a smattering of Latin on this job, if nothing else, Morpurgo thought.

"Next to a determination to speak English," Dukinfield was saying. "in such a way as to suggest that his most urgent need is a prolonged course of remedial speech therapy, the contemporary tutee seeks nothing better than an opportunity to demonstrate his contempt for the tutor to whom he – I suppose I am also obliged to say she – must defer before being bundled out to hawk a miserable talent in the marketplace."

His predatory nose lifted as if to strike. "Therefore why me, pray? Indeed, why this college? Why not St Antony's?"

First Spencer, now St Antony's. He should not forget that, at Oxford, unrevealing façades concealed a quantity of classy brain-power.

St Antony's, a post-graduate college with a reputation in the field of Eastern European languages and political studies. More to the point, a favourite SIS recruiting ground. Dukinfield had all but trapped him, yet instinct told him it was less deliberate than an arrogant mind attempting to impose itself on a perceived inferior.

"No previous knowledge!" Dukinfield's smile was sharp as sliced lemon. "To the extent of failing to inform yourself that Aske went on to St Antony's. I fancy I prefer my terminology to yours. Excessively positive vetting."

He might, Morpurgo saw, have to lean on Edmund Dukinfield. "You were his tutor during a crucial period. St Antony's comes later."

"Crucial?"

"Formative." Why so sharp a response?

"Ah." The man was undoubtedly suspicious. "You are not aware that my becoming Aske's tutor was in a sense fortuitous?" Not only an elocutionist, but pedantically perfectionist in his use of the language.

"Let's assume that I'm aware of nothing, Dr Dukinfield."

"Then one must assume your unawareness of the fact that Slavonics was not Aske's first choice?"

"Let's assume that I'm not even sure what Aske's subjects were."

"Really! Might one, pray, enquire just how much you do know?"

"What were Aske's subjects, Dr Dukinfield?"

"He came up on modern languages, German and French. Being" – he hesitated – "an impressionable young man, he switched after the Michaelmas term to German and Slavonics." A deliberate hesitation, more of a challenge.

"What had being impressionable to do with it?" Hadn't Haystock said something similar about Aske's switching from English to languages?

Dukinfield stroked his hair once more in token of a small victory. "He formed an attachment. A young research student who introduced him to the delights" – the smile was briefly lascivious – "of Slav culture. The girl departed. The attachment remained."

"To Slavonics?" Two girls in the young Aske's life so far. The tentative homosexuality was crumbling a little.

"German and Slavonics. You are a linguist, Mr Morpurgo?"

"Not really."

It was the answer Dukinfield had hoped for. "Germanic and Latin-based tongues are relatively easy for the English student with an aptitude. Slavonics present difficulties. You have my word for it. They are – you won't wish me to assume that you knew this – my subject. For an Englishman, his tongue part Latin, part Germanic, they are, one might say, another world."

"Which Aske conquered?"

"One is obliged to suppose," Dukinfield said grudgingly, "that the boy would have obtained his first in Chinese had the girl been from Peking."

So Simon Aske had got a first. "He had an aptitude?"

"It must be conceded." With extreme reluctance. "Aske was a brilliant linguist. No doubt that was why Spencer recruited him."

Morpurgo sat silent.

Dukinfield's hand went again to his hair, lingering there while he looked at Morpurgo past the crook of his elbow. "Trotsky," he began, and stopped, the small smile spiteful. "In such circles as yours, *persona non grata*, doubtless, but if I may?"

Morpurgo gestured assent. So he reads Trotsky in the original Russian. Well, sod him!

"Trotsky said, in free translation, 'Don't give me facts. Give me the laws that govern them.' I incline to subscribe."

Morpurgo cocked his head.

Dukinfield's eyelids fluttered. "As one understood from Spencer, positive vetting is substantially concerned with things other than fact. Impressions? Nuances?"

"Dirt." Morpurgo was beginning to weary of Dr Edmund Dukinfield.

The eyelids fluttered again. "Wheat and chaff." He pronounced it "charff", aspirating "wheat" strongly. "To be personal" – the hand revisited the head – "is to run the risk of being suspected of . . . malice?"

Morpurgo's indeterminate gesture sufficed. "This is most distasteful." Dukinfield's tongue moistened his lips with relish.

"One's tutees. Some, contemptuous of guile, simply, as it were, turn down the volume of their ego for the benefit of the unworldly academic. Some, no personality worthy of the name, grey little learning machines. Most, two facets, one for the pedagogue, the other for their peers."

He waited for Morpurgo to enquire Aske's category. Morpurgo, beginning to enjoy himself after all, did not.

"Into which category," Dukinfield said after a deep breath, "did Aske fall? Answer: all." A lesson learned, he skipped the opportunity of a pause for effect. "Each and every variation. According to" – another heavy aspiration – "whim."

English, Morpurgo thought, as she is spoke by the fussy purist. He had the dawnings of a suspicion.

"According to mood," Dukinfield said. "Or what kind of fool he took one to be."

'Other chaps,' Haystock had said, 'think he's acting the fool. Really making fools of them.'

"Was Aske moody?"

Dukinfield said a word.

Morpurgo frowned. "Sorry?"

Dukinfield said it again. "*Litost.*" His eyes glowed.

Morpurgo, having learned from Sylvie, said, "Translation, please."

"*Litost.*" He was noticeably more assured.

"That's some kind of Slavonic?"

"Czech." Tutor cutting tutee down to size.

"Could you explain?"

Dukinfield's hand swept his hair with restored confidence. "Translate? Impossible. Explain? Well, perhaps. There is no

156

equivalent in English."

He was sleek now, the proper order of things re-established.

"*Litost.* A despair, even anguish, that comes when one glimpses, receives, unexpected evidence of one's own basic inadequacy." He clearly saw it as something happening only to others. "It applies most particularly to people who have an overwhelming" – heavy aspirate – "need to be admired. No, adored. A need for totally uncritical love, let us say. So long as one has it, one is indescribably happy, because it is the proof of one's perfection. If one is perfect, unhappiness is naturally precluded."

He saw his command of English as a proof of his perfection.

"The instant," Dukinfield said, "that uncritical love is withdrawn, one's perfection is destroyed. The ground opens up. One sees into the abyss."

*If you gaze long enough into the abyss . . .*

"Tell me, pray, do I make myself plain?"

"No." It was true. It was also calculated to please, which it did.

"No." The hair was caressed. "Your reaction is adult and mature. Not all adults are mature. And the young . . ."

"Aske was immature for his age?" From the photographs, he had had the impression of a man old when still young.

"Simon Aske" – was Dukinfield coming finally to his point? – "had the knack of matching himself to the opinions he wished others to hold of him."

An elaborately oblique way of saying that Aske was not to be trusted.

"Set out his stall to please?"

"And conversely, to affront those who gave him a sense of his own inferiority."

Guess who!

"It is," Dukinfield said, "a serious weakness of character. In my view. It quite outweighs academic ability. I said as much," he added pettishly, "to Spencer."

"I'm still not sure I get the *litost* bit." He got it as a fancy way of suggesting untrustworthiness, emotional instability.

"There were some" – Dukinfield had drawn himself up like a vindictive old woman; he *was* a vindictive old woman, Morpurgo decided – "who were not deceived. Unwilling to remain silent or uncritically admiring."

Guess who!

"The effect on Aske? Ah, there's the point! The brilliant Simon

Aske, not wholly admirable? Not perfect, after all? Oh, unthinkable! Despair! Anguish! *Litost*. But *litost* has its aftermath, Morpurgo." So he was plain Morpurgo now. "First the despair. Then the urge to revenge oneself. To humiliate those who have brought about one's own humiliation."

He looked slyly at Morpurgo. "It is, of course, for experts to interpret these things in terms of character."

Morpurgo's dislike had become a bad taste in his mouth. By inference, one exhibitionist, Dukinfield, had been upstaged by another, Aske, who had then rubbed salt in the wounds by going on to achieve first class honours.

Dukinfield had tried and failed to blacken Aske in the course of one positive vetting; Spencer's. He saw Morpurgo as an intellectual inferior with whom he might be more successful.

Stripped of the flimflam, this was character assassination pure and simple. Yet Aske *had* gone on to get a first. And the unknown Spencer *had* recruited him. He would pass the entire matter of Spencer and St Antony's over to Epworth.

But Dukinfield's was only one side of the story. Was he right in suspecting that something less obvious than Aske's academic success, something more personal, was the cause of Dukinfield's abiding rancour?

"Aske was obviously a bit of a performer. Was it just his general behaviour, or did he take it farther? I mean, acting, for example?"

"Is one to continue to assume ignorance?" Dukinfield's fingers had stopped their self-satisfied strumming.

"Beyond what I've learned so far. You've been most helpful."

"The boy was an exhibitionist. Pray forgive me if I do not display any enthusiasm."

"But did he act? I mean, drama?" Wasn't there some kind of university theatre? He should have thought of that earlier.

"He acted," Dukinfield said. For the first time he looked at his watch. "The verb" – no easy flow of words now, more a disgorgement – "is, after all, open to a variety of definitions. You have an appointment at St Antony's? Pray forgive me, a question of our respective engagements."

"Not at present. Was Aske flamboyant?" The photographs firmly in mind, he had a strong instinct to lead Dukinfield on. Exhibitionism, possibly. Flamboyance, no.

"I myself" – Dukinfield was increasingly restless – "have a luncheon engagement. The boy occasionally rose to flamboyance. You may recollect my saying that I find this kind of thing distasteful. I hope I may be considered to have fulfilled my obligations as a public-spirited citizen."

The opening appeared. Experience took Morpurgo through it. "I imagine you make frequent visits to Eastern Europe, Dr Dukinfield?"

"In that" – there was an underlying tautness now – "I cannot assume your ignorance. In view of your Foreign Office connections, that is. I am a British citizen, but my subject is Slavonics. My visits are professional, academic, and of course, officially documented."

Things came together. That overbearing perfection of language and diction. "Yes, of course. Your date of naturalisation. . . ?"

"What has this to do with Aske?"

Bull's-eye. "I'm sorry. Nothing, really." Be apologetic, but keep the man off-balance. "We were talking about Aske's acting ability."

Dukinfield brushed that aside, giveaway spots of colour in his cheeks. "The details of my naturalisation are a matter of record. Which you will not expect me to believe you have not seen."

Biting off words, he said, "I have been in this country since the forties, but this kind of interrogation can still stir up unpleasant recollections." In view of his willingness to slander Aske, that took some swallowing.

"It is something the British are singularly slow in grasping. Those of Jewish descent . . ." His animosity had now been divided between Aske and Morpurgo.

Skilled interrogation being part science, part art and part – a small but vital part – pure instinct, Morpurgo said, without prior thought, "Did Aske make fun of you? I mean, as a refugee or something?"

The latent fury emerged, shrivelling that hitherto confident voice. "You knew. You were aware when you came." Rage had seized Dukinfield like rigor mortis. "You and Spencer, putting your heads together. No previous knowledge!"

He stood up abruptly. "Pray allow me to see you out. Do what you will. I retract nothing. Not one word. The man is malevolent. Evil behind a mask of meekness.

"Small wonder," he said at the door, and flecks of spittle flew, "national security is so frequent a source of scandal. None is safe. All are maligned. The Nazis were no worse. Jewry as the butt of mockery is Jewry still only one step removed from the death camp and extermination." The door slammed.

Arriving at his car, Morpurgo experienced a small annoyance.

"This your vehicle, sir?" The motorcycle policeman was young, burly, with a mechanical politeness that might have been issued with his machine.

"Yes. Anything wrong?"

The man put his weight against the car and heaved. It moved. "Handbrake not set, or brakes faulty. Offence under the Road Traffic Act, sir."

He could produce his pass and clear himself at once, but the PC might put in a report. It might make ripples.

"I'm sorry, officer. I could have sworn I'd put the brake on."

"See your driving licence and insurance, please, sir." The PC had not been issued with a smile. "Have to make a report, sir. Up to the super to decide whether to prosecute. Have those brakes checked, sir, if I was you." All for momentary forgetfulness due, undoubtedly, to preoccupation. An older and less zealous officer would have dismissed the business with a caution.

He drove off towards the hunch which had been the unwitting parting gift of Dr Edmund Dukinfield, naturalised British citizen of Middle European Jewish origin, permanently scarred.

*     *     *

Walking into the Playhouse from the Regency urbanity of Beaumont Street, he was met by a small, dark, friendly girl with a gipsy skirt, a gamine look and a certifiably infectious smile.

"Mr Morpurgo. Anita Parry, Mr Haley's assistant, we spoke on the phone. Would you like to come up?"

Sylvie moved among such types as theatre directors. Morpurgo's own fuzzy image was of someone with a personality twice as big as Lotta Boyle's. Peter Haley was, if anything, less outgoing than Morpurgo, a man who would have slotted comfortably into a seminar of middle-range business executives once they had abandoned their three-piece deskwear for a not too wild evening in the bar. About forty, with close-cropped, straw-coloured hair and the hollow cheeks of the vocational zealot, his quiet voice annihilated the preconception.

"It's very good of you to see me at such short notice."

"Yes, it is." Haley's smile took away the sting.

Waving Morpurgo to a sofa he returned to a glass-topped, sub-Bauhaus desk with a litter of papers and a fountain of decorative ivy in a pot. The room, Georgian elegance fallen upon hard times, had two tall windows with wrought-iron balconies and a mini-Adam fireplace before which a *Monstera deliciosa* posed skimpily. Flaking walls were patched with theatrical prints.

"I didn't know the Foreign Office had a research department."

"It covers a multitude of sins."

"Like a posh set and a slick production. Any sin in particular?" There was a sharp mind behind the soft voice.

"We hope not. We have to find out."

"I see." Haley waited. More overpowering personalities than Morpurgo's had occupied the worn sofa.

"Bloke recommended for a rather important post," Morpurgo said. "We have to dig deep."

"Obviously. The sixties are a long time ago."

"The early sixties. He was a member of the university dramatic society."

Haley took a file from a drawer. "Does he lose the job if he got bad reviews? Before my time, like most things except the problem of paying the bills. The Foreign Office wouldn't happen to have a spare quarter of a million?"

"Banker's draft? Or used oncers?" They both laughed. Haley came to sit with him. The atmosphere kicked off its shoes.

"It's not the reviews," Morpurgo said. "More the people he knocked around with. You get a different story from the academics."

"I'm sure." The file had been thumbed through many times before. " 'Aske, with an *e*,' I think you said. You're sure he was a member of OUDS?" He smiled. "Ow, oh, ooh, take your pick."

"Not sure of anything. I'm just the one who has to get on with it."

Another smile. "Sounds familiar. And he appeared here at the Playhouse." Haley was running a finger down a page. "Beginning of the sixties."

"Late fifties, early sixties, I think."

"When we've checked, we'll look at the programmes. Did he claim to be any good?"

Morpurgo shrugged.

Haley smiled once more. "Don't tell you much, do they? OUDS people tend to be like the little girl who had a little curl."

"When they're good, they're very very good, and when they're bad they're horrid."

"Occasionally," Haley said, "they can make you squirm. Are you much into theatre?"

"I go occasionally. Never have much time."

"Mr Average Bum-on-seat. Well, if he was keen, he'd try out in his first term. Show promise and he'd be in the next major, anything from spear-carrier up."

He pointed at a page. "Say he came up in '59. He could have been in *Measure for Measure*, February of the following year. After that . . ." – he continued down the list – "'60, *The Devil's Disciple*, three or four goodish parts for an up-and-comer. Then *Henry IV*, Pirandello, not the Bard. In '62, *The Merchant*. After that . . ."

"*The Merchant of Venice*" – hadn't Haystock said something, by God! about a Shylock scandal? – "rings a bell."

"Does it, now?" Haley gave him a dry glance. "Take a squint at the programmes, shall we?"

They went back into Anita's office. She put down the phone. "Can I help, curse you?"

"Anita," Haley said, "is the one who runs this place; reign of terror. Please may we look at the programmes, please, please?" He took some of a set of bound volumes, Oxford blue.

"You bring 'em back," she said, "or I'll have your guts for garters."

Back on the sofa, Haley opened one of the volumes and riffled through pages of local advertising. "Suppose we said a mere hundred thousand? The Foreign Office wouldn't even miss it."

"Gold sovereigns," Morpurgo promised. "Chamois leather bag, Queen's Messenger."

"Sixty-two, then," Haley said, "since you fancy *The Merchant*." He found the first page. The producer, Morpurgo saw, was now a National Theatre luminary. He saw something else: Designed by Serena Donne.

Aske's first love? Came up the same year as Aske himself. It was like an archeological dig, another set of bones. He needed more; every last artefact, coin, shard.

Haley whistled softly, his first real sign of interest. "Some bell!"

Morpurgo bent to look.

"You said *The Merchant* rang a bell." At the tip of Haley's finger, Simon Aske . . . Shylock himself. In Morpurgo's mind shards began to piece themselves together.

Haley was looking at him thoughtfully. "As I said, before my time. But Anita . . ." He raised his voice. "Anita, spare a minute?"

"Not even a second"; but she came. He showed her the cast

list. "Oh yes," she said, *"quite* a vintage year. Peter's on telly more often than Kellogg's. Tom directing faster than people can write. Lotta twinkling away at Stratford and – "

"Whoa!" Morpurgo took the programme back. "Lotta? Lotta Boyle?"

"Charlotte Leveson-Boyle in those days." Anita put on a very superior voice. "Leveson pronounced as Lewson." She giggled. "You can see why she changed it. And Simon Aske, well, that was one of your ackshull causes celebree, wonnit?"

Peter Hayley spread his hands comically. "If she says so."

"S'right." She struck a pose. "Face like a Muppet, can't act for little pink pigs, but soon as I left school, round here, gissa job, gissa job. Anything! Programmes in the foyer, icecream in the interval, scrub the loo floors, don't care, just gissa job."

"And look," Haley said, "at her now. What *cause célèbre*, child?"

"Him. Aske. 'The Acting Leave Hoo-hah' or 'Shylock's Revenge'."

Haley sat back, mouth shaped to an "O-o-h" that never came. "Of course!"

"Aske," Anita said inevitably, "and it shall be given you. Will there be anything else I should bloody well hope not?" She went.

"Well!" Hayley's voice was very dry now. "Once upon a time . . ." He stopped. "I suppose you want it in detail?"

"Please."

"In that case" – he tapped his watch – "Anita, the *Oxford Mail, Oxford Times, Cherwell* . . ." He patted Morpurgo's arm placatorily. "Opening tonight, the bal*lay*, more temperament than a hairdressers' convention. Come down and find me before you leave."

"You just threw away a quarter of a million."

"Five quid," Haley said as he left, "would buy you the two-legged know-all. Anita!"

She reappeared. *"Wottt!"*

"Show the gentleman the OUDS archives."

"The archives," she said. "Ha-ha! The ha-bloody archives-ha! Take you all of two minutes."

It was an attic: bits of tinsel and streamers like dead flowers on a grave, a dusty jumble of box files, cardboard packing cases and cobwebs.

"Your average OUD" – Anita prepared to abandon him – "is up for three years. Chief motivation, if it has one, a belief that the stagedoor of the Playhouse opens on to Shaftesbury Avenue. It's

163

about as interested in archives as Eng. Lit. or whatever it pretends it came up for. If I were you, I'd go to the City Library."

Most of the boxes were full of trash, no rhyme, no reason. One held programmes for a fund raising production of *Dr Faustus*; lead role, Richard Burton, for God's sake! Another dusty ten minutes, slide and shuffle, poring through photo glossies. Then, Schliemann at Mycenae, a picture of Simon Aske.

A young Simon Aske, dinner-jacketed, first night party? In company with the cast? The cast of *The Merchant*? No way of telling, nothing on the back, not even a date. Anita had flattered the ow-oh archivists.

It was an Aske antic as a satyr. His eyes, brilliant with reflected flashlight, mocked. His mouth gaped like a comic mask. He had a glass in one hand, the other arm about a girl in evening dress as archaic as those distant days.

It was as if Aske had known, all those years back, that a man called Morpurgo would labour to find this picture, as if he had prerecorded some cryptically derisive message for Morpurgo's particular discomfort.

Back in her office, he showed Anita the picture. "Ho," she said, "haven't seen this 'un before. Your Master Aske, proper little bundle of mischief he looks, dunnee? As for the doxy, a roll in the hay while it was still green and growing, that's my guess, but who she is? Well, search me."

"Can I borrow it long enough to have it copied?"

"Swear on your mum's deathbed you'll let me have it back?"

"I swear." He surprised himself by saying it without a pang.

In the theatre, across a long perspective of empty seats, the stage was lit only by naked overhead bulbs. Three men and a girl, dressed in Oxfam rejects and leg-warmers, thumped through a workout while another man clapped his hands rhythmically.

"A one and *two* and a one-two-three. A one and *two* and bumpity-bumpity *bumm*." It was part of the strange new world he must somehow penetrate.

Haley materialised. "City Library's just at the top of pedestrian precinct. Hope you didn't think me rude."

"No," he said, "you've really been very helpful. I just wanted to say thank you."

"The Acting Leave Hoo-hah! Quite a story! What else might Master Aske do? Or" – Haley flickered his perceptive smile – "has he done it already?"

Morpurgo smiled his own smile and left. When he got back to his car, he had a parking ticket.

# EIGHTEEN

Sylvie was back. She had a visitor, as incongruous among her furnishings as Yorkshire pudding *chez* Bocuse.

"Now then," Trigg said. "How're you getting on? Don't look so surprised, lad. I'm just passing through."

"From where to where?"

"Is this official?" Trigg was at his most deadpan.

"Sorry. Call it polite interest."

"I don't mind letting on," Trigg said, "I'm a bit chary of your kind of polite interest, buttercup."

"How was Oxford?" He wondered what Sylvie had been discussing with Trigg.

"Interesting."

"Profitable?"

"You could say that too."

"Don't mind me," Trigg said. "Anyroad, I've a mind to get back where wind'll blow Whitehall out of my lungs."

"Whitehall?"

"Oxford?" Trigg winked at Sylvie. "Losing his grip, is this chap. Time was when he'd have known where I'd been, what I'd done and who I'd done it with."

He regarded Morpurgo benevolently. "Department of Industry, lad, that's what. It may surprise you to know that my lollies is highly regarded as a source of foreign currency. Every one that is licked by a foreigner makes a contribution to the balance of payments."

Morpurgo relaxed. "Your Austrian deal's going ahead, then?"

"Is *your* Austrian deal going ahead? Happen I might make you an offer you couldn't refuse."

Morpurgo laughed. "All right, make me an offer."

"Thinking of expanding overseas, that's what. Cleethorpes operations is flourishing, no lack of orders. But exports is another matter." He drank his tea at a gulp. "How'd you like to be our man in Europe?" He heaved himself out of his chair, lumbered across for his billycock hat.

"Are you serious?"

"I don't come down from Cleethorpes to London for fun," Trigg said scathingly. "Department of Trade might call it that, and I'd not blame them. They're not folk that looks as if they have much in the way of fun. Licking Trigg's lollies is fun, and meant to be. But making 'em? There's nought more serious than that."

He gave Sylvie a resounding kiss, clapped his hat on his round head and held out his hand to Morpurgo.

"Nought's settled for certain yet, but if me and yon fellers at Ministry can put things together in a manner satisfactory to both, happen there'd be an opening for a chap like you."

"And what," Morpurgo demanded afterwards, "was all that about?"

"Don't worry," Sylvie said. "He's not closing down in Cleethorpes, just thinking of setting up some sort of manufacturing subsidiary on the Continent. He brought you a bit of news."

"I brought *you* a bit of news. About an arrogant don."

"Do I want it?"

"Let me read you something. A review of Aske's performance as Shylock in *The Merchant*. I've got a fistful. I went to the Playhouse and then to the City Library. 'The Acting Leave Hoohah', or 'Shylock's Revenge'."

"I'll kill you."

"Listen first." He began to read one of his clippings.

" 'But what are we to say of Simon Aske's Shylock? In the past two seasons, notwithstanding eccentricities, we were tempted to think we were watching the hot forging of a major talent.

" 'Even allowing for events which, whatever their importance in the matter of relations between don and undergraduate, little concern this play, we were reasonably entitled to expect from Mr Aske, in his final year and one of Shakespeare's most controversial roles, something, in skill if not in years, by season seasoned to its right praise and true perfection. It was not to be.

" 'Is Shylock a good Jew wronged, or a bad Jew deservedly humbled? Is he bad because he is a Jew, or a Jew who happens to have vices by no means exclusive to his race? Does he behave as

166

he does because of what he is, or because, being what he is, that kind of behaviour is expected of him?

" 'Is he, in short, true to type, or true to type-cast?

" 'Mr Aske gave us no answers. In the five scenes which are all that Shakespeare permits his eponymous central character, he did indeed dominate the stage like a star. But it was a dark star, a cold star, all fire damped down, all fury inward turned. For the outside world – and this included both audience and his fellow players – nothing but aloof arrogance, complacent disdain.

" 'Who would have expected "If you prick us, do we not bleed?" to be delivered at a counting table, almost as a series of asides, by a man less interested in making out a case for his humanity than displaying an ability to score debating points and simultaneously tot up his ducats?

" 'Who could be comfortable with the feeling that any anti-semitism the play contains was being evoked less by a vengeful victim of race hatred than a Jewish Nazi intellectual, an SS ideologue in yarmulka and moneylender's fustian?

" 'Mr Aske loped the stage, replete with self-satisfied manner-isms, until the loss of ducats, daughter and, at the last, his perverted faith brought him – ' "

"Don't read any more," Sylvie said. "Remember? 'If the population of Israel were two hundred million, the rest of the world might be a concentration camp.' And I asked him if he was Jewish."

"Here." He handed over the rest of the reviews. "All more or less the same. Aske sent up Dukinfield. As a caricature it must have been brilliant. Cruel, but brilliant. As an interpretation it was obviously a disaster."

He gave her another small sheaf of photostats. "This is the story behind the story."

She set them aside. "Just tell me."

"Okay, you won't believe this, doesn't happen any more, but in those days you had to get your tutor's leave to be in a play."

"I can guess. Dukinfield refused it."

"Aske pulls this plum part. Dukinfield forbids him to accept. He had the right. And, on the face of it, a legitimate argument."

"Last year. Last term. Finals coming up. Doing plays when he should have been swotting."

"That was the reason Dukinfield gave."

"Personality clash, obviously, but something more, so get on with it."

"You can learn a lot from newspaper stories, but not every-thing. Did you know Lotta Boyle was at Oxford with Aske?"

"No," she said. "I do now. You want to go back to Stratford."

"She'll know the whole story, bound to. Do you think you could. . . ?"

She smiled. "I know. She frightened the life out of you, but you're a big boy. Ask her yourself. All right, Dukinfield refused Aske permission to take the part. Incredibly authoritarian, but he had the right, so where's the scandal?"

"Aske went to the Warden. That was *his* right. He told the Warden that Dukinfield had tried to talk him out of the part because it was antisemitic. When Aske said no, Dukinfield refused him acting leave. Aske said it was censorship, pure and simple, nothing to do with the welfare of the tutee."

He grinned. "Oxbridge don accused of intellectual dishonesty? Sodomy, okay. Intellectual dishonesty!" He sucked in his breath.

"Don't look so bloody pleased. LSE's lousy with bigots."

"Aske said – listen to this – he said, all right, Dukinfield was Jewish but so was he, and he had as much right as Dukinfield to decide whether the play was antisemitic or not."

"But you told me Peter Haystock said he only pretended to be Jewish. For laughs. And that school, evangelical Protestant."

"I know. Anyway, Aske leaked the whole story to the press. *The Times* had a third leader. So did the *Guardian*. And the bingo papers turned it into what Haley's assistant called a cause celebree, a chance to send up poncey academics in general and Oxford in particular."

"You'd have enjoyed that. Anyway, Dukinfield's not the only one who thinks *The Merchant* is antisemitic."

"From the way he played the part, you could argue that Aske thought so too. Which would make him as intellectually dis-honest as Dukinfield."

"He played the part, so he obviously won the argument."

"The Warden ruled in his favour. Bloody great smack in the face for Dukinfield. Then Aske turned in a performance everyone recognised immediately as a takeoff of Dukinfield, so . . . 'Shylock's Revenge'!"

"No wonder Dukinfield doesn't like him!"

"Couldn't wait to smear him. If he'd stopped to think, he'd have realised I was bound to get at the truth."

"Did Dukinfield say Aske was Jewish?"

"Didn't say he wasn't. Aske said he was, and it wasn't

challenged." He spread his hands. "Looks as though we were wrong. Anyway, I should be able to get the whole story from Lotta Boyle." He pulled a face of mock dismay at the prospect.

"I told you Eustace Roland brought you a bit of news too. Uncle Norman's heard of some old lady who knew the Askes way back. He's following it up. If there's ought to be snapped up, he'll let you know."

"Snapped oop? Aye, well, happen there will be, happen there won't. In the meantime, there's this cast photograph as well. Lotta's bound to know everyone. That should give me some more leads."

Going over to sit at the piano, he played a few bars, Schubert's Trout theme, but stopped as Sylvie put her hands on his shoulders.

"He's not what you think." She said it decisively.

"How on earth can you say that? He's an actor. He's whatever he wants you to think."

"I don't know. But I'm sure." She let her hands slip away. "Better not .waste time if you want to see Lotta. They're off on tour."

"So what? I mean, she won't be incommunicado on tour, will she?"

"Not if you're prepared to go a long way to talk. Warsaw, Budapest, Prague, Leipzig. A couple more I can't remember."

He swung round. "She was only just learning her part."

"Stepping in at very short notice. The first Gertrude's on the sick list. I can't remember the exact date they leave. You might check for me."

"Why?"

"Oh," she said in the same moment that he guessed the answer. "Can't do a year in the life of the RSC without taking in at least a part of an Iron Curtain tour, can I?"

"Any particular fancy?" His own voice sounded strange to him.

"No. Well, maybe. Dates permitting, I fancy Prague's the pick of the bunch. I mean photographically speaking."

*       *       *

The treffpunkt – Epworth had insisted on calling it that – was an old beech within sight of the Round Pond in Kensington Gardens. Dressed for jogging, moving at the steady pace he had maintained all the way from Chelsea, Morpurgo arrived from the

Kensington side, wondering how Epworth had come to know of the tree and the head-high cavity that made it a classic letter-box. Many a Sovbloc meet and drop had taken place in the park, where it was all but impossible for an SV team to operate in secrecy, and the tree was an easy walk from the Soviet embassy in Kensington Palace Gardens.

As it happened, secrecy hardly came into things.

The chalk-marked confirmation was there. Epworth was not. In his place, as Morpurgo made his approach, was Steve Archer.

He smiled pleasantly, hatless and spruce, his usual air of an English country gentleman come briefly to town. "Johnny, good morning. Beautiful day for jogging. Not dressed for it myself, so care for a stroll?"

No one nearby who could be from Five except that, these days, anyone and everyone could be from Five, including little old ladies and kids.

"Yes, of course," he said. "Why not?"

They headed towards the Round Pond, Steve as if he were on a tour of the family estate. Which, Morpurgo thought ruefully, in a sense he was.

"Three traffic offences in less than a week," Steve said. "Isn't that going it a bit?"

"Do you want to see my driving licence and insurance like everyone else?"

"Hardly necessary, old son. In fact you can forget the whole thing." They took another two paces before Steve said, "This once."

"Good of you. I must be slipping."

"Yes." They reached the path round the pond. "You must, mustn't you? Shall we sit? I rather enjoy watching the boats."

Sunlight and a strong breeze had strewn the water with diamonds. Two or three model sailing boats scudded bravely towards Lancaster Gate. Two or three more were in various kinds of trouble. A superbly detailed scale model of an ocean-going tug, radio-controlled, ploughed a straight course in the direction of Kensington Palace.

Morpurgo had worked with Steve Archer almost from the time he was transferred from SIS field operations, back in the middle sixties. Steve's relaxed pose was just that, a pose. The Director-General of Five did not normally break into a busy schedule to keep rendezvous in the park.

Steve pointed. "Going to rescue the ketch." The tug, speed

reduced, was nosing one of the shipwrecks skilfully towards the side of the lake.

So it was a ketch, not a yacht. Steve would know. Among his top-people watering holes was the Royal Thames Yacht Club. He crewed, Morpurgo remembered sourly, during Cowes Week; bloody great ocean racers that swept over the Solent as if they owned it.

He said, "Nice to know there're still some good Samaritans about." The tug was in the control of a man in a plain peaked cap of navy blue. He handled the control box with the kind of assurance Steve Archer normally used in handling people, so why had Steve, for all his seeming ease, a deep, fixed and telltale cleft between his eyes?

Steve pointed again. "You'll remember young Sibley?"

Morpurgo looked. Young Sibley, not quite so young after more than two years, occupied a seat not so far from theirs, carefully reading a newspaper. Sibley had been his favourite among the Curzon Street juniors in his Security Directorate days. After being corrupted – they were all corrupted sooner or later – he had helped to bring about Morpurgo's downfall at Five.

Considerably later, conscience-stricken, as well as disturbed by some of the things he was required to do to freedom on the pretext of defending it, he had been corrupted again, this time by Epworth. Steve Archer didn't know that one of his bright young up-and-comers was Epworth's man.

But then, Steve himself had been Fish's man in Security Directorate, Fish had been Langley's man in SIS, and John Morpurgo, trusting Steve as his deputy in K section, had simultaneously been bedding his wife.

He said, "Good lad, young Sibley. Fancy seeing him here."

"Small world, Johnny. Fancy seeing you here." Steve took his gold cigarette case from his pocket, looked at it, then put it away. The cleft above his nose had deepened. "Stratford, Oxford and deepest Wiltshire. You do seem to be getting around."

"Culture," Morpurgo said. "Well, not much culture in Wilts, but they do a good line in prehistory."

"Have you given thought to what might happen if it went beyond parking and speeding?"

"Car's paid for. Licensed till next May. Not due its first MOT test until next year. New front tyres last February, shocking bloody price these days." He was living dangerously.

"Nobody" – it was if Steve had cautioned himself to be on his best behaviour – "knows better than you, Johnny, just how bloody expensive life can be if you get on the wrong side of the law."

"Do you mean the law?" Morpurgo asked equally pleasantly. "Or what we do?"

"You're facing a profit-and-loss review. You know how they work. Picking your nose in public can be enough to tilt the balance."

Morpurgo watched one of the boats take a gust and flop sideways. Miniature breakers burst over its bright red sail. Symbolic? "Never in public," he said, "and privately, only in Oxford, Stratford and Wilts. The Branch should have told you."

"You know what I can do," Steve told the Round Pond. "Have you picked up and taken in. Keep you away from the lawyers. Have you strip-searched, humiliated. Hold you for four days without charge if the court approves, and I can make bloody sure the court approves. Have your house turned upside-down. Your mother's house turned upside-down, empty or not. Your mail intercepted. Sylvie's mail intercepted. I can – "

Morpurgo, scuffing the ground with the toe of his shoe, happened to kick Steve's ankle. "Sorry. Take me in on suspicion under the Act? Go ahead, Steve, why don't you?"

Steve laughed almost convincingly, further proof that he had learned new skills. "Worth a try, cock; didn't pin much faith on it. You're an awkward bugger, always were. Being Epworth's poodle won't save you. Take my advice. Lie low until things blow over. I'd sooner ride round you than through."

He laid a hand on Morpurgo's arm. "No tricks on my side, no disloyalty on yours. How well *do* you know friend Epworth?"

He gave the question time to sink in. It must, Morpurgo thought, be because he was spending so much time with the politicians these days.

"No catch," Steve said. "How well do you know him?" The thing was, it was a good question.

"Tell you this much." Steve's mouth quirked. "Print him out at Mount Street on one sheet of paper."

The Mount Street computer held an amazingly large number of official fiches on an amazingly wide variety of people, but none, naturally enough, on known SIS people. There was another list, officially non-existent in the way that unauthorised phone taps were officially non-existent. From his own past experience, Morpurgo knew that he himself would be on the unofficial list.

Now he wondered about Lawrence Epworth.

Steve pressed. "Hate to repeat myself, old son, but he took you over when nobody else would. Know any more about him now than you did then?"

He held up a hand, although Morpurgo had not been about to speak. "Don't expect you to comment. Just listen." The radio-controlled tug set off on another errand of mercy.

"People in our line don't exactly go around advertising themselves. Small world and a tight one, recommendation and recruitment by word of mouth, yes?"

Spencer, unknown, had recruited Aske. Who had recommended him?

"Chaps do talk, though, right place and right time, you know that."

Yes, Morpurgo thought, chaps do talk, Steve's kind of chap in Steve's kind of place which, as often as not, was the right kind of club or the right social occasion, pretty well guaranteed to include only the right chaps. John Morpurgo had never been the right kind of chap. He had no idea – Steve was right so far – whether Epworth was the right kind of chap.

"Doesn't mix," Steve said. "Nothing against that, of course, and not to be taken too literally."

Steve Archer and Epworth saw each other regularly at meetings of the Joint Security Committee, and probably on other, even more exclusive business. None of them were exactly social gatherings, but those who attended them, no more than a handful, relatively speaking, would meet elsewhere and on less formal occasions.

Was there a country where so much real power was concentrated in the hands of so few people? Or where those people moved in circles that were so few and so select? Did Epworth move in such circles? Or belong to the same kind of club as Steve Archer? Morpurgo had no idea.

"Private schools," Steve said. "Meaning not public," and Morpurgo wanted to laugh. Private meaning eccentric, he translated; not public in the sense that the public schools, though private, were open to anyone who had the background, the means and the correct attitude to privilege.

"Fancy private schools." Steve was barely able to conceal his distaste. "Free discipline, meaning no discipline, bunch of sandalled cranks running things as far as they're run at all. Subjects like ballet and transcendental codswallop. Did you

173

know his father was a Chinese bishop?"

"You don't," Morpurgo said, "mean that literally?"

"Anhwei." Archer either ignored the joke or failed to recognise it. "Doesn't exist any more, meaning the diocese if that's what they called them out there. Know anything about Anhwei?"

"It's in China."

"Capital's Nanking. Capital of China too, from the time the Japs invaded until Mao's gang kicked out the lawful government. Hotbed of Reds after the war."

He tapped Morpurgo's knee. "Bishop Epworth retired in '55. Word is that he was pushed; too sympathetic to the Reds."

"I didn't know that."

"Good many other things you don't know. Any idea how many languages brother Lawrence speaks?"

"No." He knew Epworth spoke good German, some Spanish. He remembered being depressed at the thought that Epworth might speak Czech, and saw what Archer might be driving at. He was a little shaken to realise that he had been subconsciously moving in the same direction himself.

"More than that," Archer said. "So the word goes. A man of talents, brother Lawrence. So far as one knows."

Steve Archer, also a man of talents, but absolutely not one of the intelligentsia, had a world view that had led him to paint himself into a great many curious corners, the paint always a bright primary red.

The man with the radio-controlled tug, surrounded by children of all ages, lifted it out of the water. Young Sibley turned the pages of his paper, looked at Archer, looked at Morpurgo, looked away.

Morpurgo said, "I don't suppose he'd have got where he is without some ability."

"Oh, agreed!" Archer said, "Absolutely! No question, none at all!"

It was like one of those children's puzzles, a scatter of numbered dots. Join them in sequence and they made a picture. Steve Archer had been joining dots.

"Something else I'd like you to ask yourself," Steve said. "Don't expect you to tell me what you think. If the Aske business produced a stink, who would stand to gain most?"

He got up, his shadow across Morpurgo's face. He looked at the tracksuit and trainers with a bleak contempt.

"Told you, Humphrey Fish happened to be a friend of mine,

174

served in Berlin together. Good bloke, one of the best, don't propose to have him smeared by a traitorous little mountebank like Aske. My advice to you, Johnny, do a bit of thinking, see which side your bread's buttered. Ride straight over you otherwise, see if I don't. Day to you."

He nodded and walked off.

Beyond him, Sibley, folding his paper, strolled over the grass in the direction of Bayswater, but he gave Morpurgo a jerk of the head.

The man in the naval-style cap was collecting his tugboat and radio control gear in some haste. Morpurgo smiled to himself. Steve had left behind a Trojan duck. But the duck, though not old enough to be his father, was certainly too old to jog.

Loping over the scuffed turf at a pace kind to his own years, he came back to an earlier conclusion. For some unknown reason, Steve hoped to scare off Epworth's poodle without using any force. Yet he had said some telling things.

Who, he had asked, stood to gain most if the Aske business went public? Sylvie had already answered that question. "If the Punch and Judy man gets what he wants, he'll be God Almighty, won't he?" Now why wasn't that comforting?

*       *       *

Epworth, driven by Prettyman in a taxi that never plied for hire, picked him up at Palace Gate. "Under the greenwood tree, who loves to lie to me?"

"Who blew the meet?"

"Young Sibley got wind of it. A very good lad, young Sibley."

"Meaning you blew it. Presumably to make Steve feel the heat."

" 'Come hither, come hither, come hither,' " Epworth carolled in his sweet soprano. " 'Here shall he see no enemy.' " They headed for the river.

"Did he," Epworth asked, "mmmm – sweat a little?"

"Outwardly, the perfect English gent, smiles, threats, sweet reason. Inwardly he sweated. Half a chance and he'd be sweating me."

"Half a chance," Epworth said discomfortingly, "and he may yet."

"Who's Spencer?" The trick with Epworth was to catch him on the hop.

"Spencer? Should one know?" Epworth's trick was never to hop.

175

"Since he apparently recruited Aske, it might help."

"Ah. *Ça commence*." Epworth closed his eyes.

"How many languages do you speak? As a matter of interest."

"It isn't. A matter of interest."

"Steve thinks it is. Do we still deal with St Antony's?"

The taxi crossed Albert Bridge, a series of sharp turns, a series of short streets, some of them one-way in the wrong direction. Epworth, eyes still closed, hummed *Under the Greenwood Tree*, eventually stopping long enough to say, "We?"

"Us. The firm."

"Just as well to be sure. It's a wise man, in our trade, who knows his own friends." They debouched near the stamping grounds of Morpurgo's youth. Prettyman, whose broad shoulders might well have developed in consequence of owning a name that invited comment, took them on a tour of Wandsworth backstreets. Morpurgo took Epworth on a tour from Wiltshire to Oxford and back.

The car came to rest in an old-established cemetery. Deciding to emerge from hibernation, Epworth looked out approvingly and then strolled away from the car to examine a particularly exuberant example of the Victorian stonemason's art. "Nothing to beat a vintage burial ground for peace and quiet. And such splendidly – mmmm – uninhibited lack of taste."

*"Take him among you, angels,"* he read out. *"For he is one of you. And pride of place within your ranks Accord him as his due. He fought the good fight in this life. The Tempter laid he low. Now grant him rest and grant him peace Until we join him too."*

He gazed at something less like an angel than winged victory. "Threatening, would you say, that last line? At all events" – he stooped to read further – "the peace of the paragon lasted a mere seven years, no more than a blink in the eye of eternity. Of course, even in those days most people were Christian only in name. The same can apply to Jews."

"The Askes?" Morpurgo nodded. "Yes, I did think of that. Are you sure you don't know anything about Spencer?"

"Pseudonym," Epworth said. "Standard practice on recruiting trawls."

"But it will be on record? On the files?"

"Alas!" Epworth strolled on, reading inscriptions with the scholarly relish of an Egyptologist. "In Aske's case, no. Interesting, the – mmmm – psychology, wouldn't you say?"

"And contradictory. Except . . ."

"Yes?" Not quite so absorbed in death as he seemed.

"Lotta Boyle said something about actors having no personality of their own, only themselves when they're being someone else."

"Just like a spy."

"Were you ever one?" Archer was right, he knew practically nothing about Epworth. Knowing nothing about a man who presided over your destiny had its disturbing side.

"Every man" – another masterly sidestep – "is a spy. As every spy is an actor."

"Aske said that to Sylvie. About being an actor, not about being a spy."

"They go together, my dear Johnny." Epworth had abandoned his study of petroglyphs. "A spy must act for his life. And actors spy upon us for their living, looking for us in themselves. Interesting question, is Simon Aske a spy acting, or an actor spying?"

"There's a difference?"

"Ah," Epworth said cryptically, "now you see it." He began walking back to the car. "Of course, Archer's right. Next time it may be something more than a ticket for speeding."

"Next time?"

"Lotta Boyle would be a good start. But only a start. We must make the Director-General of Five sweat a little more."

"If Steve decides to play rough, he'll play very rough. I know him."

"Of course. That's why I must know your thoughts while you remain in blissful ignorance of mine."

"Cheers me up no end," Morpurgo said. "Go back to Stratford and I may end up in The Other Place." Five's country house in Sussex, used for other purposes beside training, had the same name, informally, as the RSC's smaller Stratford theatre.

" 'The rolling English drunkard'," Epworth quoted, " 'made the rolling English road.' If yours takes you no farther than Sussex we shall have failed to sweat the Director-General sufficiently. However, should you escape Five's invitation to a country house party, a minor airport and a package weekend in – mmmm – Ostend would be a good beginning."

"To what?" He had half-guessed the answer, but if a pattern was emerging, it was blurred and incomplete.

Epworth, getting back in the car, raised his token eyebrows toward his token hair. "If they can't deal with us, they must deal

177

with Aske. I'd much rather you got to him first."

"I thought the FO had put out a hands-off notice on Aske?"

Epworth produced his vaguest smile. "If Aske applies for asylum, he'll be in – mmmm – Tom Tiddler's Ground."

Meaning up for grabs. So he would get as much as he could from Lotta Boyle, then, for what gaps remained, go back to Vienna. And the anti-Epworth cabal would do all that it dared to stop him.

"I could understand," Epworth said abstractedly, as Pretty-man did a neat three-point turn between the forests of death, "Aske's being a Jew and denying it. But to claim to be Jewish when one's not?"

He took a last look at winged victory. "After all, the legal bloodsuckers who administered the Aske estate must have known what they were up to when they buried the Askes in a Christian cemetery, under a Christian cross." He shook his head musingly. "I wonder if we can persuade the right Mr Aske to stand up?"

Back in Trinity Road, Morpurgo said, "How do I know you won't drop me in the shit if the going gets rough?"

Epworth stopped humming something medieval. "You don't."

"Then why am I doing all this?"

"Patriotism? Marxist principles? Money?"

"Balls!"

Epworth wrinkled his nose fastidiously. "Then perhaps because – mmmm – it's there. Drop you here, if you don't mind."

Morpurgo began the long walk to Clapham Junction, small hope of a taxi, no bus in sight. Yes, he thought morosely, because it was there.

# NINETEEN

Back in that huge, shabby rehearsal room, the extraction system whispered, something hummed, the same gold-trimmed but shabby cloak was draped over the same gilded but rickety throne. In the far corner was an old piano. It was in adequate tune. He tried the opening of the Schubert C Minor Impromptu, fluffed the trill, lost his nerve at the prospect of using the loud pedal in this dead silence. Lotta Boyle came though the door from backstage. She wore a denim jacket and jeans, her tawny hair in stylish disorder.

"Why did you stop?"

"Don't like to start what I can't finish."

"Don't you then!" She crossed in long, loose strides, heels striking confident hammerblows. She was the actress all right, dominating the vast and shabby emptiness, mysteriously giving it life and meaning.

"Well, Mr Sylvie Markham, what's so special it couldn't wait?"

She was as tall as he, perhaps taller. She stood close; deliberately, he suspected.

"Can't exactly call you a kept man, can we? Just the junior partner? Mr John Morpurgo of the Foreign Office. My! Should I be flattered? Yes, I'll be flattered." For a moment or two she was a foolish woman hanging on a compliment, while a sceptical twin looked out through pale green windows.

"Is there somewhere we can talk? The Swan, perhaps?"

"This is the Swan." She swept an arm to indicate the surroundings. "At least, ugly duckling now, all that's left of the original theatre that got itself burned down. Now it's going to get a beaklift, your actual Jacobean theatre for your actual Jacobean plays."

179

She looked about her proprietorially. "Come to life, it will, just like us actors when our egos walk on stage."

"So I noticed." He marvelled at himself.

"What did you expect me to do, crawl in on my belly? Anyway, stuff the Duck, I say! Can't entertain a gentleman caller in a pub. Are you a gent?"

"Not really."

"Thought not. Sinfully proud of it, too. How's Sylv?"

"Up north poking around chemical plants."

"Poke? Sylv? Never! Our Sylv's a highborn lady." As on the previous occasion, she tucked her arm through his. It was like her face, bony and full of hidden strength. "Come on. Can't be your place, have to be mine. Bet she said I'd eat you alive."

"All she said," he lied, "was 'Say hello to Lotta.' "

As they went out into Riverside she pointed across the road. "First time I came here, waiting women, kitchen skivvies, walk-on trollops, I had a room in one of those cottages. They belong to the Company. Now I've arrayved, it's a bit farther. Do people like you walk?"

Oh yes, he walked, he said, and went on to add that it was good of her to spare him the time considering how busy she must be di-da-di-da.

"Jesus! You're making me nervous, all this *politesse*. What is it, dear? Overawed by the *ac*-tors?"

"Something like that, I suppose. Bloody stupid, really."

She produced a laugh that sounded like someone settling on an old spring bed. "Gerroff! Still, makes a change. Listen, up here in Stratford they don't give a toss for the actors. Expect us to coin our hearts and drop our blood for drachmas, but can we wring from the hard hands of peasants their vile trash? Not ber-loody likely!"

"Do all actors quote Shakespeare?" Aske had quoted Shakespeare, according to Sylvie. "It is Shakespeare?"

"It's Shakespeare, sweety. And also Shaw. Actors mostly quote when they're onstage and mostly don't when they're not, and since they're mostly not, what they mostly do is bitch." The bedsprings creaked again. "Whingeing and character assassination, that's mostly your actors' line."

"I see," he said humbly. "Are you still in a Company house?"

"No. A poor thing, but mine own. Shit! Done it again. Anyway, good investment, see? Easy lets when you're not here,

home when you are. We cross here. Give mummy your hand."
The road was deserted.

"I suppose Stratford's the actor's Mecca." If so, why had Aske
abandoned the pilgrimage?

"Stratford's the pits, especially in winter. The RSC is the actor's
Mecca. RSC spells theatre, all over the world. Telly to get your
face known, fillums to make the bread, but the theatre's where
it's at, as the man said."

"Which man would that be?" He was still fumbling his way.

"Which man? Any man! Always bloody men, innit? Specially
in theatre."

"You don't seem to have done so badly."

"No thanks to the fellers. First thing you do when you get a
part, big or small, is suss out what the producer and the lead guy
want, 'cos they're the stars, see? Not the play or the writer, Christ
no! The play was written for them, wonnit? If there's women
around, it's just to butter up their egos, be a mirror they can see
themselves in. If you're a woman and you want to get anywhere
in theatre, you'd better bloody well play along."

She emphasised her points with fierce little jabs, her voice
classless and crackling with a kind of streetwise vitality. He had
to remind himself of her background: Charlotte Leveson-Boyle of
Oxford and the Shires, a world removed from John Morpurgo of
Wandsworth.

So which was real? How could you tell? Once an actor, did you
ever really stop acting?

"You don't strike me as an easy person to push around."

"Push around?" She exaggerated her amazement. "What's
that got to do with it, then? Walk into the rehearsal room even for
the first read-through, it's not just what you are, it's what you've
been and what you're expected to be. Christ! If I walked into that
room with nothing to offer except basic me, I'd never get off the
ground.

"So I'm not an easy person to push around, but once through
the door I pretend to be, up to a point. If they push me around it's
because they think I want to be pushed. Only if I've done it all
right, I feel good too, 'cos I've screwed them without being
screwed.

"So now you know." Another creaking laugh. "Not far now.
Not getting tired, are you? I mean, me rabbiting on." Everything
about him was a joke to her for reasons not yet apparent.

"Far from it." He meant it. A spy was an actor, Epworth had

181

said, and an actor a spy, and here he was, walking along a nondescript street with a woman who could be nondescript or not, all according to what was expected of her, yet never abandon the real self that manipulated the strings of the false.

"Down here" – she turned a corner – "and we're good as there. Tell me about you."

"Nothing to tell. Did you always want to act?"

"Evasion noted. We all want to act. We all act when we can get away with it." She stopped outside a whitewashed cottage, the front door a little fancier than its neighbours. She was smiling as she opened it.

"Most of us," she said, "get caught out too often, too soon. Some of us do it professionally and get caught out anyway."

Inside, it was unpretentious and charming, one living room, straight off the street, white-painted walls of ancient plaster; a little kitchen and stairway beyond, a glimpse of a tiny terrace on which flowers were lowering their colours in surrender to autumn.

The room was a hotchpotch that ought not to have blended but did, everything vaguely rural, old-world but not Olde English. Picked up item by item, milestones in a peripatetic life.

One wall had a small family of pictures, almost calligraphic in style, yet representational. Two were heads, three full-length nudes. One of the heads was little more than a cluster of jetty brush strokes from which a pair of eyes looked out, a green moth lured from the darkness by lamplight.

"Was I getting warm?"

He came back with a jerk. "Warm?"

"Warm. Nearer to what you came for." She waved him to a seat. "Right, let's hear your lines. What's poor old Sim been up to?"

"Sim?" Now he knew one of the causes of her amusement.

She nodded her satisfaction. "Said you were a nark, right? Foreign Office? Basement bloody annexe! Come on then, what's it all about?"

"Peter Haley. He's talked to you since I saw him in Oxford."

"Wrong. Anita, old girl net. Sussed you out, she did. Drink? Scotch? Beer? Vodka?"

She shed her jacket; beneath it a shirt of emerald silk. She wore a fine gold chain about a neck whose hollow seemed to penetrate almost to the spine. Her wrists, as she poured his Scotch, displayed the same pared-down strength as the drawings on the wall.

"Sorry," he said. "I wasn't being crafty, just fascinated by a new sort of world. You used to be Charlotte Leveson-Boyle of the Ow-oh-oods. You used to know Simon Aske. I thought you wouldn't mind talking about it."

"What's he done?"

"Nothing. Just his turn to be checked out."

"That's what Anita said. She believed it. I don't."

"Let's say it's a security thing."

"Meaning secret?" She settled on the floor, lotus position.

"Things I've got to make sure of."

"Is he Foreign Office too?" She smiled. "Sort of?"

"Sort of."

"Anything I say will be taken down and used to lumber me?"

"No. Was he a good actor?"

"What if I said the only reason you've got this far is that I fancy you?"

"You don't mean that."

"Funny, thought I did. Yes, he was a good actor."

"What made him give up?"

"What makes you think I don't fancy you?"

"I'm not the fanciable type. Ask Sylvie. Would he have been successful, do you think?"

"If I fancy you, you're fanciable, sweety. Don't you fancy me?"

Yes, he did, although only now had he become aware of it. "You're a very attractive woman."

"You're a bit of a pompous twit. Sorry, didn't really mean it."

"Was Simon Aske good enough to have made it to Mecca?"

"Good enough linguist to make it to St Antony's. Whatever he wanted to be good at, he could persuade you he was. Are you good in bed?"

"What did you think of him? As an actor. As a person."

"I'd ask Sylv, only she wouldn't tell me. Sylv's a highborn lady." The laughter bedsprings creaked. "Poking! Sylv!"

He tried another tack. "You too, really, highborn Leveson-Boyle. No wonder you changed it. Did you know anything about Aske's background?"

"Do you know anything about mine? *Jeunesse dorée*, that's what you think, innit? I'll tell you how *dorée* my *jeunesse* was. My father was a society stud. My mother's a whore. I'd have had more loving care in a cats' home. I didn't change my name, I changed me. Sim showed me the way. Let's screw."

He was John Morpurgo from Wandsworth and he had been

around. Not so long ago he had been screwing another man's wife and she had been screwing him. Now he felt like a raw boy faced with his first woman.

"Was he Jewish?"

"He was Jewish when he said he was. I never saw his foreskin. Does that help?"

"If you don't feel like helping, I can't make you."

"If you don't feel like screwing, I might persuade you."

He tried to ignore it. "What do you mean, he showed you the way to change yourself?"

"I was shy. He said if I wanted to act I couldn't afford to be shy. He said it was just an excuse to avoid facing up to things."

"Was he shy?"

"Oh yes, when he was shy. But not when he wasn't. He could have taught you a trick or two."

"Me?"

He could imagine her in bed, lithe and vigorous. He cleared his throat.

"Yes, you," she said. "Rather sweet, really, a shy nark. Coconut, tough and hairy outside but full of milk. Are you hairy outside?"

"Was he popular? In the OUDS?"

"With the women. And some of the men." She looked at him under her lashes, smiling to herself. "Was he," she asked herself, "queer? Bent? Homo?" She looked up. "Gay hadn't really taken hold in those days."

"All right, was he?"

"He was gay when he was gay. And when he wasn't gay he was" – a momentary emptiness behind the eyes – "sad. Oh, very very sad. Poor Sim!"

"But you liked him."

"When he was likeable. Next time I mightn't find you fanciable. Next time, you might fancy me. Too bloody bad, cocky!"

She saw his eyes wander again to the nudes on the wall. "Me, those are," she said. "Me then, meaning the halcyon days. Oxford. Me, meaning the subject. Or object. Artists are like actors, subject becomes object, yourself in them."

"They're good. Aren't they?"

"God, are you unsure of yourself! The original" – she passed her hands over her breasts – "was better."

"Was?"

184

"Was, is. Listen, sweety, can't be anything we haven't always been – that's a good thought to keep hold of."

"But strange for an actor." It must be so, otherwise Simon Aske became more of an enigma than ever.

She was looking at him oddly. "Is it strange? What do you think actors work on? The selves they've got, what else?"

"I'm not sure I see."

"Of course you don't see. It's something you feel, and you don't feel it until you've tried it. Like screwing. Let's try."

"Simon Aske," he began.

"Sim was different. That *was* his self, to be different. No." It was as if she had decided – temporarily? – to abandon his seduction. "Sim would never have made it to Mecca. To make it to Mecca you have to start from something solid. Maybe bad, maybe good. Maybe likeable, maybe . . . Christ! I could tell you! But solid, a basic 'you', because that's what you build on."

"You make it sound as if he had" – he gestured uncertainly – "no core. No basic 'you'."

"Fluid." She gestured too, but hers was explicit, a conjuring up of something mercurial. "Some actors learn to walk on the water, but they all begin by being brought down to earth. With a bloody great bump. Sim never learned that."

"His Shylock – "

"Utterly wrong. I don't mean morally, I mean misconceived. But he did it brilliantly. Overruled everyone else – he could be very persuasive – then did something very clever but utterly wrong. Because he could see but he couldn't feel. Didn't know which Sim to come to terms with."

She hesitated, began again. "His Shylock wasn't a reason. It was a symptom."

Her hands turned and stroked like a potter's, struggling to shape something still unshaped in her mind. "You never saw him. As if he'd set out to make half of us love him and the other half hate his guts. Only the two groups were hardly ever the same, always changing, this one in, that one out, falling from grace or being . . . redeemed.

"He could understand people, see? Even when he didn't like 'em. Knew what to flatter, what to send up." Another creak of amusement. "Make him sound a right bastard, don't I? Well, he was, when he wanted, and not when he didn't. Sometimes he could just sort of fade into the woodwork, be there and yet not. But when he was there he was right bloody there, the original

185

Oxford eccentric. Count Dracula, cloak and silver-nobbed stick all as shabby as if he'd found them in somebody's dustbin. Probably had."

She put her hands over her face, conjuring up time past. "What he couldn't do was" – her fingertips thumped against her chest – "*give* himself. That's why he didn't make it to Mecca. Perhaps he knew. Perhaps that's why he went to St Antony's and" – she gave him a sly look – "wherever."

Questions pressed at the inside of his lips like a physical force but he had no intention of interrupting.

"I'd gone down by then," she said. "Off I went to London, early in the morning, see the little puff-puffs, all in a row. Fame and fortune beckoning, the bitches. Everyone said his Shylock cured him of being stagestruck, drained away all his dreams through his big toe. Wasn't that. They'd forgotten the essential non-essential Sim."

A car went by outside, otherwise Mecca was as silent as the grave.

"Go on," she said. "Your cue. Don't corpse on me."

She got up, lithe as a gymnast. She refilled his glass but not her own. She watched him. The tip of her tongue came out moistening her lips. Yes, he thought, I want her, and felt himself stir.

He said, "What was that, the essential Sim?"

Her nearly smile would have been indulgent if born, but it never was. She turned away to look through her little house at her little terrace. Was there a joke still to come?

"The essential Sim" – her hands went through swift movements of manipulating cards – "was . . . now you see me, now you don't. When you saw . . . wham! Then you looked again and . . . " Her fingers walked the air. "Gone. He once said . . . " A short hesitation. He began to understand something. "He once said his ambition was to run through time and leave no footprints. He talked like that."

"Were you ever in love with him?"

"I told you, he couldn't give. He had to hide, always in someone else. Even when he was acting, not really alive. Here" – she touched her forehead – "but not here" – her hand went to her breast – "or here." It rested on her belly. In his mind, his own hands followed hers.

"You have to give as well as take. Sim was always holding himself back. He'd have been found out if he'd gone on. He was terrified of being found out."

186

"Did you ever hear of a man called Spencer in connection with Simon Aske?" He would have to be quick.

"No."

"Know anything about his background?"

She laughed outright. "Background? He was a bloody chameleon!"

Time was running out. He produced the photograph. "Who are they all? Who's the girl he's got his arm round?"

She came very close. He could feel the warmth of her body.

"Come off it, cocky."

"Come off what?"

She studied him. "You really don't know?"

He put his hands behind him, anywhere away from her.

"I want to hear you say you don't know who she is. The girl."

"I don't know who she is."

"Jesus! That's Serena. That's his bloody wife."

"Serena?"

"Serena Donne. Wouldn't so much as give him the time of day until she decided he was going to be famous."

Back to the Haystocks, the senior language master's daughter. Back to the Playhouse. "The girl who designed *The Merchant*?"

She turned him towards the wall. "The girl who designed me." Those pictures of green eyes and naked body in a torn-off scrap of night.

"Very plausible, Serena, as an artist," Lotta said. "But not the real thing, which is why she never made it. You'll see that for yourself." Her hand slipped from his shoulder to his waist. He went on looking at the pictures. Inside him the naked ape gibbered.

"See what?"

Going Cockney, she said, "Cor, proper bleedin' old larf, innit?" Her other hand came to his waist.

"Little Dolly Dropdrawers, that's what we called her. Ignored him for the first two years, snapped him up as a very considered trifle in his last, the next John bloody Gielgud or whatever." She pressed close.

Unnecessarily loudly, he said, "But he went to St Antony's instead, and then . . ."

"Yes?" she said. "And then?" Her mouth was raised, lips parted, breath on his face.

Desperately, he said, "Well, what then?"

"Walk up the bloody High Street and ask her." She moulded

herself against him. He forgot Sylvie and Simon Aske.

But his hands passed fleetingly over the thin silk of her shirt as she slipped away. Pouring herself a drink, she said, "Last lesson in acting, cocky. Don't worry. Won't tell Sylv."

His dignity about his feet like trousers in a bedroom farce, he said, "I'll let myself out."

"Men!" she said. "Try the world from our side, chum. Even when they're tough and pink and pretty, little grey people, endlessly conspiring. Congratulations though. You held out so long I thought I'd failed my bloody audition."

\* \* \*

He found his way back past the theatre, symbol of the illusory world into which he had plunged, filled with an active hatred. Not for Lotta Boyle. For himself. She had given him a seminar on Simon Aske, a lesson in acting, and had held up a mirror for him to look in. He thought he must be the exception; little and grey on the outside as well.

He had seen Simon Aske once, a glimpse through a bookshop window, fleeting and blurred. Now he was more blurred than ever, drawn from the memories of others over a period of more than thirty years and, worse, no more likely to be the real Aske than any one actor could ever be the definitive Shylock.

If he should in due course come into direct contact with Simon Aske the man, what possible hope had he of learning anything?

Yet he had learned one thing. His knowledge of Stratford was sketchy, but a High Street was a High Street.

He walked up from the river, past a Marks and Spencer's disguised as a bank, innumerable tea and gift shops disguised as stations of the Shakespearian cross. Then everything became suddenly easy and obvious.

SERENdipity, said the fascia in eighteenth-century calligraphy; SERENdipity. An onyx writing set with a scarlet-feathered ballpoint, rummer candlelamps in rose-pink glass, flowered Wedgwood, porcelain eggs, table mats and coasters with scenes from Shakespeare.

He walked in.

"Lunchtime, but come in if it won't take long."

Changed but still recognisable after more than a quarter of a century, she had a hoarse voice, the brisk confidence of someone used to pushing people around. Heavy-breasted, broad-hipped, in a few more years she would be stout. He thought of the girl in

188

the first-night picture and mourned his own lost days.

The cigarette in her mouth jerked as she spoke, ash sprinkling the flowery coverall that stopped halfway down a hound's-tooth check skirt. Tweedy matron: gin, fags, opportunistic quicky romps with chaps from the local Conservative Club.

She was walking back down an Aladdin's cave of goodies for the status symbol market. He looked for paintings that might be hers, but they were all reproductions. So was the pembroke with a scatter of business cards: SERENdipity. The name beneath was Serena Donne, not Aske.

She looked at him, the appraisal not entirely commercial. "What were you interested in?"

He plunged. "Simon Aske."

She removed her cigarette. "Who the hell are you?"

"I have some enquiries to make. I hoped you might help me."

"Did you, then!" She stubbed out the cigarette viciously. "Spencer sent you, right? Well you can push off double quick, my boy. Closed for business, got it?" She turned her back, took a step, turned again. "I mean it. Bugger off. And don't come back. Those days have gone."

He said, "I don't know anyone called Spencer. I'm just trying to fill in a few gaps."

The look on her face, skin crazed with tiny veins like old glazed tiles, was indecisive. Her lips compressed, released, compressed. He said, "I saw some pictures you once did. I liked them."

"How do I know who you are?" As his hand sought automatically for his ID, she all but shouted. "Don't bother. See one, see all. Trouble, that's who you are, just plain bloody trouble."

She said, "Twenty years. You know that, don't you? You lot know everything."

Serena Donne, not Aske. "Since you split?"

"Split!" She had a raucous, bronchial laugh: endless cigarettes, too much liquor. It turned into a cough. She suppressed it with a fist. Her eyes, bulging, went on staring at him.

"Some bloody split! Or is that your sense of humour? Where is he, anyway? Berlin? Prague? The loony bin?" She found her cigarettes and shook one out. "Who cares? I don't, that's for sure. Twenty years! Don't you buggers ever let go?"

She said, "Which pictures, anyway?" and struck a match as if it were force that produced the flame.

"Lotta Boyle."

"Lotta! Oh, God! Scavenging!" Serena had not been happy as a name choice. "Hardly knew him. Sour grapes, I'll bet." Her cigarette dwindling fierily, she belched smoke like a dragon. "Not that it would have come to anything. Lesbie, like as not."

Not, he thought, from this side.

"I could paint, then. What did she say? About me?"

"That I'd find you in the High Street."

"You're making me miss my lunch."

Lunch was a large Bloody Mary, a small salad, their end of the pub almost empty. As they walked the short distance down the street she tried and failed to discover what he had discussed with Lotta Boyle.

"I used to work in the dump." She meant the theatre. "Sod-all to do with them now. Stage sets like New Year's Eve in Piccadilly, all hoardings, scaffolding, lights."

She had gone to Stratford from Oxford, fetching and carrying in the scenery workshop while Aske was at St Antony's. Then she had followed him on various postings before returning to the theatre workshop, a job that fell through almost at once.

She let him order another Bloody Mary. "All right, what do you want?"

"You stuck to theatre. Why didn't he?"

A loud laugh, another bout of sticky coughing blocked with a perfunctory fist. "Stuck to it? Didn't stick to me, did it? You can lose a talent, did you know that?"

"Is that what happened to him?"

"Sim? Sim's talent was for . . ." Her gaze narrowed. "What happened to Spencer?"

"No idea. I never met him."

"He can't have retired. No older than you. Not much, anyway."

"People shift around. What was he like?"

She described someone who could have been anyone of a hundred: dark, medium height, well-spoken, well-dressed. "Pukka," she said, exaggerating the pronunciation. "Pukka sahib, Mr Spencer, oh yes. You get to know the type. Oxford was full of them."

"He was an Oxford man?"

"Oxbridge. Not that he said. It just showed. Public school too. Daddy had pennies and an acre or two, that's for sure." Her cigarette burned like a fast fuse before she said in an explosion of smoke, "Good-looker, truth to tell, but not what you'd call red-blooded."

He realised she was looking at him with veiled invitation; no real liking, but a chance of getting something out of him. Little Dolly Dropdrawers!

He said, "It's really Sim I'm curious to know something about, not Spencer."

It was the wrong thing and the right thing. Wrong because he had recognised an invitation, turned it down and she knew. Right because it stimulated anger never far below the surface. She was a pilgrim to Mecca who had actually arrived, only to be turned away. Now she had her *suq* outside the walls, catering for minor pilgrims.

"Curious to know something about Sim!" She ground out her cigarette as if extinguishing life. "It *was* curious to know something about Sim. Christ!" She was venomous. "Standing there as if no one had told him the facts of bloody life then" – she snapped her fingers so that the barman looked from the other end of the bar – "vanishes up his own arse. As if he'd never seen it before. Shall I tell you how much *I* knew about him? Bugger all! Your lot probably know more than I ever knew!"

The barman was coming in response to that snap of the fingers. She waved him away.

"He *might* have been," she said, "better than anything they've seen over there." A contemptuous jerk of the head towards the theatre. "Name up in lights, London, New York, never mind this godforsaken hole. Only your lot got at him. That arrogant bastard Spencer. Sim always went after whoever could convince him he was the best thing since sliced bread."

Serena Donne, for instance; wanting to be there when his name went up in lights. Very susceptible to influence.

"London, that bloody awful place they had before Chelten-ham. Then Berlin. Of all godawful deadly holes, Berlin! Do you wonder, do you bloody well *wonder* I stopped being his camp bloody follower?"

Berlin, the great treffpunkt: Fish, Archer, now Aske.

She lit another cigarette. Her hand had a tremor. He wondered if she was nympho as well as frustrated, bitter, corrosively convinced that she had snapped up the chance of basking in fame, glory, only to have it slip through her fingers. Her own talent had slipped through her fingers, too.

Scooping up cigarettes and matches, preparing to depart, she lingered under a last brief compulsion. "We never *were* married, not really. He never could be, not to anything. Just his great

191

fantastic act of being this or that, then stepping back to watch himself. Unfaithful! I could have been unfaithful a million times."

She slid heavily from her stool. "Have you seen him?"

"No." A glimpse didn't count.

"You won't. Nobody ever did. Nobody ever will. Just don't come back here, that's all." She went without one glance back. Through the window he saw her march up the street toward SERENdipity.

\* \* \*

An aimless Cotswold meander, a late supper, a drive through the autumn night on roads that stayed empty almost to London. His lights probed ahead through the darkness. It was as if he were chasing a will-o'-the-wisp, up and down hills, round corners, through deserted towns and villages. At last he hit the city. In the cold, harsh street lights it escaped, adapting itself chameleon-like to night and neon.

He let himself into what he had to learn to call home and went upstairs without putting on any lights. He never felt the blow, the sensation of the ground coming up to meet him, any of the clichés. Like the will-o'-the-wisp he simply merged with the night.

# TWENTY

Convalescence was over. He had been expecting it for some time.

"Well, they seem to be pleased with you." Her kiss was less bestowed than applied like a dressing.

"They bloody well should be. I'm helping to boost their profits."

"Not your problem." He had still been semiconscious when she had had him transferred from casualty to the posh clinic.

He said, "Mum would have loved it here. No blacks. The nurses probably earn more than I do," behaving badly in anticipation of what was to come.

"Sid called again to ask how you were."

"I'm grateful to Sid, too."

She bit her lip. "The insurance company will pay in full for the damage, but my undeveloped films are a dead loss. The police have been round five times. I'm told it's a record. They're continuing their enquiries."

"The films are the worst thing," he said. "And the mess they made of your files and equipment."

"I don't give a damn about the mess. I do rather care about the films. And about you. The fact that they hurt you."

He rapped his head. "A thick skull has its advantages."

"A hairline fracture is still a fracture. Lying there for hours. And lucky it wasn't longer. Thank God Sid had a key."

"The people here say I'm as good as new." He grinned wryly. "That should make me better than before."

"Has Epworth been in again?" Her manner was cool, not unfriendly but disturbingly brisk.

"Yesterday evening. Didn't stay long." Another lie. He

pointed at grapes and flowers. "From Amaryllis."

"Good of her."

Not interested in Amaryllis. The omens were bad.

She sat down at last. "Johnny, I'm going to New York."

"Good. When?" The thing had been pending for long enough.

"Tomorrow."

He waited. She added nothing, but there would be more to come.

He said, "Final tests and radiology tomorrow. If everything's okay, Saturday."

"I wouldn't ask you to come with me, even if you were completely fit."

"No. I'd only be a hindrance."

"Mrs Cullin will take care of the house and do some shopping."

"I'll do my own shopping. I mean, I'm not really an invalid any more."

She looked up. "What did Epworth say?"

"Mmmmmmm, mostly." He waved the weak joke away. "Oh, nothing much. They've leaned on the police. It's just another breaking and entering."

"But it wasn't, was it?" Her look told him not to waste his time.

"Perhaps. Perhaps not. Hard to say, really."

"It is, isn't it? Hard for you to say. I'm prepared to believe" – she went to the window – "they didn't actually mean to kill you."

"Let's keep things in proportion. Somebody panicked, miscalculated. But killing . . ."

"I hoped," she said, "you'd tell me Epworth had decided to take you off."

"I am off. I've been off quite some time."

She ignored that as unworthy of comment. "I wouldn't have come back after Helga if I hadn't loved you. I thought I ought to try to live with what you do. I've tried. I can't. Not any longer."

"How's Sylvie taken it?" Epworth had asked, and he had said oh, she'd been upset, naturally, but taking it well, all considered.

"Mmmmmmm," Epworth had said.

"What are you trying to tell me?"

"I'll be away at least a week. Plenty of time to think. On both sides."

She slung her bag over her shoulder. "That's about it. I shan't come tonight. Things to do."

"Of course."

"I may not stay in New York. Things are a bit . . . fluid. Stella will know where I am."

Stella would call him Mr Markham before making things worse with her apologies.

He said, "It *could* have been a routine breaking and entering. Happens all the time in the part of the world we've moved to."

"Could have been Santa Claus, but it wasn't." She went without looking back. Things looked bad. He set himself to wait for Epworth.

The first thing Epworth said was, "Sylvie's been talking to Amaryllis. I expect you know."

Pulling a comical face seemed inadequate as a response, but better than saying he didn't know.

Epworth looked at him enigmatically. "I gather your skull's mended nicely. How is your spiritual malaise?"

"My skull," Morpurgo said, "isn't ready for that kind of thing."

"Lying halfway down the stairs," Epworth said, "and all through the night. I thought perhaps it might have settled more than one account."

Damn the man, Morpurgo thought, too bloody penetrating for his own good. It was true. He had done an appropriate penance. The burden of guilt over the way his mother had died had lifted considerably.

He said, "What did Sylvie say? To Amaryllis?"

"My dear man" – Epworth at his vaguest – "Rylla doesn't tell me anything. Did I tell you we've had to let the Branch in, by the way?"

It was his way of saying that any further investigation of the break-in would be abandoned.

Epworth had waved the big stick of security to begin with; only a paragraph in the local paper. But since it *was* security and since there were limits to what SIS could do in home territory, it was inevitable that it should go from the Mets to the Branch.

There was no mystery about what had happened. Sylvie had worked it out.

One of Five's break-in artists to deal with the alarm and locks, a couple of Al(C) guys to rummage, a minder from the legal thuggery section in Camberwell to head off interference. Morpurgo, returning late, had taken them by surprise. Minders were not chosen for their intellectual qualities. This one, reacting through his muscles, had underestimated his own strength.

Epworth said, "So we may safely assume that's that. Though one does wonder how Archer reacted."

Archer had sent the frighteners: rubbish the place but nothing physical. He would have learned soon enough just how wrong things had gone, and would be in no doubt that the source of the intrusion would be identified.

"Wasn't going to send me flowers," Morpurgo said. "That's for sure."

Once he had been assured that Morpurgo had suffered no serious harm, Steve Archer would not necessarily be overly remorseful.

Morpurgo could have been killed, but "could have been", in this game, was as good as "wasn't". The frighteners had done their job. Nothing was so certain as that Epworth would make no official complaint.

Sylvie, knowing nothing until the police tracked her down in Billingham, had been well and truly frightened.

Steve Archer's purpose had been to give Morpurgo an ultimatum, unattributable, unambiguous. Now Sylvie, too, had given him an ultimatum, equally unambiguous, totally attributable. Was that, he wondered, what she had said to Amaryllis? Had Amaryllis, after all, passed it on to Epworth?

It she had, Epworth proposed to leave the ball in Morpurgo's court. "By the way," he said, and Epworth's by-the-ways were something to watch out for, "Dukinfield, originally Durchenfeld. Jewish, refugee from the Sudetenland when we gift-wrapped Czechoslovakia for Hitler. Nothing known."

Morpurgo gave himself a grape. He didn't particularly like grapes, but Epworth was eating them all. "And Spencer?"

"Ah, Spencer. Well, we're dealing with the early sixties, of course. Post-Philby. The broad church movement. You know all about that."

Morpurgo did indeed know all about that. He was a product of the policy. A cause for regret since, over twenty years on, Oxbridge was back at the helm.

"Not sure I get the point."

"Considerable recruiting activity in the early sixties," Epworth said. "It – mmmm – made for strange bed-fellows."

"Aske and Spencer?"

"Aske and Fish."

"But Aske was recruited by Spencer. London. The old Joint Technical Language Service. Serena Donne made that plain."

"After your recent excursions," Epworth said, "little if any-thing is plain. But from St Antony's to JTLS, thence to Cheltenham out-stations. Berlin, who knows where else? Not much of a life for stage-struck Serena."

"It means that GCHQ will have his files."

"Cheltenham?" Epworth sucked in his breath. "Oh dear no!"

Morpurgo got the point. Since Washington's insistence that GCHQ be deunionised, Cheltenham was the US National Security Agency's private fief, the prime minister their honorary caretaker. To enquire about Aske at GCHQ would be like enquiring at Number Ten.

"Of course, in '61" – Epworth munched grapes – "you knew nothing of us."

Morpurgo laughed. "In '61 I was still researching working conditions in the distributive trades for the TUC. Five didn't recruit me until '64." A moment later he said, "You know that."

Epworth looked apologetic. "Yes, I suppose I do. And Steve Archer, when did you first meet him?"

Morpurgo frowned. Epworth must know that too. "Around '65. Vague recollections of him. But we didn't start working together until, oh, must have been '70 at least. Is this relevant?"

"Probably not. It's just that when he came off field work he worked for Fish until he was transferred to Five. One's mind wanders. So" – Epworth came suddenly back from wherever he had been – "Aske went to JTLS, cut his teeth translating intercepts. Transferred to Cheltenham, we may assume J division in view of his qualifications. Then Berlin."

"Special Sigint. Very sensitive for someone who seems to have been a bit of a nut. Bloody peculiar that Spencer recruited someone like that at all. I mean, not the stablest of personalities."

"My dear Johnny, the upper echelons of intelligence are full of eccentrics, never more so than in GCHQ." Epworth giggled, head atilt like a sly parrot. "The kind of people who do what we do, and do it well, are not what most people would call normal."

"Is this getting us anywhere?"

Epworth looked surprised. "Spencer is a pseudonym. Re-cruiters have used them since the broad church days, part of the security shake-up. It wasn't Fish himself, if that's what you're wondering. Your – mmmm – serendipitous lady friend seems to have a good eye for the male beast. The description doesn't fit."

Morpurgo touched his head gingerly. "Go on like this and they won't be letting me out on Saturday. Of course, we could ask Steve."

"Steve?"

"Joke. You said he was working for Fish at the time. In that case, he might have known Spencer."

"I doubt if Steve would tell. Pity. He and Spencer must have been of much the same age."

The prettiest of Morpurgo's nurses came in, thermometer at the ready. "Time for our pulse and temperature, Mr Morpurgo. And I don't see" – she looked accusingly at Epworth – "how you could possibly have had your rest."

"Just going." Epworth popped the last grape in his mouth but stayed until the performance was over, when he said, "How's Sylvie? Still taking it well?"

What *had* Sylvie told Amaryllis? What had Amaryllis told Epworth?

"Well enough to go to New York tomorrow. Business, important."

"For long?"

"At least a week." Loyalty forced Morpurgo to add, "She wouldn't go if she didn't know I'll be okay. It's been on the cards for some time."

"Well, *no* place for rest and recuperation. Which of course you must have. Did I mention that friend Aske is apparently moving firmly in the direction of Austrian citizenship? No? Pity. Incommunicado, once he crosses over."

He shrugged on his coat. "You must go away, of course. Change of scene, change of air, a little – mmmm – cosseting in Sylvie's absence. What about – mmmm – Ostend?"

\*       \*       \*

Aske had the cards. Lotta, in tights and spangles, glided through lurid light while laser beams sliced the blackness, and a beat of some kind, not music but the growling rhythm of subterranean machinery, made the air shake, the blood pound in his head.

Aske was in evening dress: silk hat, cloak, silver-topped stick. He spun the stick in a dazzling whirl, the other hand manipulating three giant cards with bewildering skill.

"Any card. Choose any card."

The pictures on the cards – tarot symbols? – changed constantly, each a separate, miniature performance, a deep significance for Jews but no one else. Lotta, naked, reminded him of some Hindu goddess, arms and legs replicated, head sliding

198

unnaturally from side to side, mouth lasciviously agape.

"Any card," Aske said. "Choose any card." The cards changed their scenes with the speed of channel-hopping television sets.

At his side, Dukinfield said, "He matches them to your opinion of him. Whatever you choose will make a fool of you."

Serena Donne, her weight oppressive on his lap, blew smoke in his eyes. "At the end of the show he vanishes up his own arse." She dug her chin into his head with excruciating force.

Bright light enveloped Aske, reducing him to the minimal: black, white, the dark holes of empty eye sockets. The three cards switched endlessly, almost but never quite merging.

"Take a card. Any card."

Lotta posed obscenely, legs wide astride, three arms pointing at Aske, eyes and smile only for Morpurgo. An immensely amplified whisper said, "They are never other than what they were. They will never be other than what they are."

The Haystocks turned in their seats to stare at him. Haystock said, "You'll have to choose, you know. We always have to choose. Then we have to live with the choice."

"To be, or not to be, that was his question." Ellie Haystock stroked the toad on her shoulder with one clumsy finger. It sank unexpected fangs. She held the finger towards Morpurgo. It dripped blood like wine.

Aske tossed his silver-headed cane to Lotta, shuffled the cards, displayed them. Each was a living photograph. Aske's own head and shoulders. The music had changed – Mozart, played one-handed on an out-of-tune piano: *La ci darem la mano*. It stopped abruptly.

The portraits on the cards, all identical now, wore the same smile. They shook their heads in unison. In unison they said, "He was never there. He can't come back from where he hasn't been. Take a card. Any card."

Morpurgo's head throbbed. Everyone in the shabby theatre waited. Everyone had the same face, Aske's face. The only noise was in his head.

He chose a card in the middle. The face on the card smiled. The smile was Lotta's. It faded. The card was blank. The two remaining cards merged their faces with Aske's. He in turn merged with the crowd.

The great whisper, Lotta's voice, said, "Now you see it, now you don't." The last word became an electronic echo: *oh-oh-oh n-n-n t-t-t-t*.

199

Haystock's voice, cracked with rage, bellowed, "Victim! One of life's natural victims! Idiot! Idiot! Idiot-t-t-t-t-t!"

Morpurgo was overwhelmed by desolation. A failure, rejected. High hopes but the wrong side of the river. Dukinfield, gleefully vindictive, said, "*Litost*".

From the empty stage he looked down on the watchers, sandcastles, glistening and shapeless, that dwindled while he stared. The assault of waves rolled through his skull with a ceaseless, deafening rhythm.

Far out to sea he heard Sylvie calling.

\*     \*     \*

On Saturday he left the clinic. On Sunday he went to Ostend for rest and recuperation.

# THE HEART
# OF SILENCE

# TWENTY-ONE

At the Schottentor he boarded a streetcar. Soon after it had clicked over the points, leaving behind the Ring with its nonstop parade of grandiosity, the city changed. It was no longer Vienna, a baroque museum, but a vast, impersonal working town on the divide between East and West.

He got off at Spitalgasse and walked through canyons of high, oppressive apartment buildings with shops and small businesses at street level. Arriving at tall double doors that would never open save in some unimaginable emergency, he was looking down the battery of labelled buttons when a black BMW pulled up.

"Herr Morpurgo." Karl-Heinz Mandel, immaculate as ever. "Welcome back. You have your passport with you?"

"Next plane out?" Morpurgo joined Mandel in the car. It pulled away instantly. "I'm beginning to get the feeling Vienna doesn't want me."

"My dear Morpurgo." The amiable Karli looked hurt. "We welcome all of our visitors. History has seldom allowed us any choice." He flipped through the passport, pausing briefly at a red-and-green stamp headed *Czeskoslovenske Visum*, good for one week after validation, then closed and returned it.

"Although," he said, "discretion is something we have learned to appreciate." The car was kerb-crawling.

The monogrammed gold cigarette case was proffered and declined. Mandel selected one of his crested cigarettes and applied the flame from his gold lighter.

"In our city we still have many thousands of known former Nazis." He had one gold tooth, visible only when he smiled.

Perhaps it, too, was engraved.

"Tolerance," he said, "is not always the product of British fair play. Sometimes it is a case of silence in return for silence. If each of us in Vienna told what he knew about his neighbour's past, life would be full of problems."

"Not just in Vienna."

"Really? In London also?" The car stopped. They had gone round the block.

Mandel removed a glove and held out his hand. "I would ask you to give my compliments to the Engineer, but we have never met. Not in person. *Wiedersehen*, dear colleague."

As Morpurgo got out, Karl-Heinz said, "Those large camps, Mauthausen for example, required resident engineers. Power supplies, water, sewage. And of course, gas." The car slid away. Morpurgo pressed the bell. A voice said, *"Herein, bitte."* A buzzer sounded. He pushed at the narrow wicket door and stepped in.

*     *     *

Engineer Stiegelbauer, pudgy pink hands embracing his corpulence through a woollen jacket with buttons and holes misaligned, was cautious.

"I regret. Herr Aske is no longer resident."

Mandel must have known that.

"Perhaps I could have his room."

The Engineer was taken aback, but only for a moment. "The room has been re-let. Good morning."

"I thought" – Morpurgo put his superior weight in the doorway – "we might talk. About old times. About Mauthausen."

Turning colour with the speed of litmus paper, the Engineer glanced involuntarily behind him. "Who are you?"

Morpurgo drew him out on to the landing. "More private. Where did Herr Aske go?"

The Engineer had come out in a fine film of perspiration. "Who *are* you?"

"I'm here with the knowledge of the authorities. Where did he go?"

"Traiskirchen." Looking behind him again, the Engineer fumbled for a handkerchief and dabbed brow and cheeks.

Traiskirchen, where, according to Toby Farrar, they sent political refugees while they decided what to do with them. Simon Aske had applied for asylum. Mandel had known that, too.

He looked predatorily at the Engineer, a mollusc-soft old man with a tyrannical wife. Did she know that her husband had helped to maintain the efficient functioning of a slaughterhouse?

"What do you know about Herr Aske?"

Again the Engineer looked behind him. The Frau Engineer was undoubtedly at home. "I have always cooperated with the authorities. When Herr Aske first disappeared, I cooperated fully."

"Herr Mandel said as much." In making it clear that he and Stiegelbauer had never met personally, Mandel had given Morpurgo carte blanche.

The Engineer's head jerked up. "You're from Department One?"

"Herr Doctor Mandel himself," Morpurgo said, "dropped me at your door."

"He was a Jew." The reference to Mauthausen made the Engineer stammer. "I mention this as a point of fact, not of criticism. A fact Herr Aske himself first revealed to me. And so – "

"Why? What did he say?" Mass murder was in another age. This was a weak and frightened old man. Morpurgo nevertheless found himself repelled.

The Engineer dabbed mechanically at his mouth with his handkerchief. "My wife . . . " As if on cue, there were sounds of movement. He flapped anguishedly.

"Tonight, the weinstube on the corner. I go to play chess. I can leave early. I'll tell you what I can. What little I can. You must agree." It would have been pathetic but for his history.

A woman's voice. "Stefan? Who is it?"

Morpurgo nodded. "Nine o'clock. Tell her I was looking for a room."

Halfway to the lift he sensed that the Frau Engineer had appeared to stare suspiciously after him. She might have the whole story in minutes, might contact authority.

But authority was Karl-Heinz Mandel, who could have had him on the next plane out but instead had told him about Mauthausen. There was no black BMW waiting for him in the street. Aske's doubtful Jewishness had become important.

*       *       *

The weinstube was softly lit, respectable, lightly populated. Unless Department One was represented by worthy middle-class citizens deep in conversation over a *kleines heller* or viertels of white wine, there was no surveillance.

The Engineer half rose, signalling his presence rather than with any idea of hospitality. He was drinking brandy. His attitude had changed.

"The mistakes of the past," he began in a low, angry voice, "are of the past." It was obviously something he had been waiting to say. "The Statute of Limitations—"

Morpurgo interrupted. "Forget it. It's Aske I'm interested in."

The Engineer swallowed brandy greedily – not his first. He would have some explaining to do when he got home. "Questions, questions. All I know, I've already told."

"Not to me."

"I don't even know who you are."

"That's best. Did Aske really tell you he was a Jew? Or are you an expert?"

The Engineer flushed. "He told me. What was it to me? I liked him. A perfect tenant. Quiet, polite. No guests. No drunkenness or parties."

"No guests? None?"

"None, in all the years."

"How long?"

"Five, six, I don't remember. The police . . ."

"Never mind the police."

The Engineer screwed up his face like a sullen child. "A solitary man. He went out, came back – "

"Where? How often? For how long?"

"*I'm* not a policeman." His brief rebellion appeared to give the Engineer a little encouragement. He signalled for another brandy, sitting stubbornly silent until it came.

"Herr Aske was a scholar. History, the Habsburgs, something of that sort. Out every morning, back every evening, libraries, the university. He didn't say. We didn't ask. We don't grill our tenants. They have their lives to live."

"He told you he was a Jew? Why was that?"

A grunt of irritation. "A thing mentioned in passing. You don't live for years under the same roof without revealing a little about yourself." More brandy, gulped. "I can't remember how his Jewishness first came up."

"Did he only mention it once?"

"Several times, don't ask me how many. Over the years things are repeated. He made a joke of it. Being a Jew. I liked him for that too." He gulped brandy. "After all, there are good Jews."

Those that are left, Morpurgo thought, but now he had a glimmer of understanding. A recollection of that quizzical face, sad, yet ready to lighten with quick amusement. Self-mockery as a defence, a pre-empting of any hostility on the part of others.

Could Fish, perhaps, have briefed Aske on the Engineer's past? Could Aske, knowing that he was to spend years with the Stiegelbauers, have revealed his supposed Jewishness to preserve his own privacy and at the same time secretly mock his landlord?

"Was he a practising Jew?"

The topic was increasingly distasteful to the Engineer. "He made nothing special of Saturdays. Ate normally. Dressed normally, no" – one pudgy hand described a circle about his skull – "little cap, nothing like that."

Another attempt to change the conversation. "A model tenant. Is it my fault he went off on one of his trips and didn't come back?" Two fat *Bürgerinnen* spilled small change on the next table while discussing whether they should have another *Trinkerl*.

How many Jews had the man sent off on trips from which they didn't come back?

"When did he begin the trips?"

"After a year or so. I don't take notes when a tenant makes a trip."

"What did he tell you about going to Prague?"

The Engineer sighed. "I made a joke. That's when he told me about his work. The Habsburgs used to own the Böhmen. The Czechs."

"A joke?"

Stiegelbauer drank more brandy, slowly, with a gleam of defiance. "I told him he should visit the Pinkas synagogue in Prague, find some ancestors maybe. Do you know Prague?"

Morpurgo shook his head, repelled by the man's insensitivity.

"No longer in use, a sort of memorial. The walls are covered with the names of all the Jews who used to live in Prague."

He was a little drunk, Morpurgo saw; not used to so much liquor, or betrayed by tension. He said, "I liked him. He was a nice man. A Jew, but quite a nice man." Astonishingly, his weak eyes filled with tears.

"He told you he went to Prague in connection with his work?"

"On the Habsburgs. The libraries there are good, that's what he said. The libraries there are good."

"Regular visits."

"Always the same day, Wednesday. And back the same day, Friday. Two nights. Always two nights. One day in the library, a day each way on the journey. The Böhmen railway system's falling to bits. Nobody cares."

"Always the same train?"

That made the Engineer titter. "Only two a day. One of 'em's a slow, but the one they call an express takes seven hours to do a hundred and twenty kilometers, best part of two at the border. He always caught the express, same back, the Vindobona. Gets you there in time to book in and get a meal."

"You said he never brought anyone home, but what about callers? This man, for instance?" Morpurgo produced a picture of Humphrey Fish provided by Epworth.

"Never."

"You sound sure."

"Never forget a face." How many faces had he managed to forget during his time at Mauthausen? How many faces did he take care not to remember? Like the one he had just denied knowing; Morpurgo was too old a hand to mistake a lie. Fish had been a caller.

"Always the same day there, same day back. At regular intervals?"

"No. Sometimes only a month between, sometimes much more. You should ask Department One – forgive the suggestion, *Exzellenz*, – save yourself time."

"What did you tell them?"

The Engineer's round face, a shiny pink globe in the diffused light, became cunning. He tapped his button nose. Morpurgo, middle-aged, decent in spite of everything, had a sudden lust to flatten it.

"A little bierstube in Lassallestrasse, near the Danube. Nothing special, it's not the best of quarters. Sometimes our clubs plays a club across the river, in Donaustadt. Sometimes . . ."

"Your chess club?" The Engineer knew more than he was about to say.

"Retired colleagues from the technical college where I – "

"About the bierstube."

The Engineer looked at his glass. Morpurgo captured it. "If you drink too much, your wife will be suspicious. About the bierstube."

"My wife!" For a moment it was possible to see the Engineer as a man who had personally supervised the injection of the Zyklon

B into the packed gas chambers. Then he was once again a compliant old man.

"The U-bahn crosses the Danube on the Reichsbridge. From Donaustadt we sometimes go straight to the bridge, cross by the pedestrian way, catch a train at Vorgartenstrasse station. The bierstube's near the station, *Exzellenz*."

"And?" Why, Morpurgo wondered, had he belatedly become *Exzellenz*?

This time the Engineer dared to give him a look of impatience; stupid foreign policeman.

"Saw him. Twice. Once leaving the stube just as we were going into the subway, didn't see us. Once" – he saved his small triumph until last – "in the stube." He made the motion of tipping a glass.

It was too pat. Aske had made numerous trips to Prague, but not at regular intervals. That the Engineer, by chance, should have come across him twice in or around a bierstube on the other side of town . . . Tonight was Saturday. Stiegelbauer claimed he had just been to his chess club. Aske always went to Prague on a Wednesday.

"Strange. I don't believe Herr Doctor Mandel mentioned this to me."

"So many questions," the Engineer said too glibly. "So many questioners." Had too many weinbrands made him careless?

Two men came into the bar, stocky citizens. One was telling a story that finished in a joint shout of laughter. The Engineer glared balefully at them. "I must go. The Frau Engineer – "

Morpurgo's hand detained him. "You spied on him, didn't you?"

Stiegelbauer briefly considered denying it. Something in Morpurgo's face made him change his mind. He puffed himself up. "I have a responsibility. As a citizen and the proprietor of a *pension*. It is my duty – "

"But you didn't report it. I wonder why?"

How much did Mandel already know? Karl-Heinz, who could be charming off-duty, if he ever was off-duty, had not picked up Morpurgo to tell him about Mauthausen as a matter of idle gossip.

"It wasn't like that," the Engineer said. "Not like that at all. But some of them, a man like Mandel, for instance . . ."

". . . might have found you hard to believe?"

The man had 'quite liked' Aske, but Aske, a Jew, had behaved suspiciously by making regular visits to Prague. In Stiegelbauer's mind, Jews were a natural cause for suspicion. But the Engineer's own past in the matter of Jews was sufficiently delicate to make him think twice before hurrying to tell authority.

"What were you waiting for?"

A chance to ingratiate himself, he guessed, but only when he had more to go on. Aske had inconsiderately spoiled things by disappearing; better for the Engineer, a former Jew-exterminator if only at second hand, to lie low.

"I quite liked him," the Engineer repeated stubbornly. "But a Jew is one thing, a communist another. When each trip starts with a meeting, a secret meeting . . ."

"Where?"

"The lorry park below the Reichsbridge. On the river bank, near Mexico Platz." Anxious now, almost ingratiating, he said, "I would have told them, but when he disappeared . . ."

"Secret meetings? Who with?"

"It was dark. How could I know? Hungarocamion, that's what it said on the truck. Budapest. They come through all the time. From the border, at Klingenbach. Spend the night in the lorry park. Then they go on." He wanted to be believed.

Toby Farrar had said something about a lorry park on the Danube, a possible meeting with a Hungarian truck driver the night before that last trip. Could Epworth know what Mandel did not?

The Engineer misinterpreted Morpurgo's silence. "It's dark down there. A patch of wasteland by the river. I couldn't see what was going on."

"Where were you?"

"The Reichsbridge. On the pedestrian walk. You can stand . . ."

The two *Bürger* had left the bar, coming to a small table against the wall. They talked cheerfully and loudly, but Morpurgo lowered his voice.

"Was he carrying anything? Before or after?"

"Nothing."

"You saw him when he came home?"

"Still nothing. Just said goodnight."

"And the next time was the last time."

Now the Engineer was a man longing to escape. "Prague next day, as usual, but something on his mind. The Frau Engineer knew it, too, spotted he hadn't done his weekly shopping, hadn't – "

"You'd better go." The Engineer went in haste.

Morpurgo sat on for a while; a lot to think about. He knew where he wanted to go, just as soon as it could be arranged. H. E. the British ambassador wouldn't like it one damn bit. That was Epworth's problem.

The Engineer would lie to Frau Engineer to explain his lateness. A drink too many with the boys, something like that. He had lied about Fish. He had lied about other things. A man who had supervised the provision of essential services to a death camp, subsequently surviving to become a respectable citizen in post-war Vienna, had undoubtedly had a great deal of practice in lying.

# TWENTY-TWO

Traiskirchen was a small town an hour's drive from Vienna, the Traiskirchen of the refugees a former Austrian army cadet school. The Russians, said the plump matron who took him to the camp director's office, had used it as a barracks during the occupation. The great stone buildings seemed disproportionately massive for the housing of those hovering between two worlds with no real existence in either.

The camp director's office, like the camp director, was large and busy. Telephones rang. People bustled in and out. Conversation was not an easy thing. Abandoning his cluttered desk, Herr Grosschmidt took Morpurgo through a miniature jungle of flourishing rubber plants to the window, where a bird in a cage sang loudly.

"So, you are here to see Herr Aske."

"If that's possible."

"Here, anything is possible." Herr Grosschmidt had a great laugh to go with a big frame and giant energy. "But you must understand, he is like everyone who has just arrived, a little" – he spiralled a finger in the air – "disoriented. A leaf in the wind, seeking a still corner."

Herr Grosschmidt, rubber plants, a contented cagebird and a talent for imagery, was clearly something of a poet in a desert of the soul.

He laid a big hand on Morpurgo's shoulder. "You understand?"

"I'll be careful."

"Here the world is no more than a few hectares across. People have little to look at, but they see it very clearly. It can disturb. Come."

They went out among the dispiriting stone buildings. Everywhere, small groups of people, some obviously struggling to make themselves understood, discussed and argued. There could be only one basic topic: Where to from here?

"In coming here" – Grosschmidt's strides were as big as his personality – "they leave behind an identity. Now they must find a new one. Sometimes they fail."

Simon Aske, his own identity seemingly in question ever since childhood, had come to a place where everyone was no one hoping to become someone.

"How long will he be here?"

"The bureaucrat's answer to most questions that matter: it all depends. 'On what?' they all ask. I keep my cards close to my chest and just say again, 'It all depends.' "

Between the blocks half the makes of car of Eastern Europe, some with trailers, some with caravans, the sum total of possessions of people who had escaped to the West in the belief that life there had more to offer.

Morpurgo was here as a representative of that superior society they had sacrificed so much to reach. What kind of representative was he? One bearing a banner with a very strange device.

Grosschmidt saved him from endlessly chasing his own tail.

"Herr Aske, it seems, is a remarkable linguist."

"I'm sure his German's better than mine."

Diplomat as well as poet. "Yours is excellent, but Herr Aske speaks German like one of us. I gather that his Czech is equally good. But perhaps you know this?"

"I've never met him."

"Really." Grosschmidt took it in his long stride. Or had he already known? He said, "As requested, he has not been advised of your visit."

Requested by whom? Morpurgo said, "I'm only here to find out what his wishes are." And over His Excellency's not only live but strongly kicking body. It had taken all weekend.

They were mainly young, the refugees, many with small children. What would they think, having sacrificed everything to begin again, if they knew they had among them a refugee from a land of vaunted liberty?

"In here," Grosschmidt said. "Since he is, shall we say, unusual, a little privacy."

A small room just inside the entrance to the block, probably once occupied by an NCO. Grosschmidt knocked. Morpurgo found himself tense: a legend was about to become flesh.

"*Bitte, komm.*" A pleasant voice. They went in.

"Herr Aske," Grosschmidt said, "a visitor from England."

"Hello," Morpurgo said. "I'm John Morpurgo. You met my wife."

A truckle bed, coarse sheets, thin grey blankets. Aske lay on the bed, shirt-sleeved in the dry heat from an old-fashioned radiator. The room was lofty-ceilinged, one small window too high to look through. He had been reading. It was the book of verse Sylvie had found him reading in Gerold's, poems by Sylvia Plath.

"I met your wife?" He looked faintly bemused.

"Now I leave you to talk. You will find me in the camp office." Grosschmidt closed the door softly.

"Sylvie Markham," Morpurgo said. "That's her professional name. You invited her to lunch."

It was as if he had known the man all his life, known him yet knew nothing of him, but he had not missed the way Aske had retreated deep into himself at the sight of a stranger. The melancholy downturn of the mouth was leavened now with a polite smile, but another Aske stood sentinel behind the eyes.

And the man was an actor, never forget it.

Still smiling faintly, Aske said, "Of course. Did she forgive me for not turning up?"

He was in faded jeans, already halfway to the image of the refugee, except that the rest all appeared to have escaped in their best clothes.

"May I?" Morpurgo sat down. From the main block he could hear the shouts of children playing some game or other in Sovbloc lingua franca. If he had been in Aske's place, the first thing he would have wanted to know was how Sylvie Markham's husband had tracked him out to Traiskirchen. And why.

Aske said, "It was very remiss. I did try to get away, but . . . well, it wasn't possible. When is her next exhibition? She's a remarkable artist. Of course, you know that."

"Yes," he said. "I do know that." He was being assessed, and was trying to make his own assessment.

But there was a difference, and he would do well to remember it. A lifelong role-player, a chameleon response to every change of circumstance. Had what had been instinctive in the boy become calculated in the man?

214

Another fact. Aske had not been chosen by Humphrey Fish for his bonny brown eyes. Of those associated with Operation Highflyer, he was the only one left alive.

"Your wife's surely not still in Vienna?" Beyond laying the poetry book on the bed, Aske had scarcely stirred.

"No." This was the thin ice. He had been practising his skating. "But she was worried about you. She – "

"Worried about me?" Aske's voice changed, curling itself about the question in almost sensuous enjoyment. "But she hardly knew me." It was as if he found the idea of anyone's worrying about him too preposterous to be taken seriously.

"In any case" – the question slipped in as a Sovbloc agent might slip in among all these refugees; natural, casual, biding time – "how did she know I was here?"

"She had some idea that you were" – Morpurgo laughed: women, who knew what went on in their minds? – "lonely, depressed perhaps, something like that. Anyway, when she knew I was coming to Vienna – "

"Business?" Aske smiled apologetically. "I'm sorry. Forgive me. None of mine." If it was acting it was smooth, but sharp-edged.

"That's right. She knew I was going to the embassy and – "

"To find out about me?"

"No. I had a meeting with a chap from the commercial section. Farrar? Toby Farrar?"

Aske shook his head, still smiling faintly.

"You've not missed much." Toby would have shrugged off the undeserved slur. "I mentioned your name and he said, 'Oh, that's the bloke who's just applied for citizenship.' Seemed quite put out about it, terribly unBritish sort of thing to do."

They both laughed. Aske put his hands behind his head. He looked relaxed. "I expect they've all heard about it."

"I wouldn't know. Not much time for embassy types."

"Morpurgo," Aske said. "Interesting name."

"I've heard it suggested it's Spanish or Portuguese. From way back."

"Portuguese Jewish." Aske touched his nose, so casually that it would have meant nothing if Morpurgo had known nothing. "The Sephardi. As opposed to Ashkenazi." He pronounced the Z Germanically, turning it into a grim if clumsy pun. "Of course, if you prefer Nordic mythology, Ask was the first man. Hitler's Adam."

215

"I don't understand. Are you Jewish?"

"Simon Benjamin?" For a moment Aske was a Jew. He laughed. "What do you think?"

He didn't know what to think.

Aske said, "Vienna's always been home from home for Jews. A good place to hide."

Morpurgo thought of Engineer Stiegelbauer. "Not any more, surely? Nearly all dead."

Aske smiled. "Precisely." He picked up the book of verse, found a page.

> " 'Ash, ash –
> You poke and stir.
> Flesh, bone, there is nothing there –' "

He said, "Ashkenazi, sometimes. Flesh, bone, nothing there. Do you ever feel Jewish?"

"No, not really." Morpurgo found himself at a loss. "What did you mean, precisely?"

"Precisely dead. Death is very precise. We were the lucky ones. Being here" – he waved a hand at the bare room – "is like coming home. Jews are used to camps like this."

A game was being played. Aske knew the rules. Morpurgo did not. Aske said, "I'm British by adoption. You wouldn't know that. Viennese Jewish family, the old tradition. Before the Nazis, one in every ten families in Vienna was Jewish. Scholars, artists, musicians, writers. Hitler didn't just murder the Jews. Hitler murdered culture."

"Your family . . ." Morpurgo began, a Christian cross in his mind's eye.

"Ash," Aske said. "Poke and stir, nothing there." He smiled.

"You were a refugee?" Morpurgo's thoughts raced through what was known but must not be shown to be known.

"*Ash*kenazi. Ask a Nazi. Poke and stir, nothing there. Except me. Sorry I can't offer you anything in the way of hospitality. There's a canteen of sorts. I couldn't recommend it. Does the embassy know you're here?"

Changes of subject, no change of tone.

"I didn't tell them I was coming."

"They'll find out. Probably won't like it." His amusement was the gloss on the underlying tristesse of a man used to being misunderstood.

216

Or playing the part of a man misunderstood. There *was* something actorish about him. Partly the way he spoke, an awareness of sound as well as content, of impact as well as sense. That face, too, a controlled mobility, what went on behind it projected or disguised at will. In short, intensely self-aware, highly skilled in concealing his true self.

Also a trained and experienced agent. Aske had run the courier service between Gossip and Fish, had even continued the Prague run after Highflyer ended in disaster. Epworth had said so.

But no, he must have got that wrong. Highflyer ended when the KGB put Gossip in a bare cell at Lefortovo; nothing more for Aske to bring back. Fish had made two or three trips to Vienna during the attempts to exchange Gossip for Sattin, presumably to consult Aske. Then Aske had crossed back into Czechoslovakia and vanished. Only to reappear more than eighteen months later, denying that he had made the trip. Denying, in fact, that he had ever been to Czechoslovakia.

He tried to rid his mind of the thought that the answer to all these questions sat no more than a yard or so away. A few days on Five's country estate would have Simon Benjamin Aske telling the truth and glad to.

Following his own train of thought, Aske said, "No, I'm afraid the embassy won't like it."

"Well sod the embassy," Morpurgo said, and meant it; no love for high officialdom.

Aske looked at him for several seconds, and there was briefly something between them. A warmth? Ridiculous! Aske laughed. " 'Villains by necessity, fools by heavenly compulsion, knaves, thieves and treachers by spherical predominance.' How did you get the Austrians to let you into this place?"

"Told them I was a friend of yours." He supposed the quotation was more Shakespeare. He said, "It's what Sylvie would expect me to do."

"You know her that well? To be sure what she would expect?" Now *there* was an odd question.

"I've been married to her a long time." An opening here. "You've never been married, or you'd know."

"No." The response was emphatic. "I suppose I've missed something."

But he had been married. And had discovered his wife in bed with another man. Sufficient reason for denying the existence of a marriage? Perhaps. Toby Farrar, on the canal bank, had said, 'If

217

Czechoslovakia didn't exist, Traiskirchen won't exist.' If Czechoslovakia didn't exist, why should a failed marriage?

Aske said, "What sort of business?" the question looping out
as unpredictably as a clay pigeon from the trap. If it was a
deliberate diversion, it was a good one.

"Confectionery." He had been prepared for it. If there was one
person he could rely on to back him up, it was Trigg.

Aske didn't follow it up. "Where is she now? Your wife."

Morpurgo snapped up another chance. "She's got this marvellous thing on with the RSC. The Royal – "

"I know." A touch of asperity. Then Aske produced his smile.
"The RSC. I remember. Did she tell you she thought I was an
actor?"

"Something of the sort." He pushed his luck. "It didn't seem
all that important at the time."

"No, I don't suppose it would." The answer appeared to
amuse Aske. "At the time." His heavy, bluish lids dropped over
his eyes as if he were looking at something outside the cheerless
room.

"I told her I wasn't. That wasn't strictly true. I almost was.
Almost very good."

He looked up. "Just think. Instead of meeting her in a Vienna
bookshop, it might have been the greenroom at Stratford.
Posterity," Aske said. "He gave up his vocation and missed an
appointment with posterity."

It was the first time he had used the third person.

He saw Morpurgo's small frown. "The knowing lens. I might
have met her behind it at Stratford. But" – he raised a hand as if to
prevent something – "*he* wouldn't have liked that. He wouldn't
care to have himself looked into as deeply as Sylvie Markham
would look."

"He? Who?"

Somewhere a radio was playing music that could freely cross
borders. Somewhere the children were playing a new game,
singing and clapping their hands.

Aske smiled his slow, secretive smile. "A manner of speaking.
There was a time when I was tempted towards the stage. A talent
as well as a vocation. There was" – his fingers, interlaced, tugged
against each other – "an inner struggle. I wanted it. He didn't, the
other me we all have. Do you know what I'm talking about?"

"You were afraid you'd fail."

The smile curled higher. The hands pulled apart. "Just the

218

opposite – afraid I'd succeed. He wouldn't have liked that. Do you understand?"

"Sylvie behind a lens," Morpurgo said, "sees nothing but the truth. Is that what you mean?" He wasn't quite sure what he meant himself.

Continuing to smile, Aske said, " 'I cannot tell what you and other men think of this life; but, for my single self, I had as lief not be as live to be in awe of such a thing as I myself.' "

A moment later he had tipped his head to laugh. It was impossible to say at what.

He came off the bed to pace the few yards between it and the bare wall.

" 'Seldom he smiles, and smiles in such a sort as if he mock'd himself, and scorn'd his spirit, that could be moved to smile at anything. Such men as he be never at heart's ease, and therefore' " – he turned away – " 'are they very dangerous.' "

Over-stressing the rhythm, he said, "He hopes you won't resent his little joke. Iambic pentameters, do you see? It's hard to stop it, once you're in the swing."

Morpurgo felt an unexpected sense of relief. This, after some initial doubt, was the Aske he had been piecing together through the past weeks. Mercurial, light-weight, a poseur and also, he rather thought, basically amoral. Certainly a man far more preoccupied with his own image than his obligations to others. In short, an actor. Sylvie, who had liked him, had been deceived.

During that last run to Prague, the man had been taken. After that, simply a matter of time.

A casebook study in psychological instability: a compulsive performer, eager to speak whatever lines would draw applause. The KGB interrogators would have made mincemeat of him.

Afterwards?

The greater part of two years in enemy territory, that was the way SIS looked at it. Simon Aske had been a prisoner-of-war in a war that never ended. For that kind of prisoner there were only two possible fates.

They were, in due course and always at a price, repatriated. Or they disappeared – as Sattin had disappeared, as Gossip had disappeared – no questions asked since none would be answered.

Simon Aske was the exception. Simon Aske had come back.

"You missed your vocation," Morpurgo said.

"Yes." Aske was febrile now. "I could have been great, you know. Only you don't. The people I worked with, they'd say I was too cold, all mind, no heart. He wouldn't let himself go, they'd say, and they'd be right. *He* wouldn't. But they'd say I was great. They'd have to say *I* was great."

Pacing up and down, with short, agitated steps and occasional glances at Morpurgo, who thought, nevertheless, that he was talking to himself.

"*They* couldn't stand aside," Aske said. "They threw themselves into their parts body and soul, nothing held back. They gave themselves. If you give yourself like that, you lose all control. Whereas *I* . . ."

He had stopped, staring up at the small window through which no sun would ever come. In the distance there was singing – not children now – sad, soulful Slavic singing, full of a sense of loss. Aske, too, looked full of a sense of loss.

People who need uncritical love – Dukinfield speaking – and find it suddenly withdrawn. After the despair comes the need for revenge, the urge to humiliate whoever has been the cause of humiliation.

*Litost.*

How had Aske felt when his coldly brilliant Shylock, calculated to humiliate Edmund Dukinfield, had produced nothing but criticism, even self-humiliation?

Little to do with his giving up the stage, according to Lotta Boyle, but might it have influenced his response when Spencer came a-wooing on behalf of Fish?

Unstable, given to withdrawal, now publicly rejected, might he not have seen it as an appropriate response to take up work of great secrecy? He liked being told he was the best thing since sliced bread; Serena Donne's characteristic cliché.

Recognition of his outstanding linguistic ability was praise in itself. To be invited, with all the trimmings of conspiracy, to join the most select of elites; might that not, in the circumstances of failure, have been irresistible?

Preposterous! So what, Morpurgo wondered as he watched Aske staring abstractedly at the window, *was* he suggesting?

Question: Just how far *would* such a man go to humiliate anyone he might feel had humiliated him? As far as to become a traitor? Not to be taken against his will in Prague, but to go there certain of a welcome, having betrayed Gossip and Highflyer in advance?

Question: Did it stop there?

Aske came back from his self-induced trance. "The things that

220

might have been. Who was it said the saddest words are 'If only'?"

No alternative now but to play his own part to the end and make his exit.

"Are you sure you're doing the right thing? Even if you were born here, England's your home."

"Yes," Aske said. "I'm sure I'm doing the right thing."

"Giving up your country is a big step."

"What if your country's giving up you? That's a bigger."

That was close, very close.

"I'm not sure I understand."

"Really? Lucky man. You like things the way they are back home?"

It would have been a shrewd thrust if Simon Aske had known all about John Morpurgo.

He said, "Not liking things the way they are is no argument for running away." How often had he said that to Sylvie?

"Change from within?"

"Something like that." But people in his kind of job were in no position to change anything. They were there to keep things as they were.

"Decline and fall," Aske said, "is like bad breath. Everybody knows about it but you."

He sat down on the bed and swung up his legs. "Tell Sylvie Markham I was touched. Tell her, when she's done with the RSC she should consider a pictorial record of Kakania. Tell her it needs her kind of truth." He stretched out his legs and turned his back.

"How long are you likely to be here?"

"For ever and ever," Aske said, "and no amen."

"I'll come and see you again. Tomorrow." He must come back. He hadn't finished. He had barely begun.

"Tomorrow" – Aske's voice was far away – "and tomorrow and tomorrow. The days are pretty long here."

Back in the camp office, every phone ringing at once, the director said, "Has he changed his mind?"

Morpurgo shook his head. "No?" Grosschmidt grabbed two phones at once. "Oh well, makes a change, a refugee from the West."

# TWENTY-THREE

After returning his rented car, Morpurgo walked aimlessly about the town, ending up high in the Belvedere gardens to look down over the city across the great sweep of lawns with their wedding-cake ornamentation of statuary. The change he had sensed on his return to Vienna was not in the city but in himself. He was no longer an outsider with a mystery to solve. He was part of it, or why had Department One made things so easy?

If Aske had come to England as a Jewish refugee child adopted by Christian parents, it provided an answer to the mystery of their Christian burial. It also went a long way towards explaining his complex and contradictory character; the more so since the boy had been sent away to endure the rigours of an evangelical Christian education.

But if Aske was his adoptive name, all that strange talk of Ashkenazi was so much nonsense. Recollecting the stark fragment from the Plath poem, Morpurgo thought that the grown man might perhaps have come to be haunted, perhaps worse, by the racial tragedy from which he had been saved in infancy.

There was truth in Epworth's remark that the spy trade was a home-from-home for brilliant eccentrics. Fieldmen, in particular, frequently had complex and poignant motivation. In a hazy way it helped him to understand why Fish, through the so far unidentified Spencer, might have seen Aske as a likely recruit.

Steve Archer would have had little patience with that kind of analysis. Like intellectual nonconformity, fancy theorising always produced a mixture of contempt and suspicion in Steve; what he called clever-clever.

The westering sun had summoned a chill wind from the

Danube. Time to go back to the city, following the path from the Upper to the Lower Belvedere past the baroque graffiti of the great. The wind was whipping back a glittering crest of spray from the edge of the cascade where Neptune and assorted Tritons gestured theatrically. He found it, as he found everything about the period, heartlessly self-congratulatory. The city had applauded itself and neglected its inhabitants as it had applauded Mozart's music and tossed him into a pauper's grave.

People like Steve Archer liked places like the Belvedere. Symbolising the division of the world between Us and Them, it was the nearest they came to culture. The reason Steve kept coming into his mind, Morpurgo thought vaguely, could only be that Aske had been recruited by Fish, and Steve and Fish had been close in those far-off days.

He crossed Schwartzenbergplatz in the shadow of the Red Army war memorial, the wind catching the water jet and swirling it up to drench the steel-helmeted hero on his high column. On the far side of the square he passed the response of the other superpower, a well-patronised McDonald's.

For himself, later, he picked a small restaurant off the Neuer Markt. Its decor aimed at a Tyrolean hunting lodge, the walls patchworked with old prints, protuberant with the heads of boar, deer and, gastronomic outcast, a leering, sly-eyed fox. Shoulder-high partitions gave it a degree of intimacy.

He ate morosely as the restaurant slowly filled up. He had failed before, more times than he cared to remember. His career, like everyone's in the security services, was a litter of unanswered questions. Failure was the norm, success the occasional carrot that lured the donkey on.

So why had he gone against his first instinct and suggested a second visit to Aske? And why in God's name had Aske agreed?

He brooded before abruptly leaving his meal to telephone.

"Herr Grosschmidt has gone home."

"Give me his home number, please."

"Sorry, sir. That's not permitted."

"Herr Doctor Mandel of Department One will be annoyed if I have to trouble him. Herr Grosschmidt will be even more annoyed when he finds out." Though Morpurgo's German was being stretched to the limit, his tone of voice was fluent.

Grosschmidt said, "Ah, Herr Morpurgo. You got my message."

Morpurgo thought fast. "I've only just got back to the hotel.

223

What's happened?" Aske had done something drastic. Killed himself? Why should he think that?

A booming laugh from the poet *manqué*. "What happens when the chrysalis decides not to become a butterfly? In this case, simple. It turns back into a caterpillar and walks away. A man is our guest when he knocks at the door and asks for entry. If he later wishes to go home to mother, still simple. I have no power to detain him. So, the authorities are informed. I pat him on the back. I wish him well. I open the gate."

"But the paperwork must take time?"

"Ah, the paperwork! Colossal! We are great bureaucrats. In this case, fortunately, no problem."

"When will he leave?"

"Herr Aske already has a residence permit. I advise the authorities, but I cannot prevent him from leaving at once. Particularly since it is now his intention to return home."

"Home?"

"England. Where else? He is very grateful to you for helping him to clear his mind."

"Herr Grosschmidt, where is he now?"

"Back in Vienna, some *pension* in the ninth district. He has stayed there before, it seems."

Like everything else to do with the visit to Traiskirchen, it was altogether too smooth, even if Grosschmidt himself believed it. He doubted whether the Stiegelbauers would have Aske back for a single night.

"My government is in your debt," Grosschmidt was saying. "We refuse no one the right of asylum, but we are a small country. There are many who say that stray cats should not be a charge on the taxpayer, even if they miaow like nightingales." He produced his jovial laugh.

One appetite lost, a stronger one unassuaged, Morpurgo settled his bill. From the alcove nearest the door he received nods and smiles. It was the two solid citizens he had last seen in Engineer Stiegelbauer's local weinstube. Returning their *"Grüss Gott"*, he went out into the bright lights of the Neuer Markt.

It was Tuesday. No matter when the Engineer's chess club met in Donaustadt, Wednesdays were the days on which Aske had gone to Prague.

*　　*　　*

Taxis were too easily tailed. He took the streetcar to the

Schottentor, the U-bahn to Donauinsel. As he walked along the platform to the exit, the closed-circuit traffic control monitor showed him that no one was following.

The Reichsbridge pedestrian walkway was deserted, sparsely lit. His footsteps echoed hollowly, no one in his wake. The slow eastward drift of the Danube, broad and desolate, was detectable only from undulating streamers of reflected light. Behind him, on the edge of the great plain stretching away towards the Hungarian border, were the vertical constellations of UNO City and the Danube Tower. Upstream, the western bank, remote in the night, reared toward the blacker blackness of the Kahlenberg Heights.

Halfway across, shouts, shrieks and distorted music echoed in the silence, too far away at first to be identified. A gang of youths on roller skates swept down on him, one of them swinging a huge stereo radio. They flew past to a cacophony of mocking yells. He walked on, his heart beating that much faster.

The walkway merged with Lassallestrasse high above the river. Below was Handelskai, only the occasional truck or car. From the river the land crossed a large patch of unlit wasteland before rising to the level of the street. Above loomed office blocks with huge neon signs; white GRUNDIG, yellow BANNER BATTERIEN.

In the lorry park, hemmed about by miniature Alps of construction spoil, were three vehicles, one small and anonymous, one a great van emblazoned with BAUMANN, GRAZ. It was the third that was of interest, a huge double-artic labelled HUNGAROCAMION. Toby Farrar had hinted that Aske had had treffs with trucks from Hungary. The Engineer had confirmed it. In Lassallestrasse he could see the bierstube and the U-bahn entrance, just as Stiegelbauer had said. Morpurgo found a way to the lorry park down a track made by the earth-moving machinery that had dumped the Alps. He picked his way quietly. Long-distance truck drivers usually slept in their cabs.

The best cover was a bulldozer leaning on its blade like an exhausted mammoth. Its cab gave him as good a view as the poor light and uneven ground could offer. It was all unprofessional, illogical, crazy.

Occasional traffic apart, the only sound came from a group of moored barges over toward the Kaisermühlen bank, where a dredging shovel, outlined against the light from UNO City, swung, dipped, disgorged in a dinosauric ballet. The night became colder, traffic less frequent, just the periodic rumble of the U-bahn to testify that the heart of the city still beat. The repetitive chug of the dredger was hypnotic.

In due course someone came down the track made by construction traffic, stumbling on the uneven ground, cursing without conviction. He could see the man now, back from a night on the town. Skirting the van from Graz, he tripped, fell against it with a thump. A sleepy voice swore at him. He held up his hands in token of apology, used one of them for a less apologetic postscript.

Reaching the Hungarian artic, he hauled himself up, grunting, to vanish inside. The stillness returned. Far across the river, the dredging shovel snored and muttered.

Any treff, Morpurgo thought, would be with this man. How much longer should he wait? Why wait at all? He was on autopilot, flying a ramshackle structure of hunch and guesswork cobbled together over some twenty years.

No, he was stuck in a bloody bulldozer in a bloody lorry park on the banks of the brown bloody Danube because he had been used, and he didn't like being used. He wanted to know who was using him, and why.

Beyond the nearest spoil heap, limned with ghostly yellow light from the Banner battery sign, the shadows put out a pseudopod. The pseudopod split off, moved, silent, from heap to heap, vanished, reappeared beyond the vehicle from Graz. It was halfway to the Hungarian vehicle before he could be certain that it was Aske.

Reaching the Hungarian artic, Aske rapped gently on the cab. It was some time before the pale blur of a face looked down. The driver seemed baffled and annoyed. If this was a treff, he had not been expecting it.

It was developing into a dispute; Aske determined, the driver gradually raising his voice. Angry now, he climbed down. He had prepared himself for sleep by removing his trousers and shoes.

He must have trodden on something sharp. He yelled, hopped, broke into a stream of abuse. The cab door of the truck from Graz swung open. A broad-shouldered, stocky figure swung down, angry to have his sleep disturbed a second time. That was the first of a whole series of events.

The lights of the third truck came on unexpectedly. Some half-dozen men tumbled out with a general scuffle of feet, barked

226

instructions and the waving of hand-held beams, Aske, the Hungarian and the man from Graz, taken by surprise, shielded their eyes from the dazzle. Someone shouted, "Police. Stay where you are."

A stakeout. In the cab of the bulldozer, Morpurgo made himself small. He, SIS, the British government, could be in the deepest kind of international trouble if he were caught in a Department One dragnet.

The Hungarian, if that was what he was, had begun to shout. The man from Graz gaped, innocent and bewildered. Mandel's men should have cut off all possibility of escape but Aske appeared to have vanished. Morpurgo heard the soft pad of feet, a light panting, then Aske went swiftly past the bulldozer. He slithered down to follow, telling himself that this kind of thing was not for sedentary deskmen within sight of fifty.

Aske made straight for the U-bahn station. So did Morpurgo, but seemingly no one else.

Keeping well back until the train came in, he boarded at the far end of the car. He knew it was too simple when a knot of teenagers moved to reveal one of the men he had seen earlier in the restaurant in the Neue Markt. The man, seeing him too, got out at the next station.

Aske was hunched in a corner. His hands, fingers interlocked, kneaded each other endlessly. Every so often he moved his head from side to side like a man in pain or anguish. Not once did he look down the car.

He rode the train to Karlsplatz. He appeared to be indifferent to the possibility that he might have been followed; indifferent to everything except whatever was going on in his own mind.

Morpurgo, too, had his pressing thoughts. His hunch as to what Aske would do had come off, but he saw no cause for self-congratulation. Someone else's hunch, since it had also included an accurate guess at what Morpurgo would do, had been altogether superior.

Aske worked his way through the throng towards the exit on the south side of Kärntnerstrasse. Morpurgo followed at a distance. The man on the train might have handed over to others. There was nothing he could do about it. A girl thrust a leaflet into his hand, more anti-nuclear propaganda. He stuffed it unthinkingly in a pocket and ran up the steps after his quarry.

Aske headed towards the floodlit Karlskirche. In the little park he hesitated, as if running out of ideas. Eventually he took a seat facing the great dome of the church. The open space, so near to the heart of the city, yet separated by the immense width of the Ring, was all but deserted, no chance of unobserved approach.

Virtually asking himself what Department One would expect him to do next, Morpurgo swore under his breath, walked on and sat down beside Aske. Aske, hunched forward, head on chest, ignored him.

Half prepared for Aske to bolt, he said, "Tell me about Spencer." Behind them, an ambulance raced along the Ring, siren wailing.

After several seconds, Aske turned his head. "Was that his real name? I often wondered." His voice lacked surprise, interest, any emotion at all.

"You didn't think Spencer was his real name?"

Aske cupped his face. "He played the same game."

"What game?" This time, Morpurgo told himself, he would not let go of the conversation, no matter how much it wriggled.

"The us-and-them game," Aske said. "Don't pretend you don't play it. Everyone plays it. The game of Slansky's shadow."

"Who's us, and who's them?" Slansky's shadow, still beyond him, could wait for the time being.

"Who's he? And who was she?" Aske laughed, nothing to do with humour. After his first look at Morpurgo he had paid no more attention.

Afraid to let the silence take root, Morpurgo said, "She? Was there a she?"

"She's dead now. We mustn't talk about her. He wouldn't like that."

"Who? Spencer?"

"Not Spencer. Spencer found him, but Spencer didn't know. Godwin bought him. Godwin knew too much."

Morpurgo produced the photograph of Fish. "Is this Spencer?" The picture was black-and-white. Fish, heavy-browed, always dark about the jowls, had been a black-and-white character.

Aske took it mechanically. "That's Godwin." The picture had brought him upright in barely suppressed agitation.

"No," Morpurgo said. "That's Fish." So Fish had been Godwin to Aske.

High-pitched, yokelish, Aske said, " 'Master, I marvel how the fishes live in the sea.' " then, dropping a rough octave, " 'Why, as men do a-land: the great ones eat up the little ones.' " He giggled, Epworth *redivivus*.

228

"I should have said 'was'," Morpurgo said. "Fish is dead now."

" 'O' " – Aske was desolate – " 'that this too too solid flesh would melt'." Sitting there in the semi-darkness, the floodlit columns and baroque dome of the Karlskirche theatrical ahead of them, he seemed to be trying to melt into the night.

*He said he'd like to run through time and leave no footprints. He said things like that.* Lotta Boyle; he could see now what she had meant.

"Tell me about Godwin." He tried to make himself sound harmless, however you did that. Fish's pseudonym had been Godwin. But Spencer?

Aske was still looking at Fish's picture. "Is he dead dead, not just dead inside?" Morpurgo had the beginnings of a new suspicion, entirely new.

Aske tore the picture down the middle, then again, slowly, methodically, until Fish was a collection of scraps. He tilted his hand. The scraps sifted to the ground. "Fly away, Godwin, fly away Fish." Morpurgo felt a frisson. For a second or two, Aske had actually been Fish, jerky, full of suppressed energy, eyes sparkling with suspicion.

"Godwin made him go," Aske said. "Godwin got past to make him do what he mustn't ever do. She drove Godwin and Godwin drove him. He had to hide deep. Now he'll have to go deeper still." He was clearly talking of himself.

It was like eavesdropping on something of which only the occasional word was in English. Fish – Godwin – had had some hold on Aske, strong enough to turn him into a courier between Vienna and Prague, strong enough to drive him back to Prague even after Gossip had been captured.

But was Aske suggesting that someone else – 'she' – had had a similar hold on Fish? Not Fish's wife, from what Epworth had said. And the postmortem enquiry had turned up no other woman. He abandoned it for the time being. A man in Aske's mental state should not be taken too literally.

"I understand" – he was a man feeling his way through strange rooms in pitch darkness – "that you want to come home. I think you should."

"Home." Aske gave the word no inflexion. He stood up, looking about him as if he had no idea where he was. He said again, "Home."

It was as Morpurgo had disappeared, as if he had never been. Aske looked about him once more, small, meaningless movements of the head, then up at the sky, where the brighter stars pricked through the city glare. He shivered, thrust his hands in his pockets and began to walk towards the distant Karlskirche.

Under his breath Morpurgo said, "Shit!" and went on sitting. It could have been the state of Aske's mind that decided him not to follow. It could have been the state of his own. It could have been that Aske would be followed in any case. He had no doubt of that.

\*　　　\*　　　\*

Karl-Heinz Mandel arrived just after breakfast. He looked sleek. The man with the smile waited near the street exit.

"Deportation order?"

Mandel laughed. "A free ride to the airport? Why not? First, a little trip."

Making for the Ring, the car headed north. They rode in a silence that Mandel clearly enjoyed. At the Schottentor the car looped north again on Porzellangasse. Morpurgo said, "What's the German for a ferret?"

Mandel lit a cigarette, still smiling. "Ferret?"

"A small animal you put down a hole to chase out a rabbit."

"Ah! *Ein Frettchen*." He smiled out smoke.

"Or perhaps I was just your bunny."

"A bunny is a rabbit?"

"Or a mug. A mug . . ."

" 'Mug' I know." Mandel patted Morpurgo's knee. "Not so stupid, or you would not have been on the Handelskai last night. We had not expected that, *nicht wahr*, Rudi?"

The man who had been in the weinstube, the restaurant and on the U-bahn nodded. "*Das war gut. Das war wirklich hübsch.*"

"He'll never go home," Morpurgo said. "I expect you know that." They came to a halt outside a glass and steel tower.

Mandel smiled more smoke. "You're familiar with such tricks, naturally. The Hungarian was very alarmed, but everything has been put right."

"Not the right man, not the right time."

"Something like that."

"Yet you thought Aske would go there."

"Strange, don't you think? As if the last time was only yesterday?"

"You talked to Stiegelbauer."

"Stiegelbauer talked. You caused him great alarm."

"Mauthausen caused a lot of people great alarm."

230

"Of course." Mandel was buttoning his coat. "Shall we go?"

"What is this place?"

"An old railway station in new clothing. Come."

Behind the glass people-file the old station had changed little from the days when the Austro-Hungarian empire stretched from Poland to the Adriatic. The other of the two men from the Engineer's weinstube was waiting. He jerked his head. "In there."

A supermarket had been added during the modernisation. Beyond was a cafeteria. Euromusic tiptoed down the frontiers of audibility. Aske, alone, hands folded like an obedient child, stared at nothing. Only one other table had an occupant, face hidden by *Die Presse*. Morpurgo and Mandel pretended to look at groceries.

At last, Aske put money on the table, picked up a soft weekend case, moved towards the exit.

They watched him board, walk down the train, settle in a seat. The man who had been reading *Die Presse* also boarded, carrying a couple of small cases. At nine-twenty the train pulled out for Prague.

"Our two countries," Mandel said, still staring after it, "have much in common, dear colleague. Though you have yet to adjust while we have had much practice. Small, stripped of empire, unimportant. In this age of giants we must export all manner of things if we are to survive."

"Come." He took Morpurgo's arm again. "Some coffee. A good ferret should not go unrewarded."

Morpurgo went without a murmur. He wondered what Mandel would say if he knew that the man with *Die Presse* was Pierre Weber, deputy head of operations, CIA. Or perhaps Mandel already knew?

# TWENTY-FOUR

"It turns out" – Trigg came straight to the point – "yon feller is a bastard."

He had telephoned not long after Morpurgo's return, "just passing through, buttercup". They were in a pub near the Strand Palace Hotel, where, according to Trigg, the Guinness was halfway drinkable "for London".

"Are you with me, lad? I'm talking about Aske." Top of Morpurgo's list of bastards was not Aske but Epworth, whose house in the woods was once again not answering the phone.

"Eh!" Trigg withered him. "I reckon that crack on the skull's let rust in. Are you interested in what Uncle Norman's found out, or not?"

"Uncle Norman's got it wrong this time. Aske's not illegitimate. He was adopted." His beer tasted sour, flat. Life tasted sour and flat. He had to see Epworth.

"Hasty-tempered, is Uncle Norman," Trigg said, "when it comes to being called a liar."

"I'm sorry. It's just that I've found out a few things myself since I last saw you."

"Aye, well, your Sylvie'd not be best pleased to know how long it took to get hold of a feller that's only just out of hospital and supposed to be taking things easy."

He finished his Guinness. "He might look clumsy, might Uncle Norman, but when it suits he can wheedle a bird out of a pussy-cat's mouth.

"There's this old lady, happen I mentioned her last time we spoke. Ada Crossthwaite – names don't come more Yorkshire nor that. Over ninety now, but according to Uncle Norman, still sharp enough to cut fingers if not handled with care.

"Anyroad, she and Mrs Aske was both members of some women's social club run by St Andrew's church in Pontefract, back in days when bingo was housey-housey. Pretty, fluffy little thing, she reckons Mrs Aske was, name of Winny. Her old man had a bit of brass, but was seemingly a right tartar. Thought the only purpose of a wife was to feed him and keep his boots shiny, gave her what for if she didn't."

He broke off to thump on the bar. "Same again, love." While Guinness creamed slowly into the glass he went on. "All in all, lass had a pretty rough time, but this Mrs Crossthwaite gave her a bit of mothering. Aunty Ada, Winny Aske came to call her.

"Right, where does this get us? I'll tell you, buttercup. One day – this is early in t'war, do you see? with the boy no more than a babe – Winny Aske gets rough end of her old man's tongue once too often and goes running to Aunty Ada crying her heart out.

"Well, what was left of Christmas port was brought out. According to Uncle Norman, Christmas must have been a right miserable affair, since there was enough port left to get young Winny Aske singing like a canary in the sun." Stopping abruptly as his glass returned, Trigg buried his mouth in its creamy collar.

"Now then" – he dabbed his mouth with the back of a hand – "where was I? Well, it's just what I said. Wrong side of the blanket, your Mister Aske. Before coming to Pomfret, young Winny, soft as grease according to Aunty Ada, had let some feller slip a bun in her oven and clear off without settling up. Tom Aske, always hanging around, never a look-in, sees his chance and pops the question."

"Marry him and he'd give the child a name?"

"Got it in one. There was nought that noble about it. He wanted the lass, didn't want the bairn though, which is why, once it was old enough to get in t'way, it was treated like summat picked up cheap on fents and fancies stall in Leeds market."

"Poor little bugger packed off to school practically as soon as he could walk."

"And his mam," Trigg said, "wasn't even allowed to see that much of him when he wasn't at school. It seems there's places where kids whose parents are abroad, or just don't want to be fashed with them, more like, can be sent during the holidays to be kept out of mischief.

"By!" He shook his big head. "Happen that's why country's so badly run; them that was privately educated getting revenged

233

for the way they were treated when they were little lads and couldn't hit back.

"Anyroad, buttercup, you can see how things must have been. Then comes the car smash and what scrap of mother love lad had had was gone.

"There was a trust to handle the brass. Aunty Ada's none too sure about any of that, but you've just about picked up trail from then on."

"Just about." It was as if he had barely begun to make sense of a mammoth jigsaw puzzle before Uncle Norman and Aunty Ada, well-meaning but clumsy, had knocked it to the floor.

"There's no doubt about this? I mean, an old lady of ninety!"

He knew before Trigg withered him again that there was no doubt.

So much for the adopted Jewish refugee child.

> Ash, ash –
> You poke and stir
> Flesh, bone, there is nothing there –

\*　　　\*　　　\*

Epworth had apparently been cleaning a very fancy .22 rifle. The room smelled of gun oil, which was perhaps why all the windows were open. No one else was at home.

"Why aren't you answering the phóne?"

"No need. You came." Epworth waved him to a chair. "Drink?"

"Thank you."

"Palo cortado viejissimo? Something of a rarity. From the Machanudo, too." He waved a glass under his nose dreamily.

"I'd rather have a drink."

"Scotch." Epworth was pained. "In the sideboard. What news on the Rialto?"

"Don't you start! Anyway" – *was* this Shakespeare? – "nought for thy comfort."

"So I hear," Epworth said. "But do go on." The link with Karl-Heinz Mandel was practically visible.

Morpurgo sloshed Scotch generously. "Tell me something first. Am I working for the country or Lawrence Epworth? And don't bloody well say it's the same thing."

Epworth's lips formed a wounded O.

"What's Toby Farrar told you?"

234

"You went to Traiskirchen."

"And?"

"You left. So did Aske – mmmm – a clean departure. The Austrians are pleased. The ambassador" – Epworth giggled – "will get over it. Now, the full story, especially about Traiskirchen." He clearly knew nothing about Pierre Weber at the Franz Josef Station.

Morpurgo ended with Trigg's newest revelation.

"Not Jewish after all," Epworth mused.

"I think they scrambled his brains in Lefortovo, but he's obviously never been normal."

"Normal!" Epworth giggled. "That word was invented by the silent majority as a form of herd protection. If one were to stack up the human race according to normality, the lumpen mass would make an Everest, with genius an endangered species in the foothills."

He went back to Aske. "Registered as the legitimate son, but to all intents and purposes an orphan even before the car crash."

"And never touched a penny of the estate afterwards. I've checked."

"Severing the last remaining link with his parents."

"I reckon," Morpurgo said, "he knew the score. I reckon his mother must have told him."

"I suppose" – Epworth resolved instantly what had taken Morpurgo hours – "one might see his assumed Jewishness as some sort of symbol. Identification with the – mmmm – rejected, the persecuted, the people Hitler tried to write out of history."

Morpurgo nodded. "Could explain his attraction to Vienna. It's that sort of place, written out of history." He half expected Epworth to deride the theory.

Instead, Epworth said, "But of course. Slansky's shadow."

Slansky was dead, an official Marxist-Leninist non-person, written out of history. For a moment Morpurgo thought he understood something, then it was gone. "He seems to have been looking for an identity ever since childhood."

"Or hiding one. After all," Epworth said wickedly, "take you. Working for covert, ultra-right-wing pro-Establishment organisations for over twenty years, keeping your conscience quiet by pretending to be an old-fashioned left-wing radical, *à bas les aristos*. Sylvie's – mmmm – rumbled you. So have Trigg and I. But everyone else – "

"What the hell do you mean, pretend?"

"You mean you really believe it? Oh dear! I do apologise. Bearing in mind your occupation, your – mmmm – innate decency strikes a good many people as the least sincere thing about you."

"You bastard!" Morpurgo said. "It was as a token left-wing moderate that I was recruited in the first place."

"Recruited then, rejected now," Epworth said. "Which is why you sometimes show all the symptoms of identity crisis. Are you a decent, freedom-loving man of the people? Or a watchdog of privileged authoritarianism?" Picking up the .22 rifle, he laid it across his thighs.

"Which" – there was none of his customary vagueness – "is the role and which the reality? Curtsey while you're thinking."

After a long moment, Morpurgo said, "You're talking about Aske."

Epworth, who had been gazing intently through the window, returned his attention. "Take a spy, for example. Sattin. Gossip. Even Aske. The very symbol of contemporary man, identity and autonomy always under threat. Just like – mmmm – yours."

Reaching for a box of .22 cartridges from the table on which his sherry caught the evening sun, he shook it absently.

"Of course, most of us don't have your problem. Take your friend Sid. He sees himself as a painter, decorator and family man. So do his family and friends. I see myself as a security expert and family man. So do my family and – mmmm – acquaintances. But you . . . And Aske . . . Always in question. Always under threat. No more secure in the world than you're secure in yourselves.

"An unshakeable sense of one's own identity, that's the first requirement. Without it . . ." He spilled cartridges into his palm.

"I know what I am," Morpurgo said reluctantly. "At least, I know what I ought to be. I just haven't had the guts to be it."

" 'To thine own self be true.' " A smile, tenuous. "Quotations are catching. Of course, Aske's is an extreme case. No strong-willed mother to make him fight for his identity. No Sylvie to help him find it. No identity at all except whatever he decided to give himself."

"How on earth was he ever recruited?"

"Spencer wasn't a psychiatrist. Spencer probably thinks psychiatry is rather disgusting claptrap."

"Thinks?"

"Thinks" – Epworth waved absently – "thought."

236

"Spencer found him," Morpurgo quoted, "Godwin bought him. We don't know who Spencer was, but we know Godwin was Fish."

"Godwin – Fish – drove him," Epworth remembered. "Fish certainly drove him to Prague the first time. I wonder what drove him back?" He rattled the cartridges, peering through the open window as if the answer might be lurking somewhere outside.

"The way you put it," Morpurgo said carefully, "Fish was up to something before he died. Dig it up and it could discredit the old guard."

"Including Archer."

"The way you put it, it's our duty to dig it up."

"Did I say duty?" Epworth considered. "I doubt it, but let it pass."

"The way Sylvie put it to me" – Morpurgo paused to give Epworth a chance of commenting on Sylvie's involvement, but he let that pass too – "if Steve and the old guard were discredited, you would be God Almighty in British security."

"Mmmmmm." Epworth went cat.

"Steve Archer asked me how much I actually knew about you. I had to say, bugger all. He went farther, suggested you weren't necessarily" – he found himself stumbling – "politically reliable."

"Meaning not one of them." Epworth giggled, but his eyes were still cat. "By the way, the profit-and-loss, dropped, lack of – mmmm – evidence."

Morpurgo ignored that. "I didn't go back to Vienna because you wanted me to. I went because I wanted to." Epworth, he reminded himself, didn't know about Weber.

"Second time round, all sorts of doors opened. Mandel's nobody's fool. Gossip obviously used someone in Hungaro-camion to get word to Aske that a trip was on. Mandel made Aske think there was something for him at the lorry park. Aske goes there. Mandel's waiting, scares the pants off him but makes bloody sure he gets away. Now he's back in Prague, I'm back here and the book is closed. Technical knockout to Steve and the cabal."

"Anyway," Morpurgo said, "that's what I thought."

He looked at Epworth. Epworth was doing his Mona Lisa imitation.

"All right, full of holes. If the KGB gave Aske a rough time, why would he want to go back? How did he get a visa for a Sovbloc country between ten at night and nine the next morning? Especially since Mandel's people obviously never lost sight of him for a minute. And so on."

He paused, but Epworth stayed silent.

"End of the line for your enquiry, isn't it?" Morpurgo said. "Fish's secret safe forever. Steve and the cabal laughing, since Moscow Centre's hardly likely to send Aske back for a replay."

"Alas."

"Only what if it wasn't like that at all?" He tried and failed to catch Epworth's gaze.

"At the time I wound up the Sattin spy ring," Morpurgo said, "the only one who came out of the shit smelling of violets was Lawrence Epworth. Made himself king of the castle."

Epworth listened and looked out of the window.

"First thing you did, took Fish off the Sovbloc desk. Fish took early retirement, then killed himself."

"Alas." Epworth's back showed all the regret of a shark happening upon a beginners' swimming class.

"Alas be buggered!" Getting up, Morpurgo wandered towards the window. "It left you sitting pretty." Nothing in the evening shadows but trees.

"My reward for being smart in the Sattin affair but a bloody fool over Helga would have been to be shunted into a dead-end job. Only kind Uncle Lawrie adopted me, his tame, neutered pussycat."

Epworth, toying with the rifle, wrinkled his nose. "Smelly stuff, gun oil."

"Sattin gone," Morpurgo said. "Fish, Gossip, Aske, all gone. All the records on Highflyer gone. Just Lawrence Epworth, high and dry, waiting to be auditioned for the role of God Almighty." He watched Epworth feed cartridges into the magazine with casual skill.

"But then," Morpurgo said, "the impossible happened. Aske came back. Aske, who knows who Gossip was, who Spencer was. Or is. The only living soul with the inside story on Highflyer. No wonder there've been flutterings in the dovecot!"

"And where" – the magazine loaded, Epworth operated the bolt, sighted along the gun toward shawms and crumhorns – "does the – mmmm – neutered pussycat fit into all this?"

"Mice," Morpurgo said, "seldom stop to check if a cat's got balls."

"Mmmmmmm. I do see. Your orders, look but don't touch. But someone has told Aske that SIS have put in a bogey. Go back to Prague or be – mmmm – quietly terminated."

"Someone. Using, say, Karl-Heinz Mandel, who wants Aske out of Austria, and doesn't care how it's done. Of course, that someone would have to know that Aske was psychologically vulnerable."

Epworth was flipping the safety catch on and off. "The people in the Vienna embassy spent hours talking to Aske just after he came back. We all knew he was – shall we say? – strange? Including Steve Archer."

He saw Morpurgo's uncertainty. "Joint Intelligence Committee. The thing's been on the agenda for weeks."

So the someone could have been Steve after all.

"Of course," Epworth said, "if your theory's correct, the original plan failed. Who could have guessed that Sylvie would actually meet Aske?"

"No one. But it was you who wanted me to go back to Vienna, not Steve. With Mandel primed to make sure that I made direct contact with Aske."

"Sylvie's right, of course," Epworth said. "If the cabal were hiding something naughty and we – mmmm – exhumed it, I would be God Almighty."

"And if Steve's right about you being the one with something to hide, and *they* dug it up, you could end up at the Bailey."

"Oh, absolutely." Epworth had gone back to being Mona Lisa. "Which is what you're inclined to think, isn't it?" He swung up the rifle with surprising speed, fired almost instantly, the sound shattering in the low-ceilinged room.

Morpurgo scrambled up, dry-mouthed, heart still thumping, angry and embarrassed. Out across the lawn, where the ancient hedge abutted on the wood, the deer's forelegs were buckling. It rolled sideways, no more than a dun heap in the evening shadows. It was a masterly shot, and the second time he had seen Epworth kill. On the last occasion his prey had been a man.

"That little roe," Epworth said, "has been nibbling our rosebuds for weeks. I've been watching her – mmmm – sussing out the ground for the past fifteen minutes. Those who grow careless must pay the price."

Morpurgo watched him set down the rifle. "Got it all wrong, did I?"

"A very nice theory. But you did rather – mmmm – leap a few gaps. Just like Steve. Why didn't you tell me about Weber?"

Was there nothing – Morpurgo poured himself a very large Scotch – the bastard didn't know?

239

Epworth said, "Did Weber say anything about his doctor friends when you met?"

Morpurgo checked himself just in time. Epworth was talking about the meeting in Hampstead, not the Franz Josef Station.

He said, "Are you the old guy who leans on a spade? No, he didn't say anything about his doctor friends."

"One of them" – Epworth drained the last of his palo cortado – "is a psychiatrist. Uses her maiden name professionally, just like Sylvie. Her maiden name is Godwin. A recognised expert on schizoid and schizophrenic disorders."

Morpurgo listened to the sound of silence.

"A question," Epworth said. "Is Master Aske's apparent addiction to role-playing perhaps something more? Does he perhaps not see it as playing at all?"

"I suggested that. Searching for an identity?"

"And I said, not searching for one. Protecting one. Remember something he said to Sylvie, back at the beginning? He acts the fool to hide the fact that he is one."

Epworth looked round at Morpurgo. " 'He'. The hidden Aske."

"Whatever he is" – Morpurgo was still struggling – "he's no fool."

"Precisely! He acts the fool and claims to be one. Double disguise for the real Simon Aske. Like spying and counter-intelligence, both sides acting out elaborate roles to disguise their real intentions."

"If you mean he's only pretending to be out of his mind, do you think I hadn't considered that?"

"What," Epworth said, "if you got it the wrong way round? What if he *is* out of his mind, and working very hard to conceal the fact? Not that '*he*' sees it that way. He sees himself as normal, but his 'normality' is to mistrust everyone, to be suspicious of everyone. And as that's 'normal', it follows that everyone else is suspicious of him, so he must keep his 'real' self hidden away. Just like a spy in enemy territory. What we call role-playing, he would call camouflage."

Morpurgo took a seat. "Have you been talking to this woman Godwin?"

"Good lord, no!"

"You've been talking to someone."

"Of course. Some knowledge" – Epworth giggled – "of abnormal psychology is essential in this business. I think we may

240

assume that Simon Benjamin Aske is schizoid – not the same as schizophrenic, not even necessarily psychotic."

"You mean" – Morpurgo tried not to sound sarcastic – "only a little bit insane?"

"Mmmm. Let's say, only occasionally. And anyway, what," Epworth asked gnomically, "is 'sane'?"

"Where does it get us?" There were things about which he was still unconvinced.

"What if it's why Fish was able to use Aske so effectively?" Epworth assumed his own donnish role.

"Sadist dominating easily influenceable schizoid. Providing him with an identity and a purpose. With some schizoids, compliance is a defence mechanism. It makes them easily influenceable.

"They tend to act, because they think everyone acts. Acting is a way of preserving personal anonymity. They like anonymity. It makes them feel safer.

"But Lotta Boyle was right. You have to give all of yourself to be a good actor. The schizoid always holds his true self back, otherwise he can never be – mmmm – master of his situation."

Morpurgo listened, reluctant to believe, already halfway convinced.

Haystock saying, "Which Simon Aske?" Lotta's remark that Aske didn't know which basic Sim to come to terms with. Ellie Haystock: "To be, or not to be, that was his question." Serena: "His great fantastic act of being this or that and then standing back to watch himself."

And Aske himself: "Vienna's a good place to hide."

He watched while Epworth produced the Shylock review and began to read: " 'Does he behave as he does because of what he is, or because, being what he is, that kind of behaviour is expected of him?' Interesting, don't you think? Even prescient. And of course, the sandcastles, melting away, pure rejection fantasy. One could – mmmm – go on."

Sylvie, too, with her camera eye, had given him a clue. "He's not what you think." Simon Aske was not what anyone had thought, and yet everything they had thought, if they had understood what they were thinking.

"Yes," he said. "I'm sure you could go on. You probably bloody well will."

Epworth, smiling apologetically, said, "The perfect agent. Ordinary everyday life the threat. The secret life the only reality.

Fish, London – Kakania, as Aske calls it – a sort of Kafkaesque nightmare, stay away at all costs. Vienna, even Prague, security, because the only security is in secrecy. What a marvellous pressure point! Fish was cleverer than I thought." He looked wistful, but there was no sign at all of pity for Aske.

"Do you know," Morpurgo said, "given a little encouragement, I think I could learn to hate you. What about Weber?"

"Suppose" – nothing could offend Epworth – "that Langley – meaning Barzelian – knew all about Aske because Fish was Langley's man in SIS. Suppose Langley, so to speak, inherited Aske in Fish's will. As soon as Aske comes back to Vienna, Weber comes to London. Where he just happens to have very good friends, one of them a psychiatrist originally introduced to him by the late Humphrey Fish. Suppose Barzelian fancied running Aske again, that marvellous pressure point, only this time for Langley."

He looked enquiringly at Morpurgo, who knew that he should now relate how Weber had boarded the Prague train at the Franz Josef Station.

A car crackled up the gravel outside. Doors thudded. There was the sound of small children. A child's voice called, "Daddy! Daddy, we're back." Morpurgo watched the second youngest, bright and erratic as a butterfly, race across the lawn towards the dead deer, bend to look, race back, small legs pumping like pistons.

Amaryllis called, "Hello, you two. Anyone want anything?"

"Not yet, thank you." Epworth was still watching Morpurgo.

"In that case" – Amaryllis's voice trailed away – "I'll remove the corpse from the lawn. Murderous monster!"

"How well," Epworth said, "she understands me. I'd still like to know what Fish was up to. They'd still like to – mmmm – nobble me."

"And me," Morpurgo said. "Sometimes you get this paranoid feeling you're not wanted."

"In your case," Epworth said, "nothing paranoid about it."

There was a hiatus, filled by the Epworth young distantly singing some unintelligible song. It took him back to Traiskirchen.

"Mmmmmmm. How did the rest go? Godwin knew too much. Godwin made him do what he didn't want to do."

"She drove Godwin," Morpurgo quoted. "Godwin drove

him." It was as if he were still sitting next to Aske in the nighttime Karlsplatz.

"She." Epworth produced his baby-frown. "She drove Godwin. Godwin drove him. 'He' is Aske himself. Godwin was Fish, who obviously borrowed his pseudonym from the lady psychiatrist in Hampstead. She used to advise SIS from time to time."

"She couldn't be the one Aske was talking about?"

"You've forgotten something. Aske said 'she' was dead."

Morpurgo watched Amaryllis cross the lawn, grasp the deer's rear hooves and tug it one-handedly out of sight. "Unless . . . You said Fish had wife trouble. I suppose Mrs Fish isn't dead?"

"Far from it. Aggressively alive." Epworth had put on his veiled look. "In any case, she didn't drive Fish. She was on the – mmmm – receiving end so far as trouble was concerned. *Not* really a nice man, dear Humphrey."

"I could have a word with her, perhaps."

"Alma Fish," Epworth said flatly, "is *not* well-disposed towards SIS. And since Aske is now back in Prague or wherever – did Dukinfield tell you he's also fluent in Russian? – one may be obliged to – " Morpurgo thought he appeared almost to welcome the disrespectful hammering at the door.

"High tea in the nursery," Amaryllis said. "Off you both go and wash your dannies. I hope your guest likes jam with his fish sticks."

He decided, after all, to save his story of Weber at the Franz Josef Station, at least for the time being.

"Incidentally," Epworth said as they washed their hands in competition with the Epworth brood, "Trigg's going to Prague. Some extraordinary scheme for combining Czech currency needs, Cuban sugar and Cleethorpes know-how to flood Europe with lollipops. Perhaps you could be his man in Prague."

"Is that why you wangled my Czech visa?"

"Not at all. I thought you might want to go with Sylvie and the RSC. After all," Epworth said, "you do really owe her something after your deplorable behaviour when she took you to Vienna."

"Is he being impossible again?" Amaryllis asked as they went into the nursery. "Why don't you just sock him one?"

# TWENTY-FIVE

Alma Fish said, "Sylvie Markham's husband. That's why I said yes. Because you're Sylvie Markham's husband." She had a high, clear voice, much younger than her years.

A mock-Georgian house in Esher, a mock-Georgian double garage; it was like finding himself in a dead man's dream – even a wisp of bonfire smoke down the autumn garden.

She said, "Humphrey never discussed his work, of course, but he liked to feed me titbits. You were a titbit."

She laughed, an unconvincing sound. "Humphrey said, 'I met Sylvie Markham's husband today. She married beneath her.' Did you know Humphrey was a snob?"

"I didn't really know him at all." 'Today' must have been that first time, at Century House, when John Morpurgo, still big in Five, was riding high on the triumph of breaking the Sattin ring.

She was tall, bony, thin, with big hands on very slender wrists. Her hairstyle came from the pages of magazines aimed a generation below. Her clothes made him think of little girls with rich mummies, playing at dressing up.

"You'd better sit down." He took one end of a sofa, she the other. She turned to face him with a mixture of wariness and anticipation, afraid he might start something, afraid he might not.

He thought she might have found her true self in the two years since her release from a chauvinistic bully, but was not quite sure whether she had gone forward or back.

"Oh yes," she said. "Humphrey was a terrible snob. And a bit of a shit, did they tell you that?" She said "shit" with a selfconscious brightness.

"I knew very little about him, Mrs Fish."

She crossed her legs, a sigh of nylon beneath a flowing skirt. She was all kinds of things she was trying not to show, he thought: bitter but childish, vindictive but curious, suspicious yet simultaneously coy.

"He was a *snob*." She said it with a curious emphasis. He noticed she used the trick every so many words, less to underline than like a child attempting adult conversation.

"It bothered him to think that your wife wasn't. I expect you think I'm being bloody rude. Humphrey taught me how to be bloody rude."

"Sylvie takes people as she finds them."

More people than Fish thought that Sylvie had married beneath her, but in any case, he had to go whichever way Alma Fish led. It was surprising that she had agreed to see him. Epworth had known about his secret meeting with Weber. Where was Epworth now?

"Humphrey didn't leave *me* as he found me. Of course, *he* thought *he'd* married beneath him."

She was still wearing her wedding ring. She turned it endlessly as she talked. "He fed me scraps. Bits of dirt. I mean that's what he dealt in, dirt. She nearly did, didn't she, your wife? Leave you."

He said, "Mrs Fish, you won't expect me to talk about that."

Her voice unnaturally vivid, she said, "The big dirt's classified, so poor Humphrey can't tell little wifey why he's always coming home tired, no" – like a foreigner showing off an idiom – "*lead* in his pencil. But he can toss her tasty shreds of other people's reputations in between pushing her around. Moral *tales*. Like playing Happy *Families*."

She had a fixed, bright smile. Her eyes moved endlessly up and down his face.

He, Sylvie, Steve Archer – who had been Humphrey Fish's friend and protégé – were among the choice items in the doggy bags Fish had brought from scandal's table. He wondered if she actually believed she could shock him. He said, "Perhaps I'd better go."

"No, don't go. How *is* dear Steve?"

"You don't still see him?"

"Sir *Stephen*? Goodness, people like him haven't time for people like me!"

It was his job to exploit this kind of thing. "I thought he and your husband were good friends."

"Used to be. Like you and he used to be . . . *what* used you to be?"

Best to leave that. "He's remarrying."

"Oh, that's nice! And do you know her?" The conversation was as unreal as children playing grown-ups

"Aristocracy. Not my style." He thought she could be led on.

"All the same in bed, isn't that what they say?"

She recrossed her legs, slid the ring almost free, slid it back again.

"And how is Sylvie Markham?"

"Well. Busy. Away, just at present."

"Busy. Away. Famous. Nice for her, but is it nice for you?"

He was a man who had had Steve Archer's wife, wrecked Steve Archer's marriage, a man who should, in consequence, have lost his own wife, especially as she had married beneath her. In a flouting of natural justice, he had been given another chance.

Alma Fish, pushed contemptuously around by Fish when alive, had been left with a pension, a house in Esher, a world of silence. Had that fact been his entrée?

Her thoughts chiming precisely with his, she said, "Do you know what it's like? No, of course you don't. 'What did your poor husband *do*, Mrs Fish?' 'Oh, he was a civil servant, quite important in a backroom sort of way.' They warned me I mustn't say anything else."

Her voice higher still, she said, "Non-person when he was here, un-person now he's gone. They read you the riot act in their smooth, bloody Whitehall way, then leave you to rot.

" '*Terribly* sorry. Of course, we *do* rely on your discretion. Sign on the dotted line and don't think we wouldn't know if you talked.' Well, I told them what they could do."

She laughed. It was a painful sound. "Only nobody *does* ask. The word gets round. Nobody says, 'Exactly why *did* your husband knock himself off, Mrs Fish?' "

She had never been beautiful, but Fish, in the strange way that such things happened, must have found her attractive. Perhaps, he thought, because she was still in some ways an overgrown schoolgirl. Perhaps Fish had had a thing about overgrown schoolgirls. He found it discomfiting to see her fighting to hold back tears.

"So why did you let me come?"

She had herself under control now, head high, posture rigid.

246

She had a good profile, bony cheeks and nose, but a touch of something different. Sylvie would find her facially interesting.

"You only worked with Humphrey towards the end, isn't that right?"

"Hardly at all, really. Just dealings. He'd already resigned by the time I went to Century House."

"Were you involved in the enquiry?"

"I was a new boy."

"But you want to talk about him now. Isn't that why you've come?"

No point in dodging that one. "Yes," he said.

She smiled, an element of triumph. "I always thought that if she took you back, you must have had *something*. I always thought that if Humphrey, Steve, the whole bloody shower didn't like you, you couldn't be *all* bad. Would you like some tea?"

"Please." It was grotesque, but if tea was the way, he would have tea.

When she came back, she drew up a small table and sat much nearer. "Do you ever hear of *her*? Helga Archer?"

"No. I think she's back in Germany."

"Not Vienna?"

"Vienna?" Did she know how much she had startled him?

She was looking at him thoughtfully, the tip of her tongue moistening her lips. She shook her head. "No, not Vienna. I *wondered* about her, you know. Come one, come all, that sort of thing."

This time – he made no attempt to hide it – he had no idea what she meant.

She saw that. "Demure little Helga. I knew *Steve* wasn't much use to her. I started to get ideas about who might be *servicing* her at the time."

"Such as?"

Another shake of the head, impatient. "Humphrey, of course! More and more impossible, the absolute *pits*! And away a lot. I wondered about Humphrey and Helga. Only then it came out it was *you* – Humphrey enjoyed telling me that – and I decided Humphrey's was his usual thing, pressure of work, something to do with all the trips he was making to Vienna."

Trips to Vienna to see Aske.

"Looking so sweet and waiflike," she said. "Patience on a monument. Was *she* good in bed?" Coming from her, the

247

question seemed grotesque.

He drank some tea, seeing the nature of the trap he had walked into. Her smile terrible in its desperate artificiality, she said, "Are *you* good in bed?" Moving nearer, she took his cup from him. Behind her, on the striped lawn, a blackbird craned, listening for telltale stirrings.

\*     \*     \*

She had played the lead, urgent, without finesse. Now she lay on her back in the overlush bedroom, her small conical breasts pointing at the ceiling. She – no other word for it – prattled, brightly.

"Fucked around by the bloody service for all those years. *Well*, one good fuck deserves another. Was Helga as good as me?" She made the crudity seem nothing more than juvenile naughtiness.

It was as if he were staring up from the foot of a cliff he had just fallen over. Except that he had jumped, anything for information, and he had hardly been very high to begin with.

She said, "If your Sylvie killed herself, how would you feel?"

She said, "How would you feel if you knew she'd killed herself because of another man and you hadn't the *smallest* bloody idea who it was?" She slid out of bed.

She said, "I know you didn't want me. I didn't want you. I had *them*. The rotten bloody service. Now I expect you want to be paid."

\*     \*     \*

"Did they tell you about the bonfire?"

He nodded, wishing himself on the far side of the moon.

"They took it away in little plastic bags, but it had rained first." She crossed to open a reproduction bureau that could have come from SERENdipity.

"Got themselves *good* and mucky. I didn't offer to let them wash. They didn't like to bother the poor bitch of a widow."

She unlocked an inner drawer in the bureau.

"While they were taking him away, before your lot came, I noticed the smoke. Down there." She nodded towards where light smoke still drifted beyond a small copse.

"Not autumn then. Do I interest you? So to speak?"

He nodded again.

"I guessed. All these years keeping me out of his life, and there it was, going up in smoke. 'Oh no you *don't*', I thought. 'Oh no you bloody don't!' ''

"Off my rocker, of course. Not every day you open the garage and find something you used to know." She spread her hands. They were trembling. "Burned my fingers, didn't I? Hurt like bloody *hell*, only I didn't notice at the time." She clutched one hand inside the other, held them to her breast as if they still burned.

"When they came they spotted the bonfire straight away. More concerned about that than poor pink Humphrey. *Ought* to have noticed I'd burned my hands, don't you think? *Should* have put two and two together?"

"We'd have noticed, Five. What Six used to call our cops-and-robbers stuff." It was just something to say.

"He used," she said, still squeezing her hands, "Humphrey, that is, he used to call you the heavy mob. Anyway, some of the stuff was only singed. I think he probably was in a bit of a hurry. To finish. Himself." Her fingers burst apart. "*Off*."

She examined her fingertips. "I expect you're wondering what I found."

He opened his lips, closed them again.

"Charred bits and pieces," she said. "Useless, really, no point in trying to pick them up. Though they did their best. She laughed. "You should have *seen* them. Grown men!" She took something from the little drawer. "Hadn't the faintest idea what I'd find. Honestly! Codes? Plans? Grubby secrets? You *don't* know, *do* you, not if you're not involved." She took a deep breath.

"Months of too tired and overwork, everything except the traditional headache, and me thinking, damn him! damn the service! and then it was all over and he was dead."

"Letters," he said. "Were there letters?"

"Humphrey said you were smart. Too clever for your own good, he said. I said I'd thought it was a good thing to be clever in the intelligence services. He said, 'Fancy Sylvie Markham being married to a blue-collar Torquemada and I wondered . . . I remember wondering whether it was Sylvie Markham he was . . .''

She came to sit down. She had an envelope.

"You get to think that sort of thing. There was even some woman up in Hampstead, some consultant psychiatrist retained by Six. Used to be, anyway. He went to see her from time to time. I did my own bit of spying. I found she was about a hundred years old. Then Vienna got to be the big deal and I decided it was that."

"You burned the letters? What was left of them?"

"Now I see what he meant. Very clever. Yes, eventually. When I got over it. Eventually. It seemed . . . better. Do you speak German?"

"A bit."

"I should have kept them." She looked towards the wisp of smoke. "He was thorough with the files. They mattered. The *bloody* service! Me, *I* didn't matter."

"They were in German?"

"Yes. Funny, suspecting little Helga. Right language, wrong woman. Austrian, Viennese or something, I suppose. I tried to read them with a dictionary. *Steamy*, I could tell that, but they don't put really steamy words in dictionaries. Couldn't ask anyone else, could I? That's why I burned them. Everything except this."

The envelope in her bag held a photograph.

The remains of a photograph. Charred, one whole corner missing, part of the glaze bubbled and blackened. It was possible to pick out a woman's face, little more.

Sylvie might know how to get some of the detail back. The fourth-floor annexe at Century House certainly would. Pictures. It had been photographs all the way through: Aske, Serena, Fish, himself with Helga, and now this. Would Sylvie appreciate the irony? He turned it over. There was writing on the back, sprawling. All that was left said: ". . . *deine immerliebev . . . Klatschi*".

Alma Fish said, "Everloving. *Immerliebevolle*."

"Yes."

"Klatschi. I don't suppose you know who she is?"

"Sorry." It was true, yet in another sense not. He had no idea who she was. He knew exactly who she was. He knew something only one other living person knew.

"What's Klatschi short for?"

"Nothing, at a guess. One of those silly nicknames people use."

She believed him. "Bitch." She said it calmly now.

He said, "Talking of names, does the name Spencer mean anything to you?"

"Not a thing. Are you sure it's nothing to do with her?"

"Positive."

"Well. That's it then?"

"You might have got your fingers burned much worse. You still could."

She managed her first real smile. "I don't think *you'll* talk."

"I've got something on you, too. Withholding information. Here." He returned the photograph. "Burn it."

"You think?"

"I think."

"But won't they . . .?"

"Never mind about them."

She said, "Humphrey always said they'd find a way to fix you, sooner or later. He said they should never have let you in."

"He's probably right."

"It's probably why I let you come."

"I know."

"*Will* they find a way to fix you?"

"I'm more likely to fix myself first."

"So if I read that you're billed for the Old Bailey . . .?"

"Just sit tight and say nothing."

"That trick cyclist I was talking about. *Her* name was Spencer, come to think. Her married name. I don't suppose that's what you meant."

"Not really." Had Epworth, then, been wrong?

"No, Anyway, wrong, come to think. Or half wrong. That was her professional name. Her married name was Godwin."

Sylvie Markham, Sylvie Morpurgo. Or did he mean Mr and Mrs Sylvie Markham?

She sat upright on a settee in a room furnished exclusively by shops like SERENdipity, everything in mint condition, everything for show. He thought he had seldom seen anyone so lonely.

She said, "He needed a psychiatrist himself sometimes. You all need one in your line."

"You're right," he said. "I've known it for years."

# TWENTY-SIX

Fish had been having an affair. It made them vulnerable to blackmail, yet they did it, these professional dealers in deceit, being men like any other men. Morpurgo had done it himself, which was why he was where he was now.

Fish had served in Berlin, made visits to Vienna, who knew where else? That the woman should be German-speaking was no particular surprise, but *Klatschi*! An intimate diminutive, he had told Alma Fish, the sort of thing he and Sylvie had used in sillier, happier days.

It was much more than that. Warren Claas, of all people, had left him the clue. When Warren, third-generation German-American, thought something wasn't being discussed seriously enough, he would say, 'What do you think this is? A goddam coffee klatsch?'

An American thing, a coffee morning where the women got together, usually to raise money for some project, always for a good yak. Klatsch was the German for gossip. Humphrey Fish's affair had been with a woman whose nickname had been "Little Gossip".

Everyone, Epworth included, had assumed that the Highflyer field agent had been a man. Now John Morpurgo – only John Morpurgo – knew otherwise.

Correction: John Morpurgo and Simon Aske.

Alma Fish had not sensed his shock of surprise. But then, she had been unwittingly capping one revelation with another. Godwin and Spencer – pseudonyms for Fish and the unknown who had been responsible for recruiting Aske – were represented in the persons of a Hampstead woman psychiatrist, one-time

252

consultant to SIS, and her husband.

Both 'nice, safe folk', friends of Pierre Weber, who had left for Prague on the same train as Aske.

That made three things Epworth didn't know.

He ought to tell Epworth. He would have done if he could have been totally sure that Epworth ought to know.

* * *

"Do you remember" – Trigg was sitting in Morpurgo's chair and very much at home – "summat I said, all that time back, when you asked me to stand in for that chap Sattin at the remand hearing? I asked why you did this sort of stuff. 'Is it patriotism?' I said. 'Or saving us from Moscow? Or is it just a job?' "

He looked up from his Guinness. "It was a good question."

"I seem to remember saying something about preferring the way we do things in this country to the way they do them anywhere else."

"You seemed none too sure of it at the time."

"I'm none too sure of it now."

"So just when I'm off to foreign parts, you get me round here to tell me stuff that could put me away for more years than I've a mind to spare, and you're not even sure why. By! I don't know how fellers like you gets picked, but it's nought to do with brains."

They sat there with footsteps clopping this way and that outside. A taxi put down a fare while its diesel engine went *tock-tock-tock*. Trigg disposed of his Guinness in a single seamless swallow. "Know what I think, buttercup? I think you're best out."

"It's like a maze. The only way out is to go on."

Trigg saw that Morpurgo had nothing to add. "All right, I've had my bit of fun. Just what are you after?"

"You're going to Prague tomorrow."

"Lollipops and spice, nought else. No Epworths, no secret service, just plain business."

"I'm going to Prague, too."

"Oh aye? And what'll your Sylvie say about that?"

"Nothing, if she doesn't know."

"She'll know if you don't come back."

"I've every intention of coming back."

"Of course you have, you daft bugger, but what if they have every intention of stopping you?"

253

"I'm what's called Sovbloc green in the trade. Not known."

Not true; he was amber. If Steve Archer were right about Epworth, he might well be Sovbloc red.

"*He'd* know, would Aske," Trigg said. "And he's why you want to go, isn't that right?"

"He's one reason." The other was Pierre Weber, who, according to Di Pasolino at the American embassy, was 'somewhere in Europe'.

"What happens if I say I want nought to do with it?"

"I'm off anyway. Vienna, then Prague. How long will you be there?"

"Direct from London, a couple of meetings with some fellers from t'Czech Ministry of Foreign Trade, a works visit, on to Vienna day after. Three nights in all." After a pause, he added, "Barring accidents."

"We could meet up as and when."

"Show 'em someone knows you're there? I'm not daft, lad."

Morpurgo grinned, the adrenaline beginning to build up. "Unlike you, I shan't be sponsored by the British embassy."

But Epworth, whichever side he was on, would put two and two together. One side or the other would know that John Morpurgo was in Prague.

Trigg reached for another can of Guinness, then sat for a long time, chin on chest. "And you've fixed it all up."

Morpurgo nodded. He had been busy since leaving Alma Fish.

"You don't need me, looks like."

"I just might."

Trigg snapped the ring on his can. "Aye lad, you just might, at that."

*       *       *

He had no idea why he was going by train, except that it was what Aske had always done. That and the fact that security was always tightest at airports.

He was tense. He had left a letter for Sylvie. He hoped to be back to destroy it before she returned from the States. Trigg was the only other person who knew. Theoretically. If his worst fears were justified, the SB could be waiting for him at Prague Central Station.

He could imagine the reactions of Steve Archer, the cabal, all those who, over the years, had queried the presence of Morpurgo, social and political outsider, in the subterranean corridors of power.

"Well, what did you expect, old boy? Said all along the chap was a crypto-commie." There would be no meetings to discuss an exchange.

One of his fellow passengers was an old lady, emaciated, a deathly pallor, but a chatterbox. He kept silent, pretending he spoke very little German, but her talk was to the world at large.

One sister and a brother killed during the war in an air raid. Another brother, a soldier, badly wounded, had survived to die of cold and hunger in the first winter of defeat.

She had managed to reach Vienna ahead of the Soviet army. Another sister, trapped in what was now the German Democratic Republic, had just died. Sole survivor, she displayed the fat sheaf of documents needed to attend the funeral in Leipzig.

*Where have all the flowers gone? Gone to graveyards, every one. When will they ever learn?* He thought of all the Warren Claases with their transatlantic contempt for has-been Europe. When would *they* ever learn? Would they even have time?

The train crawled, hour after limping hour. He thought about Simon Aske, who had two personalities. Sylvie was always telling him that he himself was two people, one public, one secret. In the security services they were all permanently schizoid.

Even Sylvie had two lives.

Trigg was the only man he knew who was all of a piece. Integrity, that was the word; integrity.

The brief high point of his own career had been in persuading Trigg to be Sattin for as long as it took to deceive.

He thought about Fish, a man who had fallen in love with his agent – what a host of unanswerable questions there! – and suffered a treble agony. He had known the KGB had her in Lefortovo. Sattin's death had put paid to any exchange. Epworth had taken his position of power. No wonder Fish had eventually killed himself.

What had Aske said? *She drove Godwin. Godwin drove him.*

Translation: the thought of what was happening to his Klatschi had driven Fish to despair. As a consequence of that despair, Aske had been forced into repeated trips to Prague.

Why? It could only have been in an attempt to make a deal with Moscow.

Gossip would inevitably have talked under the persuasion of the Lefortovo interrogators. As well as identifying Aske as her courier, she would have confessed to an intimate relationship with a senior British intelligence officer, the man who ran the Sovbloc desk in the Secret Intelligence Service.

Fish had fallen into the classical trap, the kind of thing that was custom-made for the First Chief Directorate in its fortress building on the Moscow ring road. Nothing in too much of a hurry.

Sattin was still alive at the time, still running a highly successful spy ring in the British Admiralty. One game still in progress, the other would keep, with Fish sweating blood but forced to endure his agony in silence. No wonder he had given Alma Fish such a bad time!

Then John Morpurgo had broken the Sattin ring. Another skilful delay while Moscow went through the charade of a possible exchange and Fish's trauma festered, all brought to an end by Sattin's abrupt death in custody.

After that the big catch – Fish indeed! – already weakened and in danger of losing all power to Epworth, was ready to be played and gaffed.

Moscow would not have know about Epworth. Moscow would only have known that the British head of Sovbloc intelligence was theirs for the taking.

Another classical ploy: Fish would have passed some relatively minor item of information through Aske to Prague as a token of good faith. After that, he was theirs, the question of Gossip's release academic. The price would have been stepped up trip by trip, the grip on Fish tightened beyond any possibility of withdrawal. Fish had become a doomed man.

But Aske had said something else in the Karlsplatz. *She's dead now.*

No longer interested in exchanges once Fish was entoiled, Moscow had dealt with Gossip in routine fashion, execution as a common traitor.

But then, in the aftermath of the Sattin affair, Epworth had plucked SIS like a ripe fruit.

Fish, forced out of power in SIS, became another of Moscow Centre's near misses. He had done what he could to protect his own name and that of the service he worked for. Wipe Aske from the records. Burn the files. An – mmmm – unwise quantity of carbon monoxide.

And Aske?

*He had to hide deep.*

Mentally unstable, under intolerable pressure from Fish, his mission at an end, he had simply opted to stay in Prague. Or Moscow.

Then why, after more than eighteen months, had he been allowed to come back?

He thought he had the answer to that, too: what Pierre Weber had called one hell of a job of destabilisation. Archer and the cabal lusting for the overthrow of Lawrence Epworth. Epworth silently and subterraneously working for the downfall of the cabal. Aske had been sent back as a time-bomb. He could see now that Epworth, burrowing through the dirt, had been close to striking gold when Aske had vanished for the second time.

*He had to hide deep. Now he'll have to go deeper.*

The obvious way to get around the problem of acquiring a Czechoslovak visa between ten in the evening and nine next day was not to need one, to know in advance that no obstacles would be placed in the path of return.

And to be known by the experts at Lefortovo to be schizoid, driven by the need to protect a secret identity, convinced that the price of interior liberty was eternal suspicion.

Yet Mandel had played his part in the carefully planned charade, and Weber too, so Weber had known all along about John Morpurgo, had been fully aware of his presence at the Franz Josef Station.

They reached the frontier: tarmac strip, electrified wire, watchtowers, no change in the air they breathed. The shrunken old lady said, "Now it begins."

A wave of khaki uniforms, pink young faces. Outside, soldiers with machine pistols and dogs, feet thumping heavily along the roof of the coach, dogs and men peering underneath. Passports inspected, stamped; visa approvals inspected, stamped, separated; passports reinspected. New faces; accommodation check, currency check, third passport check. How many times had Aske gone through this meticulous search for identity in disguise?

The old lady, relieved successively of passport, visa forms, letters of authority, currency exchange forms, even her black-bordered obituary letter, clasped resigned hands. "Now I am no longer a person."

How many persons was Aske? How many persons was Wandsworth-Chelsea, for-and-against, have-your-cake-and-eat-it Morpurgo, who wasn't even sure why he was going to Prague?

A whistle blew. The train lurched on; hilly countryside, empty roads, then a town much like other towns, a church unlike

257

previous churches. A station: VÝCHOD. Low platforms with checkerboard patterns of tiles.

People much like any other people, carrying cases and plastic carrier bags, picking their way over the lines to climb aboard while a red and cream Czech train, much like any other train, arrived, departed, and time and the world went by. Czechoslovakia; same world, different world; schizoid.

A Czech border control officer brought back the old lady's papers, apologised for the inconvenience, expressed his regret at her bereavement, saluted as he left.

"They weren't sure I was me." Her ravaged face sad, she showed them all the picture in her passport. An alter ego, plump-faced, ten years younger.

"Only just out of hospital when my sister died. No time for a new picture, so, yet more papers to prove I'm me. Still" – she opened a packet of sandwiches as the train groaned, jerked and began a funereal progress towards Prague – "now I exist. The Böhmen say so. Yet that was a kind man."

\*        \*        \*

The station was vast, gloomy, slashed with golden blades of late afternoon sunlight. Like the Franz Josef, it had had a huge new concourse tacked on, but no supermarket, no massively stocked bookstall, no sign at all of the good life. Half the overhead lighting was either switched off or not working. He found a cab, a battered Polski.

"*Deutsch*?"

"English."

"You want to change money?" He didn't. The man seemed to expect the refusal.

The first sight of the city was depressing. High terrace blocks of dark brick; streets, their surfaces patched and repatched, that were free not only of traffic but of parked cars. One distant glimpse of shark-tooth spires and they were at the second-rate hotel. He overtipped ludicrously.

The foyer had the same shabby air, the woman receptionist processing him as if he were an item in an endless, pointless stocktaking. He watched the appropriation of his passport with regret.

A noisy group flooded in from the street, men and women in conspicuously new clothes. He realised with a sense of unreality that they were Russians. A porter, accompanying him un-

258

necessarily to the single lift, whispered, "You want to change money?"

Wide corridors, high ceilings, threadbare crimson carpeting. He was reminded of London clubs.

The room was large and mostly empty, the wall at the side of the bed darkly smudged, the linen spotless. There was a radio, a choice of three channels. All three carried speech, incomprehensible.

Across the street were more of the forbidding office blocks, eight storeys high, gloomy, no fluorescents. Inside, people were preparing to go home. He opened the window and realised what was missing. No traffic roar. No cars. Only human voices, human footsteps, near and far, a unique and indescribable mass murmur with, distantly, the occasional grinding progress of a streetcar. A pedestrian metropolis.

Everything was suddenly infinitely depressing. In coming to Prague he had done the most idiotic single thing of his life. With nothing but a street plan of the city to study, he settled down to wait for Trigg.

\*      \*      \*

Trigg seemed to dominate the gloomy foyer. "Ahoy, buttercup. Nay, I've not gone off my chump, that's how they say hello round here. I reckon it's nearest these Czechs gets to a navy."

He followed Morpurgo up to his room. "I'm right glad to see you, lad, but I can't stay. I told 'em I'd a friend just arrived that I had to say hello to, but I'm a guest of the state and must do what's required."

Between the outer and inner doors he dropped his voice to a hoarse whisper. "Should you think you were being watched, then?" He seemed twice as large and twice as Yorkshire. There was comfort in it.

Morpurgo went to the window and opened it so that they could both lean out. The street below was dark, empty, streetlights not yet on, the life of the city going on tiptoe. "I don't think so. And I doubt this room's bugged, but you never know."

Trigg leaned closer. "I wouldn't want to see you the guest of the state. Go back to Vienna tomorrow. I'm not free before afternoon, and I'll not sleep easy for thinking you're liable to get yourself into mischief."

"I've a call to make at the American embassy in the morning. After that . . ." After that he didn't know, but there must be something after that.

Trigg drew out his pocket watch. "They're taking me to some cellar that's famous for history and beer. These Czechs reckons they're great boozers, but they'll put me under t'table with history before they do it with ale." He looked worried. "I'd ask you along, buttercup, but this is business."

"I'll be all right."

"I'll give you a ring in t'morning, but what if they tell me you've checked out?"

"If I really check out, I'll let you know."

It made Trigg no happier. "You tell me Prague isn't a patch on Cleethorpes, right? Then I'll know it's genuine."

Morpurgo laughed. "Might get me arrested anyway, but okay."

He found himself grabbed and shaken. "You daft bugger! If he's back here, do you think you'll find him? If you find him, d'you think he'll want to see you? If he wants to see you, d'you think they'd let him?"

Trigg released him. "What'd I tell your Sylvie, if ought goes wrong?"

"Nothing will, damn it!" He said it more sharply than he had meant. "I'm sorry. Tell her . . ." He punched Trigg gently. "Nothing will."

When Trigg left, the space he had occupied expanded to fill the room.

He went down to a solitary meal in a restaurant where the background music had elbowed its way into the foreground and the waiter was less interested in him than in two girls at another table. They didn't look like Služba Bezpečnosti, but how could you tell?

After his meal he found the heart of the city an easy walk, though it took him along a series of streets with only an occasional passer-by apart from a knot of people outside a shop which offered, when he stopped to penetrate its inadequate light, nothing but an extraordinary miscellany of cannibalised electrical parts.

He emerged on a main road. Streetcars ran. There were telephone booths, unlit, in which intent citizens shouted earnestly. He lingered at a closed and darkened bookshop whose windows, impressively stocked, had nothing more frivolous than travel guides and a vast range of educational literature. A huge blank wall made him pause, uncertain why until he realised there were no graffiti. Not even communist graffiti; no graffiti whatsoever.

But the sky ahead was brighter. He reached a junction where brilliantly lit subway entrances had drawn groups of bejeaned young like moths. A disembodied voice, in English, muttered, "You want to change money?" Wenceslas Square.

Shops, neon signs; but the shops had no display lighting, and the signs, mostly of foreign airlines, were conspicuous for their sparsity. Vast, almost devoid of traffic, the square with its wide traffic lanes and wide pavements dwarfed crowds that tended to cluster in front of shops with little to sell, and that of indifferent quality. He told himself it was socialism in practice, and found the other Morpurgo guiltily unimpressed.

Young soldiers everywhere; doomed to graveyards, every one? Conspicuous knots of khaki-clad police with their yellow and white cars, yet always a trailing incantation: "You want change?" He had no intention of falling into any black market currency trap, no intention of falling into any trap. He walked slowly, seemingly aimlessly, victim of his professional training, prisoner of his cultivated obsessions.

No obvious tail. But then, it would not be obvious. After all, who could disappear in a country like Czechoslovakia?

Answer: Simon Aske.

He stood at the top of the square, under the Wenceslas monument and the great dome of the National Museum, looking at the changing yet strangely inanimate scene. People seemed subdued, less concerned with their surroundings than with themselves. Somewhere not far from where he stood, the student Jan Palach had burned himself to death in 1969, in protest against the Soviet occupation. Now the crowds went docilely by, talking, eating icecream, sausage, even – the world was undoubtedly mad – drinking Coca-Cola.

Outward conformity, inner dissent? Was that schizoid, too, the split personality of those who were Sovbloc citizens, like it or not? And if so, said his own other self, was he, locked in the ambiguity of his personal circumstances, guilty of the opposite: outward dissent, inner conformity? Did that make him schizoid too?

All sense of purpose gone, he went back to his silent, inadequately lit room with its antiquated brass washbasin fittings and its chipped enamel shower cubicle that dripped maddeningly.

Long before midnight Prague died; nothing but the occasional, distant grumble of an all-night streetcar service. Leaning from his window he watched a policeman turn off the traffice lights at the intersection. The only traffic in more than an hour had been a cleansing truck brushing the gutters in a street made the darker by high white lamps craned over uneven setts.

He stayed awake far into the small hours, but there was no peremptory knock at his door.

# TWENTY-SEVEN

Breakfast was a wake for a day stillborn. Grounds floated in his coffee like drowned insects. Waiters and a handful of guests competed in unsmiling taciturnity. His one word of Czech, "Good morning," appeared to disqualify him out of hand. He was missing Sylvie more than she would have believed.

The Vindobona left Prague Central Station for Vienna in the mid-afternoon. His return ticket, now his most precious possession, was good for any day. How many days was he good for himself?

Trigg telephoned during the meal. The waiter who showed him the whereabouts of the phone muttered, "You want to make change?"

Trigg, through the sound of frying bacon, said, "By! Getting through on one of these things is less a test of patience than a way of life. How's things your end, buttercup?" All the clicks and crackles made it a phone tapper's paradise.

He said, "Not a patch on Cleethorpes, so far."

"I was calling," Trigg said, "to say that plans is changed. A couple more meetings and I'll be done. And since I've to report back to Vienna I could join you on that train. Do you think you could keep yourself out of mischief until this evening? I'd be through around seven, then we could eat at my hotel. It's a double room. I could even give you a bed."

The message was plain: stay out of trouble until seven, after which he would be lucky to lose Trigg before they were both back over the border.

He agreed to be at Trigg's vastly superior hotel on the river at seven, but that was not the end of it. "I'm being taken to lunch up

263

at that castle. After that we shall have a look at t'sights. If you just happened to be eating in t'same place, I dare say something could be arranged." Trigg's insistence was implacable.

Yes, he said, he would try to be up there around lunchtime, then cut off the call in mid-speech. It was probably common enough with the Prague telephone system, but he wasted no time in going out in case Trigg, scorning the language problem, should bulldoze his way to a reconnection.

Prague represented something as unknown and potentially menacing as the heart of nineteenth-century Africa, but his sleepless hours had at least enabled him to make a rough assessment of his risks. With Fish's past role in perspective, he felt obliged to give Epworth a clean bill of health. He was still left with uncharted minefields.

Helga and the compromising pictures, for a start. He had no idea how the piece fitted into the puzzle, but anything unexplained was a threat. Aske himself was hardly likely to have returned without being questioned about the events that had brought him back. If the links between border control, the visa bureau and the security police in Prague worked efficiently, John Morpurgo's presence would already be known.

His hope there, and it was little more than a crossing of his fingers, was that the sluggishness of Sovbloc satellite bureaucracy, plus the sheer improbability that he should have followed Aske to Prague, would keep him safe for the day or so that was the most he meant to stay.

So if a plan was a course of action with no alternative, he had a plan.

No more taxis; he had made too much use of taxis when he himself had been playing cat to other people's mice. He set out to walk to the American embassy. First the drab streets and the tramlines, then a sudden debouchment into a vast open space where a red-draped reviewing stand contrasted startlingly with surrounding Gothic, renaissance and baroque. The parade would be a spontaneous tribute to the October Revolution of the great Soviet ally. He hoped to miss it.

A fanged Gothic church, more narrow streets followed by wider, and he came out on the river, the face of the city changing as if by magic. Across the Vltava, the air patrolled by swirling flurries of gulls, the green, leaf-speckled water by swans and old men fishing from moored boats, the fortress ridge of the Hradčany dominated the skyline like a medieval print, castle and cathedral side by side above trees, pink roofs and golden stone, all in a glow of autumn sunlight.

After the stony pomposity of Vienna, it was a fairy sight. Mozart, rushed headlong to his pauper's grave in Vienna, had been given a requiem mass in Prague. Yet it was Vienna, now, that breathed the purer air.

The American embassy, some long-gone lordling's palace, was on the far side of the river, tucked away in the narrow streets at the foot of the fortress hill. To the left under the deep arched entrance was a reading room and enquiry desk. Redirected, he went through a small courtyard where stone steps climbed to gardens that vanished under copper-leaved trees.

"Weber, sir? I don't believe we have anyone of that name with us right now. If you'd care to take a seat for one moment, I'll make enquiries."

He knew in that one moment that Weber was somewhere around, knew too that he was not going to see him. But that was not the point.

The phone was replaced after a murmured and growingly terse conversation. "I'm sorry, Mr Morpurgo. Mr Weber's not in Prague presently and we don't seem to be expecting him. Mr Kowinski will be right down to see if he can help."

Damn right Mr Kowinski would be down. Mr Kowinski would be one of the resident spooks, instructions: find out what the hell John Morpurgo is doing in Prague, convince him Weber is anywhere but, report back fast.

The instructions would have come from Pierre Weber.

"Thank you, but tell Mr Kowinski not to bother. It's not important."

Crossing the narrow, cobbled street where the Czech police had their own cubbyhole to monitor the enemy's friends, he cut through another archway to Malostranské Square, headed at speed for the river through the alleyways of the old town.

He had done what he had meant to do, stirred up the bloody Yanks. They would guess he must have good reasons for thinking Weber was in Prague. They would think he had good reasons for being in Prague himself. They would have no problem in deciding that it was all to do with Simon Aske.

He wished he knew what the hell to do next.

He reached the Vltava and a bridge where baroque religious statuary postured with the awful earnestness of politicians, risking an occasional glance behind to see if there was any obvious tail. To be followed through communist Prague by both Czech security police and Mr Kowinski of the CIA would be quite a twist, but then, craziness was the name of the game.

This was tourist Prague, and the tourists chiefly spoke German. Not that many years earlier, they or their fathers could well have been patrolling these same streets in jackboots and steel helmets, or, more recently, part of the heroic Sovbloc forces that arrived in the nick of time to save the Czechs from freedom.

That was not what interested him. The standard of dress this side of the great divide was markedly lower than, for instance, in Vienna. He fancied he would be able to spot any American at twenty paces. There wasn't a CIA man in sight.

Not long after, it had turned into a fiasco. There he was, not just a stranger in Prague but a hostile agent, and no one wanted to know. Among those he was hostile to he counted the Yanks. They *must* have been asking each other questions, Weber and his friends: only one reason for the guy to be in Prague, so what the hell's he up to? Find out fast.

He could imagine Weber using whatever fancy system of communication they had to get Barzelian out of bed in his fancy house in Washington's fancy Cleveland Park district. They would never believe that if Morpurgo was still working on the Aske mystery it was just because it was there. At the time of the Century House takeover, Barzelian had made the initial mistake of underestimating Epworth. He would take it for granted that it was Epworth who was getting too close for comfort.

But too close to what, for Christ's sake?

The morning was advancing. Before long, Trigg and his official hosts, in their shiny black Tatra – he had been in this town long enough now to notice that the Tatras were the only cars that didn't look as if they might break down at any moment – would be climbing the steep slope of the Hradčany ridge to the restaurant.

He had no intention of being there when they arrived. Minor officials they might be – lollipops were hardly likely to bring out the Central Committee – but in this closed society his name, if he fell in with Trigg, might filter through. Then his tour of the town would end in Bartolomějská, where almost the entire street belonged to the secret police.

He had muffed it at the embassy. He should have waited for the solicitous Kowinski, said enough to start up a peal of alarm bells in the hope that they might give him clues. As it was, he had been too quick to lose himself in these cobbled streets, out of sight before anyone could organise pursuit under the eyes of the Czech police post just across the road.

But Weber had not been hiding behind *Die Presse* for nothing at the Franz Josef Station, let alone making the seven-hour trip to Prague. He would not give up on Morpurgo that easily, or Barzelian, back there in the American dawn, would want to know why.

Morpurgo, too, wanted to know why. Up to now he had taken care to keep a low profile for fear Moscow Centre would find him, but Weber, who knew the difference between the shifty look and the manly, unblinking stare, would gamble that his quarry would play the old hand's trick of seeking security in numbers. For fear that Weber would lose him, it was time to stand out from the crowd.

It would be like the worst kind of package tour, only one morning to do Prague.

Before Trigg should arrive there he went straight up to the Hradčany, walked past the sentries at the entrance to the presidential palace, loitered conspicuously at the centre of each great courtyard in turn, stood interminably before the high altar in Saint Vitus Cathedral, cut through to the medieval houses of Golden Lane, stayed there long enough to have been photographed, framed and sold as a souvenir.

He left by the great flights of steps below the south wall of the castle, stopped halfway down to join the changing throng anxious to see the panorama. He looked down through the tumble of pink pantiles and gabled roofs to the riverside trees, and across the Vltava at the prickle and thrust of spires and baroque domes.

Should Sylvie choose Prague as the city to cover on the RSC's Eastern European tour, she would see it without his own dimension of fear. He knew now that it was the prospect of her trip, as well as Aske's presence, that had brought him here himself; the only way he could be himself as Sylvie was being herself. He wished she were here. He wished he were not.

No one, American or Czech, touched his shoulder or murmured into his ear, not even an offer to make change. Wenceslas Square, he thought. He would climb the statue of King Wenceslas and shout: Weber, you inefficient bastard, what the hell's taking you so long?

He completed the descent, became daring, found his way back

to the Mostecká, crossed the green glide of the river by the Charles Bridge – where the hell are you, Weber? – to forage through the maze of medieval streets around Old Town Square.

His depressed mood of the previous night had gone. He had misjudged this place. Here the alleyways were cobbled, the first floors of ancient buildings jutting out to make pavement arcades. Even the red mini-banners in the shop windows, reminders of the October Revolution and the colossus to the east, failed to detract from the beauty, the sense of past glory, the feeling that the actors, far from having gone someplace else, were simply resting. Only get their act together and there could be new and better parts to play in Europe.

Claas, he shouted in his head, when Broadway, Hollywood and Pennsylvania Avenue can point to a cast list and a repertory the equal of this, that'll be the time to boast.

In the meantime, the CIA was playing hard to get.

He found himself near the old Jewish cemetery, where the tombstones jostled, fighting to escape the earth as if the dead millions of pogrom and holocaust were struggling to be reborn. He came across a restaurant, took time off to eat pork with cheese-and-ham stuffing, passed a synagogue draped with Czech and Soviet flags, came in due course to another which appeared to have been turned into a museum. Out of curiosity or something deeper, he went inside, and there was Simon Aske.

Aske was alone, and yet they were all there, thousands upon thousands, the Nazi harvest of death. Brodski and Steinberg, Nachman and Rosenfeld, and Yawitz, Goldfarb and Kisch, engraved in mind-numbing numbers, as much an endlessly repeated pattern as a roll-call.

"I told him," the Engineer had said, "he should visit the old synagogue, maybe find some ancestors."

Aske had not moved, had not, so it seemed, even heard him come in. He stood staring at the curving wall. Morpurgo, coming up behind him, knew what he would see.

*Akenazi . . . Askenazy . . . Ash . . .*

Aske turned. He should have been startled, even shocked. Instead, he looked at Morpurgo, looked beyond him, looked back. Morpurgo thought he had never seen him look so sane.

He said, "Well!" and looked beyond again. He said, "This . . . is an unexpected pleasure." He smiled, but his eyes couldn't stay still, constantly slipping past Morpurgo towards the entrance. An old woman, bow-legged, kerchiefed, bent over a stick, appeared from an inner room to stare in silence.

"Klatschi," Morpurgo said. "I think you probably used to meet her on the train. Did you know who she was?"

Aske's eyes darkened, their flickering movement stilled. The muscles of his face softened yet simultaneously set, the hovering smile quite gone. He said, "Poke and stir. Nothing there," and it was as if those whose names in their tens of thousands covered the walls had poured their combined anguish into his voice.

Behind them the heavy door swung open. The old woman, without haste, shuffled back to wherever she had come from. Three men, spreading out a little, came down the bare flagstones, their footsteps loud in the cold, inscribed emptiness. No need to wonder; they had all the hallmarks of the secret brotherhood of which he was a member.

"You will come with us, please."

Only much later did he realise how his own background and training had betrayed him. Unflawed, he would have asked who they were, demanded identification, made a fuss. Instead he said, "There must be some mistake. I'd like to telephone the British embassy."

They treated it exactly as Special Branch would have treated it, back home. They ignored it. Two of them took his arms, no force, just plenty of experience. The man who had spoken, vaguely reminiscent of Warren Claas, flat, Central European features and Americanised English, followed behind.

In the narrow street a car waited; no gleaming official Tatra, but a drab Skoda, inconspicuous, looking, like most of the cars in Prague, as if it might break down at any moment. There were passers-by, curiously preoccupied. None of the three had even looked at Aske. So far as Morpurgo knew, he was still standing there, motionless as he had been after the mention of Gossip in the affectionate diminutive.

\*     \*     \*

The train came in, a green monster escaped from Berlin the walled city. They had kept him to themselves, well down the platform, moving casually away if anyone came near. Few people, he noticed, came near. Not one word, on either side, had been spoken.

The compartment was empty, all seats reserved. No one else boarded that section. His own ticket was still in his pocket, his baggage still in his hotel room. Abrupt departure was becoming a

269

routine. This time he had no resentment, only an immense desire to be gone.

A whistle blew. The man who spoke English, if you could call American English, left the compartment, sliding the door shut behind him, all without haste. Moments later he saw the three of them descend the steps of the gloomy subway leading to the concourse. No one looked back. They knew he would not get out. The coach groaned, jerked. The cavernous station slid into the past, taking with it public conformity, private dissent, the sound of silence.

Soon countryside rolled by, green woods and hills, idyllic. A deer and its fawn stood motionless in golden stubble, staring as the shadow of the train flickered past under a sky with clouds that had come from the west and would pass to the east without hindrance.

Tábor, Veselí, Vychód; his mind divided between future and past. Then no-man's-land, the khaki wave. The whistle blew. The train moved. The wire, tarmac and guard towers, brilliantly lit in the encroaching darkness, faded into memory.

Gmünd. Louder, more confident voices. Brighter, more confident lights, blazing prodigally along streets where cars moved as if they could never break down. An Austrian State Railways inspector checked his ticket.

He became aware of an immense lifting of the spirit, John Morpurgo, token lefty from backstreet Wandsworth, back in the capitalist West. He was ashamed, but only because the Czechs were stuck with their own country.

Someone was coming down the corridor. He fumbled for his ticket before remembering that it had already been inspected. Tucked in the same pocket was the leaflet thrust into his hand at the Karlsplatz station as he had followed Simon Aske out into the capitalist night.

*MENSCHENKETTE*, it said at the top. A human chain.

Tomorrow, in Vienna, part of a Europe-wide series of demonstrations in support of nuclear disarmament. It would link the American and Soviet embassies, five kilometres across the heart of the city. It would not link the two halves of the split-brained world.

The footsteps stopped. The door slid back. Weber came in.

"Hi! This seat taken?"

Morpurgo released his breath, then gave him the leaflet.

Weber smoothed it on the seat. "How was the trip?"

"So-so."

"Fine city."

"Sorry we didn't meet. We could have done the sights."

"You and me?" Weber folded the leaflet carefully. "In Prague? Barzelian would slip his trolley." He jerked a thumb at the receding lights. "Gmünd, me. Just a quick visit."

"Is that where you were going the day I saw you board the Prague train with Aske? Gmünd?"

"Great little place, Gmünd. Those crazy dots over the U, real cute." Weber smiled his pothook smile.

"Okay," he said. "Just kidding."

The train picked up its first real speed, swishing through the light-speckled Austrian night like a thing released.

"If we're not born mad," Weber said, "it doesn't take long to learn. My shrink friend says you have to be crazy to be normal in a world like this." He smiled his crooked smile. "You never met her. The one with the place in Hampstead."

"The one Fish introduced you to."

Weber closed his eyes, pretending to think. "Sure, that's right. Some kind of professional relationship. She went off him and took to me. I always said you have to be crazy to be a shrink."

"Advised Fish on how to handle schizoid personalities?"

"Went off him," Weber said obliquely. "Got the idea he was using her for purposes she wouldn't approve of." Opening his eyes to look straight at Morpurgo, he said, "Friend Fish was not altogether normal himself."

"One of the SIS people who think the road to the future runs through Langley."

"The word was," Weber said, "he changed his mind. Took another look at the future, decided it ran through Moscow. Mind, that could have been no more than gossip." He drew the folded anti-nuclear leaflet through thin fingers.

"Does gossip inerest you? That kind of gossip?"

"Where would we be without it?"

"Maybe it's gossip, maybe just uninformed guesswork."

"Don't knock the trade," Weber said.

"Some kind of deal. She'd pass over what she could. In due course, he'd get her out. Only the stuff got better . . ."

". . . and better . . ."

". . . and Humphrey Fish had his sights on the top slot at Century House. H.F., for High Flyer. Something bigger than Gossip. Couldn't bring himself to call a halt to the one or carry out

271

his promise to the other."

"Love," Weber said wistfully; "it's wonderful. Did you cast someone for Cupid?"

"Aske," Morpurgo said, "and it shall be given, seek and ye shall find." Weber groaned.

"Fish had some guy who recruited for him under the name of Spencer. Spencer dug up this longuistic whizz kid in Oxford who also happened to have a talent for acting."

"No kidding?" Weber smiled his crooked smile.

"Every actor," Morpurgo said sentenuously as the train racketed over points, "is a kind of spy. Every spy is a kind of actor."

"Kind of a split personality," Weber said, "only Fish didn't find that out until later."

"But when he did find out, he took advice, found he could handle it. Even found it had advantages. Orphan, loner, a natural inclination to cut himself off from his past, even to invent new pasts to suit any particular purpose. Say a Viennese Jewish refugee, family all gone to the gas chamber."

"Mauthausen?" Weber gestured apologetically. "First name that came to mind. You know?"

"Fish was a bit of a sadist."

"Primary qualification for top slots."

"Aske was terrified of losing his secret identity. Afraid Fish might expose him, but pretending not to be because that would be putting himself still deeper into Fish's power. Pretending – acting – was what suited him best. So long as he's acting he's able to feel he has everything under control. It's *his* skill and *his* intelligence that are keeping him safe."

"Where" – Weber was thoughtful now – "did you get all this stuff?"

"Hampstead, just before I came away. Your friends are back from their conference. Laid my cards on the table; she liked that, your Mrs Godwin. Or should I say Doctor Spencer?"

Weber, more thoughtful than ever, rummaged, tossed something over.

It was a set of contact prints, uncut: Morpurgo with Helga in the Kärntnerstrasse. The negatives were there too.

Morpurgo looked up.

"Us," Weber said. "We took them."

"Helga . . .?"

"*Nashi*, as Moscow says. Ours."

Morpurgo looked at them again. "But why?"

"Barzelian figured we might need them. A little leverage."

"On *me*?"

"Not you. Epworth. Picked you up when you were down, right? If brother Lawrence had struck paydirt . . ."

". . . and become God Almighty . . ."

"Right! Epworth recruited Helga Archer when she went back to Germany, got her to offer herself to the opposition. I guess you didn't know that."

No, he said, he didn't know that.

"We poached her. I guess *he* doesn't know that. All he knows is that he recruited her and she set you up. Wouldn't have looked good if those pictures had shown up at the profit-and-loss, evidence that the Hauptverwaltung had turned her and used her against his . . ."

". . . neutered pussycat," Morpurgo finished savagely.

"Wouldn't have stuck," Weber said cheerfully, "but it sure worried the hell out of him. Every little helps. Still, no matter now, right?"

"No matter now." Morpurgo's suppressed bitterness gushed up. "The neutered pussycat blown, expelled from Czechoslovakia. Don't pretend you didn't know. Don't pretend you weren't there. Gmünd!"

"Sure I was there," Weber agreed. "What's the problem?"

"Since when did the Sovs play live and let live? They let me go for a purpose. Do you think for one minute they won't . . ." He stopped abruptly. "What's so funny?"

Half amused, half compassionate, Weber said, "You owe Langley this reserved compartment and your ride to the station. When someone says, 'Come with us, please,' do you always go so quietly?

"Trouble is, you British have forgotten how to say 'Kiss my ass' to Uncle Sam." He smiled wryly. "Always excluding a one-off called Trigg. We had to square him, or he'd have raised hell back there."

He leaned forward to return Morpurgo's leaflet. "Gave us a bad time, junior, when you dropped by the embassy. But nothing to the time we had trying to keep out of sight while you all but stood in the street and hollered, 'Come and get me!' As for the holocaust memorial!" He wagged his head. "Want to tell me what made you think he'd be there?"

They hadn't spoken, had kept him to themselves at the Central

Station, had put him on the Vindobona knowing he wouldn't get off one minute before the train pulled into Franz Josef Station. All that had mattered was to get him away from Aske, from Prague, without revealing that they were not SB but resident CIA cryptos. They had taken huge risks.

"No," he said, "I don't want to tell you. I may quite possibly never tell anyone anything again." He looked at the leaflet. *MENSCHENKETTE*. A human chain.

"Slansky's shadow." Weber was watching with a lurking sadness that reminded him of Aske. "That say anything to you?"

He shook his head. This time he wanted answers, not questions.

"You've heard of Slansky?"

He sat silent.

"Jewish Secretary of the Czech Communist Party and Vice-Premier until 1951." Weber was going to tell him anyway. "Arrested as a Zionist traitor during the Stalin purges. Found guilty, rigged trial. Hanged. Want me to go on?"

He chose to take Morpurgo's silence for assent.

"Up there on the Hradčany, in the presidential palace, there's a picture of the Central Committee, made just before it happened. Slansky was in it, right next to Gottwald. They touched him out; you can do anything with pictures, ask Sylvie. But for those who know where to look, his shadow's still there."

He looked for a reaction from Morpurgo, but got none.

"Okay," he said. "So they take the picture down, right? Only who's going to suggest it? Slansky doesn't exist. Slansky's a non-person. You can't take a picture down without giving a reason, and Slansky's a non-reason. And you can't tell someone to get rid of that shadow, because non-persons don't have shadows.

"So there it stays. Everyone on the Central Committee knows about it. No one is going to be the one to do something about it, because to do something about it you have to show that you know about it, and if you know about it you know there was an official goof. But the state never goofs."

He rotated a finger. "So on and so on. *Ad infinitum*. You want to know where Aske comes into it, right?"

Morpurgo sucked in one cheek.

"Sure you do," Weber said. "Fish was using Aske to make his pitch to Moscow Centre for the release of Gossip. Moscow Centre was only interested in stringing Fish along, because Gossip was already dead. Aske guessed that eventually. Don't ask me how,

274

he won't talk about it. When he made those trips to Prague he would catch this train back to Vienna, the one we're on right now.

"She would come from East Berlin on the same train as far as Prague. When she got off she left him her stuff in one of the toilet compartments. They never talked, never even met, but he got to know what she looked like. She looked a bit like his mother might have looked if she'd lived and developed a little sense."

Morpurgo looked up briefly.

Weber took it as encouragement. "When Aske realised they'd done a number on her – he was in Prague at the time – he slipped a gear. Went deeper, that's how he puts it. Started back from Prague on his return trip, dropped off the train somewhere on route, Tábor, Veselí, he won't say. Fluent Czech, hell of an actor, I guess he could have got away with it for weeks, months.

"Fails to show up in Vienna and the Stiegelbauers report it to the police. You know most of the rest. When the Austrian authorities made an official enquiry, the Czechs thought Western security had figured the game, thought they were operating a sting. So they just clammed up: they knew nothing about Aske and that was the end of the line."

The train pulled into some station or other. People boarded. Two of them, senior citizens, indecently well-dressed after Prague, opened the door to the compartment.

Weber stuck a thumb in each ear, waggled his fingers, grinning like a madman. They retired indignantly, retreating far down the corridor. Weber went on as if nothing happened.

"At some stage or other, Aske was picked up. Maybe just gave himself up, wouldn't put it past him. It put the Czechs in a double bind. Can't let him return to Austria because he isn't in Czechoslovakia. They'd told the Austrians so, officially, and the state is never wrong."

His smile never so lopsided, he said, "Simon Benjamin Aske, alias Slansky's shadow."

"But the Czechs let him come back."

"Uh-uh." Weber waggled his head gently. "Moscow Centre sent him back. Eventually. When the guys at Lefortovo were convinced he was schizoid but not psychotic. When he'd convinced them the best news he ever had was that Humphrey Fish, who'd made his life a torment for years, had killed himself."

"But" – he had to know all of it now – "Aske didn't know Fish by his real name. He only knew him as Godwin."

Weber chuckled. "You've forgotten. Moscow knew from

Gossip that Fish was Godwin. It suited them to tell Aske. English-speaking, Czech-speaking, Russian-speaking, German-speaking, and a hatred for the man who might take over SIS one day. Moscow Centre had plans for Aske."

Morpurgo gave up his pretence of disinterest. "But Aske came back, for Christ's sake!"

"Sure he did. They sent him back. Great destabilisation ploy: first set the British and the Austrians snapping at each other, then wait for the spin-off between Five, Six and Whitehall. Nearly worked, didn't it? But they were smart, too. A last test for a man they had big plans for back there on the Moscow Ring Road; make quite sure he's kosher."

"How could they doubt it, after Lefortovo?"

"They didn't doubt Aske. But did this new guy rumour said had taken over in SIS have Aske down for a left field play while they were covering middle and right? That's why we – Barzelian – fixed to have him chased back."

"Fixed to have *me* chase him back. I did manage to work that out."

Weber chuckled again. "You think Warren said all those bad things on the Century House roof for kicks? We knew Sylvie was going to Vienna. We knew Epworth would have you go with her if he had to hide you in her baggage."

"And you had a deal with Mandel."

"Smart guy, didn't care how it was done, just so long as Aske was out of his hair. Of course, we convinced the Austrians Aske was Moscow, not that they needed any convincing."

He watched Morpurgo trying to tease out something that stayed obstinately entangled.

"*Nashi*," he said softly. "Ours. Meaning Simon Benjamin Aske. Ours right from the time Fish was using him to set up a deal over Gossip and he found out Moscow had already had her tidied away. Warren Claas smelled a rat, all the hollering Fish was doing at that time. That's when I was ordered to cosy up to those nice folk out there in Hampstead."

Morpurgo closed his eyes briefly, re-running Traiskirchen, re-running the scene in the Karlsplatz. "Are you trying to tell me Aske's not really schizoid? Not crazy? That it was all just . . . acting? But the Pinkas Synagogue? That, just acting?"

"Sure he's crazy." Weber was no longer smiling. "Always been crazy, his kind of crazy, crazy like a fox. Now he's our kind of crazy. And sure he was acting. Only he doesn't act for a living. He acts for his life."

"He could have been good," Morpurgo found himself saying. "If he'd been an actor instead of . . ." He stumbled, repeated, "He could have been good."

"He'll need to be," Weber said bleakly. "You only flop once in his kind of big time."

He buttoned his coat. "Fish is dead. Gossip is dead. Don't ask me who she was, we don't know. Just that she's dead because there was nothing more in it for Moscow. Barzelian isn't dead. Aske is Barzelian's boy now. Like it or not, Aske is going to be Barzelian's boy in Moscow Centre. Barzelian has a lousy sense of smell."

He peered out at the night. "I think we'll be in pretty soon. I'm putting in my resignation, incidentally. Why do you think I'm telling you all this?"

\*　　　\*　　　\*

Epworth had insisted on his presence at the final recording of the Cornysh Consort's album. It was just over. The recording engineers had gone to the pub before removing their gear.

"Look at these!" Archer stormed into the former church regardless of whether or no the recording sign might be on.

He thrust the press clippings under Epworth's nose, oblivious of his surroundings. Outside the high double-glazed windows leaves were streaming before a high October wind as if in terror.

Ignoring the clippings, Epworth nestled the crumhorn in its case and fastened the catches meticulously. "We have them. Our man in Vienna couldn't wait to get the news from – mmmm – Aix to Ghent."

"Why is *he* here?" Archer swung round on Morpurgo like a man finding his favourite club occupied by squatters. "And why the devil do I have to come here? Aren't you ever in that bloody office of yours?"

"I presume" – Epworth counted his reeds, snapped down the lid of the box, slipped it into a pocket – "you came because Wriothsley said you'd find me here. You're just too late. You could have heard the final takes."

He waved absently at the last of the Cornysh Consort, who, across the great width of bare floor, gave him an almost imperceptible nod and thumbs-up as he left.

"All SIS chaps, the Cornysh," Epworth said reassuringly, turning back to Archer and the flourished extracts from the Austrian press. "No one else here. Do feel free."

"A woolly-hat anti-nuclear demo!" Archer was outraged. "Woolly-witted woolly-hats, still wet behind the ears and well laced with commies, anarchists and agents of sympathy."

"Oh." Epworth looked reproachful. He pointed at a photograph under the heading: *FRIEDENSKETTE AUF DEM STEPHANSPLATZ* "An Under-Secretary of State, three members of parliament, the head of the Austrian Human Rights – "

Cutting him short, Archer jabbed a finger so violently at the paper that it tore. "Never mind them! That's their business, bloody politicians, only there to have their picture taken anyway. But this . . . this . . .!"

It was a good likeness of Morpurgo, hand in hand with the politicians and the woolly-hats forming the human chain as the great bells of St Stephan's had thundered apocalyptically through the city's noon.

Archer brought himself to speak to Morpurgo. "Haven't ever had all that much time for you, you know that, but up to now I've at least given you credit for . . ." He choked. "What in the name of God made you do it? It's all over Whitehall."

"They held out their hands," Morpurgo said. "They said, 'Come on. Join us.' So I did." It was near enough to the truth.

"So you did!" Archer was still fighting for self-control. "If they'd asked you to shout their bloody slogans, would you have done that too?"

He turned back to Epworth. "You're his boss. He's got to go."

"Harmless infiltration," Epworth said. "In pursuit of – mmmm – enquiries."

"What infiltration? What enquiries, for God's sake?"

Epworth watched trees lashed silently by the silent wind, the sound-proofing isolating them from the world outside. "We made some progress with a man called Godwin. There's a bit of tidying up to do over a chap called Spencer. A bit tricky, it was rather a long time ago."

After that they listened to Archer's impassioned, partly incoherent speech in silence until he stopped abruptly. .

"Are those damn things turned off?" He pointed at the clustered microphones.

Epworth looked shocked. "I told you. All gone. You just missed the last takes. Tomkins, you'd have enjoyed it."

Breathing heavily, Archer said, "Humphrey Fish was a good man. Humphrey Fish is dead. All right, maybe there was dirt. I don't know and I don't want to. Muckraking is bad for the service, bad for the country. I had no idea Aske was what he was when I recruited him at Oxford. Anyway, he's a traitor."

He crumpled the cuttings and tossed them at Morpurgo's feet, speaking of but not to him. "No way of hushing this up, but the profit-and-loss showed his record is good. Such as it is. I'll speak for him, but he has to go. Leave it to you."

He stalked out.

Raising his voice towards the microphones, Epworth said, "End of take. Wind back and bring it to me, please, and don't leave anything for those recording engineers to find."

To Morpurgo he said, "He's right. You'll have to go. That plane leaves in just over an hour. Even if you catch it, you'll still arrive in New York far too late to take Sylvie out to dinner, always assuming you're forgiven. After all the trouble he's been to, Trigg will be – mmmm – proper fed up."

As Archer had said, he would have to go. He would be allowed to resign. He would not tell Epworth that Helga and Aske were Langley's, because he was going. He went.


Bath, 1983 –
Roussillon, 1985

# Top Fiction from Methuen Paperbacks

While every effort is made to keep prices low, it is sometimes necessary to increase prices at short notice. Methuen Paperbacks reserves the right to show new retail prices on covers which may differ from those previously advertised in the text or elsewhere.

The prices shown below were correct at the time of going to press.

| | | | |
|---|---|---|---|
| ☐ 413 55810 X | **Lords of the Earth** | Patrick Anderson | £2.95 |
| ☐ 417 02530 0 | **Little Big Man** | Thomas Berger | £2.50 |
| ☐ 417 04830 0 | **Life at the Top** | John Braine | £1.95 |
| ☐ 413 57370 2 | **The Two of Us** | John Braine | £1.95 |
| ☐ 417 05360 6 | **The Good Earth** | Pearl S Buck | £1.95 |
| ☐ 413 57930 1 | **Here Today** | Zoë Fairbairns | £1.95 |
| ☐ 413 57620 5 | **Oxford Blood** | Antonia Fraser | £2.50 |
| ☐ 413 58680 4 | **Dominator** | James Follett | £2.50 |
| ☐ 417 03890 9 | **The Rich and the Beautiful** | Ruth Harris | £1.75 |
| ☐ 413 60420 9 | **Metro** | Alexander Kaletski | £2.50 |
| ☐ 417 04590 5 | **Sometimes a Great Notion** | Ken Kesey | £2.95 |
| ☐ 413 55620 4 | **Second from Last in the Sack Race** | David Nobbs | £2.50 |
| ☐ 413 52370 5 | **Titus Groan** | Mervyn Peake | £2.50 |
| ☐ 413 52350 0 | **Gormenghast** | Mervyn Peake | £2.50 |
| ☐ 413 52360 8 | **Titus Alone** | Mervyn Peake | £1.95 |
| ☐ 417 05390 8 | **Lust for Life** | Irving Stone | £1.95 |
| ☐ 413 60350 4 | **Depths of Glory** | Irving Stone | £2.95 |
| ☐ 413 41910 X | **The Agony and the Ecstasy** | Irving Stone | £2.95 |
| ☐ 413 53790 0 | **The Secret Diary of Adrian Mole Aged 13¾** | Sue Townsend | £1.95 |
| ☐ 413 58810 6 | **The Growing Pains of Adrian Mole** | Sue Townsend | £1.95 |

All these books are available at your bookshop or newsagent, or can be ordered direct from the publisher. Just tick the titles you want and fill in the form below.

**Methuen Paperbacks**, Cash Sales Department,
PO Box 11, Falmouth,
Cornwall TR10 109EN.

Please send cheque or postal order, no currency, for purchase price quoted and allow the following for postage and packing:

| | |
|---|---|
| UK | 60p for the first book, 25p for the second book and 15p for each additional book ordered to a maximum charge of £1.90. |
| BFPO and Eire | 60p for the first book, 25p for the second book and 15p for each next seven books, thereafter 9p per book. |
| Overseas Customers | £1.25 for the first book, 75p for the second book and 28p for each. subsequent title ordered. |

NAME (Block Letters) ................................................................................................

ADDRESS...................................................................................................................

................................................................................................................................